"I want children. I always have."

Clay turned from her. "I can't take that risk. Not with you." He strode off in the direction of the barn.

Amity watched him go. What had he meant by that—that he couldn't take that chance with her? For a moment she allowed herself to think it meant that he loved her, then pulled herself back to reality. Clay did not love her, and he never would. The sooner she accepted that fact, the better.

But she could not deny the fact that she loved him. She felt it all the way through her body. She loved him, and she wanted to have him hold her and to lie beside him in the dark and even to do the secret things that a husband and a wife did together, the things that she'd never thought she would want to do....

Dear Reader,

From a haunted ghost town to a widower with five daughters, there is something for everyone in our titles for December.

There is trouble brewing in DeLoras Scott's *Springtown,* and Chance Doyer and Amanda Bradshaw are right in the middle of it. This intriguing tale is sure to delight DeLoras Scott fans who have been patiently waiting for her next book.

British spy Anne Hargraves is on a mission to expose Queen Victoria's would-be assassin, when she finds herself falling for one of her prime suspects in *Dangerous Deceptions* by Erin Yorke.

Promises To Keep from Nina Beaumont is the sequel to *Sapphire Magic.* In this tale of an American woman's journey to unravel the mystery of her birth, the heroine returns to Vienna at a time of political turmoil.

Amity Becker is a mail-order bride in Lynda Trent's *Beloved Wife,* the story of a young woman who is overwhelmed by her handsome new husband and his five unruly daughters.

We hope you enjoy this month's selection, and, from all of us at Harlequin Historicals, we would like to wish you and your family the very best of the season.

Sincerely,

Tracy Farrell
Senior Editor

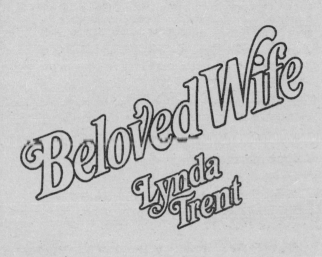

Harlequin Books

TORONTO • NEW YORK • LONDON
AMSTERDAM • PARIS • SYDNEY • HAMBURG
STOCKHOLM • ATHENS • TOKYO • MILAN
MADRID • WARSAW • BUDAPEST • AUCKLAND

Harlequin Historicals first edition December 1992

ISBN 0-373-28754-2

BELOVED WIFE

LYNDA TRENT

started writing romances at the insistence of a friend, but it was her husband who provided moral support whenever her resolve flagged. Now husband and wife are both full-time writers of contemporary and historical novels, and despite the ups and downs of this demanding career, they love every—well, *almost* every—minute of it. The author is always glad to hear from her readers.

For John and Annette
and dreams come true

Chapter One

1887

Amity Becker touched her gloved hand to her hair to be sure every strand was in place. Even though her hair was more red than brown, she always referred to it as brown, and as it tended to curl more than her elderly aunts thought was proper, she was ever conscious of keeping it in place. Amity had tried diligently to please her maiden aunts since coming to live with them in their Charlotte, North Carolina, home at the age of ten when she was orphaned, but throughout those fourteen years she had rarely succeeded.

Aunt Ophelia and Aunt Dorcus were old maids as much by choice as by necessity, and as they had little use for men themselves, they always discouraged boys from calling on Amity. Their younger sister, Amity's mother, was the only one of their generation to marry. Their only brother, a confirmed bachelor, had died young and was remembered with more veneration than Raymond probably had deserved.

Amity had longed for years for a beau to come calling, but as the time had passed and no young man had dared to brave her formidable aunts, she had tried to accept her destiny as a spinster.

Then one day a new minister had come to the church she and her aunts attended, and with him had come his wife and an unmarried son named Emmett. Amity and Emmett had become friends right away, that term seeming best to her to describe their relationship. He never actually called for her at her house as a beau would have, but rather they often walked out in the evenings when her aunts thought she was with her best friend, Dorothea Kendrick.

She had loved the time she had spent with Emmett and had looked forward to each of their clandestine meetings. That is, until recent events had changed things. As she prepared to slip away to see him once again, she was afraid to think what Emmett's reaction would be to what she must tell him.

Hoping to hide her nervousness, she squeezed her cold lips together trying to make color come back into them. From the parlor, Aunt Dorcus called out to her, "Amity, are you stepping out?"

"Yes, Aunt Dorcus. I told Dorothea I would come by this evening and sew on the quilt she is making for her grandmother."

Aunt Ophelia said, "Don't be late. It's not proper for a young lady to walk about at night alone."

"I'll be back early." Amity repressed the urge to point out to her aunt that Dorothea lived only three houses away and that she would hardly be in any danger. Nor was it necessary to remind them that at twenty-four she was scarcely a young lady anymore.

She let herself out of the house, passed through the gate in the white picket fence surrounding her aunts' yard and then forced her feet to take her down the street to where Emmett was to meet her just past the Kendricks' house. Nervousness left her hands cold in spite of the white gloves she wore. Spring had settled in, and the days were already warm for Charlotte. She blamed the excitement of spring on what had happened between Emmett and herself during their last meeting.

Amity's heart pounded as she remembered that terrible night. Emmett had picked her up in his father's buggy, rather than on foot as usual. They had ridden out into the country even though Amity had told him they would be taking a great risk in her coming home late. He had only laughed and teased her about being tied to her aunts' apron strings. Once they were away from town, he stopped the buggy in a secluded spot and started kissing her. Amity had heard that once a man became excited in that way there was no stopping him. And since she had kissed him back, she felt she was somehow to blame for what had happened after that.

Emmett was waiting for her just where he had said he would be, and although she wished that this time he had stood her up, she was relieved to see he was on foot. She had avoided him for two weeks, even at church, and he was pacing as if he was eager to see her. She tried to bolster her confidence by reminding herself that he was obviously glad to see her, but it was of little help.

"I thought you weren't coming," he complained when she drew near. "You're late."

"I'm sorry. I had agreed to sew the buttons on a dress for Aunt Ophelia. I came as quickly as I could."

"I have a surprise for you." He grinned and winked.

"Oh?" Her spirits lifted. Maybe he was going to propose, and she would not have to be embarrassed after all. She wondered if he had bought an engagement ring, but decided he probably had not. As a preacher's son, he would most likely buy his wife a plain gold band. That was fine with Amity.

"Do you remember that house over on Baker Street?"

"The one we saw for sale? Yes."

"I've bought it."

"You have!" Her excitement soared. He *was* going to propose.

"I've already moved most of my things in. I wanted to tell you, but I haven't seen you lately."

"I've been busy."

"Would you like to see it?"

"Go there now? I couldn't possibly. It's nearly dark. What would people say?"

"If it's dark, no one will see us go in." His grin broadened. "We won't have to settle for damp grass anymore."

She wished he had phrased his last statement differently. "We should set a date and let it be known, shouldn't we? I could bring one of my aunts or maybe Dorothea with me to see your house. That way there can be no talk." She smiled at him. "I never expected you to buy a house before you proposed. What if I said no?"

"Propose? I'm not proposing marriage." Emmett backed away and frowned at her. "Where did you get that idea?"

Amity's mouth dropped open. "But you have to marry me." She glanced around to be sure no one could overhear them. "You remember what happened last time we saw each other."

"I never mentioned marriage. You've got it all wrong."

"But you did. At least I thought you did. Even if you didn't, we must be married." She blushed. "You had your way with me and...and I think I'm in the family way." There. She had said it. The words sounded even more dreadful aloud than they had in her mind.

Emmett stared at her. "You can't be. We only did it once."

"Don't talk so loud. What if someone hears you?"

He backed away. "No, you don't. You're not trapping me into marriage."

"Trapping?" She felt as if her world were crumbling. "Emmett, I don't understand. You said you loved me!"

"A man says all sorts of things at a time like that. I didn't mean it."

"But you must have!" Her fingers knotted in the strings of her reticule, and she wadded it into a ball in her distress.

"I'm seeing a girl I knew in Winston-Salem. We had an understanding before I ever moved here."

"What? That can't be. You never mentioned her to me."

Emmett tried to grin and bluff his way out of it. "I would be pretty stupid to tell one girl about another, now, wouldn't I? She and I are going to get married in the summer. That's why I bought the house. I figured you and I could use it between now and then."

Amity stumbled backward, her head shaking slowly. "I don't believe you. You forced yourself on me."

"Forced you? That's a lie. You let me take you for a ride out in the country. You had to have known what I had in mind. You never tried to stop me."

Tears sprang to Amity's eyes. "You seduced me and had no intention of doing the honorable thing! What am I to do, Emmett? What can I do?"

He shrugged. "Those aunts will help you raise it. You'd better not tell anybody it was mine, though. I'll deny it. Nobody has seen us going out together, and I've never come to call at your house. Nobody would believe you, anyway."

She heard a ringing in her ears and wondered if that was what one heard as one was about to faint, then anger flared in her. "Don't you ever speak to me again, Emmett Hamilton. If you do, I'll...I'll slap you!" She gathered up her skirts and ran from him as tears streamed down her face.

Darkness was falling fast, yet she couldn't go home, at least not until she had regained her composure. Seeing she was even with Dorothea's house, she brushed aside the gate and hurried up her friend's walk. Fortunately Dorothea answered the door. Amity whispered in a broken voice. "I have to talk to you!"

Dorothea let her in and called to her parents, who were apparently in the back of the house. "It's Amity. We're going up to my room."

They hurried up the stairs, but Amity didn't feel safe until the bedroom door was shut behind her. Dorothea stared at her, her face filled with puzzlement. "You're crying. What happened?"

"It's terrible. Just terrible!" Amity sat on the window seat, and Dorothea sat beside her. She pushed the curtains aside and looked down at the corner. Emmett had gone.

"You look as if the end of the world has come."

"It has." She wet her lips nervously. "I don't know how to tell you."

"We've been friends for years. You can tell me anything."

"I've been . . . indiscreet."

"Indiscreet?" Dorothea's eyes widened. "You don't mean with a man!"

Amity nodded miserably. "I thought he loved me. He said he did! All he wanted was to . . . you know."

"That's terrible! Who was it? I didn't know you were seeing anyone but Emmett Hamilton."

Amity nodded harder. "It was Emmett."

"No! He's a minister's son!" Dorothea leaned forward and took Amity's hand in her own. "Why would you do such a thing?"

"It wasn't my fault. I let him get too carried away and . . . well, I guess he couldn't help himself. Dorothea, I think I'm going to have a baby."

Silence hung in the room. Finally Dorothea said, "A baby?"

"Now you know why I say it's the end of the world."

"Surely Emmett will marry you. It can't be so bad. You said he told you he loved you."

"He plans to marry a former sweetheart from Winston-Salem. He told me so tonight."

"He can't! Not now. Did you tell him?"

"Of course I did. He didn't care. He said if I tell anyone he's the father, he will deny it and everyone will believe him because he's a minister's son and because no one knows I've been seeing him."

"I know about it."

"Would you be willing to testify to that fact?" Although Dorothea did not speak, the look of horror on her face answered the question. "I thought not." Amity buried her face in her hands. "My aunts will kill me."

"No, they won't."

"You don't know them as well as I do. They won't even let me have a man visit in the parlor. This will be the end of them. I'll be disowned. Dorothea, what can I do?"

"Let me think. There has to be some way out of this. Are you positive you're . . . that way?"

"I think so. I'm not sure exactly how to tell. I didn't have my time of the month this past week."

"That's bad. When my sister was expecting, that was how she knew." Dorothea's eyes were round. "Is there a cousin or someone you can visit for a while? A long while? You could put the baby up for adoption and no one need ever know."

"I don't have any cousins. Only my aunts."

Dorothea went to her writing desk and began rummaging through the lap drawer. "Maybe if I write to Aunt Mabel," she said uncertainly. "She lives in Spartanburg."

"What excuse could I possibly give my aunts for visiting your aunt for several months? That would never work."

Dorothea's eyes fell on a letter she had received that morning. She picked it up and turned to Amity, her face alight with hope. "This is it. You could elope!"

"I could what? I told you that Emmett is marrying someone else."

"Not with Emmett. With Clay Morgan." She came to Amity and handed her the letter. "He's the man I told you about I've been writing to in Texas. The widower with two children."

"What are you talking about? I don't know him at all, and he doesn't know me."

"He doesn't know me, either. You could tell him you're Dorothea Kendrick, and he would never know the difference."

"I told you not to answer that ad. I don't care how curious you were—what sort of man would advertise for a wife?"

"A lonely one. Maybe there's still a shortage of women in Texas. His wife died, and he needs a mother for his children. He's written me several times, you know, and he seems quite nice."

Amity shook her head and stared at her friend. "You expect me to marry a complete stranger? I could never do that!"

"Do you have a better idea? He needs a wife, and you need a husband. You've read his letters. You said he sounded nice."

"I wasn't thinking of him in regard to marriage, and neither were you. I told you to write him and apologize for falsely encouraging him."

"It's a good thing I didn't, or you'd have no place to go."

"No. I'm not going to marry a man I've never met. The idea is preposterous."

"It was only a suggestion."

"I should be going. I told my aunts I would be home early. I'll plead a headache and go up to bed. They're both firm believers in headaches. I couldn't possibly talk to them tonight."

"You'll have to eventually. If you're going to have a baby, they'll have to know."

"I'll cross that bridge when I come to it." Amity tried not to think what that would be like. "I don't suppose you know how long I have before people will begin to notice?"

Dorothea shook her head. "My sister had to start letting her dresses out in about three months, but she's taller than you are. Otherwise, she might have been showing earlier."

"Thank you for talking to me. I don't know what I would do without you."

"Keep Clay Morgan in mind. I'll keep writing him until you see if you have another choice."

Amity nodded, but she was determined to find some other way. She couldn't imagine herself as a mail-order bride. That was something a low woman might consider, or someone who had no prospects at all. She hated to admit that the latter description fit her all too well.

At her aunts' house, Amity tried to slip up the stairs unnoticed but was heard. "Is that you back so soon?" Aunt Dorcus called out.

"Yes, I have a headache and came home early."

"Come here and let me look at you."

Amity straightened her shoulders and reminded herself that she looked no different now than she had earlier that afternoon. Reluctantly, she went into the parlor.

Both aunts were knitting shawls for the church's charity cases as they did almost every evening. Amity had once teased them that all the poor in Charlotte must have at least one of their shawls. Her aunts had not been amused.

"You look flushed. Doesn't she look flushed, Ophelia?"

Aunt Ophelia studied her niece. "She seems pale to me. I think she's needing some of that spring tonic Mama used to give us."

Amity suppressed a groan; she hated the taste of that tonic. "I think it's just the change in the weather. If I could go up and lie down, I'm sure I'll feel better by tomorrow."

"That might be a good idea," Ophelia agreed, though she never liked to agree with anyone. "Your eyes are red. Hay fever, is my guess."

"It's the goldenrod," Dorcus put in. "It gets to me every year."

Amity was glad to escape upstairs. Her aunts had eyes that were entirely too sharp. There was no way to prevent them from noticing her problem unless she did something soon. She changed into her nightgown and pulled down the covers of her bed even though it was still early. She wanted to lie in the dark forever and never have to face anyone again.

She buried her face in her pillow. How could she have been so foolish as to allow Emmett to take her on that buggy ride? She knew it was wrong, but at the time it had merely seemed daring, not bad. She had never thought he would get so carried away. Once she had realized what he was going to do, she had fought against him, but it had not mattered. Emmett was strong as well as determined. Now that she thought back on it, he hadn't seemed to care that she was hurt and frightened.

Embarrassment flooded over her. She had given her virginity to a man on the grass in the woods like some tramp! It didn't matter that she hadn't wanted to—her aunts and all her upbringing had taught her that. If a man got too carried away, it was the woman's fault. Amity groaned. It hadn't been her fault! No matter what everyone might say, it hadn't been! She had thought Emmett loved her or she wouldn't have ridden out of town with him in the first place. The injustice of her situation exasperated her, and she clenched her fists under the pillow.

The next few days did nothing to help Amity's situation. On Sunday, from his father's pulpit, Emmett announced his engagement to the young woman from Winston-Salem. Everyone congratulated him and seemed as pleased as could be to hear that he and his bride would make their home in Charlotte. Because no one knew Amity had had any involvement with Emmett, no one tried to spare her feelings—least of all Emmett, who looked through her as if she were a perfect stranger.

The following week, Amity went to Dorothea's house, and together they composed a letter to Clay Morgan accepting his proposal of marriage and asking that he send money for a ticket to Texas as soon as possible.

"I feel like a heel and a liar," Amity said as they posted the letter.

"Better a small lie than a baby out of wedlock," Dorothea said.

"I'd like to know what you'd consider a large lie," Amity retorted.

The following week, Clay Morgan sent money for the train ticket and word that he was looking forward to meeting his bride-to-be at last. He was to be at the station when the train arrived.

"I'm terrified," Amity whispered as she packed her clothes in the steamer trunk. "What if my aunts come home before I'm gone?"

"They won't if you hurry. I never knew you owned so many things. Will we be able to get them all in this trunk?"

"We have to. It's all I have. They'll never forgive me. Never."

"You're getting a new start, and Clay Morgan seems very nice. If you're not happy, you can come home again. Then if you have a baby, everyone will assume it's his."

"That's true, isn't it? If he's horrible, I can always leave.... Pack faster. The tea my aunts have gone to won't last forever."

In less time than she had thought possible, Amity was packed. She looked around the room that had been her refuge since she was ten. She felt surprisingly little regret at leaving it. She went to the bed and propped the farewell note she had written to her aunts on the pillow. By the time they would find it, she would be on her way to Texas.

The man who worked for the Kendricks carried her trunk downstairs and put it on the buggy. Amity and Dorothea climbed in as if this were only a ride to the store. When they reached the train station and the trunk was loaded on the waiting train, Amity turned to Dorothea. "I'm so frightened!"

"Don't be. You're having an adventure. I'd never be so brave."

"I've never wanted an adventure. Not really." She looked at the train. "I've never wanted to see Texas. What will I do among Indians and buffalo and cactus? I must be out of my mind to even consider this." The words had no sooner left her mouth than she saw Emmett and some of his friends drive by. They saw her, too, and from the sly grins on their faces, Amity knew, without a doubt, that they knew all about her buggy ride with Emmett.

Her cheeks blazing, she turned to Dorothea. "I can never thank you enough."

"If it works out, I may be able to come see you someday."

"Yes, oh, yes. I'd never be able to endure it if I thought we would never see each other again." From down the street, she heard one of Emmett's friends shout something unintelligible at her.

Amity didn't spare them a glance. She hugged Dorothea and lifted her skirts to climb onto the train's steps. With the conductor steadying her elbow, she boarded the train, then made her way into the passenger compartment and found a seat. Through the smoke-hazed window she found Dorothea and waved goodbye. In only moments the train made a hissing sound and lurched forward. She was on her way.

She had heard that Texas was little more than an endless prairie with cowboys and longhorn cattle and Indians who still caused trouble from time to time. But instead of that, the terrain of the eastern portion of the state where Ransom was located proved to be quite similar to Charlotte, North Carolina. There were enormous trees and clear streams that poured into mud-red rivers. And from what she had seen from the train, it appeared that the people there seemed more interested in farming than ranching. As to the Indians, she had yet to see one, and she hoped that never changed.

As the train slowed to a stop at the Ransom train station, she peered out the window with nervous anticipation. This station, like most of those she had passed on the trip, was painted a mustard yellow with dark brown trim, apparently conforming to some sort of railroad company standard. A number of people were milling about, all dressed more or less the same as those in every little town she had been through, though here she did see a few men wearing buckskins, and the women's dresses, for the most part, were less stylish than she had seen back East.

Squaring her shoulders, she stepped out onto the wooden platform and looked around, trying to appear more confident than she felt. It had not occurred to her until she had already left Charlotte that she had no idea what Clay Morgan looked like. Dorothea had given her all his letters but none of them contained a description of him. An older man standing at the far end of the platform shot a stream of tobacco juice into the weeds nearby, and suddenly she was filled with dread as she realized that he might be the man she had agreed to marry. Amity shared her aunts' disapproval of chewing tobacco—though they had always been quick to add that a pipe such as their dear departed brother Raymond had smoked was acceptable. When the man looked in her direction as if he was sizing her up, she swallowed hard against the lump in her throat. Then, thankfully, he called out a greeting to a man who had gotten off the train with Amity, and she knew for sure he was not her intended.

Moments later, Amity's trunk was deposited onto a baggage cart on the platform and a teenage boy pulled it over to Amity and offered to load it for her into her buggy or wagon. Quickly she looked about again but saw no sign of anyone who had come to meet her. With a sinking feeling she waved the boy away. What if he did not come to get her at all? She had no money, having spent what little she had on meals during the trip, and had neither a place to stay here nor a way to return to Charlotte. With a great effort she tried to look composed.

By this time, the crowd she had seen earlier had dispersed. Those leaving Ransom had boarded the train, and those meeting arriving passengers had made contact, gathered their baggage and gone on. What kind of man could forget to pick up his bride? With rapidly mounting panic, she sat on the baggage cart next to her trunk and tried to slow her breathing.

"Miss Kendrick?" a deep, male voice called out from behind her, causing her to flinch.

For an instant, Amity froze, terrified that the grizzled old man she had seen earlier had come back for her. Quickly concluding she had no alternative but to answer, she drew a deep breath as she stood up and turned around.

As her eyes swiftly scanned the man, relief washed over her. He was nothing like what she had expected. She had thought any man who needed to advertise for a wife would be at least homely and perhaps older than his letters had indicated. This man, however, was not much older than she was and was handsome in a rugged way that appealed instantly to the woman in her. "I'm Miss Kendrick."

"I'm Clay Morgan," he said, and when he smiled, she felt her heart skip a beat. His teeth were straight and white, and his wide, friendly smile made him even more attractive.

"It's nice to meet you," she said awkwardly. She had no idea how to talk to him. "I'm glad you came to pick me up."

"I could hardly forget something as important as that," he said, then paused as he stared at her with his head slightly cocked to one side. "You don't look the way I pictured you."

"I'm sorry." Her hands went to her hair. "I must be a mess after the train ride."

"I meant you're prettier and younger than I had expected."

"I am?" She wondered for the first time what Dorothea had written in her letters. Dorothea was younger than Amity and was prettier, in Amity's opinion.

"You'll have to forgive my bluntness. I tend to say whatever I think."

"You're quite a surprise to me, as well," she frankly replied, then caught herself. "So is Texas. I thought I'd be coming to a desert."

"That's west Texas. Most people get it confused." He indicated her trunk. "Is that all your luggage?"

"Yes. I only have the one trunk."

Amity watched with awe as he lifted the trunk with no sign of any strain and carried it to his wagon, which was parked on the opposite side of the building. She knew for a fact that the trunk weighed more than she did, and she had to hurry to stay with him.

"I guess we ought to be married before we leave town," he said conversationally, tipping Amity a bit off-balance.

"So soon? I mean, we just met."

"I know, but you can't stay at my place without us being married, unless you want to cause talk."

"I never thought of that. Of course I couldn't."

He put the trunk on the wagon bed and turned to look at her. "If I'm not what you want, this is the time to say so. You can still get back on the train and go home."

Amity lifted her head. "No, Mr. Morgan. I've not come halfway across the country to change my mind. I'll stay if you'll have me."

He smiled again. "I didn't ask you to come until I was sure you were the woman I want. You aren't the only one to answer my ad."

"I'm not?" She couldn't believe there were other women who would consider such a thing. "Were they serious?"

"Most of them. But you were the only one that interested me."

"Mr. Morgan, there's one matter I have to clear up."

"Surely under the circumstances you can call me Clay. What matter?"

"My name isn't Dorothea Kendrick. It's Amity Becker. I wrote to you under that name because I wanted to remain somewhat anonymous until I knew you better."

"Amity. I like that. I don't blame you. I know this is a big step for you."

"You have no idea," she said dryly.

"Then you agree we should be married before we leave town?"

"Yes. That would be best." She let him hand her up onto the wagon seat, and as she slid over so he could climb up beside her, she watched him from the corner of her eye. Every time he touched her, she felt a reaction all the way through her body. Did he feel it, too? She would be mortified if he guessed how he was affecting her. If he felt anything, he gave no sign.

In relative silence, he drove them a short distance to a small house beside a white frame church and helped her down from the wagon. Taking another deep breath, she followed him into the church, and in less than ten minutes, she was no longer a spinster but was Amity Morgan, wife of Clay Morgan.

"That was fast," she said. "I thought it would take longer."

"I had told Brother Crowe to expect us today, even though I wasn't absolutely sure you would be on the train. I'm glad you were."

Curious, she looked at him. "What if I had disappointed you in my appearance?"

"As I told you in my letters, I want a mother for my children. Your personal appearance would not have mattered, so long as you were neat and clean. That you're young and pretty is a bonus."

"I feel I must be honest with you. I'm not young. I'm twenty-four." She waited for his response.

"I consider that to be young. I'm thirty-three," he added.

She glanced at him. She had thought he was younger. "Your letters indicate you have young children. Five and eight years, I believe you said. You must have married late."

His failure to reply and his closed expression suggested that he did not want to talk about it.

"I like children. They're girls, you said?"

"Yes. I have daughters."

Amity wondered why he was being so withdrawn all at once. "I hope you won't think I'm prying, but how long have you been a widower?"

He drew in a deep breath as if he was considering whether or not to answer. "Six months. My wife died in childbirth, along with our son."

"Oh." She had assumed it had been at least a year. Then she remembered her manners. "I'm sorry. It must have been a great blow to you."

"Yes. Yes, it was. Elsa was the best of wives."

Amity had no idea how to respond. He sounded as if he was still in mourning for her. So why did he want a wife bad enough to advertise for one? Dorothea had been writing to him for over a month. "Are there no single women in Ransom, Mr. Morgan?"

"Call me Clay. Yes, there are."

When he made no further effort to explain himself, she folded her hands in her lap and silently contemplated the situation. As they headed east out of town along a road roughly paralleling the railroad tracks, she surmised the farm he lived on must have been one of those she had seen from the train. She glanced at her hands, and her thoughts changed course. Although her gloves covered it, on the third finger of her left hand she now wore a gold wedding band. She could feel it whenever she pressed her fingers together. She was this stranger's bride.

Bride. Amity's eyes widened. Until this moment, she had not given thought to the fact that as his wife, she would be sharing his bed. She looked at him sharply, then turned away again quickly. He would know she was not a virgin the moment they became intimate!

Panic rose in her. What would he say when he discovered this? As she struggled to calm her skittering thoughts, it occurred to her that at her age, he might believe her if she told him she was a widow. Amity had never been good at lying, but she knew she would have to do so. "Mr....Clay, I have something I must say to you."

He glanced at her, then back at the horses. "What's that?"

She moistened her lips. "I may have led you to believe something that's not true. I'm not...that is, I'm a widow."

"You are?" He looked surprised. "You never mentioned that in your letters."

"I should have. It was terribly remiss of me."

"How long ago did it happen?"

"Long ago. Years." She told herself she would have to do better than that if he was to believe her. "I was only married a short time. I've lived with my two maiden aunts for years."

He turned the team of horses into a lane that led off the main road. Ahead she could see a large farmhouse.

"I hope you won't hold it against me," she said. "I thought I should tell you now before I meet your children."

"Yes." He paused for a moment. "I don't hold it against you. It gives us something in common."

She felt a surge of relief. They were nearing the house, and she looked at it with interest. It was two-storied and painted white with blue shutters. The upper story had a fish-scale design on the sides and several dormer windows. A porch swing hung on the deep porch, and there were flowers along the fence that separated the yard from the surrounding pastures. "You have a beautiful house," she said. "It looks well cared for."

"Amity, there's more I should have told you, too." He spoke as if he was reluctant to bring it up.

"Oh? What's that?" It seemed odd to have a man she had known for only an hour call her by her first name. "Look. There are your children. How adorable they are!"

Two girls had come out onto the porch. Except for the fact that one girl was slightly taller than the other, they looked amazingly alike. Each had a pretty face and hair so blond it seemed almost white. As she watched the anticipation in their faces, another girl joined them. "Is that a cousin? She looks just like your daughters."

"Actually that is my daughter."

"Then which of the others is not?" Amity was confused. She thought the larger of the first two seemed too old to be the five-year-old, and the last child looked older than eight. As she watched, a smaller girl came around the corner of the porch and joined the others.

"As a matter of fact, they all are. That's what I was about to tell you."

She paused. "Three children. Well, that's not such a great shock. It's only one more than I expected." She hoped he would confirm the number. They all looked as alike as any children Amity had ever seen.

"Actually, I have five children. All daughters."

"Five?" Her confidence waned. "You have five children?"

"My oldest is Hallie, and she's visiting relatives with her aunt and won't be home until later in the week." He parked the wagon at the gate, and after climbing down, he extended his hand to her.

For a moment, Amity could only stare at the girls on the porch. Her world was changing even more quickly than she had ever thought it could. Finally, she noticed Clay's extended hand and allowed him to help her from the wagon and lead her through the gate and up the walk to the porch where the children were waiting silently on the porch. "Girls, this is your new mother. Amity, this is Kate, Jemima and Laura. The little one there is Rosemary."

None of the girls said a word, so Amity took the initiative. "I'm glad to meet you. I'm looking forward to getting to know all of you."

The girls exchanged a look, turned and scurried into the house. Amity stared after them.

"It may take them a while," Clay said by way of apology. "They were against me marrying again, especially to a woman they don't know."

"I can hardly blame them." She tried to smile. "Maybe Hallie—is that her name?—will take to me more readily. I have patience. I'll win them over."

"I hope so." He went back to the wagon to get her trunk. Amity hoped desperately that Hallie would be friendlier than her sisters. She hoped even more desperately that she was capable of being a mother to five girls.

Chapter Two

As Clay pulled his new bride's trunk from the wagon bed, he hoped he had done the right thing. Amity looked capable enough, and she was neat in her appearance and spoke as if she was educated. But she wasn't Elsa. He ached for Elsa with every breath he drew and was certain he always would. He had loved her wholly, as she had loved him. Six months ago she had died trying to give birth to his son. The boy had died, too, but Clay had been so grief-stricken over the loss of his beloved wife that he had scarcely noticed.

The following weeks had been hell. He could not accept the fact that Elsa would never speak or laugh again or work in the house she had loved or among the flowers she had planted. For a time he had willed himself to die, as well.

Then Elsa's sister, Gretchen, made him aware that he had five daughters who were dependent on him. His and Elsa's children. This had forced him to pick up the burden of living again. It had also forced him to see that he needed someone to take care of the children while he was working in the fields.

He had hired a succession of housekeepers, each of whom left the job after only a matter of days. They said his children were unmanageable and that Gretchen was constantly coming over from her neighboring farm and causing problems. He had spoken to Gretchen about the housekeepers' complaints, but she seemed puzzled as to what they had meant. She had admitted that she had come over occasionally to be sure the children were being treated kindly in their father's absence and to see that the housework was being done, but Clay could hardly fault her for that. She only had been trying to help. At least that was what he wanted to believe.

The truth was he was not sure what to think of Gretchen. She had been married to Hall Harris for several years by the time he met her sister Elsa. A year after he and Elsa were married, Hall died, leaving Gretchen a childless widow. She and Elsa had been as close as any two sisters could ever have been, and as Gretchen had no children to tend and her house was on the hill just beyond the river, she spent almost as much time at the Morgans' house as she did at her own.

Since Elsa's death, however, Clay occasionally had felt uneasy in Gretchen's presence. She seemed to have taken him, as well as his children, under her wing. At times her manner was annoyingly proprietary and at others it was uncomfortably flirtatious.

Clay had decided his best course, all things considered, was to remarry. A wife would be more committed to staying than would a mere housekeeper, and the children were in need of discipline. Clay had never been good at correcting them, possibly because his own childhood discipline had consisted primarily of beatings, sometimes for reasons he had never figured out. And he was determined that his beloved girls would never know the misery he had suffered. But knowing no alternative, he had done nothing to quell their bad behavior. Elsa had been able to make them mind with a shake of her head or a firm word. But Elsa was gone.

He had tried to court several of Ransom's eligible young women, but none of them was willing to go out with him. They all had known Elsa and said they were uncomfortable with the idea of being courted by her husband. And, too, they were familiar with his children, and he could hardly blame a single woman for not wanting to take on five children, especially since the housekeepers had spread the word that Clay Morgan's children had become particularly unruly since their mother's death.

Clay shouldered the trunk and headed toward the house. The girls had gone inside, and Amity was left standing alone in the yard, looking as if she might be considering leaving. Without a word, he walked past her and into the house with her belongings. When he had given up on finding a wife in Ramsom, he had taken desperate measures and advertised for a wife. He had not told his children or Gretchen of the ad, primarily because he doubted anyone suitable would answer. Then when the woman who called herself Dorothea wrote back, he had not told them because he wanted to be as certain as possible that she was all she purported herself to be. He and Dorothea, or Amity as it turned out, had corresponded frequently for over a month, he had asked her to come to Texas, and here she was.

He heard her come into the house behind him and glanced back to see her expression. The house Elsa had kept so clean all those years was far from that now. He had been without a housekeeper for the past two months, and he had never learned to keep a house himself. Even if he had, it would not have mattered. Each evening when he came in from working the fields he was tired, and the reminder that Elsa was gone and never again would be there depressed him so that he had let the house go. He had told Hallie to do what she could, but she was only thirteen and was not old enough to be good at cleaning and keeping the younger children in line.

Amity had stopped just inside the door and was looking around the disheveled room, her mouth open. "It hasn't always looked like this," he said defensively. "I don't have a housekeeper, and the girls aren't old enough to be much help."

Amity made no reply.

Clay went through the parlor and into the hall. "The children sleep up there," he said with a nod of his head toward the stairs. He carried her trunk toward the back of the house.

Amity hurried to catch up with him. She had never been in such a messy house in all her life. Messy? No, it was *filthy.* She held her skirts close to her legs to avoid the dusty baseboards.

As she followed him through the dining room, which seemed to be the hub of the house, he looked at her and said, "The kitchen is in there. Can you cook?"

She nodded, then said, "Yes, I can cook."

"Good." She could hear the relief in his voice, but chose to ignore the implications of that.

Through a row of windows in the dining room, she could see a large porch and at one end a well. She was relieved to see that the porch was covered. At least she would not have to draw water in the rain; she doubted this house would have a pump in the kitchen.

"This is where you'll sleep." Clay opened the door he had indicated and went into a small bedroom.

Apprehensively, Amity poked her head through the doorway, and with relief saw that this room was relatively clean. As she was mentally giving him credit for at least keeping his own bedroom tidy, he said, "My room is across the dining room. It's the door beside the sideboard."

"Your room?" Her head jerked up. "You have a separate room?"

He avoided her eyes. "I thought you would be more comfortable with this arrangement. After all, I'm a stranger to you. I'm not a man to force myself on a woman."

Amity clasped her hands so he would not see them tremble. "I made a bargain to be your wife. I'm willing to keep my end of the deal."

"This will work out better. You'll have your privacy."

Before she could say more, he turned and left for the fields. She stared after him, unsure what to do. She pressed her palms against her flat stomach. She *had* to share a bed with him or she would never be able to convince him the child she carried was his. After seeing the condition of his house, she no longer had any qualms about her lie. But she had never thought he might want separate bedrooms.

As she slowly removed her gloves and put them on the bed, she chastised herself for not thinking all this through more carefully. If she had not stressed how long her fabled husband had been dead, she might have been able to say her child was his. No, she corrected, that wouldn't do, either. No widow would marry so soon after her husband's death. But what was she to do?

From the room over her head she heard the sounds of children scuffling, then suddenly they were quiet. Five children. What on earth was she to do with five girls? "Thank goodness they aren't boys," she consoled herself. "Girls, at least, are docile."

She closed the door to her room and opened her trunk. Her first order of business was to clean. This house had to be cleaned from top to bottom. And she certainly could not do so dressed the way she was. Without pause to consider the difficulty of the onerous task ahead, she began changing clothes.

So she would have more room to breathe, Amity left off her lacings and put on her oldest dress. This was not the way she had expected to spend the afternoon of the day of her wedding, but she had no choice. She tried to put aside her regrets. What was done was done, and if she had not come here, she would never have had any marriage at all and a life filled with shame.

Bracing herself, she went first to the kitchen. At the door she stopped and could only stare. No one had washed dishes in a long time. The black iron stove had rust spots where spilled liquids had been left. The table was relatively bare compared to the sink and counter, but the oiled cloth was soiled with spilled food and grimy from not having been washed.

Anger flared in her. How could Clay expect his children to live, let alone eat, in a place like this? Amity searched the kitchen until she found a clean apron and started washing dishes.

To Clay's credit, there was a pump in the kitchen, and as she worked her way through the dishes, she was delighted to discover that the dishes had a pretty pattern of pansies and wildflowers. They were much more attractive than the utilitarian white ones her aunts owned. The glasses were stemmed goblets with a thumbprint indention along the base of the bowl and were large enough to hold a generous amount of iced tea. She wondered how the younger children managed the large glasses until she found some smaller ones with roses printed on the side. Elsa had evidently loved flowers.

When she felt the kitchen was clean enough, she turned her thoughts to preparation of the evening meal. First she put a pot of dried beans on to cook, then realized she would not have enough time to kill and pluck a chicken. Fortunately she discovered a ham hanging in the smokehouse. She found cornmeal and flour in the pantry and set them aside for corn bread. With so much other cleaning to do, a dessert would have to wait until another day.

The next room Amity tackled was the parlor. Clothing, all dirty, was strewn about. Pinafores and aprons and stockings in all sizes had been left draped over chairs and side tables. She found one sock that had to be Clay's under the wood box on the hearth. She piled all the soiled clothing in one large heap on the porch. A laundry basket had not yet surfaced.

The plates and glasses she found went to the kitchen, and as she set them next to the sink, she reflected that it was a good thing she had come when she did, because there had not been so much as a clean saucer in the cupboard on her arrival.

The parlor had potential, she thought. It was a nice size, and the wallpaper was a lovely pattern of rows of pale rosebuds and twining greenery. And once it was clean, it would be cheery with sunlight pouring through the windows. Beneath the clutter on the floor, she found rugs, hand hooked with flower designs in shades of pink and rose. Elsa had worked hard to make a nice house. It was a shame her husband had not cared enough to keep it that way.

Amity heard a noise and turned to see four pairs of eyes watching her from the stairs just past the parlor door. When the girls realized she had noticed them, they all stared at each other. Amity was afraid they might leave again, so she smiled and said, "Hello. Would you girls like to come talk to me?" She had no intention of putting them to work before they at least had exchanged some pleasant words.

The girls giggled and ran upstairs. Amity sighed. She certainly had her work cut out for her here. She wondered when Hallie would be home. As the eldest, she must have some sway over her sisters, and no doubt she would help Amity make friends with the others.

As Amity crossed the dining room on her way to the kitchen to wash the dishes she had found in the parlor, she paused. What did Clay's room look like? She had never been one to snoop, but she needed to know exactly what sort of family she had married into. She crossed the room and opened the bedroom door.

This room was much larger than her own. The furniture was golden oak, carved with an oak-leaf design. On the floor were several hooked rugs, similar to the ones in the parlor, and the bed's counterpane was nubby with candle-wicking. Across the foot of the bed was a quilt with a flower pattern, and as the bed was not made up, she could see two other quilts beneath the counterpane. Clothes were scattered here and there, but the room was generally cleaner than the rest of the house. Amity felt some relief.

A dull thud accompanied by giggles overhead drew Amity's attention. What were the girls doing up there? She heard a squeal and more giggles. She decided it was time for her to see what was happening.

At the top of the stairs, Amity stopped to get her bearings in what could only be described as an open sitting room. Ahead of her, beneath the window that overlooked the front porch, was a deep window seat. On the left side of the room were two doors, on the right only one. A moment later the ruckus resumed, and she could tell the noise was coming from behind the second door.

Amity went to the door and tapped. Instead of an answer, she heard a muffled scream, which was covered at once by laughter. Without hesitation, she turned the knob and pushed the door wide open. All four girls were piled on the bed, tussling with the covers. The sheets were pulled half off the mattress, and one of the pillows had split a seam and was losing its feathers. As Amity watched in horror, the older girl swatted her next older sister with the pillow, and feathers spewed into the air. The two younger ones squealed and dived under the quilts.

"What on earth are you doing?" Amity gasped.

All four girls stopped instantly and stared at her.

"You! Which one are you?" she demanded of the eldest.

"I'm Kate."

"You're much too old to be acting like this. What would your father say?"

"He would probably say to hit her again," Kate said as she drew back the pillow to whack the other girl.

Amity intercepted the pillow and pulled it away, causing even more feathers to fill the air. "I doubt it," she said in a commanding voice that would have done her aunts proud. "Which of you lives in this room?"

"I do," Kate said rebelliously. "I share it with Hallie."

Amity tried not to show as much anger as she was feeling. "What about the other girls?"

Laura, the five-year-old, pointed at the wall. "We live in there."

"Who lives across the hall?"

"That's the boys' room."

Amity held her breath. "What boys? Surely there aren't more of you!"

"The boys haven't been borned yet," Rosemary, the smallest girl, said solemnly. "When they are, that's where they will sleep."

"I see." Amity drew herself up to gather her authority about her. "Kate, you start straightening this room immediately. Gather all the feathers and bring them downstairs to me. I'll stuff them back into the pillow and resew the seam. You other girls, go clean your own room. I'm sure it needs it."

Kate lifted her chin. "I'm not supposed to clean. That's your job."

Amity knew this had to be handled properly. "You're mistaken. I don't live up here, and I'm not the housekeeper. From now on, you girls will be expected to straighten your rooms before you come down in the morning. Do you understand?"

Although the girls failed to answer, they did exchange a look. Amity could see she was not going to be popular around here.

In a gentler voice, she said, "I want you girls to like me, and I want to like you. Since your father married me, I'm your mother and—"

"No! You're not our mother." Kate glared at Amity, her white-gold hair coming loose and falling about her face. "Our mother is dead."

"We don't want you for a mother," the next oldest said.

The youngest looked up silently, her eyes filling with tears and her tiny chin trembling. Amity went to her and picked her up. She had already made a big mistake.

"I know I'm not your mother and I never will be. I only meant that I'm more than a servant around here and that I want you to accept me." She smiled at the small girl. What was her name? Rosemary? "How would you like it if I made a pound cake for supper?"

Rosemary looked doubtful but she finally nodded.

Amity hugged her and put her down. Maybe a dessert was more important than a clean parlor. She could not possibly clean the entire house before mealtime, and she knew from experience that food was a sure way to a child's heart. "Pound cake it is. In the meantime, clean your bedrooms."

She turned and went into the sitting room. After a pause, she went to the door across the room and opened it. The room had a cold, unused feel, but it was clean. She stepped inside and saw a cradle, much used and probably made by Clay, beside the window. Her heart turned when she saw it had sheets neatly folded on the tiny mattress. She looked around. The room had been set up as a nursery. A bed, such as would be used by a baby, stood on one wall, and the chest of drawers was opposite it. The curtains at the window were white but were starting to collect dust. This room had been prepared for a baby in the not too distant past. She remembered that Elsa had died in childbirth and that the baby had been lost, as well.

Sadness filled her. Clay apparently had been so devastated by his loss that he had not been able to put away the things and let his daughters use the room, even though they must be crowded with three of them in the end room.

Amity felt a tug on her skirt and looked down to find Rosemary staring at her. She knelt so their eyes would be more on a level. "What is it, Rosemary?"

"We aren't supposed to open this door. Papa will be mad if he sees you doing it." She looked at the tiny cradle. "I slept in that when I was little. Papa said so."

"He must love you very much to make such a pretty little bed."

Rosemary nodded, quite seriously. "He does. We're all his favorites."

Amity smiled. How could anyone not love this small girl? "I'm sure you'll all soon be my favorites, too."

Rosemary smiled and bounced off to join her sisters. Amity left the nursery, closing the door behind her. Maybe it was not going to be totally hopeless. At least Rosemary cared if she got in trouble or not. Realizing it was later than she had thought, she went back down to the kitchen and started the cake that she hoped would reconcile the girls to having a stepmother.

When Clay came home that night, he was greeted at the door by the aroma of food cooking. For a moment he thought of Elsa, then realized it was only Amity. But at least it was food. By the way it smelled, she could indeed cook.

He was no more than halfway across the parlor when Kate and Jemima stopped him.

"Papa, she has to go," Kate said firmly. "We won't have her here."

"What's happened?" He glanced in the direction of the kitchen. "What did she do?"

"She told us to clean our rooms," Jemima said.

"Good. I've been telling you to do that for weeks."

"Yes, but she *meant* it," Kate said. "I think she wanted to spank us."

Clay frowned. "There will be no spanking around here. Did you clean up?"

The girls nodded, but he had his doubts. Jemima could never lie and get away with it, and her green eyes were averted. Kate said, "We think she was in the nursery."

"She has the right. You girls aren't giving her a hard time, are you?"

"Us, Papa?" Kate asked in weighty innocence.

Rosemary came into the room. "She's making me a cake. Can you smell it?"

Jemima sighed in exasperation. "It's for all of us, silly. Not just for you."

"She asked me if I wanted a pound cake and I said yes." Rosemary nodded as if that settled the matter. After a moment she added, "I can share it."

"Thank you," Clay said with amusement. He looked around. "I see she's been cleaning."

"Do we really have to keep her?" Jemima asked. "Even if we don't like her?"

"Yes, we really do. You don't know yet if you like her or not. Give her a chance."

Kate said in telling tones, "She said she is our mother now."

Clay's frown returned. "She must have meant stepmother."

"That's not what she said."

"I'll have a talk with her. No one can take your mother's place. Why did she say that?"

"I don't know. We were just playing in my room like we always do, and she came up and said it."

"It's true," Jemima said. "I heard her. We all did."

"Let me handle this. I want you girls to be as good as I know you can be. Try to get along with her. We need a woman around here."

"I don't know why," Kate said. "We were doing all right without her."

"You run along. I need to wash up before supper. Why don't you go into the kitchen and offer to help? She might like that."

"Yes, Papa," Kate said.

He went to his room and shucked off his sweaty work clothes. His girls were good, just headstrong. He hoped Amity would see that. None of the housekeepers had. As he poured water from the pitcher into the basin, he wondered if he had done the right thing in marrying Amity before he really got to know her. True, he had corresponded with her several times during the past month, but that had given him no information about how she would be with children. But she had known to expect them—or at least two of them, he amended. Surely if she didn't like children, she would have been warned away.

He knew very little about her, he was realizing now. Her details about her life had been sketchy. She had lived with her aunts and regularly attended church and social gatherings, but that was really all she had told him. At least she had seemed clean and friendly, and she had been willing to come to Texas and marry him. He was not asking for much more than for her to be kind to his children and to keep his house. Clay had no delusions about love. His love was buried with Elsa.

When he was presentable, he went to the kitchen and could hardly believe his eyes. With all the accumulated dishes and grime gone, the kitchen was almost back to normal. "Where are Kate and Jemima?" he asked.

"I haven't seen them in an hour or so. I assume they are upstairs cleaning their rooms."

So they hadn't come to help Amity as he had told them. "How did it go today?"

She stirred the beans before answering. "I've been busy."

"So I can see. The kitchen looks good. The food smells great," he added. "I guess you can cook after all."

She looked over her shoulder at him. "I wouldn't lie about such a thing."

He felt a twinge of guilt. "I'm sorry to spring all the children on you, but I was afraid you wouldn't come if you knew there were five of them."

"I should have been given the courtesy of being told beforehand, nevertheless." She began ladling the beans into a serving dish.

"And I guess the house wasn't as clean as it might have been."

She shot him a look that put him on the defensive.

"The girls are too young to see to it, and I have to be in the fields all day. It's enough that they look after each other."

"Is it? Surely they have chores to do. I've had chores since I was a small child."

"They had chores, but after losing their mother... I think it's been hard enough on them without them having to work, as well."

She put the bowl of beans on the clean table. "I wasn't suggesting that they be sent to sweatshops. If you have no objections, I'll assign them chores appropriate for their ages."

He frowned as he went to the cupboard to get the plates so he could set the table. He recalled his own childhood chores. Even as a boy, he had been made to work as hard as any man, and it had never been good enough for his stepfather. Why had he not thought of all this before he found a stepmother for his children? "Why don't you draw up a list and we'll discuss it?"

"Very well."

After putting the plates around the table, he sat down and watched her move about the kitchen with what he thought was dispassionate interest. "Do you ever smile?" he surprised himself by asking.

"Certainly. I smile often."

"Not since you came here, you haven't."

"You must admit that I've had a difficult day. First I find you have five, not two, children, and then I learn I'm to salvage a house that looks as if a hurricane had gone through it." She wadded up her apron and opened the stove door. After wrestling the corn bread out and onto a trivet on the table, she wiped her damp face on the apron before adding, "Not to mention the fact that your children are running wild, and I find I'm to be a wife in name only. You didn't want a wife, Mr. Morgan, you wanted a permanent housekeeper."

That hit too close to home. "You can still return to Charlotte. Our marriage hasn't been consummated."

"Nor will it be, I assume."

He could not blame her for being upset. He had meant well, but he could see how she would be less than pleased. "Then you'll be leaving?" For some reason he was reluctant to see her go.

For a long time Amity was silent. Then she said, "No, I won't be leaving. I only wanted you to know that I resent being maneuvered like this. I don't like manipulation, Mr. Morgan, and I won't sit still for it in the future. You have to understand this."

"I agree. You know the worst now. You aren't the first to tell me the girls are getting out of hand or that the house is falling to rack and ruin. If it wasn't, I wouldn't have advertised for you. But you must have wondered at my having done that unless there was more to the bargain than I was saying."

"No, actually I didn't. I must be unusually naive. I took you at your word."

That made Clay feel even worse for having deceived her. His word had always been his bond. "I'm glad you're staying. Would you mind telling me why?"

"I have no place else to go."

He watched her thoughtfully. What could she mean by that? She had a family who supposedly loved her. She had whatever life she had come from. For the first time, it occurred to Clay that she might have been less than truthful in her dealings with him, as well, and for that reason, she was willing to overlook his transgressions. "Are you going to insist on calling me Mr. Morgan as if I'm your employer?"

"Only if I'm to be treated as an employee." Her dark eyes met his squarely. "I'm to be your wife or your housekeeper, but not both."

"I can't move you into my room," he said flatly. "I'm still grieving the loss of my wife, and it wouldn't be right for either of us, or to Elsa's memory."

"And the girls?"

"Except for not sleeping in my room, you'll be my wife and their mother. But be kind to them. I won't have them mistreated or worked harder than their years can bear."

"I would never mistreat a child."

"I'm glad to hear that."

She surprised him by smiling. "You, on the other hand, are a different matter. If we're to have a relationship built on mutual respect, you have to show me the respect you expect as your due."

"That's fair."

"Then I think you should be the one to speak to Kate and the others about how I'm to be treated. We will all get along better if the positions of authority are clear from the start."

"You certainly talk different from the way you sounded in your letters."

"Do I?"

"I'll talk to the girls. I gather they sassed you?"

"Only Kate and the next oldest one. Jemima, is it? Rosemary actually tried to keep me out of trouble. I looked in the nursery, and she warned me you would be angry if you knew. If I've overstepped my bounds, I apologize."

He was silent. He had almost forgotten the nursery was there and still waiting for the baby that would never arrive. "That restriction doesn't apply to you. I didn't want the girls playing in there."

''I understand.'' She turned her back on him and went to the drawer where Elsa had kept the silverware. ''If you'll tell the girls to wash up, I'll have supper on the table.''

Clay went to find his daughters. He was rather awed by Amity's firm air and wondered how Kate and Jemima had found the courage to talk back to her.

Left alone in the kitchen, Amity drew in a deep breath to calm herself. She had been afraid to confront Clay on the matter of his daughters and the magnitude of his lie, but he had not only *not* lost his temper with her but had shown respect for her authority. Evidently, her fear of conflicts made her appear more formidable than she actually was. Before now, she had assumed everyone could see past her front and know how often she felt shy and unable to cope. Perhaps her perception of herself was wrong.

Chapter Three

In the days that followed, Amity had ample opportunity to watch Clay interact with his children, and she was moved by the love she saw between them. The girls clearly doted on their father, and he was devoted to them. That everyone more or less ignored Amity was uncomfortable to her, but she had to admit that she was a stranger to them all.

What worried her more than anything was the fact that Clay made it plain to her that he did not want the intimacies of marriage. He was still married to Elsa in his heart, and he would have no substitute. Amity hoped that, in time, his stance on that issue would change, but with each passing day, the luxury for her to wait patiently diminished. If she was pregnant—and she had reason to think she was—she would have no hope of convincing Clay the child was his unless they made love.

Further complicating things, now that she was getting to know Clay, she was having second thoughts about lying to him about the child. He was a good man and he had been kind to her, and his only deceitful act toward her had not been self-serving. And he was a terrific father who dearly loved his children. How could she lie to him about something so important? Yet how could she not?

On the fourth day at supper time, Amity heard a buggy arrive out front. As they had had no visitors since her arrival and she was naturally curious, she hurried to look out the window. A woman who appeared to be somewhat older than herself and a teenage girl were climbing out of a buggy. She knew at once that must be Hallie and her aunt.

Amity rushed around straightening the rugs and chairs in the parlor. She wanted to make a good impression on the girl. Was the aunt Clay's sister or Elsa's? She couldn't remember. So much had happened on the day of her arrival, the details were a blur. She went back to the porch to tell Clay of their arrival.

"Papa?" the girl called out in a clear voice as she came into the house. "Look, Aunt Gretchen. We must have a new housekeeper."

Amity felt a sense of pride. In the few days she had been here, she had worked miracles on the house. It was almost clean enough to satisfy her own high standards.

Clay hurried past her and swept his daughter into his embrace. "Hallie! It's good to see you. Did you have a good trip? Hello, Gretchen."

Amity took a deep breath and stepped into the parlor. Hallie bore a striking resemblance to all Clay's other daughters except that her eyes were blue, not green. Her pale blond hair was pulled back in a thick braid and tied neatly with a white ribbon that matched the trim on her navy dress. The woman beside her also had blond hair and blue eyes and strongly resembled the children. When Amity stepped into the room, Gretchen stopped talking to Clay and stared at her.

Clay turned and paused for a minute. "This is Amity Morgan. Amity, I'd like for you to meet my sister-in-law, Gretchen Harris, and my eldest daughter, Hallie."

Amity smiled. So the children looked like their mother and her sister. That made sense because Clay had darker hair.

"Hello, Miss Morgan," Gretchen said after a moment. "You must be one of Clay's cousins. Will you be visiting long?"

Amity's eyes met Clay's, prompting him to say, "No, this is my wife."

Hallie spun and stared openmouthed at Amity. Gretchen's reaction was almost as extreme.

"I've been writing to Amity for some time now, and she agreed to come to Texas to be my wife. We were married last week."

"Married!" Hallie's head whipped to her father. "You married without even telling me you were going to?"

"You weren't here. I told your sisters."

Amity smiled at the girl. "I hope you and I will be close friends." She was not going to make the same mistake she had earlier with the others of referring to herself as the girl's mother.

Hallie's eyes filled with tears and she bolted from the room.

Clay frowned after her. "I have to talk to her. Make yourself at home, Gretchen." He left in pursuit of Hallie.

Amity found herself alone with Gretchen, who was regarding her with no friendliness at all. "Would you like a cup of coffee? Or some tea?"

"No. Are you really Clay's wife?"

"Yes. Yes, I am. We were married the day of my arrival. We agreed it wouldn't be proper to do otherwise."

Gretchen walked around her as if Amity were a heifer she was inspecting. "Why is it I've never heard of you? How long have you known Clay?"

Already, Amity disliked the woman and did not at all appreciate being stared at in such a way. "I have no idea why he never mentioned me to you. We've written each other for several months."

Gretchen's eyes narrowed. "He was writing to you with Elsa barely in her grave? Where are you from?"

"Charlotte, North Carolina."

"No wonder you don't sound as if you come from around here."

Amity drew herself up. Gretchen had pushed past discourtesy straight into disrespect.

"Why were you and Clay in such a hurry to be married? Why couldn't you have waited until Hallie and I returned from our trip? There's a perfectly good boardinghouse in Ransom where you could have stayed."

"You'll have to ask Clay about that." Amity was pretty sure Clay had been so quick to marry her in order for her not to hear how many children he had and what a handful they were. Certainly it was not because he wanted her to share his bed, as this woman seemed to be implying. She had been a virtual stranger to him on her arrival, and he had been barely more than politely civil to her since. But she had no intention of telling Gretchen this.

"I intend to do just that." Gretchen's ice-blue eyes darted around the parlor as if she was looking for something to fault. "You've made some changes."

"Yes. I cleaned house."

"You've moved the pair of Staffordshire dogs from the mantel. My mother brought them from England before she died."

"I put them on the sideboard in the dining room. Clay hasn't objected." Amity thought the matching ceramic dogs were the ugliest knicknacks she had ever seen.

"He must not have noticed. Men aren't all that observant. I want them put back on the mantel where they belong. Elsa would never have moved them."

Amity knew more was on trial here than the placement of two ceramic dogs. "I didn't like them there. The colors don't look right in this room."

Gretchen glared at her. "I wasn't discussing it. I was telling you how it must be."

"I'm afraid you're mistaken. I'm not a housekeeper here, I'm the wife. This is my house now. The dogs stay where they are." Amity had known women like Gretchen before, and she knew from experience that it wouldn't do to show any weakness before her.

Gretchen lifted her chin. "I'm afraid you're in for some surprises if you take that attitude with me."

Amity tried another tack. "Let's try to start all over again, shall we? I don't want you to have hard feelings against me. I assumed Clay had told you about me and that we were to be married. I realize this has been a shock to you, but I'm really not to blame. I understand that this is what you're upset over, and not those silly dogs.''

"My mother's Staffordshire dogs are not silly.'' Gretchen's icy gaze frosted over. ''As for your marriage, I know only one reason for having one so sudden.''

Amity's eyes widened. Then she realized Gretchen couldn't possibly know. She snapped her aloofness into place. ''Since I came here directly from Charlotte, I don't see how you believe Clay could have compromised me. Nor do I intend to stand here in my own house and be insulted. Good day, Mrs. Harris. I think you know your way out.'' Amity knew she was taking a big chance. Gretchen might stay and appeal to Clay to put his new wife in her place.

Instead, she gave Amity a final glare and marched out of the house.

Amity grabbed onto the back of the nearest chair to steady herself. It was hard to believe all that had just transpired. In a matter of minutes, she had made an enemy of someone she could not afford to have against her. Still, she knew there was nothing else she could have done. At least their animosity was out in the open. ''Better an enemy I know than one who is working behind my back,'' she murmured as she had heard her aunt Dorcus say many times.

Amity's automatic identification with one of her aunts caused her even further distress. She had spent most of her youth trying to be as unlike them as possible.

Upstairs Clay was making little headway with Hallie. ''I didn't know you'd be this upset. You knew I was considering finding you a new mother.''

Hallie's sobs doubled and she buried her face in her pillow. ''She's not my mother!'' Her sisters took up the same chorus.

''Hush, all of you. I know she's not. But your mother is gone, and there's nothing I can do about that.'' He took Rosemary on one knee and Laura on the other. ''I love you girls and I needed someone to take care of you.''

"I was doing that." Hallie sobbed. "I was only gone for a week!"

"Hallie, you were doing the best you could, but you're only thirteen. You're not old enough to know how to raise the little ones, and you're not that much older than the others. I needed someone my age, someone old enough to raise you all properly."

"I'm already raised!" Hallie cried out. "I don't need a nursemaid."

"Neither do I," Kate added quickly. "We don't like her."

"Can we send her away?" Jemima asked. "I liked the last housekeeper better than her."

"The one you dropped the frog on? The same one you switched the sugar and salt with? The one who was here when you chased the goat through the wash? That housekeeper? She didn't stay as long as her predecessors."

Jemima looked down at the floor. "We don't like this one," she repeated.

"She makes us clean our rooms," Kate said to Hallie. "And she actually checks to see if we did!"

"And if our hands aren't clean enough to suit her, we have to leave the table and wash them all over again," Laura put in. "She's real particular."

"She sounds just awful," Hallie gasped. "Papa, why did you have to marry her?"

"Look here, all of you. You've managed to chase away every woman I've hired since your mother died. I had to have someone. What would your mother say if she could see the way this house was being kept? What if she saw how you girls had been misbehaving? I had to do something."

"But *marriage*, Papa?" Hallie wailed. "I don't want anyone trying to take Mama's place."

"Neither do we," her sisters joined in.

"She knows that, and she isn't trying to take her place. Amity is a very reasonable woman, as far as I can tell."

"What do you mean, as far as you can tell?" Hallie demanded. "Didn't you even know her before you married her?"

"Not very well." Clay didn't want to admit she had been practically a stranger. Now that he knew Amity, he couldn't imagine her ever answering an ad such as he had put in the newspaper.

"Then you must have met her after Mama died. How could you do it? Don't you still love Mama?" Hallie looked at him with eyes so similar to Elsa's and with a face that was almost identical to Elsa's when he had first met her.

"I'll always love your mother," he said gently. "You'll never know how much I love her. But now I can only love her memory. Life goes on and we have to live in it. I'd give anything to have her back, but that can't be. So we have to do the best we can."

"Is Amity the best we can do?" little Rosemary asked.

Clay smiled at his youngest. "Yes, and we're lucky to have found her."

"I don't think so," Kate stated. "She's nothing like Mama at all. Aunt Gretchen is more like Mama."

Hallie nodded. "You've said how much they look alike. Why didn't you marry her, Papa?"

"I don't love Aunt Gretchen. Not the way a husband is supposed to love his wife."

"Do you love Amity?"

"No."

"Then what difference would it make?" Hallie demanded. "At least *we* all love Aunt Gretchen."

"I can't explain that to you. As you get older you'll understand. There are some women you can marry without loving and there some women you can't."

"And Amity is one you don't need to love?" Laura's small brow was puckered as she tried to understand all this.

Clay knew he was saying this all wrong. "Amity and I can start off with a clean slate. If I had married Gretchen, well, it just wouldn't have worked out." He couldn't tell his young daughters that he couldn't have insisted that Gretchen live in the spare room, as Amity was. She would have expected to share his bed, and he didn't want that. He wasn't sure he could ever look on another woman with passion.

Not with his beloved Elsa in her grave. "No, Gretchen would never have been a good choice for us."

"She would have married you," Hallie said.

Clay looked at her sharply. "Did she say that?"

"No, not in so many words, but I think she would have."

"She has no right to imply any such thing to you." Clay had been uneasy around Gretchen often before Elsa's death, and more frequently since. At times she had flirted with him in such a way he could not have failed to know what she was offering.

"Aunt Gretchen didn't do anything wrong." Hallie had always been Gretchen's strongest supporter. "She couldn't possibly."

"The point is, I've married Amity, not Aunt Gretchen, and Amity is here to stay. You girls will just have to get used to the idea. She has been kind to you and she is remarkably efficient."

Hallie exchanged a look with Kate. "Maybe she's staying and maybe she's not."

"She made me a pound cake on her first day here," Rosemary said. "I shared it with everyone."

"It wasn't like the ones Mama used to make," Jemima said. "It tasted different."

"I liked it," Rosemary stated firmly. "And I like the way she combs my hair without it pulling." Rosemary had a tender scalp, and she usually hated to have her hair combed.

"You'd like anybody," Kate snapped. "You're just a baby."

"I'm not a baby!"

Clay put up his hand for quiet. "No fussing. Kate, you're not to call Rosemary a baby. You wouldn't like it if someone called you that."

Kate fell back on the bed and glared at the ceiling. Rosemary patted her father fondly.

"Give her a chance, Hallie. You don't know her. You may find you like her. She's not short-tempered, and she tries to keep the house pretty much in the same way your mother did. Meals are on time and she's a good cook."

"It's nice having clean clothes," Laura agreed. "She even irons the ruffles on my play dresses."

"Do you think she would iron my doll dresses?" Rosemary asked Laura. Because they were the closest in age, they often played dolls together. "Bertha is all rumpled."

"You can ask her," Clay said with a smile. "If she's too busy, maybe Hallie will do it."

"We have chores," Kate said looking toward the ceiling to avoid making eye contact. "I have to help churn in addition to keeping my room. Jemima has to gather all the eggs."

"Those aren't difficult jobs," their father said.

"I'm to pick flowers for the table," Rosemary said proudly. "I do it just right."

"She lets you pick Mama's flowers?" Hallie gasped. "Not her roses!"

Rosemary shook her head. "They have thorns. I pick the yellow ones and the white ones."

"Mama never put flowers on the table." Hallie glared at her father. "I thought you said she was keeping the house like Mama did."

"I said she keeps it in the same sort of way. Clean. She keeps it clean and running properly. As for the flowers on the table, what can it hurt?"

"I like them," Rosemary spoke up quickly. Laura nodded.

"Mama never let you pick her flowers," Hallie snapped.

"I was younger then," Rosemary reasoned.

Clay hugged her and put her, then Laura, on the floor. "I have to go down and thank Gretchen for letting you go with her on the trip. Are you all right now?"

Hallie nodded mutely, but she looked as if she was about to start crying again.

"I'm glad to have you back home." Clay turned and went downstairs.

In the parlor he found only Amity. A glance out the window told him that Gretchen's buggy was gone. "Gretchen left?"

Amity nodded. She looked at him with troubled eyes. "I assumed you would have told your family that I was coming. Hallie seemed to have no idea that I even existed."

Clay looked away. "There wasn't time. I received your letter saying you could come as soon as I sent your ticket and I acted at once. Hallie had already gone and I had no way of telling her. I could hardly have done it by telegram, and a letter would not have had time to reach her."

"Is she terribly upset?"

"She'll come around. Hallie has a good head on her shoulders."

"She's very pretty."

He nodded. "She looks more like Elsa than any of the others. Sometimes I look at her and it's like seeing Elsa as she would have looked at that age. She's not much younger than Elsa was when we met."

Amity turned away and didn't answer.

"Why did Gretchen leave so soon? I thought she might stay for supper."

"You may as well know. We had words."

"You did? What over?"

"She told me I should put those china dogs back on the mantel."

Clay looked at the mantel with puzzlement. "I hadn't noticed they were missing. Where are they?"

"On the sideboard in the dining room. I told her I like them better in there."

He shrugged. "I don't see what there is to argue over in that. You may put them wherever you please."

"She said her mother had brought them from England and that it was important that they remain where Elsa had put them."

"As far as I know Elsa never cared that much for them. I recall her laughing and saying what a pity it was that they wouldn't break easily."

Amity relaxed visibly. "If you'd like, I'll return them to the mantel."

"No, I never liked them. The colors are peculiar."

She smiled. "I agree."

"We should keep them out somewhere, though. They mean something to Gretchen and the girls." He thought for a minute. "I must apologize for Hallie. She was startled at the news. She isn't usually rude."

"I understand. I might have done the same thing in her place."

"She didn't know I was considering marriage, I guess. I assumed the girls knew that when I told them I was going to start keeping company again."

"Children can't necessarily understand comments like that." Amity straightened a crocheted doily on one of the side tables. "I know what she must be feeling."

"You do?"

"Both my parents died when I was young. I was raised by my maiden aunts."

Clay studied her. This was the first he had heard about her having been *raised* by aunts. What about the family she had written about?

"They didn't particularly care for children," Amity went on. "I think I was a complete shock to them. There was no one else to take me, however, and my mother was their younger sister."

"What about your brother and sister?"

"I don't have a brother or sister." Amity turned to him quickly, as if she was surprised, then a veil dropped behind her eyes and she went toward the dining room door.

"I'll have supper on the table in half an hour," she said as she left.

Clay was thoughtful as he watched her pass from sight. There were a number of things about Amity that didn't add up. He was positive she had written about an older sister who was married and a brother who was attending college in Raleigh. She had never mentioned aunts at all in her letters.

That night as Amity readied herself for bed, she thought back on the day. Hallie had been almost totally silent at supper, as had Kate and Jemima. Laura and Rosemary had talked incessantly, as was their habit, but the older girls had been too quiet. Amity wasn't accustomed to conversation at mealtimes. Her aunts had taught her to eat as quietly as possible and to leave the table before starting a conversation. Clearly, none of the Morgan girls had ever been taught this.

She had tried to be friendly to Hallie, but every time their eyes met, she had seen definite dislike in the girl's expression. Amity blamed Clay for not telling the girls ahead of time. She realized now that the girls who had been at home must have only expected her for a matter of days before her arrival. It was no wonder she was having difficulty with them.

Amity drew her brush through her long auburn hair. She studied its color in the lamplight. It was no wonder to her that Clay didn't find her attractive. Her aunts had made no secret of the fact that her red hair flawed what little beauty she might otherwise have had. Amity was accustomed to the fact, but she still silently rebelled against it. In their youths, her aunts, like her mother, had had comfortable brown hair, as had their revered brother, Raymond. Amity's father, however, had had more than a touch of red in his hair, and she had inherited her auburn coloring from him.

She allowed herself to think about Emmett Hamilton for a moment. He had called her pretty. He had wanted her enough to get her into trouble, but not enough to marry her. Amity put him from her mind. What did it matter if Emmett had said she was pretty? Obviously Clay didn't share that opinion.

She went to her bed and lifted the covers to climb in, but before she swung her hips onto the bed, something alerted her to be cautious. Carefully, she pulled the covers back all the way, and there on her sheets sat a frog.

Amity reached across and picked him up. "Which one did this, I wonder." The frog only regarded her and wriggled.

As it was late and everyone was already asleep, Amity did not bother to put on her wrapper in order to take the frog outside. She opened her door onto the dark dining room and gingerly felt her way across to the door.

As she stepped onto the porch, the boards beneath her feet felt cool, and a breeze lifted her nightgown and billowed it around her. Amity had no fear of the dark. She went down the steps and put the frog in the grass. "Go back to the pond and next time hop faster," she advised. "I could have stepped on you."

She looked up at the black sky and the powdering of stars. When she was a girl, she had wished on stars. Then Aunt Ophelia had caught her doing it, and had scolded her soundly for being superstitious. What had it mattered? she thought rebelliously. She picked out a star and said softly, "I wish I may, I wish I might, have the wish I wish tonight. More than anything I want them all to like me."

At once she felt foolish. She was a grown woman of twenty-four years, and here she was standing in the yard wearing nothing but her nightgown and wishing on stars. What if someone saw her?

Amity hurried back into the house.

Clay continued sitting motionless on the stump by the woodpile, just as he had been when Amity had come unexpectedly out of the house. What had she been carrying? A frog? He had heard her tell it to hop back to the pond. Kate, he decided. She had no qualms about picking up a frog. Hallie and Jemima were afraid they would get warts. Tomorrow he would have to speak to Kate about not putting frogs in Amity's room.

Unbidden, the recollection of every detail of the scene he had just witnessed came back to him, the way she had looked standing there in the moonlight, the way she had taken time to stare into the heavens and the wish she had made. He felt a bit guilty about not letting her know he was there, but she had been dressed only in her nightgown, and he had not wanted to embarrass her. Not that he could see her all that well, anyway. He had heard her plainly enough, though. She had wished they would all like her.

Before now, Clay had thought remarkably little about what Amity might or might not be feeling. Now, it occurred to him that he had been insensitive in that regard. She must have had dreams before coming here to be his wife, but he had no idea what they might have been. Why had she come? She was pretty. If she loosened her hair and wore dresses that were less severe and somber, she might even be beautiful. She could have married any of several men, he was sure. Surely, men in Charlotte were not blind. So why had she chosen to come here and marry a total stranger?

Then there was the matter of the discrepancies in her background. He could see why she would write him under a fictitious name in order to preserve her privacy in case he turned out to be a cad, but why fabricate a family when she had only two aunts? Which version was a lie?

He thought of her straitlaced manner. She moved and spoke as a person might who had never been around others of her own age. Spinster aunts might instill such a formal manner. Why had she not learned more social graces from her friends, however? He could not imagine Amity ever flirting or dancing or even laughing aloud. She had a pleasant demeanor, but her smiles were rare and often she stopped smiling if she noticed he was watching her. Why was she reluctant to smile? She had pretty teeth, and when she smiled she became strikingly beautiful.

Clay shook his head brusquely. He had no business thinking Amity was beautiful or caring if she was. She was here to be a mother to the girls, nothing else. He had no intention of noticing anything about any woman ever again. Elsa had been gone less than a year, and whenever he thought of her, he felt a grief so strong it became a physical pain. Even if he didn't still love Elsa, he didn't want to fall in love again. Life was too precarious. If he loved again and she died, too, he was not sure he could survive it. No, it was safer and better in every way for him to keep his emotions bottled up inside.

He recalled Elsa, and how it was the birth of his child that killed her. None of the births had been easy. Elsa had had narrow hips and had been such a fragile woman. His son had been too large and had been turned the wrong way. Even with the doctor's help, she had been unable to give birth to him.

Clay recalled the tragedy of that day to the depths of his heart. The doctor had come out and told him in simple terms that Elsa was gone. Clay had not believed it at first, not until he was taken into the room and he had seen Elsa lying too still and cold on the bed, her marvelous light hair still damp with the sweat of her efforts. His grief had nearly killed him. His grief and his guilt. The baby boy had lived a few hours, but it, too, was unable to survive the birthing. Gretchen had been there, and she had taken care of everything. Clay had no idea what he would have done without her help.

Elsa and the baby boy had been buried together in the family cemetery between their road and Gretchen's. Elsa lay by her parents and a brother who had died in infancy. Gretchen had commented in her grief how her family seemed unable to birth strong sons. Clay had only wanted his wife back. As much as he had wanted a son, he would have chosen to live barren forever if that could have returned his Elsa to him.

He gazed at his dark and silent house. Now another woman lived there. A woman he barely knew. A woman who stood in the dark in her nightgown, a frog at her feet, and she had wished upon a star that he and his daughters would like her.

Clay slowly got up from the stump. He owed Amity more than she had received. She had interrupted her life, whatever it had been, to come to Texas and be a mother to his children. He certainly was obliged to show her more friendliness than he had. He resolved to get to know her better in the hope his daughters would see his efforts and do the same.

Chapter Four

As Amity became more accustomed to hearing the sound of children all around her, her shyness abated and so did her aloof manner. She had rarely been around children, even before her parents died. At first she had found them rather fearful. After two weeks at the farmhouse, however, she began to listen to the sounds of girlish laughter and the pattering of footsteps as if they were a normal part of her new life.

She had no difficulty adjusting to keeping the house. She soon found a house in Ransom wasn't all that different than one in Charlotte. Farm life was a bit trickier, but she was a quick learner. Her one difficulty was in milking. Clay showed her how, much to Amity's embarrassment, but she still couldn't seem to master it. Clay assigned the chore to Hallie, giving the girl one more reason to resent Amity.

As every morning, Amity thanked Hallie when she brought in the bucket of milk from the barn. Hallie, as always, pretended not to have heard her. While Amity strained the milk into the pitcher and washed the milk bucket, she wondered how to become close to the girl.

"Hallie, would you like for me to make you a new dress? I saw some blue calico at the dry goods store that would be so pretty with your eyes."

"No. Thank you," she added as an obvious afterthought. "I'd rather wear the dresses Mama made for me."

Amity refrained from pointing out that the dresses wouldn't last forever. It was sometimes difficult to remember, since Elsa had been gone six months when Amity arrived, that the family was still in mourning. Neither the girls nor Clay wore black or even the black arm bands or onyx jewelry, but they mourned just the same.

Clay overheard her offer, and when Hallie was gone, he came to her. "That was kind of you."

"I enjoy sewing. I'd like to make all the girls a dress when their mourning is over."

He was silent for a minute. "Some mourning is never over." She knew he was referring to himself. "The little ones are already mending. Rosemary and Laura laugh as easily as they did before."

"They are still babies, really. They mean no disrespect." She rarely knew how to talk to him. This was one of the few conversations they had had that didn't revolve around chores.

"I know. I keep reminding myself that it's better for them this way."

"When my parents died I was a year older than Jemima. My aunts insisted that I wear black for the entire year. I was new to Charlotte and wanted to make friends, but they turned down every invitation as long as I was in black."

Clay looked at her with interest. "That must have been hard on you. You were just a child."

"They meant well. They loved my parents and it hurt them to see me forgetting the pain and getting on with my life."

"I gather I'm to glean a lesson from this? Do you think I'm too hard on the girls?"

"Not hard. I'd not use that word. I think you might remember that they are all so young. I don't think mourning is in a child's nature once the worst pain is over."

"That's why I don't dress them in black. Or myself. We're trying to get on with our lives."

"Are you?" she asked, not believing what he had said was true. Out of kindness for him, she had stopped short of saying that it seemed to her that he was acting as if he had buried his wife only days before.

His face expressionless, he said, "I have work to do at the barn." Then he left.

Through the kitchen window Amity watched him cross the yard. Lately she had found herself watching him more and more often, wondering who this man was. Although his head was slightly bent as if he was deep in thought, his steps were sure and his movements purposeful. His body was lean and firm, and while he possessed more strength than any man she had ever known, he was also better coordinated, even graceful. At night Amity often found herself remembering how his muscles rippled beneath his shirt when he would lift some object too heavy for her or when he was romping with the younger children. Even when he was sitting still, he exuded strength.

Breaking from her revery, she began making plans for dinner. On her way out to the smokehouse to get a ham for supper, the chickens followed her expectantly, clucking softly in hopes of an extra handout of food. Amity liked them and spoke to them in a low voice so no one would overhear her and think she was odd. The hens clucked back.

As Amity pulled the leather latch on the smokehouse door, a strange noise caught her attention. She listened more carefully. Was that someone crying? As she circled the building to investigate, she found Laura sitting on the grass just beyond the raised boxes where the hens had their nests. Amity hurried to her and bent down to see what was wrong with her. "Laura? Are you hurt?"

Laura shook her head but would not look up.

Amity became concerned. She had seldom seen any of the girls cry and then only because of some bump or bruise during their play. As she sat down on the grass beside Laura, the girl surprised her by crawling into her lap. Amity held her while she cried. At length, when Laura's sobs grew softer, Amity said, "What happened? Did one of your sisters hurt you?"

Laura shook her head and held up her doll. It was her favorite, the one she always took to bed with her. One of its rag arms was torn off. "Shep did it. He killed Betsy."

Amity took the doll and examined the arm. "She's not killed. I can fix her as good as new."

"She'll never be the same. Mama made her, and now Shep has chewed her arm off."

Amity understood. Laura wasn't crying because the dog had torn her doll. She was crying because Elsa wasn't there to mend it. "Will you let me try? I know how important Betsy is to you."

After a moment's consideration, Laura nodded. "Can you really fix her?"

"I promise I can." Amity stood and brushed the grass from her skirt. She took Laura's hand and led her to the house. "I had a doll a lot like Betsy when I was just about your age. My mama showed me how to mend her. Would you like for me to show you how she taught me to do it?"

Laura nodded. "I guess so."

Amity smiled at the girl and took her inside for a sewing lesson.

Clay, who had seen Laura sitting in the grass from the barn, had been coming to see about her when Amity found her. He had seen the entire exchange. Although he wasn't close enough to hear what was said, it was clear what was taking place. He was full of thought as he returned to his chores. Amity was trying to fit in and she was kinder to the children than she was to him. He could see the youngest ones were being won over by her.

That bothered him, in a way. He wanted all his children to be happy, but he discovered he also expected them never to put anyone in Elsa's place. Was that unreasonable?

He jabbed the pitchfork into the hay and tossed the hay to the other side of the loft. He remembered how the sun had touched fires in Amity's auburn hair. Elsa's had been paler than gold. She had been beautiful in a gentle sort of a way. In the past few days he had found himself comparing her to Amity, and at times Amity had fared better in comparison.

His muscles bunched as he sent more of the loose hay to the floor above the hayrack. He would never forget Elsa. Never. But he thought how pretty Amity had looked when she had smiled at Laura, and how trustingly the girl had taken Amity's hand. Clay worked harder.

That night as Clay was washing up for supper he heard a sound he hadn't heard in a long time. He heard a woman singing. He paused, water dripping from his face and hands. Amity was singing. He would have said she didn't know any songs, she was so coolly aloof to him.

He opened the door a crack and peered into the dining room. She was showing Jemima how to set the table. Jemima smiled at her and sang the chorus with her, only stumbling a time or two on the higher notes. He closed the door softly. How had she known Jemima loved music? Elsa had often sung with the girl, and Clay knew she had a remarkable voice for her age. At eight she could play fairly complex songs on Gretchen's piano, even though no one had taught her much more than a scale.

He finished cleaning up for supper and went into the dining room. When Amity saw him, she stopped singing and moved silently about her business of putting the meal on the table. He smelled the aroma. Even if supper was generally the leftovers from dinner, she always saw to it they were warmed and served as if they were new to the table.

He sat at his place. Amity sat opposite to the chair that had been Elsa's. Their eyes met and he looked away. How often had he done that with Elsa? Amity's cheeks were pink as if she were blushing when he glanced at her. Was she embarrassed because their eyes met or was she angry at him for looking away? He couldn't read her meanings the way he could Elsa's.

She was helping Rosemary fill her plate with food. The girl sat beside her where Amity could help her cut her meat.

Amity bent toward her to tell her to hold her fork properly. The domesticity of the scene tore at Clay's heart.

"She holds her fork just fine," Hallie suddenly said.

Amity looked up in surprise. "She needs to learn the correct way so she won't be embarrassed when she's out in public."

"We never eat anywhere but here or at Aunt Gretchen's." Hallie was glaring across the table at Amity. Laura had stopped eating and looked as if she were about to cry again.

"Hallie!" Clay said more sharply than he intended. "Stop arguing and eat. Where are your manners?"

Hallie turned her angry eyes on her father, stood up and threw her napkin in her plate. "I don't eat where I'm not wanted!"

Clay half rose to go after her, but he saw the tears in Laura's eyes and how Jemima was staring at him with a stricken look on her face. "Don't be upset," he said to them. "Eat your supper."

Amity frowned at him. "Would you like for me to go up and speak to her?"

"No." He knew that would make matters worse. Hallie seemed to truly dislike Amity, though he couldn't see why. Amity apparently was trying to win her over as much as she was trying with Hallie's sisters.

Amity picked up her fork and stabbed it into her peas. Clay knew he should have been more polite in his refusal. Was it too late? "Hallie will eat when she's hungry."

"I wasn't worried about her eating."

He glanced at the other children. He didn't want to get into a discussion in front of them over why Hallie felt she could be rude to Amity. He knew Hallie was behaving in a deplorable way and he suspected she might behave even worse when he wasn't around, but he could understand why. Hallie missed her mother more than the younger ones did. She was fighting harder not to have Amity replace her.

The meal passed in a strained silence. None of the girls ate much, and they asked if they could be excused before the meal was over. He gave them each permission. As Kate left the table, she took a thick slice of corn bread with her. "For Hallie," she said.

Amity frowned. He looked down the long table at her. It seemed too long and empty without his daughters filling the chairs. "When I was a girl, I was expected to sit at the table for the entire meal."

"I see no reason to do that. The ones that are through eating just pick at the ones who aren't."

"That's why manners are taught. And Kate took food up to Hallie. How will Hallie ever learn to behave if she's pampered when she's rude?"

"I don't think any of my children will improve by being starved."

"I wasn't advocating starvation. It wouldn't hurt her to miss supper since it was her choice to do so."

Clay frowned at Amity. "She will never accept you if you continue to treat her so harshly."

"Harshly? How am I being harsh?" Amity seemed amazed. "I didn't send her from the table. I didn't even correct her deplorable manner of speaking to me. I assumed you would," she added.

"I was raising my children before I ever heard of you. I don't need your advice." His voice was sharper and louder than he had intended. She had a way of getting under his skin, and he didn't like being that vulnerable to her.

Amity put her fork down and folded her hands in her lap. She watched him as he tried to eat.

"Well?" he said at last.

"I'm waiting for you to finish before I leave the table." Her tone of voice was frigid.

Clay put down his fork. He couldn't eat with her staring at him so accusingly. "I'm through." He stood up and abruptly left the table.

In his room he lay fully clothed on his bed. How had the meal gone to pieces so completely? He felt as if emotions were growing so thick he could almost see them in the air.

Through the closed door he could hear Amity clearing the table. By the sounds she was as angry as he was.

He knew Hallie had behaved poorly and that he ought to take her to task, but Elsa had always been the one to reprove the children and Clay didn't know exactly how to go about it. When he spoke to them harshly they cried and he came away feeling as if he had been cruel. He recalled his own childhood and told himself Hallie didn't need discipline. In time she would learn from his example. He would never be as hard on his children as his parents had been on him.

He hoped the dishes wouldn't break under Amity's anger. She was clearly as upset as he was.

Amity rarely stayed angry, and by the next day she was ready to forget the unpleasantness at supper. She was showing Jemima a new stitch for her sampler. Jemima, who was much better at singing than at sewing, was resisting.

"It's not that difficult," Amity said in a reasonable voice. "If you use a shorter thread it won't snarl like this." She picked the knot from the sampler and handed it to the girl. "Try again."

Hallie had come into the parlor and was watching them with growing irritation. "She doesn't have to do that if she doesn't want to."

Amity looked up and kept her face a careful mask. "She must learn to sew. All girls need to know how, whether they ever do it or not."

"I'm never going to sew," Hallie stated. "When I'm married my husband will buy all my dresses ready-made, or we'll hire someone to do it for me."

"You must plan to marry a rich man," Amity said with some amusement. "Not everyone is that lucky."

"Are you talking about Papa? Did you want to find a richer husband but had to settle for us?"

Amity looked at her in surprise. "No, that's not what I meant. I'm quite happy here."

Hallie wasn't ready to let the matter drop. "You never talk about where you came from. Why did you agree to marry Papa in the first place? You didn't know him. Aunt Gretchen says she thinks it's peculiar, and so do I."

"I had my reasons." She took the needle and thread from Jemima and helped her thread it.

"I'll bet you're escaping from some lurid past," Hallie said, her blue eyes glittering as she closed in for the kill.

That hit too close to home. "Ladies don't bet," Amity said coolly. "And how do you know the word lurid?"

"Aunt Gretchen said it and she told me what it means. It means a scarlet past. But I see you already know the word, don't you?"

Jemima was staring at them, and Amity knew she had to take a stand. "Yes, I know the word. I know the word because I read books and because I have an education. When you're out of school, you'll know a number of words, as well. Now we're trying to work on Jemima's sampler. Please go play somewhere else."

"Play! I'm not a child."

"Then stop acting like one. At your age, you should be a help to your sisters as well as to your parents, rather than to stand about doing nothing."

"You aren't my parent. You're only a stepmother. You don't count around here."

"You're wrong." Amity wished she hadn't begun this, especially with Jemima listening to every word. "Now run along. You're upsetting your sister."

"You don't even sleep with Papa," Hallie said, pushing her advantage. "That proves you don't count."

Amity stood up and glared at Hallie. "That's quite enough! What are you thinking of to talk like that in front of Jemima? Much less to say such a thing to me?"

Hallie gave her a smug smile. "Wait until Aunt Gretchen hears you have separate bedrooms." She whirled on her heels and left the room.

Amity stared after her, then remembered Jemima and sat down. "Where are we?" She was so upset she couldn't think straight, let alone keep her fingers from trembling. "Are you tired of sewing? We can do this another time."

"No, I want to learn how." Jemima frowned at the cloth in her lap. "Why do you and Papa sleep in separate bedrooms? Mama always slept in his bed. If you're married to him, why are you in the guest bedroom?"

Amity sighed. Hallie had certainly opened a can of worms this time. "It's because we don't yet know each other that well," she said carefully. "Usually when a man and woman marry, they have known each other for a long time. Most people are engaged for a year and have gone out together a year or two before that."

"Why did Papa order you out of a newspaper?"

"He didn't order me. Parcels are ordered, not people. He needed a mother for you girls. I wanted to leave Charlotte. It was that simple."

Jemima smiled. "He got you for us?"

"More or less."

"Good. Show me again how to do that stitch." She leaned nearer Amity so that her arm pressed against Amity's side.

Amity was always surprised by the girls' spontaneous affection. She couldn't imagine ever cuddling up to one of her aunts. Even her own mother, for that matter, hadn't been one to encourage cuddling. Jemima and her younger sisters, however, seemed to take it for granted that they were loved and that adults were made for cuddling. Amity hugged her and showed her again how to make the stitch.

When Hallie left Amity and Jemima she went in search of her father. She found him in the cow barn. "Papa, I have to talk to you."

"Hello, honey. What's on your mind?" He was mending a cracked step that led up to the hayloft.

"Do we really have to keep Amity?"

He stopped what he was doing and looked at her. "Of course we do, I'm married to her."

"You don't sleep in the same room." Hallie thought since that had worked so well with Amity she might try it on her father. "I don't think that means you're really and truly married."

"You don't know what you're talking about."

"Yes, I do!" She hated it when people talked to her as if she were Rosemary's age.

He stopped working again. "Have you been talking to Aunt Gretchen?"

"No, but I wish I had. I miss her coming over every day. We haven't seen her since Amity came here."

"Gretchen will call again when she gets used to the idea that I have a wife."

"You should have married her."

"I don't love her the way a man ought to love the woman he marries."

"You don't love Amity at all!"

Clay turned back to his work. "You're discussing things you don't know anything about."

Hallie glared at him. "I want to go live with Aunt Gretchen."

"No. That's out of the question."

"Why is it? She loves me and I love her. Why can't I live where I can be happy?"

"You're part of this family. You'll stay with us."

"Amity is mean to us when you're not around," Hallie said with sudden inspiration. "She's only nice when she thinks you'll see what she's doing."

Clay looked up. "Mean? In what way?"

Hallie thought fast. "She's in the parlor trying to teach Jemima to sew on that stupid sampler and Jemima is crying." Hallie's imagination climbed. "Amity slapped her and told her she's a foolish girl!"

"I don't believe it." He looked as if he might, however.

"It's true. If you ask me, she treats the babies even worse when she knows no one is around. Kate hates her. She pulled Kate's hair the other day," she added for emphasis.

Clay glared at the house and dropped the hammer on the step. He strode off, and Hallie had to run to keep up. Her heart was pounding with excitement. Maybe he was going to send Amity away at once!

Clay let himself into the house by way of the kitchen so he could approach the parlor unseen. He could hear voices, but they didn't seem to be arguing. Hallie crept along at his side, and she looked as pleased as if she had won a battle.

At the parlor door he stopped and listened. Hallie put her ear to the door, and it struck him that she seemed to know exactly how to eavesdrop.

"Let's try it again, Jemima," he heard Amity say. "What if we sing it?" There was a pause, then Amity sang, "We put the thread in here and then we draw it out. We put the needle here and we twist the thread about. Then we poke it back through the cloth and a French knot is left. Now you try it."

Jemima's voice lifted in the makeshift tune. "I put the thread in here and then I draw it out. Look, Amity. It didn't tangle!"

"That's good. Just go slow and take your time. We put the needle here and we twist the thread about. That's it!"

"I did it! I did it!"

Clay frowned at his eldest daughter. "She's not crying, and Amity isn't hitting her. How do you explain this, young lady?"

"I guess she stopped." Hallie turned her innocent blue eyes up at her father. "If you don't believe me, ask Kate."

The door opened and Clay was embarrassed to have Amity look from him to Hallie and back again.

"I thought I heard voices," she said.

Hallie turned and dashed away. Clay smiled. "I was just passing by."

She didn't look convinced but she seemed not to know what to think. Clay backed away from the door and crossed the dining room. As he went to the barn, he fumed at Hallie for putting him in such an awkward position. What must Amity think? Even better than that, why had Hallie lied? Did she dislike Amity so much that she would sink to that depth to be rid of her?

Clay didn't know what to make of it.

In the parlor, Amity was puzzled over finding Clay and Hallie listening at the door. Why would he do that? Hallie had looked triumphant, but Amity couldn't see why. Jemima was making up a song to sew cross-stitch and didn't need Amity's attention. Amity picked up the dress she was sewing for Rosemary and tried to think about something else.

She hadn't felt well all that day. Since early that morning she had been out of sorts, and it had taken a great effort not to snap at every one who crossed her...in this house that meant several people. Hallie was the worst transgressor, followed closely by Kate. The girls seemed determined to make Amity's life as miserable as possible. There had been no more frogs in her bed, but she had found her sheets removed, her gowns in knots and the bristles clipped from her hairbrush.

Amity hadn't said anything to Clay. There was nothing to be gained by it, and she refused to sink to the level of telling on the girls. She knew in time they would either tire of their game or she would catch them in the act. A dull headache was beginning to throb in her temples. At least Jemima seemed to be able to sew as long as she could do it to music. That was a minor triumph for her side.

"Will you excuse me, Jemima? I'm not feeling well, and I think I need to lie down for a while."

Jemima looked up and nodded. "I'll come find you if I forget how to do something." She sang softly as she made another French knot.

"Yes, you do that." Amity went into her room and closed the door. She ached all over, especially in her middle. Perhaps, she thought, she should loosen her lacings. When she started to remove her skirt, she realized what was wrong. She had started her monthly course.

Amity buried her face in her hands in relief. She wasn't pregnant! Until now she hadn't allowed herself to think about it, but now relief washed over her. She found herself crying and didn't even try to stop.

There was a knock at the door. Jemima said, "Are you all right? Are you crying?"

"No," she called out, her voice shaking. "No, I'm just fine."

She took care of her needs but she couldn't seem to stop crying. The month of worrying and Emmett's rejection and her flight from Charlotte all poured out in tears. She didn't have any reason to need a husband, after all. If she had just been patient she could still be in Charlotte and not here in a farmhouse, married to a man who would never love her, with five girls who were usually more than she could handle. Amity's tears flowed faster. She rarely cried, but now she couldn't seem to stop.

There was a louder knock on her door. "Amity? What's wrong? Jemima says you're crying."

Before she could answer he turned the knob and came in. "You *are* crying," he said, almost as an accusation.

"What if I am? I'm allowed to cry, surely." She saw Jemima tiptoeing up to see around her father. "I'm fine." Jemima went away. Clay did not.

He came farther into the room. "What's wrong? Did one of the girls say something to upset you?"

"No, of course not." She couldn't tell him about Hallie's rudeness. He would think she was foolish for crying now about something that happened nearly an hour ago. All the same, she cried harder when she thought about it. She was married to a man whose daughters hated her.

"I don't believe you."

Amity threw her handkerchief at him. "Stop saying that to me! I don't lie." This made her cry harder.

"I wasn't trying to upset you more." Clay came to her and awkwardly patted her shoulder. "Was it Hallie?"

"It's everything!" She couldn't tell him the tears had started in relief. Nor could she seem to stop crying. "I'm no good at being a mother!"

"Is that what you're crying about?" He sounded as confused as she felt. "Here." He handed her a clean handkerchief from his pocket. "I never know what to do when a woman cries."

"Well, you may as well get used to it, because you're surrounded by them," she retorted.

"Now what's this about you not being a good mother?"

She couldn't look at him. "They don't like me." In her upset state of mind she believed all she was saying. "I try so hard and they still don't like me!" She was remembering how Hallie's eyes had shone with dislike. "What have I done to make them hate me?"

"They don't hate you. Who told you that?"

"I'm not an imbecile," she snapped. "I can tell when I'm not liked." She had never been a weepy woman, but she couldn't stop the tears, and this upset her almost as much as Hallie had. "Maybe I should leave here and let you all go back to living the way you were. It's not easy, trying to fit in where I'm not wanted."

Clay put his arms around her as if she were no older than his children. "You're just upset. Elsa used to get like this, too."

Amity pulled away. She couldn't bear to hear one more word about the saintly Elsa. "Just leave me alone. You don't want me. You don't even know me! None of you do. You don't have any idea what I think or feel or anything else. You haven't tried to get to know me at all. Admit it!"

"You may be right."

"You know I'm right! Not one of you has tried to find out what I'm like. You just want me to clean your house and cook your meals and nothing else!" Amity had never spoken like this to anyone in her life, but she was pushed beyond her endurance. "If you want me to leave, just say so!"

"I don't want you to leave."

Amity didn't believe him. She was surprised when she felt him turn her toward him and he put his arms around her again. This time she leaned against him and let the tears flow. She had turned away from her aunts and friends and everything she knew, all to marry a stranger who didn't want her, and she hadn't been pregnant after all. The injustice made her tears sting her eyes.

"Do you want to leave?" he asked, his voice softer than she had ever heard it.

Amity was about to nod when she thought about what she had left. There was no real love between her aunts and herself, and she suspected they were relieved to have her gone. Emmett had told his cronies what had happened or they wouldn't have shouted at her like that at the train station. By now half of Charlotte might think she was a scarlet woman. She missed Dorothea, but soon Dorothea would be certain to accept some young man's proposal and become a wife, and the gulf between them would widen. She had nothing to return to.

Amity felt a tug at her skirt, and she looked down to see Rosemary. The child silently held up a flower she had picked from the garden. It was pulled hastily and its head dangled on the stem. Amity felt her heart go out to the girl. Pulling away from Clay, she knelt to accept the flower.

"Don't go away," Rosemary said, her large green eyes filling with tears. "I like you."

Amity hugged the girl. Past her she could see Laura clutching her doll, and Jemima. When she held out her hand, they ran to her, nearly knocking her over in their exuberance. Amity sat on the floor and hugged them. She was aware of Clay watching her and she looked up at him. "I won't be leaving." She waited to see if he was in agreement.

After a moment he nodded. "Good." He turned and walked hastily from the room. Amity held the girls to her. Whatever might come of this odd marriage, she was in it and she would stay.

Chapter Five

"Chick, chick, chick," Amity called to the hens. She had formed a pocket to hold the chicken feed by gathering the bottom corners of her apron, and as she tossed a handful of the feed in an arch, the hens came running. She enjoyed feeding them. They were always so grateful.

She had slept little that night. Remembering how she had cried in front of Clay was a constant source of embarrassment to her. Her aunts would never have let themselves go like that. At times she found it so hard to maintain her aloofness. She wasn't able to do it at all with the three younger children. She smiled at the memory of how Jemima could sew only if she could sing the stitches. What on earth would Aunt Dorcus say about that?

Clay had gone to the fields without waiting for her to cook his breakfast, but with the biscuits and fried sausage that had been left over from the night before gone, it appeared that he had at least eaten something. She assumed that this change in his routine was because he was displeased with her for sobbing as if she were a foolish girl. She still didn't know why she had acted that way. Relief, she supposed. Knowing she wasn't carrying Emmett's child had been a tremendous relief.

A hen pecked at her shoe, reminding her she had been ignoring them, and she tossed another handful of feed to them. The hens, clucking their approval, scurried about willy-nilly after the grain, but the rooster, sporting his shiny red and black feathers, merely strutted about as if he were too proud to eat with his harem. He did, however, peck at the food that came his way.

"Good morning," Clay said.

Amity jumped and nearly spilled the feed from her apron. "Good morning. I thought you were in the fields."

"I was. I got an early start today. I couldn't sleep."

Amity pretended to be more interested in the chickens. She did not want to talk about the tears she had shed the day before, and she certainly did not want to admit that part of her own reason for sleeplessness was because of her thoughts of how wonderful it had felt when Clay had put his arms around her. No, she would not talk about either of those things, and if she could learn to control her thoughts better, she would not think about them again, either.

"You're wearing your hair different."

"Yes. I don't know why. I just did it differently today," she said defensively.

"I like it. You look younger with it like that."

Amity glanced at him to see if he was teasing her. She hadn't worn her hair like this in years, though Dorothea did. It was pulled up in a twist on top of her head, but the sides were soft about her face. By now she knew tiny tendrils had escaped and were curling about her neck. Was he making fun of her? "I should have pinned it tighter. My hair sometimes gets the best of me."

"I think it's pretty."

She turned and frankly stared him. "Pretty? It's red." At once she blushed. She always tried to think of her hair as brown. Her aunts had said red was such a decadent color.

"I know. I've always liked red hair."

"Now I know you're teasing me. No one likes red hair. Why aren't you in the fields?"

"I wanted to be sure you were okay this morning."

She forgot the hens. "Why wouldn't I be?"

"You barely spoke at supper last night and went to bed as soon as you finished in the kitchen. I was worried about you."

"No one has worried about me since I was ten." She remembered herself and turned away. "As you can see, I'm quite all right."

"I've been thinking about what you said—that no one here cares about you except as a worker and that I haven't even tried to get to know you."

"I didn't put it quite like that, I'm sure. I was upset or I wouldn't have said anything at all. Please forget it."

"No, you're right. In the springtime the farm takes a lot of my time, but it doesn't take as much as I've been giving it. I've been wrong. You came all the way out to Texas under false pretenses and I've treated you badly."

She shot him a questioning look, then realized he meant his own lie about the number of daughters he had, not hers. "I've wondered since I got here why you felt you had to marry a stranger in order to get a housekeeper."

"My daughters can be quite a handful, as I'm sure you've noticed. I couldn't keep a housekeeper."

"They only wanted someone who would tell them when they were going too far. I haven't had any real trouble with them." This was not true, but she was not going to let him know that. Hallie was becoming a thorn in her side, and it was getting worse every day.

"How do you do it?"

She shrugged and dumped the remainder of the feed on the ground. As she dusted her hands on the apron she said, "I just let them see that I was in charge and that I wanted them to behave."

"I had one housekeeper who insisted on being allowed to spank the little ones."

Amity's disgust for such reprehensible behavior caused her cheeks to flush. "I've never noticed it helps much to beat on a child. I was never beaten and I don't intend to abuse others in my turn. Rosemary and Laura are good children. They mind without spankings."

He nodded as if he had hoped she would say that. "The older girls must be a help to you. Elsa had taught them quite a bit about cleaning a house and so forth."

"She had? That is, yes, they are. Jemima is particularly good at her chores." She had a suspicion Jemima was secretly doing some of her older sisters' chores for them in order to keep peace, but she hadn't yet found proof of it.

"I think it's time I quit neglecting you and introduced you to our neighbors."

"I assure you, I don't feel neglected, and I already know Gretchen. I met her the day Hallie came home."

"I meant our neighbors on the other side, the O'Flannerys. Sean and I have become good friends, and I think you and Fiona might like each other."

She wondered if his assumption was due to the fact that Fiona and Elsa had been friends. At times she felt as if the entire family was trying to mold her into Elsa's image. "I'd like to meet them."

"You must get lonely out here at times."

The absurdity of that notion with five children in the house put a smile on Amity's face. "I can assure you, Mr. Morgan, I never get lonely."

"Are you ever going to call me Clay?"

They had reached the service porch by the kitchen. Amity paused at the bottom step. "I feel odd calling you by your first name. I know many wives in Charlotte who have called their husbands by their last names their entire marriage."

"It sounds too much like my father. Please call me Clay."

She looked up at him. "You and your father are at odds?"

"My real father died when I was no more than a baby. Morgan is the name of the man who married my mother and adopted me. You might say we're at odds. We haven't spoken in fifteen years, and I'll see them rotting in hell before we speak again."

Amity's eyes widened. "Why on earth would you say that?"

He drew himself up taller, as if he had already revealed more than he had intended. "Let's just say they both lacked your kindness. I'll be back for you about mid-afternoon, and we'll go visiting.''

''Yes. Yes, that will be fine.'' She watched him go, intensely curious as to what his mother and stepfather had done to make him so distant from them. She had felt a reserve in him—even from that first day, as if he was, at times, expecting to be hurt—but she had told herself it was only her imagination. Now she wasn't so sure. She untied her apron as she passed through the porch and dropped it on the pile of washing she was to do the next morning.

Hallie had watched the entire exchange between her father and Amity from the open parlor window. She couldn't recall a single time her father had come in from the fields in the middle of the morning, and she knew he was becoming interested in Amity. When she realized she had knotted her hands in her skirt as she watched them, she smoothed the material so it would not wrinkle and tamped down her feelings of anger and frustration. If she was going to get rid of Amity, it would have to be soon, but she was at a loss for what to do. Suddenly, an idea sprang to mind. If anyone knew what to do about this, it would be Aunt Gretchen. Without a moment to spare, Hallie bolted from the house.

Gretchen's house was a mile and a half by the road, but Hallie, like all her family, took a shortcut through the woods and over the bridge across the stream that separated the two farms. She reached the house in a matter of minutes. As always, she went into the kitchen without bothering to knock. Gretchen had always made it clear that her house was her nieces' as well, and Hallie felt as much at home in one as she did in the other.

Gretchen was sitting at the table peeling potatoes, while the girl who kept house for her stirred a pot of soup meat on the stove. Both smiled at Hallie. ''You've been running again,'' Gretchen said. Then she looked at her more closely. ''Nothing is wrong, is it?''

''I'll say it is!'' Hallie spoke openly in front of Libby, ignoring the servant's presence as her aunt had taught her to do. "Papa came in from the fields to talk to Amity. I think he's starting to like her."

"He did? He quit work and came all the way back to the house? What did they talk about?" Gretchen carried the potatoes to the pot on the stove.

"I couldn't hear much of it. The window was open but they were in the kitchen yard. I think he said he didn't want her to be lonely and that he was glad she came to Texas."

Gretchen frowned. Libby made no comment. "Come into the parlor, Hallie. I have some mending to do and we can talk better in there."

Hallie followed her aunt through the familiar house feeling that in some ways this house seemed to have more remnants of her mother than her own did. The succession of housekeepers and Amity's scrubbing had changed things so much at her own, she no longer felt at home there. Here she could imagine her mother might come through the door at any moment.

She sat in the chair beside the one Elsa had always favored. Gretchen sat on the sofa and picked up her basket of mending. As she fit the darning egg into one of her stockings, she said, "I've never known Clay to quit work in the middle of the day without reason. Elsa once said that he often stayed in the fields past mealtime if he was busy."

"I know. That's why I ran over here. Papa was looking at her the way he used to look at Mama. You know, as if he was listening to what she was saying."

Gretchen nodded. "I know the look. I won't lie to you, Hallie. This could be bad."

"We have to get rid of her. Kate and I are doing all we can without Papa knowing. We don't do our chores half the time, but Jemima sneaks behind us and does them before Amity sees that we haven't. Laura and Rosemary act as if Amity hung the moon." Her last words were tinged with disgust.

"They're just babies. They would forget her if she left." Gretchen shook her head sadly. "I just can't get over your father marrying so soon after Elsa's death. It's beyond disrespectful. It's shameful.''

Hallie's eyes filled with tears. "I miss Mama so much. Already I sometimes have a hard time remembering what her voice sounded like."

Gretchen leaned forward and covered Hallie's hands with her own. "You must remember! As long as we remember, she won't really be gone. You owe it to your mother."

"I know, Aunt Gretchen, but it's hard. Yesterday I caught myself laughing with Kate over something, and it was just like old times. I could hear Amity working in the kitchen below our room and for just a minute I thought it was Mama and that all this had been a nightmare. I nearly cried when I realized it wasn't."

"You're a good daughter. I only wish you could have been mine."

Hallie toyed with a seam on her skirt. "Would you have married Papa if he had asked you?" she asked suddenly. "Kate says you would have."

Gretchen shot her a look. "Perhaps. It would have been only right since you girls are my nieces and I could keep the family together that way."

"Do you love Papa?" Hallie met her aunt's eyes. "Is there some deep and secret love between you?"

"What a question!"

"I read a book once where this woman and this man were in love and fate kept them apart. Is it like that with Papa and you?" She was surprised to see her aunt blush.

"I've always cared about your father. My Hall died when you were so young you can't remember him, but he was nothing like your father. Hall was short and didn't know the first thing about farming. He worked in Ransom and went to work in the buggy every morning."

"Who took care of the farm?" Hallie knew the answer, but she loved to hear about the past the way Gretchen told it.

"I did. I hired Libby's father the week I married Hall and came to live here. He's been with me ever since. As soon as

Libby was old enough to help around the house, I hired her, too. That family owes a lot to me.''

"If you had married Papa, what would have become of your farm?''

Gretchen laughed. "Goodness, girl, I don't know. I guess I would have rented out the house and a few acres and brought the rest into the marriage. If your father had married me, he would have doubled his wealth overnight.'' She gave Hallie a level look. "What about Amity? Does she have any money?''

"Not that I know of. She never talks about herself. All I know is that she lived with her aunts before she came to Texas. I think she said once that she's a widow.''

Gretchen looked thoughtful. "She could have a small fortune if she was widowed. And she may be her aunts' heiress, as well, in time.''

"You think Papa married her for money? He can't love her. They don't even sleep in the same room.''

"They don't?'' Gretchen put down her mending and stared at Hallie. "They have separate bedrooms?''

"Yes. That must mean he doesn't care much about her. Right, Aunt Gretchen?''

Gretchen smiled. "I'd say that's exactly what it means. Tell me, Hallie, have they ever stayed in the same room at all?''

Hallie shook her head. She wasn't too sure what her aunt was getting at but it seemed important. "She's been in the guest room since the day she came. And she calls him 'Mr. Morgan.' Just like that, like she barely knows him.''

"She does?'' Gretchen looked immensely pleased. "I'd say we have a chance. If they are that distant, she may still leave.''

"Then why would Papa come all the way in from the fields to see if she's lonesome?''

"Maybe he forgot something and was just being polite.''

Hallie relaxed. "That could be it. They don't talk all that much. Not like Mama and Papa used to.''

"Of course not. Your papa loved your mama. Hallie, if we can chase Amity off, would you object if I married your papa?"

"Oh, no!" Hallie sat up eagerly. "I'd love to have you live at my house!"

"Well, I'm not making any promises, but we'll see."

Hallie jumped up. "Now I *have* to get rid of her. I'll tell Kate we have to try harder."

"You do that. Now remember, don't let your father see what you're doing. He would be angry, and I don't want him upset with you. And you mustn't tell anyone what I said about maybe marrying Clay. That has to be our secret."

"All right." Hallie loved secrets. Over the years she and Gretchen had shared many. Even though Gretchen was several years older than Hallie's mother had been, and older than her father, as well, she treated Hallie as if she was an equal in many ways.

"I'll tell you what. Tell your father to bring you and the other girls over for Sunday dinner. Just like he used to do."

Hallie's face clouded. "All right, but he's sure to bring Amity, too."

"That's okay. It will give me a chance to talk to her and suggest that she should go back where she came from."

"I've already done that."

"It might go farther if it's said by someone her own age."

Hallie thought Gretchen was probably quite a bit older than Amity, but she nodded. Adults seemed to lump all their ages together until they were really old. "I'll tell him."

"Good. Now you run along before you're missed. I'll see you on Sunday."

Hallie's heart was light as she went home. If anyone could get rid of Amity, it was Aunt Gretchen.

Amity was ready to go with Clay to meet the O'Flannerys by the time Clay had finished cleaning up from work and putting on clean clothes. Although she had not allowed herself to admit it, she missed having a woman her own age to talk to and was eager for companionship. Now that she had the housework under control, she had been homesick, and she especially missed Dorothea.

When she stepped out of her room and saw Clay crossing the dining room toward her, she paused. She had never seen him dressed in anything but work clothes, and the change was startling. He was wearing gray trousers, a tan vest over a white shirt and a deep blue coat. He had washed his hair under the pump outside, and as she observed how neatly combed it was, she also realized he was not using pomade to keep his hair in place, apparently because he did not need to. He was the most handsome man she had ever seen.

She nodded, not trusting herself to speak. As they went out to the buggy, she tied her bonnet ribbons under her chin. The buggy had a top but she did not want to risk getting freckles. As he was helping her into the buggy, she noticed she had forgotten her gloves, but she was too anxious to meet the neighbors to delay things by going back for them.

"Are the O'Flannerys expecting us?"

"Yes, I saw Sean this morning, and he said Fiona has been wanting to meet you."

"Then why didn't she come over? I've wondered why no one has come to welcome me." When she heard how that sounded, she added, "I mean, in Charlotte that would be only proper."

"It is here, too, but Fiona is expecting a child soon and she isn't able to travel. She had trouble with the birth of her last, and Sean has made her promise to take it easy with this one."

"Oh." Amity was startled to hear him discuss such a subject so frankly. According to her aunts, no man would ever admit to knowing such details, especially not about a woman who wasn't his wife. According to Aunt Dorcus, Amity's mother had not told her father she was expecting until he noticed it by her appearance. Aunt Ophelia had soundly approved such measures.

The O'Flannery house was closer than she had expected. It was on the slope of a hill beneath a huge sycamore. The house was so similar to Clay's she wondered if they had helped build each other's houses. Several children, all boys but one, were playing in the yard when they drove up. All of them stopped and stared at Amity.

Clay called out a greeting to them, and added, "Go tell your parents we're here, Brady."

The second tallest boy ran to do as he was told, and Clay stepped down, then turned to help Amity out of the buggy. As she rose, her skirts tangled about her legs and she almost lost her balance, but Clay quickly put his hands on her waist to steady her, then lifted her to the ground. Amity gasped at the intimacy of the physical contact, but he seemed to think nothing of it. She hurriedly rearranged her skirt.

A man and woman came out onto the porch and the man hurried down the steps to meet them. "You must be Amity," he said with a grin and a delightful accent. "Clay has told me so much about you."

She glanced at Clay. He barely knew her. What had he found to tell?

"Come in, come in," Sean was saying. "This is my wife, Fiona. Those hoodlums there are my boys."

The girl spoke up. "I'm not a boy, Pa." She grinned at him.

"That's right, that's right. I keep forgetting her among all the others. That would be Kathleen."

"Stop teasing the child and behave," Fiona said with a laugh.

As Amity went up the steps, the girl went back to playing cowboys and Indians with her brothers. Neither of her parents seemed to see anything wrong with Kathleen hiking her skirt up and charging after the boys, emitting chilling war whoops. And after a moment's thought, Amity agreed. Her aunts' automatic presumption that such behavior was inappropriate seemed out of place here, and now that Amity looked back on it, a number of her aunts' taboos seemed outmoded altogether. Without another glance at the yard, Amity said, "You have pretty children, Mrs. O'Flannery."

"Thank you, but call me Fiona. We don't stand on ceremony here." The woman's voice, like Sean's, was colored by a lilting accent. "My children are easy to spot. They're all redheads."

Sean grinned. "Where do you suppose they got it?" His hair was black, but Fiona's was flaming red.

"From the leprechauns?" Fiona teased. She opened the door and stepped inside to allow her company to enter first.

Amity had known people back East for years who would never have been so informal. Evidently everyone here used first names. And she was beginning to like it.

"Have a seat, Amity. Tell me about yourself. Did you have a good trip out?"

"Yes, thank you. It was a long train ride, but it was interesting. I had never seen much of the country."

Fiona nodded. "We came here from Ireland. We sailed for America the day we were married, as a matter of fact." She cast a fond glance at Sean. "I think he wanted to get me away from my kith and kin before I changed my mind and went home again."

"I wasn't sure the ocean would stop her, but I had to try." Sean winked at Amity.

She could see this couple was still in love even though they must have been married for years to have children as old as theirs were. Amity could not recall ever seeing a couple who were so demonstratively in love. The sight was heartwarming.

"You were wise to get a wife from back East for the same reason," Sean said to Clay. "You're farther from your in-laws." He smiled at Amity. "Fiona's brothers would have beat me to a pulp if she had ever so much as shed a tear."

Amity didn't know how to talk to them. They were more open and outgoing than any couple she had ever met. Her old shyness rose and she tried to tamp it down. She wanted very much to be able to laugh and joke as easily as they did. "Actually, I have almost no family. I lived with my maiden aunts most of my life. I was orphaned by the age of ten and I have no brothers or sisters."

"That's terrible!" Fiona said, looking as if she really meant it. "No family?"

"My aunts took good care of me, but they never encouraged visitors. Coming to Texas has been quite an adventure for me."

"I thought you came from a family with a sister and a brother," Sean said in confusion.

"I was wrong about that," Clay said. "She was raised by her aunts."

Amity had almost forgotten Dorothea had naturally told Clay about herself and her own family. "I was trying to protect my privacy," she said. "I had no idea who might show up on my doorstep some day."

"A wise decision," Fiona said. She wrapped a shawl about her more closely, but Amity could see she was large with child. Amity delicately averted her eyes.

"We were glad to see Clay marry again," Sean said. "He stays too much to himself. We were afraid for a while there that he would never pull out of his grief."

Amity glanced at Clay. "He loved Elsa. It was only right that he would grieve her passing."

From the look of surprise on Clay's face, Amity wondered what he had expected her to say.

"I was glad to see Gretchen didn't move in," Fiona said with the directness of a close friend. "I liked Elsa, but her sister is another matter. I told Sean it would be a miracle if she didn't show up on your doorstep, bag and baggage in hand."

"Now, Fiona," her husband said, "we shouldn't talk about her like this. It's not charitable."

Fiona stood and said to Amity, "Come to the kitchen and we'll make some coffee. These men think they can't talk without a cup in their hands." She swatted at Sean as she passed. "At home it was the pubs. Here, it's the coffee cup."

When they were out of earshot of the men, Fiona said, "It was true what I said. I don't want you to think I was speaking out of turn."

"You must be mistaken. She's Clay's sister-in-law. Surely she would have had no intention of marrying her own sister's husband."

"Out here things like that happen. I've known for years that Gretchen is carrying a torch for Clay."

"No, that's impossible. Elsa has only been gone six months."

Fiona nodded. "I know."

Amity was shocked. She went with Fiona into the well-scrubbed kitchen and automatically helped her take coffee cups from the cupboard. "Surely, Gretchen would not have made it known that she wanted Clay even with him married to Elsa, would she?"

"Not so most people would notice it." Fiona went to the pot of water that was always kept simmering on the back of the stove and ladled out the proper amount for coffee. She took down a can of coffee she had already ground and began dipping it into the top of the coffeepot. "My family always said I have a second sight. Maybe they're right. I know Gretchen has been wanting Clay ever since we moved here. We've been here since our Brian was a baby, and he's fourteen now."

Amity didn't know what to say.

"At that time, Clay had just married Elsa, and Gretchen had been married to Hall for a while. It was about two years later that Hall died, as I recall. I knew the minute I saw Clay in the same room with her how it was with Gretchen. I haven't been able to like her since."

"Surely Clay didn't return this affection."

Fiona laughed. "Clay? He never saw it at all, or if he did, he ignored it. No, when he married Elsa, there wasn't another woman in the world."

Amity ran her finger over the pattern on the tablecloth. "What was Elsa really like?"

"She was like an angel. Her hair was the color of your girls' hair, and her eyes were blue like Hallie's. She was always soft-spoken and gentle, and you could tell she worshiped Clay."

Amity felt a twinge of jealousy and at once felt guilty. "It's not easy stepping into the shoes of an angel."

"No, but you can do it." Fiona sat the coffee on the stove to perk and smiled at Amity.

"I'm not so sure. Were you close friends? With Elsa, I mean?"

"Not as close as I would like to have been. Gretchen kept most others away. I don't know if it was because Elsa was that close to her, or if Gretchen was afraid of losing her sister's affection to someone else, but you seldom saw Elsa without Gretchen tagging along. Elsa had more company than I would have wanted, even from my own sisters, bless them. It would be way too much with the likes of Gretchen."

"So she's not like Elsa?"

"They were as alike as soap and cheese. No, Clay wouldn't have wanted to take Gretchen in Elsa's stead, even if I'm sure it was offered. And I have to admit that when I saw the way she was heading after Elsa was gone, I went to Clay and told him. I don't think it was a surprise to him. Gretchen must have started putting herself in front of him almost at once."

Amity nodded slowly. "That would explain a lot." It would give Clay a reason for having wanted a mail-order bride. If Gretchen was that determined to have him, she could have warned away all the other single women in Ransom—it wasn't that large a town. In order to find a bride other than Gretchen, Clay might have been forced to find a stranger and to marry her as quickly as possible. Or maybe he was so lonely and devastated over Elsa's loss that he had to have a woman in the house and didn't want one who would remind him of his beloved wife. Amity knew he couldn't have found one more opposite if he had searched to the ends of the earth. "I'm not like Elsa," she said aloud.

"No, and you shouldn't be. Elsa is gone. Clay is still living, and one thing that is sure about life is that it changes."

Amity wondered if Clay had taken into account that all women weren't living saints, and that he might get one that had given herself so foolishly to a man just because he said he loved her. Amity was suddenly filled with regret over what she had done with Emmett. If only she had waited for her husband. But then she thought again and knew that if she had been more resistant she would still be at her aunts' house and not here where life was rushing at her pell-mell.

"It's odd," Fiona said as if to herself, "what turns life can take."

Amity jerked her head up. Had Fiona somehow divined her thoughts? Then she saw Fiona was looking at a dish with a pattern on it.

"My grandmother owned this dish," Fiona said. "It sat in my ma's cupboard all my life until I married Sean and came here. Ma sent it with me so I'd have a bit of Grandma with me. Whoever would have thought it would end up in America?"

"Life does move in mysterious ways," Amity agreed.

Chapter Six

Amity had not looked forward to having Sunday dinner with Gretchen, but since this had been a tradition with her new family, she went along with its resumption without comment. The meal proved to be as difficult as she had thought it might be.

Gretchen talked only to Clay and the children. With each dish she passed, she reminded Clay how Elsa had loved it or had served it on such and such occasion or how she had craved it when she was carrying this or that child. The girls delighted in hearing it. Rosemary said, "What did Mama want to eat before I was born?"

"With you it was honey. Do you remember, Clay? You drove all the way to Jefferson for it because there wasn't any in Ransom."

"I remember. It was in the winter and I nearly froze." He grinned and winked at Rosemary. "It was worth it, though. Look what a sweet little girl it produced."

Rosemary giggled and squirmed atop the books Gretchen had piled on the chair for her to sit on.

"Careful," Amity said. "You'll topple off."

"No, she won't," Gretchen said as she put her arm around the child. "Not with her aunt Gretchen right here to catch her."

Amity bit back the rejoinder that flashed to her mind. She was not sure she could put up with visiting Gretchen on a regular basis. Guiltily she wondered if jealousy was her motive rather than the fact she simply didn't like the woman. Lately she had become all too aware of Clay as a man, and she was growing less indifferent to hearing how happy he had been with Elsa and how perfect she had been.

Clay had been seated at the head of the table, Gretchen at the opposite end. The seating arrangement had not escaped her. Pretending to be listening to Kate, who was seated on Clay's right, Amity took the opportunity to observe him. He was the sort of man who would be noticeable in a crowd. Amity thought if he were to be dropped into her group of acquaintances in Charlotte, he would cause a stir in every woman's heart, married or single.

Today he was dressed in his Sunday best. She would have thought a man so accustomed to working on a farm would be ill at ease in a tie and starched collar, but Clay seemed to be at home in whatever he wore. His tanned skin contrasted sharply against the stark white of his shirt collar, and his eyes seemed greener than usual. His brown hair looked soft and slightly windblown, and she had the most peculiar urge to touch it. Not to straighten it, but to run her fingers through it. She looked away hurriedly. To Jemima she said, "Eat your beans."

"She doesn't have to eat her beans at my house," Gretchen said with a beaming smile at Jemima. "You shouldn't force her, if she's already full."

"She can't possibly be full. She's hardly eaten a bite." Amity knew from experience that Jemima would spend the meal talking and start to eat when everyone else was ready to leave the table.

Obviously ignoring Amity's comment, Gretchen said, "Clay would you mind taking a look at my mare while you're here? I believe she's favoring her near back leg, and Jake doesn't know the first thing about animals."

Clay nodded. "I'll see to her before we go."

"Do you remember when I bought that mare? It was at the same fair where Elsa won a blue ribbon for her fig preserves *and* for the quilt." Gretchen laughed and touched the corners of her mouth with her napkin. "She always did win in one category or the other, but that year she won it in both.''

"I remember."

Amity refrained from saying she had won ribbons in both categories. Her aunts had taught her that it was unattractive to blow her own horn. She wished, however, that her trunk had been large enough to accommodate one of her quilts. She personally thought that her work was better than Elsa's. "When is the fair?"

"In the spring. You missed it by no more than a week." Clay smiled at her. "We'll go next year."

"You mustn't feel awkward if you enter something and it doesn't win," Gretchen said. "The competition here is stiff."

Amity started planning the quilt she would enter. Surely there was something she could do at least as well as Elsa. And she doubted the competition in Ransom would be as tough as that in a city the size of Charlotte.

As it was Libby's day off, Amity helped Gretchen clear the table after the meal. Hallie tried to help, but Gretchen waved her off with a wink. "We'll take care of this. You go into the parlor and entertain your father."

Amity rolled up her sleeves and prepared to wash dishes while Gretchen dried them and put them away. Gretchen was finally ready to talk to Amity.

"You'll never know how often Elsa and I did this exact same chore," she said as she ran a dish towel over a plate. "She would wash and I would dry." She paused and handed the plate back. "You missed a spot."

Amity saw nothing on it, but she washed it again.

"She was so sweet and kind. I just don't know what we will do without her."

"I'm sure you must miss her. Was she your only sister?"

"Yes, she was all the family I had left. Except the girls, of course. My nieces are very dear to me. Naturally Clay misses her most of all. The younger children have grieved and are over it, but Clay will mourn her all his life."

Amity handed her a plate steaming from the dishwater and made no comment.

"They were so close, Elsa and Clay. It's hard to imagine one without the other. Everyone in town says the same thing. Elsa was loved by all."

"Hallie and Kate still miss her, too. It's hard to tell with Jemima. She's so complex."

"Nonsense. She's just a child. She misses her mama. It's only natural that she would at her age. I imagine she just doesn't talk to you about it because she is afraid you'll be upset with her."

"I would never upbraid a child for talking to me about her deceased mother." She glared at Gretchen. "The very idea!"

"Not in so many words, perhaps, but children can tell." Gretchen laughed. "Children seem to know so much more than we usually credit them with knowing."

"All the girls are quite intelligent."

"Of course they are. Intelligence runs in my family, if I do say so myself. Elsa could hear a bit of music once and play it perfectly on the piano."

"Jemima must have inherited her musical ability from her. She already has a remarkable voice." Amity was determined not to let Gretchen goad her into speaking against Elsa. She was positive that anything she said that Gretchen thought she could use against her would be repeated to Clay. She was glad Fiona had told her what Gretchen had in mind with Clay.

"Elsa could sing like an angel."

"I had an idea you'd say that." She handed a serving platter to Gretchen. "Was there anything she couldn't do perfectly?"

Gretchen thought for a minute. "No, not unless you'd count it a fault for her to spoil Clay so. She was always thinking of ways to make him happy."

Amity dunked a skillet in the soapy water, just for an instant imagining that it was Gretchen's head.

After what seemed an eternity, the dishes were finished, and Amity was glad to escape to the parlor and to conversation with someone other than Gretchen. Clay and the girls were there, with Jemima playing a duet on the piano with Kate. Amity sat beside Clay and listened. The younger girl was already more talented than her sister. She wondered if there was some way to get music lessons for Jemima. Ransom wasn't so far that Amity couldn't take the girl to town for lessons.

Hallie went to the glass-fronted secretary that stood in one corner. "May we see the scrapbook, Aunt Gretchen?"

"Of course you may."

As she removed a thick book from the shelf, Hallie cast a sideways glance at Amity. Her lips curved in a smile that wasn't altogether mirthful. Hallie put the book on a table and opened it with reverence. Her younger sisters crowded nearer. "Here's the card Mama sent you on your birthday the year Kate and I had chicken pox. Remember? We were inside, sick, and couldn't go out and play, so she let us cut out pictures to glue on it."

Kate crowded closer. "I remember that."

"So do I," Rosemary said.

"No, you don't," Kate argued. "You weren't born yet. Neither was Laura. Jemima was the baby then."

"I'm not a baby!" Jemima quickly pointed out.

Her sisters ignored her. "Look," Kate said, "here's a note I wrote when I was first learning to write. Look how funny it looks. I made all my *k*s and *s*s backward."

"I wouldn't take gold for that note," her aunt told her.

"Here's the Christmas card from the year Laura was born. We thought she was going to be born on Jesus' birthday." Hallie pointed at the card with ice skaters on it.

"I want to go ice-skating some day," Laura said. To Amity she asked, "Does it snow in North Carolina?"

"Yes, we get a good snowfall every year." Amity was relieved to finally be able to join in the conversation. "Does it snow here?"

"Not much," Clay answered. "We're more likely to get ice storms. Sometimes the cow ponds freeze over, though, so Laura may get to skate in her shoes."

Amity had not noticed until now, but Clay had become quieter the moment the album was brought out. Was he missing Elsa so much he was unable to speak? She looked at him more closely. There were deeper lines than usual bracketing his mouth, and he looked as if he was suddenly tired. His expressive eyes were sad as he watched his daughters poring over memories that could never be relived.

"Look at the picture Kate drew!" Hallie said.

"Did you really save that, Aunt Gretchen?" Kate exclaimed. "I did that years ago."

"I've saved everything you girls and Elsa ever sent me," Gretchen said in sad tones. "It's all I have in life."

Amity looked at the picture. Drawn by a young and rather unsteady hand, the sketch was of a happy family, the mother and father holding hands and three children standing beside them like stair steps. She looked away and told herself she was worse than an insect to feel so jealous of a dead woman.

"I had better go take a look at that mare," Clay said, abruptly. Hastily, he strode out.

As Amity watched him go, she wanted to follow him and try to mend the hurt he was feeling, but there was no way for her to do that. She wasn't Elsa.

"Why don't you girls run upstairs and see what I've put in the guest room for you?" Gretchen said as she closed the scrapbook. "I've been busy since you were here last."

As the girls tumbled out, Amity resisted the urge to remind them not to run in the house. This was, after all, Gretchen's house, and she knew Gretchen would countermand that instruction as she had all the others.

Gretchen smiled after them. "I made them all new pinafores. I didn't know if you could sew or not, and I wanted them to have something new."

"I sew."

"You don't talk much about yourself, do you?" Gretchen turned her cold blue eyes on Amity. "You say you were brought up by aunts?"

"That's right."

"How did you and Clay meet?"

"Didn't he or the girls tell you?"

"Hallie said something about him advertising for you in a newspaper." Gretchen made a gesture with her hand that showed how impossible that must be.

Amity knew she was being baited, but she decided to play the innocent rather than call Gretchen's hand. "We began a correspondence through a newspaper advertisement. After a while, he wrote and proposed and I accepted."

"You mean you never saw one another before you came out here? No, you couldn't have. He was married to Elsa for fourteen years, and since that time he has been in mourning. It must be sad for you to be married to a man who is so grief-stricken."

Amity decided a small lie was worth trying. "He's not all that grief-stricken any longer. He's putting his life back together. We've married and that's a new beginning."

Gretchen's eyes glinted with jealousy. "Yes, but it's a marriage in name only. We can't really count that. I mean, it's not like you and Clay are sharing a bedroom."

In the silence Amity could hear a clock ticking somewhere in the house and the muffled sounds of the girls as they found their new pinafores. "What makes you think we don't share a bedroom?"

"It's true, isn't it? We're a close family. There are no secrets between Clay and myself."

Amity abruptly stood up. "I think it's time we left." She went to the stairs and called for the girls to come down. Gretchen was glaring at her. Amity paid her no mind. Above the girls' protests, she marshaled them out.

By the time they reached the buggy, Clay was coming from the barn. When he saw Amity loading the children into the buggy, he increased his pace. To his puzzled expression, Amity said firmly, "It's time we were leaving." The girls raised their protests, but Amity pretended not to hear them. It was one thing to have to listen to Elsa's praises, but when Gretchen started denying Amity had rights as Clay's wife, it was time to go.

Clay gave her a probing look, but without question he helped her into the wagon and climbed up beside her. "Goodbye, Gretchen. That mare looks sound to me. We'll see you in a week or so."

Gretchen stood by her gate and waved her handkerchief at them as if they were going halfway around the world and not just across the bridge and over the hill. Amity sat ramrod straight and refused to acknowledge her.

In an undertone, Clay said, "What happened?"

"Nothing I intend to discuss at the moment." She was quite aware of the children sitting within hearing distance. She held her body stiffly erect and tried not to flinch when the buggy hit ruts in the road. How could Gretchen have been so rude? And why did it bother her to admit that she and Clay didn't sleep together? Many married couples she knew maintained separate bedrooms, and they were still solidly married. She knew why. Her own marriage had never been consummated, and therefore she was not sure how secure her position might be.

She glanced sideways at him. Did she want it to be consummated? After her experience with Emmett, she wasn't sure she wanted physical attentions from a man. It had hurt her and she had felt degraded. Yet Clay stirred a longing in her that made her want to be touched by him. She hastily jerked her attention forward. What was she thinking of?

Gretchen waited until the next day before going to town. She knew where her friends were likely to be and was pleased to find a small gathering at Lola May Grizzard's house. When the maid showed her in, several of the women exchanged surprised looks, which they quickly covered. Gretchen wondered if she had been the topic of their conversation.

"I didn't know you were coming to town today," Lola May said as Gretchen sat beside them and accepted a cup of freshly brewed coffee.

"We were just saying how little we all see of you these days," Clematis Osgood added.

So they had been discussing her. Gretchen gave her a smile that she didn't really mean. "I've been mourning Elsa and don't get out much anymore."

"We saw Clay's new wife in church yesterday," Lola May said. "She's quite pretty."

"Do you think so?" Gretchen stirred her coffee and put the spoon aside. "I think she has a pinched look about her mouth. I'm afraid it means she has a bad temper."

Clematis leaned forward. "Does she really? Wherever did she come from? None of us knew she was in the offing until we heard he was married."

Gretchen arranged her face in sorrowful lines. "Don't breathe a word of this, but she's a mail-order bride! He never met her at all before the day they wed."

"My grandparents were like that," one of the younger women said. "Their parents arranged it and they met on their wedding day."

"That was in Europe," Gretchen retorted. "We don't do things like that over here. We certainly don't do it that way in Ransom, Texas!"

"Why did he do it?" Clematis gasped. "Surely there was someone here he could have married." It was well-known she had a niece she had hoped to marry off to someone before the girl became much older.

Gretchen shrugged, her gesture telling volumes of what she thought about it personally. "I suppose he had some reason."

"Does she really have a bad temper?" asked Lola May.

"All I can say is that the two times I've been with her, we've come close to having words, and one or the other of us left abruptly."

The women collectively sucked in their breaths. "Those poor children!" one young woman said in a saddened voice.

"Indeed." Gretchen sipped her coffee. "If only he had confided in me, I could have offered him better counsel. But he didn't."

"Why would he want to marry a stranger?" Clematis persisted. "Why would she?"

"She talks very little about her past, if you know what I mean." Gretchen met their eyes hoping to impart more than her words.

"You don't mean she has a *past?*" Lola May exclaimed.

"I'm not saying that. You didn't hear it from me. All I can say is that *I* would have some difficulty leaving my home and going halfway across the country to marry a strange man unless I had a sound reason." She paused to let the women draw their own conclusions.

"She's not a wanton, is she?" Lola May demanded. "Clay didn't go to that extent!"

"Clay wouldn't do that. Not as a mother for his girls," Clematis argued. "I'll bet she's *divorced!*"

Gretchen looked noncommittal. "Please don't ever say I told you anything. It would kill Clay if he knew anyone thought ill of him. Though we can hardly blame Clay. He hadn't met her until she arrived by train. One can write anything at all on paper and make it sound truthful."

Clematis shook her head. "If only he had waited a little longer. My niece might have asked him to come to dinner, and who knows what might have come of it?"

Gretchen, who had spoken to the niece and had made it plain that she considered Clay to be her own property, nodded. "I suppose we'll never know. Assuming she stays, of course."

"She has to stay. They're married," the youngest woman of the group stated.

"Myrtle, you can be such a ninny," Lola May said. "If she has a checkered past, who knows what she may do."

"It's true," Gretchen agreed. "For all we know, she has a husband in every town on the eastern seaboard." Gretchen let them marvel at that possibility as she drank her coffee and helped herself to a tea cake. She knew these women.

Word would be all over town before dark that Amity was a woman not to be accepted in polite company.

Clay was having a problem. He had decided on Elsa's death that if he couldn't die and be with her physically, he would remain true to her memory. Although he had found himself a wife, he had done so in such a way that he was excused from actually living with the woman as a husband normally would. The problem was that he hadn't counted on the new wife being Amity.

At first it had been easy. She had been cool toward him and seemed no more interested in consummating the marriage than he was. She had even seemed relieved to have a room all her own, or at least he had convinced himself that this was so. All had gone well until the afternoon he found her crying.

When he had gone to her and had put his arms around her to comfort her, he had been no more interested in her as a woman than any stranger he might encounter in town. But when he had touched her, something had happened.

He was not sure what that something was. It had not felt like this with Elsa. With Elsa he had slowly fallen in love until he could not remember a time when he had not loved her. He wouldn't call his attraction to Amity love. He firmly believed love had to have time to develop and that it might take years, perhaps months, but certainly not weeks.

He had told himself it was only that she was a woman and he had been celibate for six months. For a while he had believed it. Then he had taken her to meet the O'Flannerys, and he had seen her as a woman.

She had worn a dress he hadn't noticed her wearing before. He couldn't remember exactly what it had looked like, something more frilly than her plain housedresses. All women's dresses looked more or less alike to him. But the color had been blue.

Amity could not possibly have known that blue was his favorite color; the dress was one she had owned before coming into his life. But the shade of blue was brighter than the colors she usually wore, and it had made her look younger and prettier. It had curved close to her body like her other dresses, but the lace at the neck and the blue ruffle at the bottom of the skirt softened her usual coolness. Her dark eyes had been bright at the prospect of meeting new people, and he had wished he was able to see them light up that way for him.

He put down the ax he was sharpening and looked toward the house. Amity was in there, and while she was not Elsa, he was finding that it no longer mattered. They were opposites in many ways but somehow that made it better. Elsa had been so good, so sweet, he sometimes wondered what she saw in him and whether she would continue to love him. If Amity were ever to fall in love, he had a feeling it would be forever.

Fall in love. He shook his head. What was he thinking of? He had no business wanting her to fall in love with him. He had vowed to be true to Elsa and he should be ashamed of himself for having such thoughts. Besides, Amity was often so cool toward him that he doubted she cared for him at all.

But he had seen her smile at Rosemary when the child was playing with her dolls, and he had seen the softness on her face when Jemima played the piano in the front parlor. There was more to Amity than coolness. Perhaps a great deal more. She puzzled him, and he had always been drawn to a mystery.

She had never told him why she had insisted on leaving Gretchen's house so imperatively the past Sunday. He hadn't asked again, and she hadn't volunteered any information. Knowing Gretchen, it could have been any of a dozen things. He only visited her because the children loved her and because she was a living tie to Elsa. He wondered what she had said to cause Amity to head for the buggy with the children in tow without even knowing he would be ready to leave. Amity was like that. She could make up her mind and not have to discuss it with anybody, not even him.

Suddenly, Clay leaned the ax against the barn wall and stood, thinking how thirsty he was. He knew his thirst was only an excuse to see Amity, but nevertheless, he let himself dwell for a moment on how good a glass of cool water would taste. Or maybe there was some of the lemonade she made for the girls. He walked to the house.

He went in the kitchen door, since he had been in the feed lot earlier and his boots were too dirty for the parlor. He opened the icebox and took out a cold pitcher of lemonade. From the screened porch he heard voices. Without trying to eavesdrop, he found himself listening to a conversation.

"My mama did that better than you do," Hallie was saying. "She could sew better than anyone."

"I'm glad to hear that." Amity's voice was cool and reserved.

"And she was prettier. Papa thought she was the most beautiful woman in the world."

Clay started listening closer.

"Hallie, I'm glad your father loved your mother," Amity said. "That's as it should be. If she had lived, I'm sure they would have lived happily forever. As it turned out, she wasn't able to stay with you. No one is to blame for that, least of all me. Why are you so determined not to like me?"

"Because none of us want you here. Papa just asked you to marry him during a weak moment. Aunt Gretchen says that it's not a real marriage if you don't sleep together."

"Your aunt Gretchen can be wrong." Amity's voice was not raised, nor did she sound as if she cared what Gretchen might have said.

"Don't you say my aunt Gretchen lies!" Hallie shouted. "She never tells me anything but the truth! You take that back."

"I think you should go to your room until you can calm down." Amity sounded as if she would brook no nonsense, yet her voice was still measured and calm. Clay wondered how she managed to do that.

"I won't and you can't make me!" Hallie ran out through the kitchen door, and as she slammed it behind her, she found herself facing her father.

Clay frowned at his eldest daughter. She had always been his favorite, though he tried not to show it to the others. She looked more like Elsa than her sisters, and that had blinded him to her difference in personality. Quietly he said, "Go to your room, Hallie, and don't come down until you're ready to apologize to Amity."

She looked as if she would refuse, but Clay didn't give an inch. After a long minute, she turned and slammed out. He heard her stomping up the stairs, and seconds later her bedroom door slammed shut.

Amity opened the door to the parlor. "I thought I heard someone in here."

"I heard what Hallie said. I've sent her to her room until she is ready to apologize."

Casually, Amity brushed the loose hair from her eyes, and he wondered if she was really as calm as she appeared to be. "In that case we may never see her again."

"Does she always talk to you like that?"

"Not always. Sometimes you're in the room." She opened the top door of the icebox and chipped a chunk of ice to drop in his glass of lemonade.

"Why haven't you told me?"

"I'm not one to go running about telling tales. I can handle Hallie. She's just more difficult than the others. She still misses her mother very much." Her brown eyes met his and he knew she was holding the tears back with an effort.

"We all have to accept what life hands out."

"That's not much comfort to a thirteen-year-old girl. She's still young enough to feel childish and old enough to feel she can behave like an adult. It's a difficult time, I suppose."

He wondered what Amity's life had been like when she reached that age. Had her aunts been loving toward her or had they quelled her rebellion the most effective way they could? "I have a feeling you have a rebellious streak yourself," he said aloud.

"Me? What gives you that idea?"

"It would take a certain amount of rebellion to come to Texas and marry a stranger. What did your aunts think about it?"

"I have no idea. I left while they were gone from home."

"You did? You're full of surprises."

Amity turned away. "Yes, I suppose I am."

Clay put his hand on her arm and turned her to face him. He could feel her skin warm and soft beneath the cloth. He dropped his hand. "I'll talk to Hallie. And to Gretchen. Is there anything else I should know?"

"No. There's no need to speak to Gretchen about the subject. It would give her far too much pleasure to see that Hallie is so against me. I think the best approach to take with her is to ignore her until she gets tired of causing trouble and leaves us alone." She lifted her eyes to his as if she half expected him to argue with her.

He wondered again what Gretchen had said to cause Amity's anger when Hallie's outburst hadn't upset her nearly so much. He said, "Gretchen had no business saying anything to Hallie regarding our having separate bedrooms."

"How did Gretchen know?"

"I have no idea. I assume Hallie told her."

"Not you?"

"Of course not." He frowned. "Did she say that?"

"No, I only wondered how she knew." Amity lifted her chin and said, "I was sewing on the back porch. Would you like to sit with me?"

"No, no. I only came in for a drink." He was too aware of how good it had felt to touch her. "I need to get back to work."

She nodded and left him standing in the kitchen. Clay wondered if he had been right to insist on separate bedrooms, but he immediately shook the idea from his mind. She was happy living apart from him, and that was best for everyone. If they shared a bed, she would eventually find herself with child. That was the other thing he had promised Elsa at her grave. He would never again create a child and endanger another woman's life. That was one promise—whether he fell in love again or not—that he intended to keep.

Chapter Seven

As Amity packed her family's lunch with care, she thought about how much she had been looking forward to the church picnic all week. Although she had managed to hide her excitement, as was seemly, she knew she was more delighted at the prospect than were the children. She missed her friends in Charlotte, particularly Dorothea, and had come to realize that she had visited with them a great deal. Although she was busier now that she had her own house and family, she missed being able to walk to Dorothea's house or see friends in the market daily. Ransom was too far for her to go there and back in a matter of minutes, even by buggy, and Fiona was so busy with her own brood, she and Sean seldom visited.

After checking to be sure she had remembered everything, she closed the picnic basket lid and hurried off to get herself and the girls dressed and ready.

The church, painted pristine white and topped with a short steeple bearing a cross, sat on a green square of grass on Ransom's main street. Not unlike many Protestant churches in its basic style, this one's distinguishing feature and the pride of its membership was its beautiful colored-glass windows, sheets of pale green with yellow marbling, that had been brought by steamboat from New Orleans to Jefferson and by wagon, packed with straw, from there to Ransom. As Amity was accustomed to seeing jewellike windows in the church she had attended in Charlotte, she did not share the same level of appreciation for the windows as the other members, but she would have been the last person on earth to ever say so.

"Look," Kate said in exasperation. "We're the last ones to get here. Laura, why do you have to be so slow?"

"I forgot where I put Betsy," Laura said in her own defense. "I couldn't come to a picnic without her." She hugged her doll closely. Rosemary, who was clutching Bertha, nodded in agreement.

"We're not late," Clay said as he reined in his horse to park the buggy beside the others. "It's not noon yet."

Hallie lifted her head to look among the other people. "Do you see the Jimmersons?"

Kate glanced around. "Over there. By the oak," she whispered.

"Can we eat by the oak, Papa?"

"Who are the Jimmersons?" Amity asked as Clay got down from the buggy and held up his hand to assist her.

Jemima said, "Hallie likes Peter Jimmerson. He doesn't like her, though."

Hallie glared at her sister, who grinned back. "I do not! I'm only being polite to him."

"Then why did you spend all that time pinching your cheeks before we went into church last Sunday to make them pinker?"

"Be quiet. You're just a baby."

"Papa, Hallie called me a baby."

Clay ignored them. "Where would you like to put our picnic?" he asked Amity.

"How about under the oak?" She hoped Hallie would see she was trying to make peace.

The oak was broad and shady, and Amity was glad to see it was noticeably cooler beneath it. The summer had arrived with a vengeance, and even though it was barely June, the days already were hot and still. Fiona had also picked a place in the shade of the tree, and the sight of her red hair shining like fire put a smile on Amity's face.

"Hello. We were wondering if you'd come," Fiona said as Amity approached. Her oldest son, Brian, grinned shyly at Hallie, but Hallie ignored him.

Quinn O'Flannery, who was four, went directly to Rosemary and Laura and began showing them the toy soldier his father had made him. Amity watched the children as she spread the quilt on the ground. "We nearly forgot Betsy," she explained.

"I see. No picnic would be complete without Betsy. I can remember when my Kathleen wouldn't have left the house without her doll." Fiona winked at Kathleen. The girl grinned, secure in her maturity of seven years.

Amity leaned closer and whispered to Fiona. "I didn't realize Brian is carrying a torch for Hallie."

Fiona looked at her eldest son, who was watching Hallie's every movement. "He has adored her since he was old enough to tell girls from boys. Unfortunately it's not returned."

Hallie was smiling from beneath her eyelashes at another boy who was sitting on the far side of the tree with his family. He seemed as uncaring of Hallie's attention as she was of Brian's.

Amity sighed. "I wouldn't be young again for anything."

"I would hardly call you over the hill," Clay said with a laugh.

She blushed. Lately he had given her several compliments, and she was not at all sure how to take them. She had never had any young man other than Emmett Hamilton pay her attention, and she was not practiced at the art of exchanging banter. She wondered if Fiona could tell she and Clay were husband and wife in name only. At times she felt as if there were a beacon over her head announcing the arrangement to all who cared to see.

Clay set the heavy basket on the quilt and Amity sat down and began to unpack it. "Come eat, girls. Then you can go play," she said quickly as Laura, Rosemary and Quinn started toward a group of other children playing in the sunshine.

Hallie gave Amity a thoroughly exasperated look. "I'm rather too old to play," she snapped. She hurriedly glanced at the blond-haired boy to see if he had overheard.

Amity pretended not to have heard her. "We have fried chicken, Jemima. Your favorite."

Kate pushed at the chicken with the end of one finger. Although she made no comment, Amity knew she was thinking that her mother made it better than Amity ever would. "We like German potato salad."

Amity opened the jar of potato salad. She had assumed potato salad was all alike. To Fiona she whispered, "What's the difference?"

"Add mustard," Fiona murmured. "And use a good bit more vinegar."

To Kate, Amity said, "You'll like this. Try it. Next time you can help me make it, and we'll do it the way you are used to having it."

Kate wrinkled her nose, being careful not to let her father see. Amity pretended she didn't see it, either. A public picnic was no place for Amity to openly correct any of the children, and Kate knew it.

"We would have to sit here," Hallie said in undertones. "Now Peter Jimmerson will think I'm sweet on him."

"You are," Jemima said smugly. "He'd have to be blind not to know it."

Hallie swatted her.

Amity's head jerked up, and in a demonstrative whisper, she said, "Hallie! A lady never hits anyone."

Hallie openly glared at her and turned her head. Clay had been talking to Sean, but he saw the exchange. He frowned at his eldest daughter and shook his head at her in warning. Hallie pretended not to have seen him. "I'm going to take my plate and go eat with Fern Grizzard and her family."

"No, eat here," Amity firmly stated. She had almost finished putting the food on the quilt.

"Papa, may I eat with Fern?" Hallie called to Clay.

"Sure, honey." He went back to his conversation with Sean.

Fiona looked from Amity to Hallie to Clay. She made no comment, but Amity was embarrassed to know her friend understood now how her relationship was with the children. Hallie triumphantly filled her plate and marched off toward the Grizzard family, who were seated under a nearby trio of pine trees. Kate did the same and followed her. "I see you have your hands full," Fiona said. "Clay must not have heard you tell her she had to eat here," she added tactfully.

Amity couldn't tell if he had or not. She was too upset over having Hallie, and usually Kate, as well, go against her every wish. "I thought she would be pleased at eating practically beside the Jimmersons. She seems to think I came over here just to embarrass her."

"Don't you remember how it was with your first boyfriend?" Fiona said with a laugh. "She's thirteen. She'll be embarrassed for the next several years about one thing or another."

Amity would have been embarrassed to admit that she had never had a boyfriend in the real sense, and especially not at thirteen. "My aunts would have been fit to be tied if I had acted like Hallie. Kate isn't so rebellious when Hallie isn't around, but together they can be trying." She looked to where Hallie and Kate had gone. They were talking to a girl who appeared to be about their age and were looking in Amity's direction. "I never know what to do with her." She put the younger children's plates in front of them and helped Rosemary with the food on hers.

"Give her time. She's not a bad girl. She'll come around. As long as you and Clay pull together as a team, it'll work out. I'm sure he must not have heard you tell her to stay here."

Amity wished she could believe her friend.

Across the way Hallie was saying in a mournful voice to Fern Grizzard, "She told me to find some other place to eat. I had so hoped to eat with Papa."

Fern's eyes widened. "She told you that you can't eat with the rest of the family?"

"Me, too," Kate chimed in. "She doesn't like us."

Lola May Grizzard had overheard the conversation. "That's terrible! Someone should speak to Mr. Morgan about this!"

"No, no," Hallie said quickly. "It will go too hard on us if Papa finds out. We try to make him think everything is all right. He's still so sad over losing Mama, you know."

Fern nodded in sympathy. "I would hate to have a stepmother. That must be awful."

Hallie sighed and poked at her food. "You'll never know the half of it, Fern. You truly won't."

"She's not mean to you, is she?"

Hallie looked at Kate, than at Fern. "When Papa is around she's as sweet as honey. As soon as he's gone, she's like a different person. We work all day and still can't please her."

"Even Rosemary has her chores," Kate said in a solemn voice.

"She's only a baby!" Lola May exclaimed. "What chores could she possibly do?"

"Gardening," Hallie said in all seriousness. "Amity told her, 'Rosemary, you're in charge of the flowers.'"

"Her exact words," Kate put in.

Lola May frowned at her husband. "Someone ought to talk to Clay Morgan and set him straight."

Her husband replied, "Don't butt in. It's none of our business."

To Fern, Hallie said, "You see where she put the picnic. It's practically in the Jimmersons' laps. When the buggy stopped, I mentioned that Peter and his family were under the oak and right away she said that was where she wanted to eat, too. She had to know that would make it look as if I were chasing after him."

"Anyone would know that," Fern agreed.

Casually, Lola May asked, "Why did she come to Ransom? No one in town seems to know where she came from or who she was before they married."

"She lived in Charlotte, North Carolina," Kate told her.

"We have no idea who she was," Hallie put in. "I never heard of her before I came home from visiting cousins with Aunt Gretchen and found her married to Papa."

"We didn't have much more warning," Kate said. "Papa told us she would arrive in two days and there she was."

"Disgraceful!" Lola May frowned at the Morgan family across the way. "I see she's being friendly with that Fiona O'Flannery."

"They are the best of friends," Hallie said.

"I've never trusted immigrants," Lola May said. "If they have nothing to hide, why would they leave their own country and come here?"

Hallie didn't quite follow that logic since she knew everyone in Ransom, except the Indian called Sam, was descended from immigrants. She ate and tried to look dismal at the same time.

"Is it true," Lola May asked, leaning around her daughter, "that she has had several husbands?"

This was news to Hallie, but she said, "We don't like to talk about it."

Lola May straightened and gave her husband a telling look.

"I feel so sorry for you," Fern said. "It's too bad you can't move in with your aunt Gretchen."

"And leave Papa?" Kate asked in surprise.

"I'd love to live there," Hallie said. "I'm rather amazed that Amity hasn't insisted that I do so. I guess she either doesn't want people to talk, or she is trying to separate me from Mama's family."

"That's terrible!" Fern looked at her mother. "Isn't that terrible, Mama?"

"It's a disgrace, pure and simple. Someone should take her to task." She glared at her husband, who continued to eat and show no interest in the conversation.

Under the oak Clay had joined Amity and the younger children on the quilt. "What's this?"

"Potato salad," Laura said. "It's not yellow, but that's what it is."

"I didn't realize there was more than one way to make it." Amity said in her own defense. "I've always made it this way."

Clay tried it. "I like it better like this. Usually potato salad tastes too much like vinegar and mustard."

Amity smiled in relief. The younger girls tried it, and Rosemary nodded in agreement. "Me, too." She tried feeding a bite to her doll.

"You've gone all out," Clay said as he picked up a wishbone of chicken. "This is the best picnic lunch we've ever had."

He sounded sincere, but Amity was feeling vulnerable and besieged with doubt. Her anger at him for his having countermanded her order to Hallie and Kate already had faded, and she wished she could accept his compliment without reservation. She wanted with all her heart to believe he was trying to make her feel accepted.

Rosemary was eating thoughtfully. Unexpectedly she said, "What was your other daddy's name?"

"What?" Amity had no idea what she was talking about.

"Your other daddy. The one you were married to before Papa."

Amity blinked. She had never expected this. "I . . . his name was, well, Emmett. Emmett Hamilton." She felt distaste at saying Emmett's name in front of Clay. It rang like a sour note in her ear.

Clay glanced up. "Then why wasn't your name Amity Hamilton rather than Becker?"

"I took my maiden name back. More chicken?"

"I'm still eating this piece."

"What did he look like?" Rosemary persisted.

"I don't want to talk about him." She knew she was being short with the child, but she wanted to put a definite end to the subject.

Clay looked at her as if he was surprised, but said to Rosemary, "Some things are too hard for a person to talk about, honey. Just finish eating so you can go play."

Rosemary turned all her attention to her plate.

Amity couldn't look Clay in the eye. She wished she had never said Emmett's name. Of course he would wonder at her having a different name. Why had she ever told him a lie in the first place? She hated to lie and this was one of the reasons. So often a lie had a way of doubling back on its originator.

Across the way two of Hallie's friends had joined the Grizzards. "I haven't seen you in a month of Sundays, Hallie," Ollie Jane Pearson said. "Where have you been?"

"I've had too many chores to come visiting," Hallie replied. "I have a new stepmother, you know."

Mavis Fraser, Ollie Jane's closest friend, nodded. "We heard about her. My mother had thought to come visit her, but she's been too busy."

"Tell her thank you, but not to bother. Amity can be rather off-putting to people, and I wouldn't want your mother to be offended."

"Why wouldn't she be friendly to Mother?" Mavis was a bit slower than most of Hallie's friends.

"She's not friendly to much of anybody, except Fiona O'Flannery," Hallie replied. "It's nothing special to your mother."

Ollie Jane looked across at Amity. "She doesn't look unfriendly."

"Of course she doesn't here." Hallie glanced at her friend in exasperation. "How else would she act at a church picnic? You should see her at home." She poked Kate. "Isn't that right?"

Kate nodded. She had been doing more listening than talking, and she was growing uncomfortable. It was one thing for them to try to make Amity want to leave their home, but Hallie was bringing in the whole town. Kate was torn between wanting to support her sister and being loyal to her father. He must have had some good reason for marrying Amity, even if Kate didn't know what it was.

"She's awful," Hallie expounded freely. "Worse than the stepmothers you read about in books."

"How sad for you!" Ollie Jane seemed as impressed as if she had heard every detail of the most awful occurrences. She whispered, "Someone told me she has a checkered past. Myrtle Smith, I believe it was. She knows your aunt rather well."

"I remember her. We don't like to talk about Amity's past."

Lola May frowned slightly. "Does she allow you to call her by her first name like that?"

"She insists on it. I guess she thinks it makes her seem younger." Hallie looked thoughtful. "We don't know how old she is, really."

Lola May's face lit up. "She's older than she looks?"

Hallie shrugged. "I'd be afraid to ask her."

"Poor Hallie. Poor Kate," Mavis said plaintively.

Kate frowned. This was reflecting poorly on her father, and she felt compelled to defend his choice of a new wife. "I don't think she's all that old. She has to be younger than Mama was. She doesn't have any gray hair."

Lola May, who had more than a few gray hairs, said tartly, "That doesn't mean a thing. Women with dark hair can hide it by using a walnut rinse when they wash their hair."

Kate didn't correct her, but she had seen Amity washing her hair under the pump in the kitchen and Amity had used no rinse of any kind, just soap. Kate was growing more and more uneasy with the conversation, but she could see no way of leaving without seeming to be in Amity's camp. She put her plate aside. She wasn't hungry anymore.

Fern said to the newcomers, "She makes little Rosemary do the gardening."

"Not really!" Ollie Jane seemed thoroughly shocked. So did Mavis. "She's too young to do that!"

"Our life is not as easy as it once was," Hallie said mournfully. "If only Mama hadn't had to die."

Kate couldn't take any more. "Excuse me. I have to take my plate back."

"Will you take mine as you go? I don't want to be trapped into having to stay over there."

Kate took Hallie's plate and walked across the church lawn. At least Hallie had given her an excuse for not returning. Jemima had gone to play with Kathleen O'Flannery. Kate sat on the quilt and watched her family. Amity was telling Rosemary and Laura a story about a frog that thought he was a prince. Clay was leaning on one elbow and listening to the story with almost as much interest as the younger children. Kate didn't care about the story, but she was fascinated by the way Rosemary and Laura were hanging on to Amity's every word. They seemed to actually like Amity.

Amity was shy about telling a story to the little girls in front of their father, but Rosemary had insisted. She had been half afraid he would tell her not to fill their heads with such nonsense, but this was Rosemary's favorite. Amity had always had a gift for telling a story, but her aunts had expressly forbidden it. They had said it wasn't good for children to hear about talking frogs and singing fairies, and that Amity should fill her mind with more edifying subjects. But Clay didn't seem to mind.

As she told how the frog fell in love with the beautiful princess, she noticed Kate had joined them and was paying more attention than Amity would have expected. Across the way she could see Hallie with several people. Now and then they all looked at her and whispered among themselves. Amity told herself she was being foolish. What could they possibly be saying about her? She turned her full attention to the story.

When the tale was finished and the frog had been turned into a handsome prince and married the princess to live happily ever after, Clay smiled at her. "You tell stories better than anyone I've ever known."

Amity felt herself smiling. Had she finally found something she did better than Elsa? She expected Kate to object, but the girl was being unusually quiet. "Who is Hallie sitting with over there?"

Clay glanced across the yard. "That's the Grizzard family and a couple of her friends from school. I'm surprised they haven't come over to meet you. Usually a new face in Ransom is cause for curiosity."

"They're talking about other things," Kate said hurriedly.

Amity gave her a searching look. To Clay she said, "I've been rather surprised at our lack of company, too. I've been here for over a month. It would seem everyone in town has heard by now that you have a new wife. In Charlotte, out of courtesy to a newcomer, we would all have been on the doorstep before she finished unpacking."

Clay nodded. "I'd have said the same about Ransom. We don't live that far out in the country."

"That reminds me," Amity said. "I wanted to ask you if I may find a suitable piano teacher for Jemima. She so loves music, and I think she has a natural talent."

"I thought you played the piano. Why don't you teach her?"

Amity shook her head. "I'm not that good, and Jemima is too talented for me to risk teaching her wrong. I've been thinking I could make a quilt and sell it to pay for her lessons."

"I can pay for them." Clay watched his middle daughter at play. "Is she really talented?"

"Indeed, she is. And she has an unusual voice, as well. That's why I'm offering to pay for the piano lessons. I'd like for her to have singing lessons, too."

Clay rubbed his chin while he considered her proposal. "I've always thought she was unusually good, but I'm her father." He nodded. "I know who to talk to. I'll have her signed up to start as soon as possible."

Kate pretended not to be paying any attention. She knew Jemima had wanted music lessons above anything else but had been afraid to ask for them since their mother was gone. Kate's estimation of Amity rose.

The next night Amity finished her work early in order to cook a particularly good meal. Although no one knew it, this was her birthday. Amity hadn't made a fuss over her birthday since she was nineteen, but this year she felt different about it. This year she was no longer an old maid.

She made a pound cake and put a ham on to boil. She wondered when Clay's birthday might be. And the girls'. It hadn't occurred to her that she had no idea when any of them had been born. She made a mental note to ask Jemima to write the dates on her calendar. All children needed a special meal and a cake on their birthday, even if her aunts had discouraged it for her as frivolous. Amity remembered the way her parents had celebrated her birthdays and how it had made her feel special and wanted.

She went into the dining room and put a white cloth on the table. The kitchen was too small for all of them to eat in there, as she had in Charlotte. At first it had seemed odd to her to use the dining room at every meal, but she was getting used to it. She remembered how the very air in her aunts' dining room had seemed to be frozen in place, and it was always several degrees cooler than the rest of the house, even in the summer.

As this was a special night, she had sent Rosemary out to gather more flowers than usual for the table. She smiled when the little girl, with her flower basket over her arm, trotted back in with them. Rosemary was such a delight and was so eager to help.

In the large china cabinet opposite the sideboard, Amity had found a set of plates when she was dusting that were prettier than the ones they used every day. The plates, stacked neatly behind the cupboard doors, bore a hawthorn blossom design and were encircled by a narrow band of gold. They were not as nice as the plates her aunts had used on Sundays, but they were perfect for special occasions.

Amity took out the plates and began setting them on the table. She was almost finished when Hallie came into the room. Hallie stopped dead in her tracks. "What are you doing?" she asked rather sharply.

Amity glanced up. "Setting the table for supper. Would you like to help me?" This was a rhetorical question since Hallie never volunteered to do anything at all around the house.

"You're using Mama's best china!" Hallie made it sound like an accusation.

"Yes, I suppose I am." She hadn't thought of it as the best china but in retrospect she realized it was. "It's pretty," she added.

"You put it right back! Mama's parents had that brought over from Germany and you have no right to use it!"

Amity hesitated. "What good is it unless we use it?" she asked. Her aunts had owned a set of china that they always referred to as "Grandmother's things" that had been too fragile to use, but this china looked sturdy enough for even the smaller girls as long as Amity was supervising.

"What good is it?" Hallie hissed. She was clearly upset and not merely pretending. "It's Mama's *china*."

"Hallie, we will be careful with it. Tonight is special and I thought—"

"No! You aren't allowed to use Mama's china. Not ever!"

Amity frowned. "Your father never said that I shouldn't. I was trying to explain when you interrupted me." If one of her aunts had said this to Amity, she would have folded immediately. Hallie put her hands on her hips and glared at her.

As the situation was growing worse with each exchange, Amity heard Clay's footsteps in the kitchen and breathed a sigh of relief. He came through the door and stopped. "Why is Elsa's china on the table?" he asked.

Amity whipped around to face him. "I put it there!"

"Papa, tell her, this china is not to be used for everyday. I don't want her to use it *ever*."

In the same tone he often used to correct Rosemary, he said, "Amity, we never use this china. It came from Germany, and even Elsa didn't use it."

"Will you tell me what earthly good china is if you don't use it?" Amity demanded. She was tired of having this family cross her at every turn.

"Maybe we could use it at Christmas," he suggested.

Amity knew she was being illogical, but she didn't care. "Do you mean to tell me that I can't use china in my own house?"

"I'm only asking you not to use *this* china. It means too much to the girls. It was Elsa's," he added as if that was explanation enough.

Amity knotted her hands in the folds of her skirt and said with frigid tones, "I think more is at stake here than a set of dishes." Hallie's expression from behind Clay's shoulder drove Amity to say, "You may be in charge of running the farm, but the house is up to me."

"Since when?" he demanded. "I was under the impression I was head of the house."

"Are you saying I have no authority at all?" Amity's temper rarely flared to this extent, and she was trembling with anger.

Clay looked uncomfortable but he refused to back down. "A family must have a central authority, and I'm it."

"Is that right? Where do I figure in this hierarchy?"

"Second in command," he snapped.

Amity saw red. The days had been too hot and too filled with underlying stress. "I refuse to be second in command to anyone in my own house."

"I might point out that this house was mine before I ever heard of you!" Clay retorted.

Hallie's eyes met Amity's, and the girl gave Amity one of her maddening smiles. Amity jerked her head up higher. "Feed yourselves, then. Since you want to be in charge of everything, you can serve supper!" She stalked into her room and slammed the door.

Amity sank down onto her chair and buried her face in her hands. She couldn't believe she had let herself be goaded into speaking like that to anyone, let alone to Clay. And she did so with one of his children observing it all. She wished she could disappear and start all over.

She turned to the open window and unfastened the top button of her blouse. She was so hot. The kitchen was already as hot as an oven when she was cooking, and the summer had barely started. How hot did it get in Texas? She had thought the summers in Charlotte were bad. Amity's temper had always been too quick when she was over-heated.

Why hadn't she thought to ask about the dishes before she used them? She could, in retrospect, think of a dozen ways the scene could have been avoided, but at the time, all she could think of was Hallie's imperious manner and infuriating smile.

She watched the evening turn into night and heard the sounds of her family passing food back and forth and talking as they did every night. They didn't seem to care, or even to notice, that she was not at the table. Amity felt her tears rise, and this time she did nothing to try to check them. No one here cared a bit for her, and this was her birthday. It didn't matter that no one was aware of that fact. Amity let herself cry.

Chapter Eight

The next day Amity was still feeling hurt over the incident with Elsa's china. She felt betrayed by Clay, even though she knew she had been in the wrong, because he had taken Hallie's side. Reason told her that if Elsa's china was that important to the others, she should not use it. If anything had been broken, Amity would never have forgiven herself. Still, she thought Clay had owed it to her, as the girls' stepmother, to discuss the matter with her in private.

Elsa seemed to continue to dominate the house, and Amity disliked the way she was beginning to feel about her. Clay was still as married to Elsa as he had been while she was alive, and Amity hated being jealous of a dead woman.

To ease her conscience, Amity filled a jar with water, got her gardening gloves and visited the tiny cemetery that lay between her farm and Gretchen's. She had seen it often in passing, but she had never stopped. Elsa's grave was easy to find. There were only a handful of headstones. She lay near her parents and not too far from Gretchen's husband, Hall. Her stone read, ''Elsa Louise Morgan and infant son, November 5, 1886. Gone but not forgotten.''

Amity wryly thought the inscription was particularly apt in this instance and at once felt guilty. This was a woman who had been genuinely loved by all who had known her, a woman taken in the prime of her life from young children and a loving husband. With her lay the son Clay had yearned for, whom Elsa had died trying to give life to. Amity could no longer feel any animosity toward her.

She knelt on the limp grass and put on her gardening gloves. The grave hadn't been well tended lately, and that surprised her until she thought how difficult it must be for Clay to face this chore. His heart must break every time he saw Elsa's grave. This, at least, was one pain she could spare him. Perhaps in doing this, she might come to understand how he could still love this woman more than one of living flesh and blood.

She pulled the weeds from the grave and smoothed the bare dirt. Perhaps she could buy seeds at the general store and plant flowers that would cover the ground and keep weeds from getting a toehold. Clay and the girls might like that.

Someone, probably Clay, had planted a rosebush near the headstone. In the heat and unremitting dryness it looked as if it was on its last legs. Amity carefully poured the jar of water on the rose and watched the water seep into the thirsty earth. The bush had one tight bud, and Amity examined it to determine that it was white, not red as she would have assumed. Had white roses meant something special to Elsa or had that been the only color available at the time in Ransom?

She wondered a great deal about Elsa and whether she had been as perfect as everyone said. How could anyone be? Amity privately thought that it would be difficult to live with someone who made no mistakes, never spoke sharply—even when she was tired to the bone—who never burned the supper or curdled the milk or forgot a name. How could a person like that understand an ordinary person's needs and feelings?

Once again she read the headstone. She was no closer to knowing the enigma of Elsa than she had been before, but for some reason she wasn't as resentful. It wasn't Elsa's fault that Amity made so many mistakes in running the house and handling the children. If Elsa had been as perfect as she was said to have been, she would not have wanted Clay to feel lonely and brokenhearted. She would have wanted him to put his life back together and get on with living.

Amity walked back to the house and put away the water jar. She wondered what sort of seeds would provide flowers hardy enough to withstand Texas summers.

In spite of the heat, she worked hard scrubbing and polishing the house. It was a pretty house, though she hadn't been able to tell that at first. The floors were made of wide pine planks, as were the windowsills and door frames. The walls were papered in prints that were brighter and cheerier than any her aunts would have chosen. The house was beginning to feel like Amity's home.

Her only real problem was the way she was starting to feel about Clay. He seemed to be in all her dreams lately, and at times the recollection of those dreams was enough to make her blush in the light of day. In her dreams Clay held her and kissed her and even made love to her, though she always woke up at that point. The dreams left her aching for a fulfillment she was not sure existed and that she was certain would be denied to her. Clay never intimated that he wished their sleeping arrangements were any different or that he would ever suggest changing them.

Amity wondered what she could do. She had no knowledge of how to entice him, much less how to make him fall in love with her. Not for the first time she wished she had Dorothea's knowledge of how to flirt. Dorothea had not been a flighty girl, but she knew how to talk to a man and how to make one become attracted to her. Amity had never learned how because she had never had the opportunity to practice.

Did Clay ever think about her beyond wondering whether she had a meal ready or if she needed something from the store? Amity could not tell from the way he spoke to her. Their conversations were all about the girls and what work needed to be done around the farm or house. She had never once talked to him about a personal subject. They had exchanged no dreams or hopes or fears. The strongest emotion they had shared had been last evening when she had become so angry over the china. Today she felt ridiculous.

When Clay came to the house for dinner, she found it difficult to talk to him, especially in front of the children. She thought that was one of their largest problems. They were never alone. Hallie was still smug, presumably over the china incident. Kate was unusually quiet, and Amity wondered what was going on in her head. Since the church picnic Kate had been less talkative than usual and not as often in Hallie's presence. Amity assumed the girls had had a falling out and would make up in their own good time. Clay seemed as uncomfortable in her presence as she was in his, and this made her more withdrawn than usual. The meal was passed in comparative silence.

Afterward she stacked the dishes in the kitchen and was about to wash them when she realized Clay had gone out onto the porch. Perhaps, she thought, she could find him alone and be able to apologize about the china without an audience. She removed her apron and touched her hair to be sure it was in place. Not that it mattered how she looked, she thought regretfully. Clay never noticed. It occurred to her that it was good she had always been plain and was accustomed to it or she would have been devastated by his inattention. She had never thought she would find anything that made plainness a desirable trait.

Clay was standing on the porch and staring at the brassy sky. Amity thought at first he might be praying, because he was standing so still. Then she realized he was only studying the clouds as if he was calculating whether or not it might rain. The sky was an odd color. The clouds that had moved in since she went to Elsa's grave were lowering and sooty in appearance. The air was taking on a greenish tinge.

She went out to stand beside him. "Do you think we'll get rain?" She looked at the clouds.

Clay shook his head. "I don't know. I can't smell it. Can you?"

Amity sniffed the air. It was dry and hot. "Maybe the wind is blowing from the wrong direction."

"The mule was acting strange in the field. He kept twitching his ears and looking around as if he knew something I didn't."

She voiced the word she had tried not to think. "Tornado?"

"It's the right weather, but the clouds are too uniform. I'm not sure what to make of it."

"Maybe you should wait before going back to the field. There's no shelter out there."

"I have to get the rest of the corn planted in the ground or we won't have a crop to harvest." He shook his head. "This sure feels strange."

"I wanted to talk to you," Amity said. Far in the distance thunder purred.

"Was that thunder?"

"About what happened last night. I was entirely in the wrong and I—" Her words were cut off as a bolt of lightning split the air and deafening thunder made her ears ring. She flinched, her heart pounding as another crash, almost as loud echoed about her.

Clay pulled her toward the door. "Go inside. It's not safe with lightning so close."

"Look!" she exclaimed. "What's that?"

A thin spiral of black smoke was rising above the trees. As they watched it thickened and belched skyward. "Something is on fire." Clay stepped nearer the porch rail. "It's coming from the direction of the O'Flannerys' house."

Amity hurried to stand beside him, her fear of the storm forgotten. "Do you think it hit their house?"

"I'll find out." He left the porch in a run and hurried toward the barn.

Amity raced after him. Fiona was her friend, and Amity knew Fiona would have her hands full if the house was on fire. As Clay saddled his horse, Amity dragged the saddle she used to her own horse.

"You're not coming!"

"Yes, I am. Fiona will need me."

He didn't take time to argue with her, and when he was through saddling his horse, he reached past her and tightened the cinch on her saddle. Amity yanked her skirts out of the way, not caring how much leg she showed, and climbed in the saddle. The animals were skittish from the weather, and her horse bolted after Clay's as soon as it felt Amity in the saddle.

They rode across country, dodging limbs and jumping creek beds. The smoke was denser and blacker, and Amity could smell burning wood. For a panicky moment she wondered if the woods were on fire and if they were riding to their deaths. She had never seen a forest fire, but she had heard terrible stories of how people and animals could be surrounded by fire before they knew they were in danger.

They burst from the woods and onto the field belonging to the O'Flannery farm. Ahead Amity saw flames snapping and dancing from the roof of the barn. Fiona and her children were lined up at the well, Fiona drawing water and handing the buckets to her older children, Brian throwing water on the buildings between the barn and the house. Amity's horse tossed his head and rolled his eyes at going near the fire, but she forced him on.

Clay was there first. He threw himself from the saddle and shouted over the roar of the flames. "Where's Sean?"

Fiona, her eyes wide and terrified, pointed toward the barn. "He went in to get the animals. They came out but he hasn't. He's been in there too long!"

Clay grabbed a bucket of water and poured it over his head, then ran for the barn.

Amity tied the horses and ran to help Brian throw water on the chicken house and the outbuilding nearest the barn. Even at that distance the heat made her skin crawl and prickle. She saw Clay duck his head and dash into the barn. Black smoke rolled out of the double doors and boiled toward the sky.

Clay held his breath as he hunted frantically for Sean. The sooty smoke was everywhere, and he almost lost his bearings. The stall doors were open and the stalls empty except for the last one. It made sense that Sean would have gone that way. Clay could hear a horse squealing in terror and steel-shod hooves banging against the stall walls.

Clay finally reached the last stall and shoved open the bolt that locked it. The horse lunged past, its hooves barely missing Clay in its rush. As he bent to dodge the horse, the smoke cleared enough for him to see Sean lying nearly at his feet.

Clay picked up Sean's limp body, threw him over his shoulder and stumbled off in the direction the horse had taken. His lungs were hurting from the need to breathe, but Clay refused to give in. If he couldn't see, he certainly couldn't take in air. His muscles were tense with the effort and he charged onward. Just when he thought he had run in the wrong direction and was trapped in the back of the barn, the air cleared and he found himself in the yard.

He eased Sean onto the grass and bent over him. Sean immediately began to cough and gasp for air. Relief swept over Clay. He likely would be all right.

As Clay stood, someone threw herself into his arms. He instinctively held the woman and suddenly realized it was Amity. "Are you all right?" she demanded, her words muffled by his chest. "Are you burned?"

He shook his head. "I'm not hurt." Fiona was bending over Sean and crying as she touched his face and hands. Amity stayed in Clay's arms. He knew he had come close to dying with Sean in the barn, and now that he was safe he felt shaken. Amity held him tightly as if she would have lost a great deal if he hadn't come out safely. Clay was surprised how good it felt to have her in his arms, how good it felt to have her arms around him. All too soon she pulled away.

She looked embarrassed as she stepped back from him. Her eyes met his, then dropped. She turned and hurried to help the O'Flannery children toss water on the outbuildings. Clay let her go, but his mind refused to release her.

The barn was lost. They all knew there was no point in trying to save it. Clay concentrated on keeping the fire contained to the barn as he waited for it to burn itself out. Sean got to his feet and stood by Clay. His skin was pale and his hands were shaking visibly. "I nearly died in there," he said in a voice hoarse from smoke. "I lost my way and couldn't find how to get out."

"The same thing nearly happened to me." Clay looked at Amity, who was listening but keeping her distance.

Fiona put her arms around her husband, their youngest child clutching her skirts fearfully. "Thank God you're all right. No horse is worth it, Sean O'Flannery. A horse can be replaced. You can't be."

Sean grinned at her. "Is that so? I was trying to save that dun mare you put such store in."

She buried her face against his shirt. "I don't care. I'd rather have you."

"Thanks to Clay you can have both." Sean's eyes met Clay's. "Thank you."

Clay looked away and grinned. He was always embarrassed in the face of gratitude. When he looked at Amity, he found she was watching him, and this time she did not look away. Her cheeks were streaked, but he didn't know if it was from tears or sweat. Her no-nonsense facade was gone, and she looked as vulnerable and as frightened as any woman he had ever seen. Silently, Clay held out his arm to her. Amity hesitated but came to him.

Her hands felt small on his waist, though he knew how capable they were. She was not as tall as he would have said, either. She had to tilt her head to gaze up at him. Her hair had come loose and was all but tumbling down, but she hadn't noticed it. Clay longed to touch it and see once and for all if it really was as soft and as thick as it seemed. Her face was paler than ever and her eyes seemed huge and almost black with repressed emotion.

He pulled her close and cradled her head against his chest as he watched the barn burn. He could have lost more than his life. He could have lost her. More than once he had seen her run perilously close to the flames to put out a finger of the fire that was trying to reach the other buildings. Her long skirts could have caught fire so easily. He tightened his grip about her.

She was so small in his arms. He had known she wasn't a large woman, but he was surprised to find she felt almost delicate in his embrace. She carried herself with so much dignity he had never noticed how petite she was or how well she would fit next to a man's body. He lay his cheek against her hair and smelled smoke. Just the thought that he might have lost her was making him shake all over again.

Amity became aware again of where they were and that they were not alone. She pulled away and glanced self-consciously at Sean and his family. Then she turned and began to pin her hair up. Clay wondered what was going on in her mind. Had she embraced him simply because he was there and alive, or had she meant it more personally? He had no idea. Amity was a complete mystery to him.

Lately she had been showing up in his dreams with alarming regularity. He had come to grips with the fact that he was starting to care more about her than was in line with the promise he had made at Elsa's grave, but in his dreams he more than cared for her. She had laughed with him in a way he had never heard her do in reality, and she had been relaxed and free with her love for him. In his dream as he reached for her, he awakened and found himself alone in the big bed. The dream had been occurring more often than was comfortable, and his body ached for her in a way that he thought would certainly shock her.

Amity seemed so unapproachable, so dignified. She was well-educated and was a city-bred lady with refined sensibilities in direct contrast with his. Elsa had had some of these same traits. But Elsa had lived on a farm all her life, and Clay hadn't found her unapproachable, though he had never ceased to be amazed that she had chosen him for a husband. Amity was pretty in a more vibrant way, but she had an innate coolness that kept Clay at a distance. Today that coolness was gone.

The barn finally collapsed and the fire started to die out. Instead of one huge blaze, it became several smaller ones.

Clay helped Sean and his two older boys shovel dirt onto the fires to put them out. Fiona and Amity held the two younger children, who were nearly as frightened now as they had been during the height of the blaze. When he looked over his shoulder, Clay saw Amity sitting on the grass, the boy and girl crowding near her, and he wondered why small children loved her so much when he, a grown man, was half afraid to approach her.

When the barn was reduced to smoldering embers, Clay said, "We'll rebuild it. We can add the tack room you wanted."

Sean nodded, still too upset to talk.

Fiona came to him. "We haven't lost so much. We're all safe and even the animals are unharmed. A barn is only an object." She smiled at Clay. "We had never built anything before we built the barn. Now we know more about how to do it."

Clay pointed to a level place not far away. "That would be a good place for the new one. It's not as close to the house."

Sean narrowed his eyes to study the place. "I almost built it there to start with. Remember? You said that's the spot you'd have chosen if you were me."

"That way you don't have to clear away all the debris before we start. I can talk to the other men at church and see who can lend a hand. We can have it up in no time if there's lumber to be had."

As they discussed the barn, Amity watched Clay. His face was streaked with soot, but he had never looked more handsome to her. His brown hair was grimed in places, and his clothes were the worse for wear. It made her want to go to him again and put her arms around him. Amity blushed as she recalled how shamelessly she had done that only moments before. She, who had never made a public demonstration of affection in her entire life, had hugged Clay as if she were completely shameless. She wondered what he thought about it. She found men so impossible to comprehend.

At last it was safe to leave the barn, and once the men had agreed on a building date, it was time to go. Amity mounted her horse and waved to Fiona, Sean and the children, then turned her horse toward her home. She wondered what Clay would say to her when they were alone. Would he reprimand her for embracing him? She was afraid she would cry if he did. Holding him in her arms had felt better than anything had in her life. His arms around her had given her the strength to go on fighting the fire even though her muscles were so tired they trembled.

They were almost to the house before Clay spoke. "I'm glad you came with me. You were a big help."

She glanced at him. "I couldn't desert friends when they were in need." After a pause she added, "You nearly died in the fire. I can't seem to forget that."

His eyes met hers. "If anything should happen to me, you would have the farm and my daughters. You'd have a place to live for the rest of your life."

Anger flared in Amity. "Do you think that's what I care about? A place to live?" She had much more she wanted to say but she didn't trust herself. She slapped the reins on her horse's rump and galloped to the barn, leaving Clay to return alone. A home, indeed! How could he think she was more interested in the house than in his well-being? She made sure she was busy in the kitchen until he had gone out to finish up his work in the field.

At supper the girls were full of questions about the fire, and Amity was relieved of having to make conversation. Clay patiently told and retold the events of the afternoon. Hallie seemed unusually interested in whether or not Brian had been hurt, and Amity wondered if the girl was really as disinterested in the boy as she pretended to be.

Afterward, she cleaned the kitchen as usual, and Jemima dried the dishes and put them away. Amity was becoming close to the three younger children. Jemima often volunteered to help her with chores, and when Amity drove the buggy into Ransom to take Jemima to her music lessons, they had had time to talk and really get to know each other.

Amity didn't know for certain how a mother felt about her children, but she didn't see how she could love her own child more than she had come to love these three.

Kate was still a mystery to her. She had helped set the table, even though it wasn't her night to do so, and had volunteered to stir the vegetables while Amity had poured the iced tea. Amity was almost afraid to hope, but it seemed that Kate was beginning to accept her. That left only Hallie, but Amity saw no improvement there at all. The older girl still actively disliked her and made little effort to hide it.

With her kitchen chores finished, Amity went upstairs to help Rosemary and Laura get ready for bed. Rosemary was still worried about the O'Flannery barn, and Amity had to reassure her over and over that their own barn was in no danger. That night she made the bedtime story longer than usual, and she was glad to see Rosemary and Laura were asleep before she finished. Amity smiled at Jemima, and the girl smiled back before turning on her side to go to sleep.

From the next room Amity could hear Hallie and Kate in conversation, but she couldn't discern any words. She considered going to tell them good night, but refrained. The few times she had tried, Hallie had treated it as an invasion of her privacy. Amity went downstairs.

The lower floor was quiet, and she thought Clay must have already gone into his bedroom. She wondered if he really went to bed that early or if he spent the time reading or deciding what work to do the next day. There was so little she knew about him. The dining room that separated their bedrooms might well have been as large as the Sahara Desert, so effectively did it keep them apart.

Amity went into her bedroom and removed her clothes. She had washed her hair and bathed after coming back from the fire, but she was glad to escape the tight waist of her dress. All her muscles were sore from carrying buckets of water, and her back twinged whenever she moved too quickly. She slipped on her cotton nightgown and took down her hair.

That afternoon it had almost fallen down around her shoulders. Amity had been embarrassed when she realized it. There she had been, streaked with soot and her hair tumbling all about her, and hugging Clay. She must have looked like a slattern! She couldn't imagine either of her aunts letting themselves get into such a state, not even if they were fighting a fire in a burning barn. What must Clay have thought?

She sat by her window, but no breezes were blowing from that direction. Since she thought she had the house to herself, she decided it wouldn't hurt to sit on the porch until she was relaxed enough to go to bed.

Moving quietly so as not to disturb anyone, she let herself out and lifted her head so the breeze would cool her throat. Because she was alone, she opened the top button of her nightgown. The night was sultry and still, but it was cooler than inside the house. Amity wished she wasn't so civilized so she could sleep on the porch where there was at least the hope of a breeze.

Even though a noise alerted her that she was not alone, when Clay stepped out of the shadows, she jumped. "I didn't know . . . I thought you had gone to your room."

"I couldn't rest." As he stepped into the moonlight, she saw he was wearing trousers and a shirt, the sleeves of which had been rolled up to just below his elbow.

She knew she should go back inside. Married or not, there was no intimacy between them, and she had no business flaunting herself before him by wearing only a thin cotton nightgown. As she backed toward the door, he said quietly, "Don't go."

She stopped at once.

"I've been thinking about this afternoon."

"I know. Rosemary was particularly upset at the idea of a fire. I had to tell her time and again that she and our barn are in no danger."

"I don't mean the fire." He looked at her, and even though it was too dark to see him clearly, she felt a warmth start in her middle and spread. "I was thinking about you holding me like you did."

"It was forward of me." She refused to apologize, however, because she couldn't honestly say she was sorry.

"Why did you do it?"

"I thought you wouldn't be able to get out of the barn. You were in there a long time."

"Is that the only reason? You must have thought the same about Sean and you didn't hug him."

Amity turned away. "Sean isn't my husband."

Clay sighed. "I haven't been much of a husband to you. Sometimes I wonder why you stay here."

She couldn't tell him it was because she was falling in love with him any more than she could say that was why she had held him so tightly that afternoon.

"I think you should know I'm becoming quite...fond of you." He sounded as if the words were hard to admit.

"Are you?"

"I had hoped you would say the same about me."

Amity tried to find the right words. "I care for you, too. I've never found it easy to talk to a man, but often I think of things I would like to say to you." She laughed nervously. "But you are never anywhere near at the time."

"I'd like to hear what you have to say." In the darkness his voice was gentle and soft.

Amity told herself not to read more into his words than he must mean. He didn't want her. Not like that. Not like he had wanted Elsa. "What sort of flowers will do well here? What kind will thrive with little attention?"

He seemed to be thinking. "I guess lantana will grow anywhere. Thrift is hardy and has purple flowers in the spring. Do you want me to dig you another flower bed?"

"No, that won't be necessary." She didn't want to bring Elsa's name into this. Not when they were actually talking about something other than the children. "I've always liked flowers," she risked adding.

"So do I. I guess that sounds strange coming from a man." He glanced at her as if he thought she might laugh at him.

"I don't think I could care about a man who didn't."

The silence grew long and Amity thought she might have gone too far. She turned away before he could go inside first. "I'll see you in the morning."

Clay felt lonely when she was gone. He had hoped she would stay and talk, but he supposed she was exhausted. She liked flowers but didn't want him to make her a new bed. She was more independent than any woman he had ever known. And more intriguing. He never knew what she was thinking, and at times it drove him to distraction. She would drop some tidbit into his mind, like this question about flowers, and then not speak of it again.

Clay wished she had stayed to talk.

Chapter Nine

During the O'Flannerys' barn raising, Fiona had news for Amity of a party in the offing. "It's the yearly watermelon festival," she said. "It's Ransom's largest party until the Thanksgiving harvest dance. All the young girls want to go and wear their prettiest dresses."

"A dance?" Dorothea had taught Amity to dance years ago, but Amity had never had an occasion to use the knowledge.

"The grown-ups dance, too. Wait until you see my Sean on the dance floor. He was the best dancer in County Cork."

Amity was folding the checkered tablecloth from the noon meal. "Can Clay dance, do you suppose?" she asked casually.

"Lord, yes! He loves to dance. Elsa wasn't much for it, though."

Amity thought what an odd quirk of fate it was that she finally found something at which Elsa did not excel, and it happened to be something that she was not at all sure she could do, either. "I know a little about how to dance, but I haven't had much practice. Clay likes it, you say?"

"I've heard him say he wished there was a dance every Saturday."

"Do you suppose Sean could teach me how to dance better? I know it's an imposition, but if Clay enjoys it . . ."

"It's no imposition at all! I won't be able to dance this year." Fiona patted the rounding of her stomach. "The babe won't be here until later in the month. Sean will be glad to have a partner."

Amity laid the tablecloth in the basket. "You say it's a dance the girls enjoy? Hallie, for instance?"

"Yes, she's old enough to be wanting to dance with a boy this year." Fiona shook her head. "I remember those years when I was at a dance and afraid no boy would want to dance with me, and even more afraid that if one did, I'd step all over him." She laughed. "Was it like that where you come from?"

"I suppose. I rarely went to parties." She looked across the yard to where the men were at work on the barn. "You can't imagine how different it is here from the way I grew up. My aunts meant the best for me, of course, but I was so secluded from others my age. There are so many things I don't know. Like how to attract Clay, for instance." She blushed at the admission.

Fiona brushed the rest of the crumbs from the top of the trestle table that had been moved into the yard to accommodate the men for dinner. At Amity's words she looked up in surprise.

Amity turned away. "We didn't really know each other before I came here. I suppose you must already know that."

"Sean and I had wondered."

"We became acquainted through letters." This was mostly true. She had read the letters Clay sent to Dorothea. "We didn't actually meet until I arrived here. Our courtship and engagement were rather unusual. At times I'm sorry, but under the circumstances it couldn't be helped." She didn't add that she was afraid that Clay might not have chosen her if they had met before their wedding day.

"I'm not a pretty woman, nor am I young," Amity said. "I realize that. I'm afraid that Clay wishes I might have been more of both."

"No, he doesn't. He and my Sean are as close as brothers, and Sean says Clay is happy with you."

Amity searched Fiona's face. "Clay said that?"

"Apparently so. Are you happy with him?"

Amity smiled. "I am. I'm happier here with Clay than I've ever been in my life. There are parts that are difficult— my problems with Hallie, for instance, but that's nothing compared to all the rest of it. The three younger girls are so precious to me, and Kate is starting to come around, I think. I hope."

"Hallie will, too, in time. Losing her mother hit her hard."

"I know, and I can't fault her for wanting to be loyal to Elsa."

"It's Gretchen, if you ask me. She's keeping Hallie stirred up."

"You think so? That had occurred to me, too, but I was afraid to mention it."

"You know Gretchen is no friend of mine." Fiona sat on the bench where the men had eaten. "I'd chase her away and be done with it."

"I can't do that."

"I know, more's the pity."

Amity looked around. "I would have expected some of the other wives to come to the barn raising. In Charlotte the women never miss a chance to get out of the house and get together. I thought half of Ransom would be here."

Fiona sighed. "So did I. At least some of the wives sent food for their men. We didn't have to cook it all."

"Why do you suppose they stayed away?"

"I have no idea."

Amity wished she did not have a feeling of foreboding about the wives' absence.

Because rain had been scarce for the past several months, all the farmers in the area were becoming concerned about their crops, and like in so many other households, money was becoming scarce around the Morgan home. Amity knew buying cloth to make Hallie a party dress was an extravagance they could not afford. However, she had noticed a trunk of clothes in the attic and she thought perhaps there might be something there that could be used to make the girl a party dress.

The trunk she sought was in a dark corner, next to her own trunk and a box packed with baby clothes. She pulled the trunk over to a spot near the eave where the light was better and opened it.

It was filled with dresses. Amity lifted first one and then another. She knew these gowns had to have been Elsa's, and she was surprised that Gretchen had not taken them. Unable to quell her curiosity, she stood and held one to her. Elsa had been shorter and thinner. This didn't surprise Amity. She had assumed Elsa's physical proportions would have been perfect, too.

Near the bottom of the trunk was the sort of dress she had been searching for. It was pale blue and would go beautifully with Hallie's eyes, just as it must have matched Elsa's. Foamy white lace, not yet yellowed by time, encircled the wrists and frothed down the front. The full skirt was as wide as any ball gown, and she was sure Hallie would look beautiful in it as she swept around the dance floor. Amity had no doubt that with only minor alterations, it would fit Hallie.

She returned the other dresses to the trunk and closed the lid. She was smiling as she descended the steep stairs. Hallie would be so pleased when she discovered she had a new dress for the dance. Amity might not have much experience with dances, but she knew young girls set a great deal of store by what they wore to such occasions.

In her sewing room behind the stairs, Amity laid out the dress on the table she used for cutting material. Not much alteration would be necessary. Hallie was flatter in the chest than Elsa had been, and she was not quite as tall yet, but these alterations would be fairly simple. With her sewing scissors, Amity carefully removed the bodice from the skirt, then started unstitching the lace at the wrists to shorten the sleeves.

"Amity, where are my..." a young female voice called to her.

When she turned to see who it was, she discovered Hallie standing in the doorway with her mouth open, staring at the dress. "Oh, Hallie, I had wanted this to be a surprise!"

A look of horror replaced the surprise on Hallie's face. "You're cutting up Mama's best dress!"

Amity looked at the table then to Hallie and suddenly realized that Hallie did not understand what was going on. "I'm remaking it for you."

"You're ruining it!" Hallie ran to the dress and gathered all the pieces to her. Tears rose in her eyes and ran down her cheeks. "Why would you do such a terrible thing?"

"I thought . . . I'm making you a new dress for the watermelon festival. I thought you'd be pleased."

"Pleased! Pleased that you're destroying my mother's clothes?" Hallie's voice rose to near hysteria.

"Hallie, calm down. I didn't mean anything wrong by it. I only wanted—"

"You wanted! That's all you care about—what you want!" Hallie hugged the dress to her and glared at Amity. "You don't care a thing about us!"

"That's not true! Hallie, listen to what I'm saying. I'm sewing this dress for you to wear to the party."

"Wait until Papa hears about this!" Hallie turned and ran from the room.

Amity went after her, but Hallie reached the porch before she did. She ran to where Clay sat sharpening his scythe. "Papa! Look what she's done now!"

Amity halted a few steps back as Clay lifted the bodice and skirt and stared at them. She could tell by the look on his face that he recognized the dress. Why hadn't she thought to ask him first?

"She's ruined it! She hates us and she hates Mama!" Tears streamed down Hallie's face.

Amity found her voice. "I don't hate anyone." To Clay she said, "I tried to tell Hallie that I'm remaking the dress for her to wear to the watermelon festival dance. I thought she would be glad to have something of her mother's for her own. It's a pretty dress and would look so nice on Hallie. It's a shame to let it go to waste where it will never be seen again.''

Clay handed the dress to Amity. "I remember this one. Elsa wore it at the last dance we ever attended."

Amity groaned. Leave it to her to have picked the dress most likely to hold memories for Clay as well as for Hallie. "I can restitch it. I had no idea the dress was so special."

Clay drew in a deep breath. "No, I think it's a good idea for it to be used." He looked at his daughter. "Wouldn't you like to wear your mother's dress?"

Hallie touched the skirt almost reverently. "I never thought of it like that, I mean, that I would be wearing something of Mama's. But wouldn't you mind?"

"No, I don't mind. I think it was nice of Amity to think of it for you."

Hallie glared at her. "If she hadn't been going through Mama's things, she wouldn't have known it was there."

"I wasn't prying," Amity defended herself. "I had seen the dresses earlier when I took something of my own up to the attic."

"Hallie, the attic, like the rest of the house, is Amity's domain now," Clay said to his daughter. "She has a right to look into whatever she pleases."

"I don't want her going through Mama's things."

Clay looked as if his sadness over not having Elsa was closing in on him.

"I would have used one of my own dresses," Amity said to Hallie, "but I don't have one this nice, and I didn't think you'd want one that had belonged to me."

"You're right! I'm not wearing your cast-offs!"

"Hallie! That's enough." Clay frowned at her. "Where are your manners? You never used to talk like this."

"I didn't have a reason to when Mama was alive. Amity coming here has changed everything!"

Clay took his daughter's hand. "Honey, your mama would still be gone whether Amity was here or not."

Hallie tried to blink back her tears, but they coursed down her cheeks despite her effort.

Amity began to fold the dress. "There's no rush on this. The dance won't be for weeks yet. Maybe there will be rain soon and the crops will be better than we have been expecting. I'll restitch this one." She didn't want to meet Clay's eyes and see the loss he was obviously feeling, as well.

Hallie surprised her by saying, "I would rather have Mama's."

"You would?" Amity stared at the girl.

"I was just surprised, that's all." Hallie touched the soft blue fabric. "I'd rather have a dress Mama made and wore. I can take it up myself. Mama taught me how to sew."

"All right." Amity should have known Hallie wouldn't want anything that came from her hand.

Hallie gathered the dress to her and hurried into the house. Amity looked at Clay. "I didn't mean to cause so much trouble over the dress."

"It's just cloth," he said as he met her eyes. "I wouldn't have thought Hallie would have behaved that way. You meant well."

"I remember a time when I was a girl and I wanted a blue party dress more than anything. I assumed Hallie would feel the same."

"Did you get it?"

"Get what?" she asked in confusion.

"The blue party dress."

Amity shook her head. "I wasn't able to attend the party so I didn't need it after all."

"I know so little about you."

"There's little to tell."

Clay moved over on the step to make room for her. "Sit here beside me and talk to me while I sharpen this blade."

Amity hesitated, then did as he asked. "It seems odd to see you at home at this time of day."

"The crops don't need tending yet and the fences are mended. I'm trying to get my tools sharpened and repaired for the harvest. Watermelons will be ripening soon, if they make it at all." He glanced at her. "Tell me more about this party and why you didn't go."

Amity folded her hands in her lap. "There's not much to tell. It was a dance and one of my friends—" she remembered in time not to say Dorothea's name "—had taught me to dance. She is younger than I am, and this was to be her first dance. I had hoped to go with her, but my aunts needed me at home, so I didn't go."

"What did you do instead?"

"We canned tomatoes."

Clay gave her a searching look.

"I didn't mind," Amity lied. "My aunts were already aging, and I wanted to help them. They took me in when my parents died and I owe them a great deal."

"They haven't written you since you came here. I've mailed several letters from you to them, but none have come in return."

"I know. I hope their health isn't bad." Amity unconsciously rubbed one hand over the other. "They were considerably older than my mother and are more like grandmothers than aunts."

"Surely both of them wouldn't be too sick to write."

"No. That would be unlikely, wouldn't it." She knew they weren't answering her letters because they were displeased with her, but she felt too guilty to admit that.

"You told me once that you left without telling them ahead of time. That you left a note for them."

"I had forgotten I told you that. Yes. It seemed to be the best way at the time."

Clay smiled at her. "One of these days I want you to have a blue party dress."

Amity blushed and lowered her eyes. "I'm too old for that. I could never wear blue at my age."

"You sound as if you're a hundred years old. Why do you do that?"

She had no answer. Her aunts had raised her to feel as if she was as old as they were. They had also convinced her that no man would want her for a wife, but here she was.

"May I ask you a question?"

"Certainly."

"Do you find me, well, attractive?" She held her breath, scarcely believing she had asked him such a thing. "No, no. Don't answer that. It was a foolish question. Forget I asked it. I have to get back to work." She rose and was about to hurry inside when he caught her wrist.

"I find you quite attractive."

She felt as if her world had stopped spinning as she gazed into his green eyes. She didn't know what to say. Clay's tone conveyed that he not only was attracted to her but that he found her desirable as a woman.

"I've never been very good at giving compliments," he said softly. "I wasn't brought up to know how to say nice things to a lady. Polish is one thing that is nearly impossible to learn on your own. I know I must be rougher and less gentlemanly than the men you knew back East, but I have come to care for you a great deal."

Amity could only stare at him.

"I look at you sometimes when you don't notice. When you're sewing by the lamp or when you're telling a story to the little ones. When you're nowhere near, I think about the way your voice sounds and how the red in your hair almost glows in the sunlight."

Amity reached up with her free hand and touched her hair. "I know it's too red, but there's nothing I can do about it. It's always been this color."

"I like it."

She felt as if her knees were turning to jelly. "You like the color of my hair? Even if it has red in it?"

He smiled at her, and she found herself smiling back. "I don't think I've ever seen hair that was prettier."

She cautioned herself not to read too much into that compliment. Naturally he had meant to say, "Except for Elsa's blond hair." Everyone liked blond hair best, and Elsa's must have been beautiful. "Thank you," she remembered to say. "No one has ever said that to me." She lifted her skirts to go into the house and he released her wrist. She could still feel the warm pressure of his fingers on her skin, and the thought touched her heart. Even after Amity was in the house and busy with her chores, she found she was still smiling.

On Sunday morning Amity herded the girls into the buggy and let Clay help her onto the seat beside him for their ride to the church. She glanced at him from the corner of her eye. He had said nothing about going to Gretchen's for dinner afterward, and she had been relieved. Hallie was less pleased, but these days Hallie was usually displeased about something or another most all the time.

Behind her she could hear the girls talking about this and that to the accompaniment of the horse and buggy's tingle and clop. Amity was beginning to feel like a real part of the family. These days Rosemary turned to her naturally for help in fastening buttons and combing her hair, and Laura talked to her as if Amity had always been with them. Jemima was still enchanted by her music lessons and often asked Amity to come hear a piece she had learned to play or sing. As they had been getting ready for church, Kate had even asked Amity's opinion on which dress to wear.

She loved being a part of a large family. Now that she was used to the almost incessant noise in a house filled with children and becoming adjusted to the idea of a house that constantly needed straightening, Amity found she liked it. She would rather straighten the rugs a dozen times a day in Clay's house than do it once a week in her aunts'. She did not feel guilty that she had run away from Charlotte and had no desire to return to her former life, but she sometimes wondered if she should. These days she felt less and less as if she owed her aunts fealty for the rest of her life. After all, they had had a choice about taking her in and had done so of their own free will.

"What are you thinking?" Clay asked under the noise of the buggy and girlish laughter.

"I was having uncharitable thoughts about my aunts."

"What are they like? You never talk about them."

"Aunt Dorcus is the elder of the two, and she is fond of sewing. Aunt Ophelia is a better cook."

"Are they widows?"

"No." The thought of either of her aunts as a wife brought a smile to Amity's face. "They are both spinsters." *Just as I could have been,* she thought but did not say.

"By choice?"

She glanced at him. "I have no idea. We never talked about anything like that."

"What did you talk about?"

"Church, mainly, and about who was being born, getting married or dying. They are both active in a number of charities."

"That's what *they* do. What about you?"

She thought for a minute. "I suppose I did pretty much what they did. There wasn't a great deal of choice. I don't mean that they were unpleasant to me, only that I had few friends my own age."

"You didn't? I would have thought you would have had many friends."

"I didn't get out often. As I've said, my aunts are elderly, and they needed me to stay home and look after them."

"Then why are you here?"

Amity changed the subject by saying, "Isn't that the O'Flannery buggy?"

Clay looked past her and waved. Sean and Fiona waved back. From over her shoulder, Amity saw Hallie quickly look away when Brian waved at her. Amity suppressed a smile. Hallie was trying too hard to appear to be unmoved by having seen him. She thought there was more interest there than Hallie was willing to admit.

They arrived at church in time for a bit of socializing before the service. Amity nodded to some of the women she knew by name, but to her surprise, most of them turned their heads as if they hadn't seen her. Fiona and Sean caught up with them. Their children had scattered like a flock of quail as soon as the buggy stopped.

"Look at them," Fiona said. "You could pick out the O'Flannerys from the crowd even if you had never known any of us."

Amity knew what she meant. The O'Flannerys' characteristic red hair stood out easily among all the blonds and brunettes. Fiona whispered, "We're hoping for another girl this time. Sean has enough sons to help with the crops, but Kathleen and I will be hard-pressed to cook and clean for them all. You're lucky to have girls."

Amity wasn't so sure this was true, but she smiled. "Did you ask Sean if he will help me practice my dancing?"

"I did and he's willing."

"Good." Because Clay enjoyed dancing, she was eager to be prepared for the upcoming dance.

They strolled near Lola May Grizzard and Clematis Osgood. "Good morning," Amity said to them.

Lola May didn't answer at all and Clematis only uttered a terse, "Good morning," then turned away.

Amity stared after them. "Why is everyone being so cool toward me?" she whispered to Fiona.

Fiona shook her head. "I have no idea. Maybe it's me they're avoiding."

"Why would they do that?" Amity noticed none of the other women seemed inclined to speak to them or even to meet their eyes. At a distance she saw Gretchen talking to Myrtle Smith. Myrtle darted a glance at Amity and slightly turned so that she could pretend not to have seen here. Amity moved closer to where Clay was talking to Sean.

Soon the bells began to ring, and they went into the church and found their usual pew. Although this church did not have assigned family pews as her church in Charlotte had had, Amity had noticed before that people almost always sat in the same places in the sanctuary. Today, however, the seats directly in front of and beside them were conspicuously vacant. She glanced around to see if the church was less crowded than usual, but found a full complement of the congregation was there, only seated differently.

After the choir sang, Brother Crowe began his sermon.
Amity had difficulty keeping her mind on what he was saying. Why was everyone behaving so oddly? Hallie was sitting with Gretchen as she frequently did on Sundays. The
other girls were squirming beside Amity and Clay, as usual.
Amity lifted Rosemary into her lap to encourage the girl to
sit quietly. Rosemary laid her cheek against Amity's shoulder and played with the row of tiny buttons down the front
of Amity's dress.

The service seemed to be unusually long, though it probably was not, and Amity was glad to escape into the fresh
air. In the summertime, churches were typically hot despite
their high ceilings and open windows. She joined the other
women under the oak tree to exchange pleasantries before
going home to Sunday dinner. Rather than avoiding her
again, Lola May, flanked by Clematis and Myrtle, appeared to be waiting for Amity.

"Good morning," Amity said uncertainly. Fiona stepped
beside her.

Lola May wasted no words. "I have been hearing some
unsettling information about you," she said, her second
chin quivering. "In view of our having asked you to join our
Wednesday Ladies' Sewing Circle, I think it's my place to
question you about these matters. It has recently been
brought to our attention that there may be more to your past
than you've let on."

"I have no idea what you're talking about." Amity had
been invited to join the sewing circle soon after her arrival
in Ransom, but she had been too busy to attend.

Myrtle said, "Were you married before you came here?
What of your family?"

Without waiting for an answer, Clematis put in, "I have
distant kin in Charlotte, and I can check out anything you
say."

"We believe you to have a past that precludes your join-
ing in our society," Lola May said scathingly.

Amity stared from one woman to the other. "You have no
right to ask me anything, and I am under no obligation to

answer you." She had seen women like these before, who were more interested in preserving their small, stagnant realms of power than in the truth. Her aunts had usually been the ones questioning a newcomer's suitability for this or that club, and Amity was mortified that anyone would question her own.

Fiona stepped forward, her eyes blazing. "What do you mean by saying such a thing to Amity? What's the meaning of this?"

Lola May fixed Fiona with a cold eye. "You are aligning yourself with the wrong person. You haven't been accepted to the circle that long yourself."

"Nor do I care to be if this is your way of treating people," Fiona retorted.

Amity lifted her chin. "I come from a good family in Charlotte. Who they are need not matter to you. Why are you asking me these questions in the first place?"

"It's been brought to our attention," Lola May said, "that you may not have come from such a sterling background. That you may, in fact, have misrepresented yourself to all of us."

For a dreadful minute, Amity thought Emmett Hamilton had somehow sent word to Ransom that Amity was a fallen woman. Then she realized that such a thing was ridiculous. "I have more to do than to justify myself to you. If you'll excuse me, I must join my husband and daughters."

As she walked away she heard the women exchange hushed but angry comments. She did not turn her head. Fiona hurried to catch up. "What was that all about?" Amity demanded when she was able to speak. "What have they heard about me?"

"I don't know, but I'm going to find out," Fiona said with a reassuring pat on Amity's arm. "Don't let them get you down. I've been to the sewing circle, and more gossip gets done than sewing."

"I can live quite happily without ever belonging to any sewing circle," Amity assured her, but nevertheless, she felt betrayed. Who was talking about her behind her back, and why would anyone want to spread ugly rumors about her? Guilt touched her. There would be no reason to spread rumors. The truth about her having let Emmett have his way with her and her subsequent flight from Charlotte would be bad enough. She glanced at Clay. What would he say if he ever found out she was a fallen woman?

Clay joined her at the buggy and called to the children. She could tell by the set of his jaw that he was angry. She noticed the men seemed to be clustered in much the same way as had been the women. She lifted her head. Whatever was being said about her, she would not give them the satisfaction of seeing her tremble.

All the way home Clay was silent. Even the girls were chattering less than usual. Concern knotted like a cold ball in Amity's middle. What had Clay heard? She knew it had to be a malicious lie made up by someone for some reason she could not fathom, but the women's accusations had touched too close to the truth.

At the house, Clay motioned for her to come with him to the barn to unharness the horse. As Amity watched him unfasten the buckles, she stood in silence, not knowing what to say. After a while, Clay said, "I heard some talk today at church. Talk about you and why you came to Ransom."

Amity waited, her eyes riveted to his face. She said nothing in her own defense. She had lied to Clay about too much already.

"I told them that if anyone had anything to say about my wife, they had better say it directly to me."

Her mouth dropped open. "You said that?"

He looked at her over the horse's back. "Of course I did."

"Clay, I . . ." Amity paused. She could not tell him the truth. Not like this. What if one of the girls came out and overheard her? "Never mind."

He walked around the horse and put his hands on Amity's shoulders. Amity felt his touch race through her.

"We stand together, you and I. That's the way it has to be. I made sure everyone knows it."

Amity gazed up at him, her eyes wide. He was defending her when she deserved no defense. When she had decided to come to Ransom, she had not known him, and she had seen nothing wrong in taking advantage of his offer. Now she knew him, and she was, despite her efforts to the contrary, falling in love with him, and she was in too far to admit her duplicity now.

She turned and ran for the house. Clay called after her, but she did not stop until she reached her room. She had based her marriage on a lie, and suddenly that seemed very wrong indeed.

Chapter Ten

Amity's eyes flew open at the sound of someone banging on the side door. Her room was dark but a glance out the window showed the sky was turning the filmy gray that preceded first light. She grabbed her cotton wrapper and thrust her feet into her house slippers. Who could be at the door at this hour?

She hurried into the dining room as the knocking came again, this time louder than before and with an urgency that demanded immediate attention. Clay's door opened at the same time. He was wearing only his trousers, and his hair was tousled from sleep. Amity found herself staring at him in the weak light of the lamp he was carrying. She had rarely seen a man without his shirt on, and Clay was better built than any she had seen.

She pulled her wrapper more securely about her and ran for the door. Clay hurried, too, and was on her heels by the time she reached the door and pulled it open. As he held the lamp over her head, they could see Sean O'Flannery standing on the porch. Sean looked as if he, too, had just tumbled from bed, but instead of the panic or fear she expected to see on the caller's face, he was wearing a wide grin.

"Fiona's having the baby! I'm on my way to get the midwife, and I was wondering if one of you would mind riding over to stay with Fiona until I get back."

"Of course I will," Amity said quickly. "How is she doing?"

"Just grand. I've got no reason to worry, but you know how it is at a time like this. I hate to leave her alone with all the little ones still asleep."

"I'll get dressed right away."

Sean called out his thanks as he jumped off the porch and ran toward his horse. Amity closed the door. "Fiona's having her baby," she said as if Clay had not heard the entire exchange. "Isn't it exciting?" To her surprise, he looked more concerned than happy. "What's wrong?"

"Nothing. I was just remembering. That's all."

Amity recalled how Elsa had died, and reached out and touched Clay's bare arm in commiseration. His skin felt warm and firm, the hairs prickly beneath her fingers. She knew she should pull her hand back, but she couldn't. He looked as if he needed the contact. "Fiona will be fine. Sean wasn't worried."

"Most fathers aren't." He looked away from her. "My stepfather seemed not to care what my mother went through with every baby." He shook his head. "Get dressed. I'll go wake Hallie and tell her to look after the others until we can get back."

"You're going, too?"

"Of course. Sean is my friend. He'll need someone to pace with him." He finally smiled.

Amity hurried to dress. Only when she was in her room and happened to glance at her reflection in the mirror did she realize her hair had pulled free of her thick braid and had fallen about her shoulders like a cape. What must Clay think of her? She yanked a brush through it with one hand while she found her clothes with the other.

She dressed quickly and coiled her hair into a decorous bun on the nape of her neck. She could hear Clay crossing the dining room, his boots resounding loudly on the pine floor. With a quick glance in the mirror to be sure she was all together, Amity hurried out to meet him in the barn.

Although the sky overhead and to the west was still dark, all signs of the stars were gone, and in the east she could see a pearl-hued paleness. Soon the sun would be up. It was not as early as she had first taken it to be. Clay was saddling her horse as she came into the barn. His own mount stood ready beside hers.

"I didn't think to stop by the kitchen and pick up any food. Do you think I should? I've never been to a birthing."

"Fiona will have plenty. She always seems to know, somehow. Unless I miss my bet, she spent the day yesterday cleaning and cooking. Elsa was like that. Just before a birth, she could never sit still and had to be up working at something."

Amity wondered if she would ever know about it firsthand. She had always wanted children, though she had given up the thought when she entered her twenties and had no prospect of a husband. Now she found the old dreams resurfacing.

Clay bent and held his cupped hands for her foot, and she let him toss her onto the horse, then she settled her skirts about her. Amity had seldom ridden a horse before coming to Texas, but she had found the sidesaddle easy enough to conquer. She curled her right leg about the pommel and put that foot into the short stirrup and the other foot into the long one.

They rode toward the O'Flannery house at a canter. Amity had no idea how long it took to have a baby, because discussion of such topics were strictly taboo in her aunts' house. As an only child, she had not had sibling births to learn from, and none of her closest friends had been married. She and Dorothea had speculated about such things in whispers late at night when they were of an age to sleep over at each other's houses, but Dorothea had known no more about it than had Amity. Now she was about to learn.

The O'Flannery house was lit up in welcome. They left their horses at the fence and hurried up to the door. Brian, who had been watching for them, greeted them at the door. "Mama is up in her room. She said for Miss Amity to come up as soon as she got here."

"How is she?" Clay asked.

"She says she's fine." Brian tried to seem nonchalant but his wide blue eyes revealed his concern.

"I'll go see her." Amity walked briskly past the boy and smiled at his brothers and sister who were clustered in the parlor. "You're not to worry. Your papa has gone to get the midwife, and it will be all over soon." She hoped she sounded as if she knew more than she really did.

She had never been upstairs in Fiona's house, but she had no trouble finding the room. Fiona heard her on the stairs and called out to her. Amity hurried into her room. Fiona was lying in the big bed, her rounded abdomen bulging under the covers. When she saw Amity, she smiled.

"We both came. Clay is downstairs with the children. What would you like for me to do?"

"Have a seat and talk to me. There's nothing to do for hours yet. I told Sean not to wake you."

"We would have been up in less than an hour anyway." She sat in the chair beside the bed. As she watched, Fiona's face grew pink with the strain of a contraction and her hands knotted in the quilt. "Are you all right?"

Fiona nodded as the pain receded. "It's the same as the others. Have you never been at a birthing?"

Amity shook her head. "I may not be much help."

"There's not much to do, really, but wait. Nature will do the rest."

"Should I go down and make breakfast for the children?"

"No, Sean will do that when he gets home. It will give him something to do." She laughed. "I suppose Clay is down there looking as if it's the end of the world?"

Amity nodded. She didn't see how Fiona could be so calm about all this. Especially since the last birth Fiona must have attended had ended in death for the mother and baby.

"Clay is like that about babies being born. Even before he lost Elsa he was afraid of birth. Sean said Clay told him he had been too aware of what his mother went through with his half-brothers and sisters."

"He said something about that. You don't mean he was present?"

"As I understand it, there was only one room and the nearest neighbor was miles away."

Amity felt shocked. "Surely he was sent to the barn along with the others or something! Who would want her children present at a time like this?"

"There are some peculiar people in this world. I've lived on two continents and have seen a lot, and I can tell you people can be strange." Fiona paused while another contraction gripped her. "And some parents simply don't care what their children go through."

As the sun was coming up and the room was quickly becoming light, Amity blew out the lamp. Beyond the window, she could hear a rooster crowing. She brushed the curtain aside to see if Sean was on his way back yet, but there was no sign of him.

For almost an hour, Amity talked to Fiona about inconsequential things and tried not to worry about her having the baby before the midwife arrived. Amity knew too little about birthing to handle it alone. Fiona was becoming restless, but she assured Amity it was from the coming birth and not because she sensed anything was wrong.

"Have you seen the baby things I've made?" Fiona asked. "My mother even sent me a cap and blanket she knitted, all the way from County Cork. She's sent me a new one for every baby. I wish she could be here."

"Do you miss her a great deal?"

"Aye. I knew when we came here that I'd likely not see her or the others again unless we failed and had to return home or they were able to save enough to move over. My parents would never leave the old country, though, not even for the gold of kings. My mother was a bit of a midwife herself. When I'm having a baby, I always wish she was beside me."

"It's terrible, but I can barely remember my own mother." Amity went to the crib and picked up a tiny gown that was waiting to receive the baby. "I was ten when she died, but she had been sick for years and rarely left her room. Just after she died, Father was killed in a carriage accident and I went to live with my aunts. Now I find I remember my parents best from the tintype that was made on their wedding day. I don't recall either of them looking that young. I was born after they had been married for a number of years."

The sound of horses outside drew Amity to the window. "It's Sean and Mrs. Willis." She hid her relief. Fiona's contractions were coming much closer together, and she could tell they were more painful, as well.

Clay went out to meet Sean. He greeted Mrs. Willis, whom he knew from Elsa's lyings-in.

"Where is she?" Mrs. Willis asked as if she had little faith that a man would have any sense about such matters and might just as easily as not take his wife to the barn to give birth.

"She's in our room." Sean glanced at Clay. "Have you heard anything?"

Clay shook his head. "Amity hasn't been down. I made breakfast for the children."

"Boil water," Mrs. Willis commanded. "And get those little 'uns out of the house."

Sean turned to Brian. "You and the others go start your chores. I'll come tell you when it's over."

Brian looked as if he wanted to argue, but instead, he did as he was told and shepherded the others out. Clay saw them going toward the barn with the youngest, Quinn, asking questions that his older brother was ignoring. "I know how he feels," Clay said to Sean. "I was the oldest, and you feel you ought to do something, but you can't. It's a bad feeling."

"It's not much different from what a husband feels."

"True." He went into the kitchen with Sean. "The biscuits are on the stove." He poured some coffee for Sean and himself. He was accustomed to the rituals of waiting for a baby to make its appearance in the world.

Sean took a biscuit, bit into it, then put it aside. "I can't eat. Do you reckon she's hurting too bad?"

"She hasn't cried out." Clay handed the coffee cup to Sean. "You may as well have a seat. You know how long this may take. I already have the water boiling."

Sean looked at the pot as if he had never seen it before. "Why do you reckon Mrs. Willis always has us boil water? Have you ever known her to use any of it?"

"I never thought about it. I guess she has some reason." He could hear the women moving about upstairs.

Sean was listening, too. "I know she's going to be all right, but it always makes me nervous. Maybe it's not knowing what's going on."

"It makes me nervous, too."

Sean ducked his head. "I'm sorry. I forgot for a minute there."

"That's okay. I was afraid of childbirth long before I lost Elsa. Fiona will be fine." He smiled for Sean's benefit. "Maybe you'll get another girl."

"Maybe. My Kathleen was the first girl born in my family in over eighty years, though. Sons run in my family."

"I can't say the same." He thought about the tiny son the doctor had placed in his hands the day Elsa had died. Clay had known by the baby's color and size that he wouldn't make it. The baby hadn't lived through the day. "I always thought I wanted a son."

"Amity is young and strong. She'll give you sons."

Clay glanced at Sean. Even his best friend didn't know he had never slept with Amity. Clay couldn't tell him. He wondered what Amity thought about it. The one place he and Elsa hadn't been in perfect agreement had been in bed. Although he had never hinted of it to another living soul, Elsa had not enjoyed making love. He didn't know if he was inept or if the difficulty was with her, but no matter how hard she tried to pretend, he had known Elsa had never thoroughly enjoyed it. No, he wouldn't put Amity through that. She had been through enough in coming halfway across the country expecting a man with two children and finding five. Besides, he didn't want to endanger her life with childbearing.

The hours crept by. Amity watched Fiona grow more and more silent as she concentrated on delivering the baby. Mrs. Willis was a woman of few words, and by the color of her nose, Amity suspected she drank more than her fair share, and often. She was sober now, however, and in full command.

She had put a sheet through the brass rails of the headboard and tied the ends in a knot for Fiona to pull against when she had pains, and she had placed a kitchen knife with a huge blade under the mattress to cut the pain. She had offered Fiona a leather strap to bite on rather than to take a chance on cracking her teeth. Everything that could be done was being done. In the meantime, Mrs. Willis sat by the window crocheting, mostly in silence.

Amity tried not to pace, but she was sensing the same urgency that filled Fiona. When a contraction came, she went to the bed and wiped the sweat from the woman's face. Fiona smiled. "That was a strong one."

Mrs. Willis put aside her yarn and hook and came to the bed. She lifted the sheet and peered under. "You don't have much longer to go."

Fiona's pains suddenly changed. Now the contractions were lasting longer than the intervals between them. Amity covered Fiona's hand as she pulled against the knotted sheet. For the first time, Fiona let out a groan. Mrs. Willis got a pair of scissors out of a pouch in the bag containing her yarn and put them on the bed, then pulled the sheet out from the foot. "Push," she commanded. "Push harder."

Fiona strained to obey and her face reddened with the effort. Sweat dampened her red braid, and a small blue vein stood out at her temple. Amity reminded herself to breathe. In less than five minutes, the baby was born, and Mrs. Willis handed it to Amity. "You wash her up while I see to Mrs. O'Flannery."

Amity had never held a baby in her life. It was a girl, and she was an odd putty color and as wrinkled as an old woman. "It's a girl, Fiona." Fiona laughed and lay back on the pillow. Amity took the baby to the washstand and laid her beside the bowl to sponge her off. Although the grayish color bothered Amity, she thought it must be natural since Mrs. Willis hadn't mentioned it.

In short order, she sponged the baby clean and wrapped her in a soft receiving blanket. "Mrs. Willis, come look at the baby. Is she all right?" Amity didn't want to alarm Fiona, but something didn't seem to be right. Weren't babies supposed to cry when they were born?

The midwife came to her and peered over her shoulder. "All babies are an odd color when they're born," she said offhandedly, but she kept watching the baby nevertheless. "She should be turning pink by now, though."

Amity put her ear close to the baby's face. Whispering to Mrs. Willis so Fiona could not hear, she said, "I don't think she's breathing properly."

"What's wrong?" Fiona demanded. "Why don't I hear her?"

Mrs. Willis pushed Amity aside and bent over the baby. She opened the baby's mouth and made sure her throat was clear of mucus, then pinched the tiny nose shut and covered the baby's mouth with her own and blew air into her lungs. Behind her, Fiona was struggling to sit up. Amity went to her.

"What's wrong? Is she breathing?"

Amity took Fiona's hand. "She is having some problems, I think." She didn't know what to say to reassure Fiona. Surely the baby would live. It was shaped so perfectly and Fiona had worked so hard to have her!

Mrs. Willis didn't spare breath or thought on the new mother, giving all her attention to the baby. She pulled her from the blanket and plunged her into the cold water in the washbowl, then held her by her feet and slapped the tiny buttocks. When there was no response, she laid the baby down, breathed into her again, then dipped her again into the water. This time the baby responded with a series of bellows, each stronger than the one before. Sure the baby was breathing normally, Mrs. Willis gave a satisfied nod and handed the naked baby to her mother.

As Fiona cradled the baby in her arms, the tiny girl roared at having been born. Amity found herself smiling as tears ran down her cheeks. Fiona was doing the same. Mrs. Willis made no comment, but she looked inordinately proud of herself.

Downstairs, when Sean and Clay heard the baby cry out, they looked at each other. "It came faster than the others," Sean said as he got to his feet and took several steps toward the stairs. "It sounds healthy."

"What do you think? Is it a boy or a girl?" Clay asked with a grin. "This is your last chance to guess."

"Sounds like a boy to me."

Clay shook his head. "I say it's a girl."

They stopped at the foot of the stairs when they saw Amity coming down with a bundle in her arms. She was smiling and her eyes seemed brighter than usual.

"Well?" Sean said. "Is it all right? How about Fiona?"

"Fiona is doing fine."

"Do I have a son or a daughter?"

Amity pulled the blanket aside and Clay slapped Sean on the shoulder. "I was right! You've got a girl."

Sean grinned so widely all his teeth showed. "A girl. She sounds healthy."

Amity did not tell them they had almost lost the baby. Clay didn't need to hear that sort of news with what he had been through with the loss of his last child, and if Fiona wanted Sean to know, she would tell him. "Fiona says you're to name her."

Sean reached out and touched the baby's tiny hand. "We're going to call her Adeline after Fiona's mother. Adeline Moira O'Flannery."

Amity smiled. "That's a pretty name." She touched the baby's red fringe of hair. "She will be a beauty."

"Aye, that she will. She already looks like Fiona. Doesn't she look like her, Clay?"

Clay grinned and winked at Amity. "She's the spitting image."

"Is it okay if I go up to see her?" Sean gazed longingly upstairs.

"She's expecting you. Here. Take Adeline with you."

Sean took the baby, holding her as if she might break. "Is she too little? Seems like she's smaller than usual."

"You've just forgotten how small newborns are, I imagine. Fiona says she is the same size Quinn was when he was born and that she seems larger than Brady was."

"Fiona should know. She's good at remembering things like that." Sean went upstairs to see his wife.

"Come sit on the porch with me," Clay said. "You look a bit pale."

Amity was glad to step out into the cooler air. Mrs. Willis had insisted on keeping the windows in Fiona's room closed, and it had been uncomfortably warm for Amity. She sat on the porch swing and Clay sat down beside her. "Fiona will be fine," she said when she saw the worried look on Clay's face. "When I came down with the baby, Fiona was laughing and talking. Mrs. Willis says the baby is healthy and there's not a thing to worry about."

"Good." He looked toward the barn. "I should go tell the children."

"Why not let their father do it?"

Clay sat back in the swing and set it in motion with his toe. "Rosemary was small like that. We thought we would lose her for the first few weeks."

"She was? You'd never know it to look at her now."

"She came early, Mrs. Willis said, and that was why. Even so, Elsa had a hard time, and I thought I was going to lose her before the birthing was over." His face clouded and he stopped talking.

Amity put her hand on his. "I know today has been hard on you."

"It was rough on Sean, too. He pretended not to worry, but a man can't help it. Not when it's your wife and baby."

"I'm sure that's right," she said, but she had no way of knowing and felt uneasy. She removed her hand from his.

"The last baby came early, too. I don't know what happened. Mrs. Willis came out to get me and said that I should come inside. I knew then that Elsa wouldn't make it."

Clay's pain was etched on his face, and Amity wished she had some way of easing it. Maybe, she thought, if he talked about it, the painful memory would soften. She had a feeling he had never talked about it with anyone. That would not have been his way. She remained silent and waited for him to continue.

"She was in the bed and her skin was as pale as the sheets. Mrs. Willis hadn't taken the time to change her gown or anything. Anyone could see she was going fast. She took my hand and her fingers were cold. As cold as if it were winter already. She tried to smile at me, but we both knew. Then I noticed the baby wasn't crying and I looked over at it. Mrs. Willis was holding it as if she was trying to warm it. I knew it was alive because its hand moved, but that was about all it did. Elsa told me it was a son. I don't think she knew there was anything wrong with the baby." Clay's voice broke and he stopped.

Amity put her arm around his shoulders. She could see the tears in his eyes and she wondered if he had ever let himself shed them before now.

"I knew she was slipping away. I tried to hold her back, but there was nothing I could do. A moment later, she was gone. I made her a promise right then and there, that I would never put another woman through what she had just been through. That I would never marry again." He glanced at her. "I had to break part of that promise."

"Do you regret it?" she asked softly.

His eyes met hers and she saw more than pain for Elsa there. She also saw a ragged yearning that she couldn't understand.

"No. No, I don't regret marrying again. I'm telling you all this so you'll understand why I sleep in one room and you in another. Now that you've seen what childbirth is like, you'll be glad, I think."

Amity stared at him. "Fiona is fine. Most women come through many births without real danger. Having babies is a natural function." What she was saying was so important that she failed to blush. "I thought you just didn't care for me in that way."

"Not care for you?" He gazed at her as if her words made no sense. "You thought I didn't want you?"

"What else was I to think?"

Clay stood abruptly. "Now that you've seen it firsthand, you can understand what I'm sparing you."

"I want children. I always have."

He turned from her. "I can't take that risk. Not with you." He strode off in the direction of the barn.

She watched him go. What had he meant by that—that he couldn't take that chance with her? That was the sort of thing a man would say to the woman he loved. For a moment she allowed herself to think he had meant it that way, then pulled herself back to reality. Clay did not love her and he never would. The sooner she accepted that fact, the better.

But she could not deny the fact that she loved him. She felt it all the way through her body. She loved him, and she wanted to have him hold her and to lie beside him in the dark and do the secret things that a husband and a wife did together, the things that she had never thought she would want to do. With Clay she instinctively knew the act of love would not be degrading and that he would be better at it then Emmett Hamilton had ever dreamed of being. The thought brought a blush to her cheeks, and she stood abruptly and tried to compose herself so she could go into the house.

Thinking lascivious thoughts about Clay would accomplish nothing. She would stay here with Fiona for the rest of the day and see to it that her family was fed. By tomorrow

Sean would have found a girl to come in and do the cooking and cleaning until Fiona was on her feet again.

Amity glanced toward the barn. Clay was such a contradiction in some ways. He was so strong and virile, yet there was more gentleness in him than anyone might suspect. He felt emotions deeper than any person she had ever known. She was willing to bet he had never told anyone, not even Sean, what had transpired the day Elsa died, or about his rash promise at her deathbed. Amity had always been logical, and she could see how that promise could ruin both their lives, but she was empathetic enough to honor Clay's wishes. Still, she thought, it wouldn't hurt to let him know she was willing to become his wife in every way. Surely that couldn't be wrong.

She went into the O'Flannery house to start dinner.

Chapter Eleven

All day the sky had been brassy, and there had been no breeze at all. Everyone's nerves were on edge and even the farm animals were restless. Hallie had found it impossible to tolerate Amity's presence in the house, and against Amity's objections, she had gone to her aunt's house.

"She told me not to come, but I did anyway," Hallie said to Gretchen. "I guess she'll be mad when I go home." She didn't really believe Amity would be mad at her, but she knew saying so would get her more sympathy from her aunt. Amity seldom lost her temper with her or her sisters, but Gretchen didn't know that. Hallie held one of Gretchen's sofa pillows in her lap and toyed with the silk fringe. "I wish I could live here."

"I wish you could, too. Have you asked your father lately? Perhaps if you make it plain how you hate Amity, he will be more reasonable."

"There's no need to ask him. I already know the answer." Hallie avoided her aunt's eyes. Lately Amity had not seemed as much an ogre as Hallie reported to Gretchen. Even if she had been, Hallie didn't really want to move out of her father's house. That was her home. "I don't suppose you could move in with us? Maybe we could make up some excuse."

Gretchen gave a mirthless laugh. "Can you see her allowing that? It would never do. If your father and I had married, well, that would have been a different story."

Hallie glanced at her. "You really would have married Papa if he had asked you?"

"What a question!" Gretchen said, but she smiled. "Perhaps."

Hallie tried to imagine her aunt and her father married. Gretchen resembled Elsa, but there the likeness stopped. "I can't imagine you two married."

"Apparently neither could he," Gretchen said tartly.

"I didn't mean it like that." Hallie was quick to try to make amends. "It's just that I'm used to you living here." She looked around the house. "I've always liked it here. It reminds me of Mama."

Outside, thunder rumbled in the distance. Gretchen looked up in surprise. "Was that thunder? Maybe we're finally going to get some rain."

Hallie went to the window. "It's getting awfully dark outside. Maybe I should go home before it starts." She had never liked storms. "Once it starts to rain, it may keep it up for days. Papa doesn't know where I am."

"And it would be just like Amity not to tell him in order to worry him," Gretchen said as she got up to light the lamp. "I can't imagine how he abides that woman."

Thunder roared again, this time sounding much closer. "I think I should start back," Hallie repeated. "It's not difficult to get over the footbridge at the stream, but you know how wide the creek can get."

"Very well. If you think you should." Gretchen gave her a commiserating look. "I wouldn't want you to get in any trouble at home."

Lemony lightning flashed and Hallie hurried to the door. "If I run, I may not get too wet." The approaching storm's lightning display was making her as nervous as it was the horses in Gretchen's pasture. They were running and kicking up their heels—a sure sign that a big storm was approaching.

Hallie gave her aunt a quick hug and slipped out the door. The rain was holding off, but the sky was heavy and as dark as evening. She gathered her skirts and ran toward the foot-bridge.

Amity looked out the window. Hallie was not home, and she was worried. Fortunately, the other children were all safely inside, as evidenced by the familiar murmur and occasional squeal from overhead. Moments before, she had seen Clay go to the barn to put away the mule and plow. Soon he would be at the house. She went onto the porch, hoping the sky only looked so dark because she had been in the lamp-lit parlor, but she found it even more threatening than she had thought. There still was no breeze blowing, and the air was a peculiar greenish color.

Amity tossed aside her apron and started down the steps. She had to be sure Hallie was in a safe place. Resolutely she started toward Gretchen's, sure that Hallie had gone there.

Clay looked out the barn door in time to see Amity go by. He called to her, but thunder stole his words. Where could she be going with a storm about to break? He ran after her.

When he caught up with her, he said in a teasing manner, "Isn't this a bad time to go out for a walk?"

"I'm looking for Hallie. I'm almost positive she went to Gretchen's, and I'm afraid she is on her way back and will be caught between the creeks."

"Hallie has more sense than to set out in a storm. She'll wait until it's over."

Amity shook her head. "I don't think so. I can't explain it, but I feel she may be in danger." The first fat drops of rain beaded the dust at their feet. "I'll only go as far as the creek."

Clay looked at the heavy clouds. "It's already storming north of here. The creek may have already started to rise though the storm's not here yet. You go back and let me check on her."

"No, I feel responsible. We had words before she left, and I'm afraid she is still angry with me."

Clay frowned. "I told Hallie to stop being so rude to you. What did she say this time?"

"It's not important, and anyway, I'm not going to stand out here in the rain and discuss it." She started toward the well-trod footpath that linked the two houses. The storm was coming fast, and she could not shake the feeling that Hallie was in danger.

"I'm coming with you."

Amity didn't argue. They hurried through the woods and soon were nearing the creek. Amity could hear the water before they could see it. The creek, normally as placid as buttermilk, was churning with red mud and was three times as wide as usual. On the opposite side, huddling in wet clothes, was Hallie. The rain was pounding all about her.

Through the storm Clay shouted, "Go back to Gretchen's house! Don't try to cross the creek until the water goes down!"

"I can't, Papa. The footbridge washed out behind me!" Hallie looked as if she might be crying, but with the rain streaming over her it was impossible to tell.

Amity caught Clay's arm as he headed for the creek. "Look how fast it's running! Can you make it?"

"I have to. I can't leave her over there."

At the edge of the creek were several large trees draped with thick muscadine vines. Even before Clay had time to move, Amity got a firm grip on one of the vines and waded into the water as far as the vine would allow her to go, then shouted, "Take my hand, Hallie."

"I can't reach you!"

Suddenly Clay was beside Amity. Taking her hand, he waded farther out, and the water swirled to his waist and threatened to sweep him away. "Come on, Hallie. You can do it if you try!"

Hallie reluctantly waded into the stream. It was rising fast and the current caught her skirts and swept them against her legs. "I'm afraid, Papa!"

"Put your hand out!"

Amity held to the grapevine and prayed it was securely looped around the tree. Clay waited in the middle of the swift water for Hallie to do as he had said. "Hurry!" he commanded.

Amity listened and looked upstream. Was that a roar she heard? She had heard of fast-rising floods, but weren't they confined to regions that were more desertlike, such as the hill country?

Her face filled with fear, Hallie forced herself to wade deeper and stumbled, but righted herself. Her pale hand reached out, and finally her fingers found Clay's. He caught her wrist and started back toward Amity and safety. Amity pulled as hard as she could. Hallie's feet were going out from under her and her skirts were billowing in the water. Amity tried not to think what the roaring might mean. With all her strength she drew them to the bank.

As Amity climbed to safety, Clay caught Hallie around the waist and shoved her up the bank. He grabbed the muscadine vine that Amity had used and pulled himself out of the water. Amity caught his arm and as she helped him to reach the bank, an additional three feet of water suddenly rushed around the bend and down the creek.

Amity wrapped her arms around Clay to reassure herself that he was safe. The water roared past, carrying three limbs and debris on its swollen currents. Clay pulled Hallie into his embrace, and Amity put her arm around the girl, too.

"Are you all right?" she demanded. "Why did you start out in a storm as bad as this one?" She had to shout to be heard over the thunder and raging torrent.

Hallie broke away and ran to the house. Amity tried to catch her, but she was too quick. She supposed Hallie thought she was shouting because she was angry, but Amity was too relieved that the girl was safe to be mad.

"Let's get to the house before we're struck by lightning," Clay yelled over the storm as he grabbed her hand and began to run.

By the time they reached the porch, rain was coming down in sheets and they were both drenched to the skin. Amity shivered and wrapped her arms around her body as Clay opened the door. Thunder boomed almost incessantly, and she could not see the barn or even the smoke-house through the downpour. Why hadn't Gretchen insisted that Hallie stay until this was over?

She wrung out her skirts as well as she could, then hurried into the house where it was safe and warm. From upstairs she could hear the other girls exclaiming over Hallie, so she knew the girl was all right. Clay had gone to his room to remove his wet clothes. Amity went to her room to do the same.

Her sodden dress clung to her skin, making it difficult to wrestle it off her body. Amity didn't know if she was chilled from the rain, or if the tremors that rippled through her were a delayed reaction to the danger they had braved, but whatever the cause, she was shaking from head to toe. As quickly as she could, she stripped to the skin, then put on her wrapper. The thin garment was not particularly warm, but it was handy and covered her body. Moving swiftly, she gathered up the heap of wet clothes and hurried them out to the service porch, where they wouldn't ruin the floor. Then she got a cloth and began drying the floor in her room.

Once the puddles were gone, she tossed the cloth onto her wet clothes on the porch and hurried back to her room. It would not do to run about wearing only her wrapper. Still cold, she pulled a quilt from the trunk in her bedroom and wrapped it around her as she sat in front of her dresser mirror and started to comb her wet hair. A knock at her door drew her attention. "Yes?" She expected it to be Rosemary or Laura, both of whom were fearful of storms.

Clay opened it. For a minute he only stood there, then he came in and shut the door behind him. "I wanted to thank you for insisting we go after Hallie. She could have been in serious trouble if we hadn't gone when we did."

Amity shivered. "I somehow knew she needed us. I can't explain it." She looked at him. "Are you okay? You look pale."

"I thought I had lost both of you when I heard the water coming downstream. I knew you couldn't hold on to the vine once the flood water hit us."

Amity looked away. "I can't seem to stop shivering."

Clay came closer, knelt beside her and put his arms around her. "You're safe now."

Amity leaned against him. She hadn't realized how much she needed to be held and comforted. She put her arms around him and held him as if they were still in danger. "I thought you would be swept away," she said, her voice muffled against his chest. "I was so afraid you would turn my hand loose in order to reach Hallie."

Clay pulled her even closer to him. She could hear the rhythmic beating of his heart. Outside the storm was raging, but in here she was safe. "I've always been afraid of storms," she confessed. "I try not to show it, but I am."

"I don't like them, either."

She lifted her head and looked into his eyes. She had seldom been so close to him. His damp hair was darker than usual from the rain, and his green eyes were the color of the pond deep in the woods, dark and mysterious. She could see his eyelashes and wondered why she had never noticed before how long and thick they were. He lifted his hand and smoothed a wet strand of hair from her face.

"Amity," he said as if her name were a word of love. "Amity, you're so beautiful."

She knew she wasn't, especially when her hair was hanging wet about her face and she was dressed only in her wrapper and a quilt, but she didn't correct him. She wanted to believe he thought she was beautiful, even if logic would tell her differently later.

He cupped her face in his large hand and bent his head toward her. Amity knew he was about to kiss her, and her heart began pounding so hard she thought he must surely be able to hear it. When his lips touched hers, she swayed toward him as if he were a lodestone to her soul. At first the kiss was gentle, but soon it irrepressibly deepened into passion. Amity returned his kiss with all the love in her heart.

For what seemed to be forever, they tasted the sweetness of each other's lips and let their passions rise unchecked. Amity felt dizzy, and she forgot there was anyone else in the world other than Clay. A need that she could not name flowed through her, one that she had never felt before. Clay recognized that need and met it with his own.

When he pulled away from her, the desire he felt for her was evident in his eyes, but she also knew he was offering her a chance to refuse him. Amity put her arms around him and drew him back for another kiss. She didn't know where this was leading them, exactly, but she was powerless to quell the passion raging within her. She wanted Clay in a way that was primeval and that would, without a doubt, shock all the ladies she had known in Charlotte.

"Papa!" she heard a voice call from upstairs. She raised her eyes to the ceiling as if she could see what was going on up there. Laura's voice came again. "Papa, Kate is pestering me. She has Betsy and won't give her back!"

Clay reluctantly released Amity. She could see it was as difficult for him as it was for her. "I almost forgot about them," he said with a shaky laugh. His eyes searched hers.

"So did I," she admitted. She knew she should look away, but she couldn't. She wanted to go back into his arms.

"Tonight," he said softly as he left to mediate the quarrel between his children.

Amity stared after him. Had he meant what she thought? That he would come to her tonight after the children were safely in bed? She looked at her reflection in the mirror. The lie about her widowhood hung all about her. She had to tell him the truth before she could give herself to him. He had to know the truth, and if he no longer wanted her, that was how it had to be. Amity shivered again, but this time it wasn't from exposure to the rain. She was afraid she would lose him if he knew what she had done. But she was too honest to continue living a lie.

As the minutes passed that evening after supper, Amity became increasingly nervous. Her palms were sweaty and her breath came more quickly than it should have. Every time someone spoke unexpectedly, she jumped. All she could think about was Clay and what the night before them might bring. Her lips still remembered the imprint of his kiss, and she had found herself smiling at odd times during the afternoon.

The rain had continued, though the storm's fury was spent, and Clay had stayed in the house the remainder of the day. He had been busy repairing a chair leg and tightening the hinges on a pesky door of the pie safe, so Amity had seen him off and on all day. However, each time they had been in the same room, one or more of the children had been present, so they had not talked, but several times his eyes had met hers, and she had read a promise in their depths.

At last the children's bedtime came, and Amity took the younger girls upstairs and helped them into their night-gowns. As was her custom, she read them a story, but her mind was not on the mischievous bunnies in the book, and she finished the tale without really hearing a word of it. Jemima came in halfway into the story and dressed herself for bed. In the next room Amity could hear Kate and Hallie doing the same. She was suddenly filled with a love for this ready-made family of hers that almost overwhelmed her. Hallie, too, was precious to her, even if the girl was more trouble than a passel of monkeys.

As she tucked the girls in for the night, she put a kiss on each one's cheek and accepted an exuberant hug from Rosemary before she settled down for the night with her beloved doll, Bertha. At the door, Amity paused and glanced back. They looked like angels in their white night-gowns and with their fair hair. Except for Hallie, all the girls had green eyes like Clay, and she could see a resemblance to him now that she knew them all better. Amity went onto the landing and pulled the door shut behind her.

She liked this time of night when she could hear the house settling around her. She was accustomed to the pops and creaks of the house and the sounds of girlish voices grow-ing fainter as one by one they went to sleep. Tonight there was the constant patter of rain against the tin roof and the sound of thunder far in the distance. It was one of the cozy nights made for closeness.

She paused at the head of the stairs. She was almost afraid to go down. What would Clay think of her and what would he say when he knew the truth? Lifting her head, she went down to him.

She knew Clay was in his bedroom and knocked before entering. He opened the door and smiled to see her there. "Are the girls asleep?"

"Almost." She went in and stood awkwardly in the center of the room. "Clay, we have to talk." She clasped her hands in front of her to keep them from shaking. "I haven't been entirely honest with you."

He studied her face. "Not honest in what way?"

"I've never been married before."

Relief crossed his face. He smiled at her and came to her. "That's all right. Were you worried to tell me that? I've wondered why you never mentioned your husband, and I had been afraid it was because he hadn't been kind to you."

"You were concerned about that?"

"Of course. I don't like to think that you were unhappy."

"There's more." She drew in a deep breath. "I'm not a virgin."

He paused for a minute and then said, "Do you want to tell me about it?"

She didn't, but she knew she must. "As you know, I'm twenty-four and had frankly given up ever having a man come to court me. My aunts had discouraged gentlemen callers, and I seemed destined to live with them forever. Then a new minister came to our church. With him came his son, a young man about my age. One thing led to another, and he began to pay me attention."

"I can hardly blame him for that."

"He said he loved me, and I believed him." Amity turned away. She couldn't face Clay and say what she must. "One night he asked me to meet him, and we went for a buggy ride. I always met him at the corner away from my aunts' house because they would have tried to keep me from seeing him, so that night I didn't think anything of it. He drove out into the country and..." Her voice faltered. This was the part she dreaded. "Well, he had his way with me."

"Did you love him?"

"I thought I might, but I know now that I didn't. I was only flattered that any man would look twice at me." She twisted her hands together. "I was such a fool. I should never have let him take me out of town, but I wasn't paying attention. I've told myself time and again that I have only myself to blame."

"You thought you loved him. Many women would have given themselves to a man if they believed they were in love."

"I didn't give myself to him. He kissed me and started to touch me. I told him not to. I said I wanted to go home, but he only laughed. He said I had led him on and that he couldn't stop." Amity looked down at her hands, shame coloring her cheeks.

"He raped you?"

Amity could only nod. "I refused to meet him again for weeks. At church I could hardly look him in the eye. Then I had reason to believe I might be pregnant." She drew in a deep breath. "I asked him to meet me, and I thought he would marry me. He had said he loved me! When I told him, he only laughed. He said he had plans to marry a girl in the town he had moved from and that he only wanted one thing from me." Tears stung her eyes. "I didn't know what to do. I had a friend named Dorothea Kendrick." She heard his indrawn breath. "Dorothea had been writing to you for several weeks and she suggested that I take her place and come to Ransom to be your wife." She finally turned to face him, her eyes large and haunted. "I lied to you from the start, Clay. Dorothea is in Charlotte, right where she's always been."

"And the baby?"

"There was no baby. I was wrong." She waited for his censure. "I couldn't come to you tonight with a lie like this between us. If you can't love me, it's all right. I know honesty is important for there to be love and respect, but I want you to know one other thing. Maybe I shouldn't tell you this, either, but…" Amity couldn't finish the sentence. She couldn't simply tell him of her love for him.

He stared at her, his eyes dark and unreadable.

Breaking the tension-filled silence between them, Amity nervously continued. "You've been so kind to me. I've seen how you love your daughters and how they adore you. You're a wonderful father and a good provider. I respect you more than I can say. If I were choosing any man that I would want to have as a husband—" she caught her breath at the risk she was taking "—I'd choose no one but you."

Clay came to her and took her hands. "You don't have to say this, Amity."

"Yes, I do. There have been too many lies between us." She lifted her chin. "I know I'm not worthy of your respect, not after what Emmett Hamilton did to me. You'd be within your rights to send me back, and I imagine you could even have our marriage annulled, since it has never been consummated. But regardless of what you decide to do, I want you to know that I hold you in the highest regard and I always will."

Clay cradled her face in the palms of his hands. "Amity, I don't think I'll ever understand you."

She pulled away. The tears were stinging her eyes. If he was going to say he loved her, surely this would have been the time.

Clay caught her arm and refused to let her go. "How could I know you and not respect you? I don't want to send you away."

She stopped. Had she not heard him right? Doubtfully she looked at him.

"You're so different from Elsa. I find myself watching you, and I never know what to expect from you. You fascinate me."

"I don't expect you to care for me as you did her. I'm not asking that. I had to be honest with you. If you want to send me away, I'll go."

"Is that what you expected? That I would be furious with you because some lout raped you and that I would blame you for what he did? It's a good thing we're this far from Charlotte, or I'd go after him and wring his neck." His voice was colored with emotion.

"You would?" She found herself smiling.

"Of course I would." He put his finger on her lips and traced the smile. Then he bent and kissed her.

"If I could do anything to alter what happened that night, I would. You deserve more from a wife than me."

"Nonsense. Don't ever let me hear you say that again." He placed another tender kiss on her lips. "I'm not coming to you as a virgin, either. I wasn't upset when you said you had been married before. From the very first I never expected you to be untouched. Why would you answer my advertisement unless you needed a new start in life? Now that I know what happened, I only wish I had been your first so you wouldn't be afraid of me."

She wondered how he knew of her fear. She had tried to hide it. "I know it will hurt. But I want you anyway. I want to give myself to you and to have you hold me all night. Will you do that? Will you let me sleep beside you until tomorrow?"

He gazed at her. "We may not get much sleep. And it won't hurt you this time."

She didn't believe him. How could it not hurt? He slowly began to unbutton the front of her dress. A quick stab of fear caused her to pull back, then he kissed her and she again leaned into his arms.

Clay was gentle with her, and as his hands slowly moved over her, removing her outer clothing, then her petticoats, she found her fear disappearing. As she stood there in her chemise, her other clothes about her feet, she was unsure where to look or what to do with her hands. She had never undressed with another person in the room since her earliest childhood. Clay seemed to understand.

He led her to the bed and helped her onto it, then removed her shoes and stockings. He straightened, and his eyes met hers as he began to unbutton his shirt. Amity did not know if she was supposed to look at him or not, but she could not help herself. He was so beautifully made. Hard muscles rippled over his torso and his skin was tanned darker than her own. Muscles ridged his stomach, and she had to fight the urge to reach out and touch him.

As he finished undressing, she looked away. "Don't be afraid of me," he said gently.

Her eyes met his in surprise. "I'm not. I just thought that I probably wasn't supposed to be looking at you."

He laughed. "I want you to look at me, just as I want to look at you. That's a part of lovemaking."

He drew her to her feet, and as he loosened the pins from her hair, it uncoiled and cascaded down her back and pooled on the bed about her hips. Clay lifted a skein of her hair and rubbed it over her skin. "You have beautiful hair. It's so thick and so soft. I've wanted to touch your hair ever since I first met you."

Amity looked at him in amazement. "You really don't mind that it's red? Somewhat red," she amended. "Red hair is considered a blemish, according to my aunts."

"I'm not your aunts, and I wouldn't change a thing about you." As he spoke, he untied the ribbon that held her chemise about her neck, loosened it and slid it low on her shoulder, nearly exposing her breasts. Amity automatically caught the cloth. Clay pulled her hands away. For a minute the fear was back. What if he thought she was ugly? She remembered how petite Elsa's clothes were and was afraid he would find her to be too large and ugly. She lowered her eyes and covered her breasts with her arms.

"You're beautiful," he said.

She looked up sharply.

"Why are you looking at me like that? Don't you know you're beautiful?"

"I'm not."

"You are to me."

She couldn't hide her amazement. That she found him pleasing, more than merely pleasing, could be no surprise. He was handsome and as perfectly formed as the Greek statues in the book her aunts had forbidden her to read. He surely could have had his choice of many women. Was it possible that he really liked the way she looked? She let herself fantasize that he would have chosen her over other women if he had met her under other circumstances. She knew that was only a fantasy, but she needed to believe it, at least for a while. She lowered her arms and let him gaze at her. She could feel her skin warming and her pulse quickening. He actually found her to be beautiful!

Clay reached past her and drew down the covers. Amity slid over to make room for him, but remained in a sitting position. Her thick hair swung over her breasts, concealing them. He lay beside her and brushed her hair back before pulling her down beside him. For a minute he only lay there next to her. "You feel so good!" he finally said.

She let out her breath in relief and put her arms more firmly around him. "I want to please you, Clay."

"You already please me. You please me by just being who you are and by wanting to be here with me like this."

"Will you show me how to make love with you?" she asked shyly. Then said quickly, "Am I too forward?"

He laughed. "No one would ever accuse you of that. No, you can't be too forward, not when we're lying here like this. I want you to enjoy me as much as I'm enjoying you." He paused as if he was remembering something. "If I frighten you or if you find any of this unpleasant, will you tell me?"

"Do you want me to?"

"Yes. I don't want to force you to do anything you don't want to do."

"Just make love with me," she whispered. That she might enjoy lovemaking was a new concept to Amity, but she didn't tell Clay. As his warm lips pressed against hers, she discovered that it was even better to kiss him when there was no clothing between them. She loved to feel the heat of his skin all the way down her body. She returned his kiss with all the love she felt for him.

When he left her lips and began planting kisses down the column of her neck and over her shoulder, all her nerve endings seemed to explode like a series of fireworks. She rolled her head back and let herself enjoy what he was doing to her. When he moved his head lower, to her breasts, she drew in her breath and laced her fingers in his hair to guide him to her. The moment his mouth found her nipple, his hot tongue darted out in a flicking motion against the pouting bud, and a moan of pleasure unexpectedly escaped her lips. She had never known anything could feel so good.

Clay took his time in loving her, teaching her what he enjoyed and learning what excited her the most. Amity felt as if she would burst with passion for him. She had no words to tell him what she was feeling, but he seemed to know.

At last, when she thought she could not wait another minute, he eased between her legs and for a moment he seemed to hover over her. Amity thought it would hurt when they became one, but instead the sensation was more pleasing—and more exciting—than any of the other things he had done. And she had loved them all.

As he began moving inside her, she matched his moves with her own in the instinctive rhythm of love. He was supporting his weight on his elbows and gazing at her. She found her universe in his eyes. An elemental need began to build in her. She didn't know where it was taking her or whether any woman had ever felt this way before. She tried not to cry out so he wouldn't know how shameless she was, but her body had a mind of its own. Clay seemed more excited than ever when she murmured his name in passion.

Suddenly she reached a point she had never suspected existed. All the nerves in her body seemed to erupt in one brilliant sunburst of sheer ecstasy. A cry escaped her, and as she held tightly to Clay, she felt him push even deeper into her. His own strangled moan was muffled in her hair. Although their movements had ceased, Amity felt as if they were drifting along in perfect bliss. Their love seemed to support them and to float them through time. For long minutes the world ceased to exist. Nothing was real but Clay and the incredible pleasure he had given her.

At length, when she opened her eyes, she found he was watching her. Her lips curved in a smile that matched his, and Amity touched his face in wonder. There were no words to describe what she was feeling, what she had experienced, but he seemed to know.

"You were made to be loved," he said softly, trailing his hand down the curve of her face as if she were infinitely precious. "You enjoy lovemaking, don't you?"

"I'm afraid I do," she admitted.

He laughed aloud and pulled her closer.

Chapter Twelve

The next morning Amity expected there to be rainbows everywhere. She and Clay had made love several times during the night, and her body still felt warm and loved. She looked over at him as he slept and her heart reached out for him. She could see the vulnerable boy he once must have been, and she felt an almost maternal desire to protect and love him.

Clay rarely talked about his childhood, but from the little he had said, she gathered it had been an unhappy one. It hurt her to think anyone had ever made him sad or frightened, though she knew it happened to many children. Her own childhood had not been that happy, either, though she had never been physically mistreated. She wanted to touch his cheek and tell him that she would do all she could to make him happy for the rest of his life, but she did not know if he would want her to awaken him.

There was so much about this husband of hers that she did not know. She had always assumed that once she married—if she married—she and her husband would be of the same mind about everything, a perfectly matched team. That certainly wasn't the case here. Yet she loved Clay as thoroughly as if he knew his deepest thoughts.

He would ask her to move her things into his room, she thought with a smile. She planned where she would put everything from her trunk and wondered if she would get half the drawers in the dresser. She had never shared a bedroom with another person, but she assumed that half the drawers would be hers. She looked around at the bedroom, barely visible in the predawn light. If this season's crops were good, maybe they could afford to buy new wallpaper. She knew it was selfish of her, but she wanted one room— this room—to have her imprint on it and not Elsa's.

She realized she was being uncharitable, and she slid out of bed. The children would be up soon and it would never do for them to see her dashing naked across the dining room with her clothes clutched to her bosom, and it was too much trouble to dress first.

Amity opened the bedroom door and listened carefully. The house was quiet. She gathered all her clothing and hurried out. It felt peculiar to be in the dining room with only her hair to cover her nakedness. Barefoot, she ran to her room and hastily shut the door for privacy.

Once she was hidden from view, she relaxed and smiled again. She had loved lying in Clay's arms all night. He had been an exciting lover, knowing all the right things to do to make her body soar in rapture. She blushed to remember how she had enjoyed the things he had done, and it seemed incredible in the light of day to recall that she had been as eager to touch and taste him and to learn his body and what he liked. She hoped he would not think she was decadent, because at the time it had seemed to be the right thing to do. There was so much she did not know and could never ask anyone.

Clay had opened his eyes in time to see Amity streak naked out the door, and the sound of her bare feet running across the dining room put a grin on his face. She was far from being as prudish as she pretended to be.

She would move her things into his room today, he thought contentedly. Before he went out to the fields he would clear some drawers for her to use. By tonight they would be living as married couples were supposed to live. He could hardly wait to hold her and kiss her again. She excited him as no one ever had. Not even Elsa, he thought without a twinge of guilt. Elsa had never enjoyed lovemaking, and he had assumed it had been his fault. Amity, however, had gloried in it. Clay knew it was time to bury Elsa once and for all.

By the time he dressed and shaved, Amity had breakfast well under way. Laura and Jemima were in the kitchen helping set the table. Amity looked up as he came in, and they exchanged the secret smile of two people in love. Clay couldn't say anything he was thinking in front of the children, but he told himself that she would be in his bed that night and that there would be plenty of time for talking then.

Amity felt warm and alive just knowing Clay was in the room. She wanted to talk to him and say a thousand things that she could never say with children in the room. Besides, she might be too shy even if they weren't. When would he ask her to move her things into his room? That was something he could say casually as he left for the fields. He could even leave her a note, though that seemed out of character for Clay. He was so direct. Amity smiled at the memory of his directness.

"You're burning the sausage," Jemima said.

Amity jumped and began taking the meat from the skillet. She would have to daydream about Clay another time. She found she was smiling.

During breakfast they talked about mundane things that didn't matter, and Amity loved it. She felt as if she was finally part of this family, even if Hallie still ignored her. Whenever Amity's and Clay's eyes met, she felt warm and excited all over, and she had to keep a close rein on herself not to let the children see. He winked at her and she blushed, though she also smiled. The children seemed to know something was different, but none of them asked questions.

Clay left for the fields before Amity finished clearing the table. He dropped a kiss on her cheek and she expected him to say something to her then about moving her things, but he didn't. She opened her mouth to ask him, but saw Hallie frowning at them and thought better of it. Amity had al-

ways been a private person and she was unable to change
overnight. So Clay went out without her knowing whether
he wanted her to move in with him or not. As Hallie and
Kate did the dishes and she started a pot of beans for dinner, she continued puzzling over it. She could scarcely move
her things into his bedroom without him giving her permission or encouragement. Surely he understood that. She was
confused.

After she had done her morning chores, she gathered up
her gardening gloves and straw hat and went to tend Elsa's
grave. She did it by habit these days. It helped her to keep
her life in perspective. Elsa might have been perfect, but
Amity was alive.

As she worked at the mundane task of pulling the wiry
grass from the grave, her thoughts returned to Clay and all
that had happened last night. He *must* mean for her to move
her things. It only made sense. On the other hand, she knew
many married couples who continued to keep separate
rooms their entire lives. Her own parents had done so. She
was positive that if her aunts had married—though the notion was most improbable—they would have insisted on
separate rooms from their husbands. Did Clay feel that
way? She wanted to ask him, but she was afraid to. She
didn't want him to think that she was out of her place, if
that wasn't what he had in mind.

She smoothed the bare earth over the grave and sat con-
templating it for a minute. The rain the night before had
washed the red dust from the headstone but had spattered
mud against its base. Amity absently wiped it clean with her
gloved hand. What would Elsa have done? Lately she had
often asked herself that question. Clay had loved Elsa, so it
stood to reason that he would approve of Amity being as
like her as possible. But there had been love between them,
and she wasn't positive Clay loved her, even though he had
certainly made her feel loved last night. She had no idea
what to do.

Unknown to Amity, Hallie had also come to Elsa's grave.
When she saw Amity there, she stopped and drew back into

the woods. Fortunately, Amity had not seen her. What was she doing? At first Hallie thought Amity was up to no good, then she saw her stepmother wipe the headstone clean. Hallie frowned. She had assumed her father was the one who was tending the grave. That it might be Amity had never crossed her mind.

She thought about the way Amity and her father had smiled at each other this morning and how he had kissed her before he went to the fields. Hallie had thought he would never do that. It had looked as if he liked her! She had to get rid of Amity fast before she put down any more roots in Hallie's family.

Once more Hallie looked at Amity and wondered why she was tending the grave, then she slipped away to go to Aunt Gretchen. Gretchen always knew what to do.

When Amity returned to the house, she was determined to do something to mark the difference in the day. Whatever Clay wanted or expected, the day was a beginning for her. She looked at the curtains in the parlor and knew what to do.

Days before she had found lace curtains in a trunk in the storeroom beneath the stairs. At the time she had wondered why they weren't being used, but she had decided they had been packed away when new ones were made. She went to the trunk and opened the lid. These would look much nicer than the cotton ones that were hanging now.

By late afternoon she had washed, ironed and hung the curtains. There were more than enough to cover the windows, which made Amity wonder, but she didn't think much about it. They might have been purchased for another room, or even another house. She didn't know if Clay and Elsa had lived here during their entire marriage, though she had always assumed they had.

She thought the curtains looked pretty on the windows, and the younger children were all excited about the change. Even Kate said she thought they made the room prettier. Hallie had been absent all day, and Amity knew she must have gone to Gretchen's without telling her, but Hallie often did this, so it wasn't unexpected. She always came home before supper.

"Aunt Gretchen, nothing is working to get rid of Amity." Hallie had spent the day with Gretchen but she still couldn't bring herself to tell her that Amity was the one tending Elsa's grave.

"You have to try harder. She's been here what? Two months? If she stays much longer, your father will be so used to having her around that he will try harder to keep her."

"That's what I'm afraid of. Do you know what he did? He kissed her before he left the house this morning!"

Gretchen's eyes grew large. "He did?"

"It was just on the cheek, but it was a kiss."

"What did she do?"

"She smiled."

Gretchen looked thoughtful. "You say they still have separate bedrooms?"

"I checked this morning and her things are still where they have always been."

Gretchen looked sad. "Do you recall what day this is, Hallie? It was your parents' anniversary."

Hallie had forgotten and she wished Gretchen hadn't reminded her. Now she felt not only sad, but guilty at having overlooked a single thing that had been important to Elsa. "It is, isn't it?"

"They would have been married for fifteen years. Their crystal anniversary." Gretchen's eyes grew misty. "I remember when my parents celebrated that anniversary. I was just about your age and Elsa was younger than Jemima is now."

"It's hard to imagine Mama being that young."

"She was such a lovely child. Anyway, Father gave Mother the most beautiful crystal punch bowl. We were both afraid to touch it, it was that beautiful."

Hallie sighed. She had often heard of the wealthy life her mother and aunt had lived before their marriages. "What happened to the bowl, Aunt Gretchen?"

"It was broken eventually. Thank goodness Mother was gone by then. She put such store in her things. She could never bear to see anything broken or misused. That's why we had such nice things," she added. "She never let anything be misused."

"It's a shame it was broken. I would love to have seen it."

"It would probably have gone to you in time. Elsa and I divided all Mother and Father's things after they were gone. The really nice things we have boxed away to pass down to you girls." She patted Hallie's knee. "You girls are just like my own children, you know."

"Why didn't you ever have children of your own?" Hallie asked with childlike directness.

"The good Lord never saw fit to send me any." Gretchen drew back.

Hallie lowered her head. Like Mama, Aunt Gretchen never liked to talk about having babies. Hallie wondered why.

"Come along. I'll drive you home." Gretchen stood and went to get a bonnet.

"I can walk. Papa won't be in yet."

"It's no problem. It will give me time to visit with your sisters. They never come here anymore, not even Kate. Why is that?"

Hallie frowned as she put her bonnet on her head. She could not tell Gretchen that the other girls no longer liked her as well as Hallie did. "I guess Amity won't let them."

"Disgraceful! She has no business raising those children."

Hallie smiled. She liked not being lumped in with the younger ones. Papa always seemed to think she was still a child.

On the way to the house by the road, they passed within sight of the small cemetery. Gretchen pulled the buggy over and stopped. "I see Clay is tending Elsa's grave. I was afraid for a while he wouldn't be able to. Naturally he would see to it today of all days. It's his first anniversary without her. I recall my first without Hall. I cried so hard."

Hallie glanced at the grave of the uncle she couldn't remember. To her, Hall had always been just a marker in the small cemetery. "Was he anything like Papa?"

Gretchen gave a short laugh. "As much like him as a mule is like a thoroughbred." She slapped the reins on the horse's back and the buggy lurched forward.

Although it was early, Hallie saw her father heading toward the house, a hoe over his shoulder. When she and Gretchen waved, he waved back. "It's a shame Papa never had boys to help him in the fields. He works so hard."

"It is a pity. The O'Flannerys seem to have more than their share."

Hallie didn't pursue the subject. She knew the O'Flannerys were disliked by her aunt. That was a shame, since she privately thought Brian O'Flannery was the cutest boy in school. With Aunt Gretchen so against the family, it wouldn't do to encourage him.

They reached the house and Hallie paused before getting out of the buggy. "Aunt Gretchen, what should I do to get rid of Amity? Everything I've tried hasn't worked. She isn't afraid of frogs or lizards or anything, as far as I can tell."

"Bide your time and watch. Eventually she will get enough rope to hang herself."

Hallie doubted it, but she nodded and climbed down from the buggy seat.

As they went into the parlor, she knew something was different. For a minute she couldn't put her finger on what it was. Then she noticed the curtains. She stared at them, her mouth open. Beside her Gretchen was doing the same. Hallie felt the roar of rage building in her and couldn't have stopped it if she had tried.

Amity had heard the buggy arrive, and when she saw it was Gretchen with Hallie, she had considered slipping out to the root cellar and pretending she didn't know they had company. There was only so much she could do in the cellar, however, so she had straightened herself and taken off her apron. Gretchen was a guest, and Amity was determined to get through this visit without a problem. Then she heard the strange noise coming from the parlor.

She hurried to the door and discovered Hallie lifting the hem of a curtain and again making that incoherent sound. Amity was confused but she said, "Hello, Gretchen. I didn't expect you today."

Gretchen turned on her, her eyes blazing. "What are you thinking of, putting up these curtains?"

Hallie wheeled to glare at her. "These are my grandmother's best lace curtains. They are to be mine when I marry! You can't have them."

Amity wanted to step back, but she couldn't afford to give an inch. "I had no idea. The other girls saw them and they never said they were important."

"Not important!" Hallie looked as if she would like to slap Amity. "Grandmother's curtains aren't important?" She was so upset her voice squeaked at the end.

"We'll discuss this later," Amity said firmly. "The curtains won't be harmed by hanging there a bit longer and we have a guest."

"I hardly think I should be considered a guest," Gretchen snapped. "Not in this house."

Amity tried to quell her temper. "I only meant that Hallie and I will discuss this later in private."

"She is my niece and I hardly think you could say anything to her that I shouldn't hear."

"She may be your niece, but she's my stepdaughter and this is my house. You're welcome here as a guest, Gretchen, but you may as well get used to the idea that matters have changed." She felt her heart sink when she noticed from the corner of her eye that the other children had gathered on the stairs and in doorways and were listening to the entire exchange. She lifted her head. "You may have a seat if you like and wait for Clay to come in, or I'll tell the others you're here."

"Clay knows I'm here." Gretchen's tone was frigid.

Amity wondered how that could be. Had Clay been to visit Gretchen? She never came for Sunday dinner, nor did they go to her house. She had assumed Clay hadn't seen Gretchen in weeks.

Hallie wasn't ready to be civil. "You take down these curtains at once! I want Mama's put back up."

Amity regarded her for a moment before she answered. "You should have told me these were your grandmother's. I asked you if there were any other trunks or belongings that were special to you."

"You asked about Mama's things! How was I to know you would try to take over Grandmother's, as well?" Hallie looked close to tears.

If Gretchen hadn't been there, Amity would have gone to the girl and promised to remove the curtains at once. She couldn't do that in front of Gretchen, however. She was wondering what to do when Clay walked in. He saw Hallie's anguished face, Gretchen's anger and the curtains.

"What in blazes are those doing in here?" he asked.

Amity turned on him. "You, too? I found the curtains. They were prettier than the ones that were hanging in here and I hung them instead."

"How dare you say Mama's curtains weren't pretty!" Hallie shouted as she gave in to her tears and ran to her father.

"I didn't mean . . . Hallie, pull yourself together."

Gretchen said angrily, "I don't think the problem is with Hallie. She's a wonderful child, and I think it's a disgrace the way you treat her and the others!"

Amity stared at the woman. "I have no idea what you're talking about."

"Don't you?" Gretchen sounded as if she didn't believe that for a minute. To Clay she said, "I came to be with you on your anniversary. Now I find that impossible. Therefore, I'll bid you farewell. My sympathy is with you." Gretchen turned and stalked out the door.

"What..." Amity started after her, realized that would never do and glared at Hallie. "What have you told her about me?"

Hallie cried harder.

"Don't shout at her," Clay said in his daughter's defense. "This would have been her mother's anniversary and she's naturally upset."

Amity glared at him. "*She's* upset? So am I! You never told me this was a special day to you."

Clay looked as if he wished he was still working in the fields. "Take down the curtains. That's one reason she's taking it so hard."

Amity lifted her chin. "Gladly. We'll go without curtains. I may not be able to choose what goes on the walls of my own house, but I can certainly choose what does not!" She knew she was being unreasonable, but she was too angry to care. She frowned at the doorway and stairs, and the other children scattered. Amity felt a headache beginning. Had this undone all she had begun with them? She went to the first window and started removing the curtains.

Thirty minutes later, Hallie had gone to her room, Clay had disappeared somewhere in the buggy, and the windows were bare and gaping. Amity felt perilously close to tears as she folded the curtains back into the trunk under the stairs. Where had Clay gone? To Gretchen? She thought it likely that he would have, in order to soothe her feelings. The idea of Clay comforting Gretchen made her tears spill over and she wiped at them with the palm of her hand. She wasn't going to give in and cry over this. She had been trained from childhood to be of sterner stuff.

The day turned into evening and the children, much subdued, came down to eat. Amity put the food on the table and the meal was passed in silence. Amity, who had always eaten in silence before coming here, felt the lack of conversation pressing unnaturally upon her. Clay still had not come home and Hallie hadn't come down.

As she finished and left the table, Rosemary whispered to Amity, "Where's Papa?"

"I'm not sure."

The child looked worried. "He's not dead, is he?"

Amity knelt beside her. "Of course not! Where did you get that idea?"

"When Mama died, she just disappeared like this." Rosemary's lower lip trembled. "Aunt Gretchen said she had gone away, but she died and she can't come back."

Amity hugged her. "Your papa is just fine. He's probably visiting the O'Flannerys." She couldn't bring herself to say Gretchen's name. "I'll bet he's home before you go to bed."

"If he's not, will you ask him to wake me up when he does come back so I'll know he's home?"

"I'll do that." Amity watched Rosemary go toward the parlor and her heart felt heavy in her chest. Where was Clay?

An hour later he returned. In his arms he carried two large boxes. Amity went to him but was afraid to touch him or to admit that she had been afraid that he wouldn't come home. He put the boxes on the kitchen table and stepped back. "These are for you."

"For me? I don't understand."

"Open them."

Hesitantly Amity got a butcher knife and cut the twine binding the top box. When she opened the lid, she saw lace. For a minute she was afraid to touch it. Then she slowly lifted the first curtain out of the box. Her eyes met Clay's.

"For the parlor windows. I thought the others looked good in there but they are to be Hallie's. These are yours."

Amity couldn't speak; she was too close to tears. She opened the second box. Inside were dishes. Not plain dishes like those used every day but really good ones with a pattern of tiny roses and rimmed in gold. "China?" she whispered.

He shuffled his feet as if he was feeling more emotion than he wanted to admit. "A wife needs her own things about her. I figured you might like these. If you'd rather have another kind, we can take them back. I had Owen Osgood go to the store and open it so I could get them.''

She still couldn't speak. No one had ever bought her china and lace curtains before, or anything else to speak of. Not as an unexpected gift like this.

''I had to talk Frank Pearson into opening the dry goods, too. He had closed by the time I got to town. That's why I was gone so long.''

''Thank you,'' Amity said at last. She held a plate to her and stroked the nearest curtain. She still couldn't believe her eyes. ''Thank you, Clay.''

He nodded. ''I'll go clean up. Is there a plate of supper for me?''

''Of course. I'm keeping it in the warmer.''

He left her still gazing at his gifts. He went to his bedroom and stripped off his shirt. After he washed, he pulled open the drawer where he usually kept his clean shirts. It was empty, and he remembered he had cleaned it out that morning so Amity would have a place to put her own clothes. But the drawer was still empty.

He looked toward the closed door. What did that mean? That she preferred to keep separate bedrooms? He took a step toward the door, but stopped. He couldn't ask her to change now. It would look as if he thought he could buy her with the china and curtains. If she had wanted to stay in his room, she had had all day to make the move.

Clay slowly went to the dresser and opened the drawer where he had moved his shirts. He was afraid he knew what this meant. Elsa had wanted her own room, though she had never come right out and said so. He had known it but he had pretended he hadn't. That had been the only bone of contention between them. She hadn't liked to sleep with him. He had felt so guilty about that after she was gone. Now he had a chance to start all over and he wanted to do it right this time. He pulled on the shirt. He had been so sure last night that Amity would want to sleep with him. The hurt was deep, and he was determined that she not know about it.

Chapter Thirteen

To Amity's confusion and dismay, Clay seemed to have forgotten the beautiful night of love they had spent. He made no reference to it, nor had he, by any sign or deed, indicated that he wanted her to move into his bedroom. Amity was glad she had waited and not taken her things in. It would have been too embarrassing to be asked to move out again.

She had no idea what she had done wrong. She thought he had enjoyed it as much as she had. Perhaps *that* was the reason—he had enjoyed it too much. Clay was determined to keep Elsa as his wife in his mind, and Amity knew he was more stubborn than any man she had ever met. She tried not to be jealous but at times she could not help it. Even though Elsa was dead, she still had a firm hold on Clay's heart, and it was not fair.

As Amity continued churning the butter, she thought about how her life had been before coming to Ransom. It had been easier. She and her aunts had never made much in the way of a mess, and the house had practically cleaned itself by comparison to this house full of children and a husband who came in from the fields in muddy boots and dusty clothes. But all that considered, she would not trade one day here for a year with her aunts.

Amity was bothered at times that she never really missed the two women who had raised her. She had to admit, however, that her aunts had done so only out of duty and not because they had wanted her. They probably did not miss her any more than she did them. If they had missed her, they would have answered the letters she sent dutifully every week. So far she had had no response from them at all. And it was just as well that way.

From her seat on the service porch, Amity could see the swing on the veranda, and as she watched, Hallie came out and sat on it, pushing the porch with her toe to get the swing started. The girl looked sad, but Amity knew she would not welcome any questions or a hug. Amity kept up the steady churning as she tried to think of ways to win Hallie over.

She had tried numerous things. New ribbons or a dress had accomplished nothing, nor had cooking Hallie's favorite meals. The girl seemed determined to be as unpleasant as possible. Now, for instance, Hallie was supposed to be upstairs changing the bed linens so they could be washed the next day. Amity had no doubt that she would find the rumpled sheets downstairs and fresh ones on the beds, but not due to Hallie's efforts. Kate and Jemima were doing Hallie's chores and thought Amity did not know. Amity was glad the sisters were so protective of each other, but it made it difficult to confront Hallie with her disobedience when the chores she had been assigned always got done.

Amity suspected Gretchen was at the bottom of most of Hallie's rebellion, because the girl was particularly troublesome and disobedient right after visiting her aunt. But part of it was because Hallie truly missed her mother, and Amity could not fault her for that. It had been only eight months since Elsa's death, and Hallie was having to adjust to that as well as to a new stepmother.

Hallie sighed and looked at the porch, then pushed the swing into an even bigger arc. From her appearance and movements, she seemed somewhat despondent, and Amity thought she might be crying. She was reminded of her own loss of her parents. Many times she had hidden behind a certain oleander bush behind her aunts' house so she could cry without her aunts knowing it. That thought made Amity more determined than ever to help Hallie. She resolved to find some way to make Hallie happy. If her efforts on Hallie's behalf also made the girl accept her as a stepmother, so much the better, but the main thing was for Hallie's unhappiness to be eased.

Getting back to her chores, Amity skimmed the butter that had floated to the top of the churn into the butter mold and poured the buttermilk into a jug and set it in the icebox. Next, she pressed the liquid from the butter and turned the butter out onto the dish. To make it prettier, she carved a design on the top with the end of a spoon. She did these things automatically. Her mind was still on Hallie.

Jemima came into the kitchen and Amity asked, "Has Hallie ever said anything about wanting something special? Something she has always wanted but has never had?"

Jemima thought for a minute. "You mean like my music lessons?"

"That's right."

"She's always wanted a pet."

Amity looked at her. "There are several dogs here. Aren't they your pets?"

"Those are mainly Kate's. Hallie has always wanted a kitten."

Amity thought for a minute. "I had never noticed. Why don't you have a cat? It would keep rats and mice out of the barn and feed bins."

"Mama didn't like cats. She said they caused ringworm and smothered babies."

Amity was about to point out that such old wives' tales as that were ridiculous, but remembered in time that Jemima was quoting her mother. "I think we should have a cat. Would that make Hallie happy?"

"I'm sure it would. She always used to play with the ones at the O'Flannerys' house, but Mama wouldn't let her bring one home."

Amity knew what she was going to do.

That afternoon when her chores were done, Amity walked over to the O'Flannerys' house. Fiona was sweeping the kitchen porch, and when she saw Amity she waved a welcome. "Come in the house," Fiona said when Amity was near enough to hear her. "I'll make you a glass of lemonade."

"Thank you. I'd like that." The day was hot and the walk had been longer than Amity had expected.

"Why didn't you ride your horse?" Fiona said as she chipped ice from the block in her icebox and filled two glasses with ice and lemonade.

"I'm here to ask a favor, and if the answer is yes, I'll have my hands too full to ride a horse."

Fiona glanced at her. "Come out on the porch where it's cooler."

When they were seated in the cowhide-covered chairs, Amity said, "Have you found a home for your kittens yet?"

"No, worst of luck. No one wants them. The cat only had two this time, thank goodness. I've known her to have half a dozen."

"Would it be all right if I take them?"

Fiona smiled. "It would be better than all right."

"Your children won't mind?"

"We have kittens here regularly. They won't mind."

"I want them for Hallie. Jemima tells me that she has always wanted a cat and that Elsa wouldn't have one."

"I've always wondered about that. I don't see how you can keep feed for your livestock without a cat to kill the mice. Elsa was afraid of cats, but she could have had one in the barn and seldom seen it."

"You mean she had a shortcoming? I'm sorry. That was uncharitable of me." She had forgotten Elsa and Fiona had been friends. "It's just that it seems she was so perfect, and I seem to do everything wrong."

"Elsa wasn't perfect. As far as I know, no one is."

"That's not the way I hear it," Amity couldn't keep the edge from her voice.

Fiona thought for a minute. Carefully she said, "Surely Clay didn't tell you that."

"Not in so many words." Amity glanced at her friend. She had had so few confidantes in her life. Could she confide in Fiona? "I came here under unusual circumstances. Clay needed a wife, and I wanted a new life, so I came. I wasn't so foolish as to think he would love me, but I'm afraid I've fallen in love with him."

"There's nothing foolish about that. Love makes life bearable. Wait. I hear the baby." Fiona hurried into the house and returned with her newest daughter. "I'm sorry to interrupt you." She gave her attention to Amity as she jiggled the baby to quiet her. "You were saying you and Clay have fallen in love. Nothing could be better for both of you."

"No, I didn't say that exactly. I said I love him. He hasn't given reason to think he feels the same about me."

Fiona looked troubled. "He cares for you. I know he does."

"I don't." Amity stood and leaned on one of the porch supports. "I don't know if he will ever love me. He's still married to Elsa." She hated to voice the words, but she felt better for having said them.

"He said that?" Fiona sounded shocked. "He never said that!"

"It's not so much what he says as what he doesn't say. Can I trust you to keep a secret?" When Fiona nodded, Amity said, "We don't share a bedroom." Her face felt hot and she knew her cheeks were red.

Fiona's mouth dropped open. "You mean you never..."

"Once. We did once." Amity couldn't look at her. She had never made a practice of confiding anything this personal to anyone and had intentionally stopped short of divulging the details of Clay's promise to Elsa and his concern over losing another wife to childbirth. Besides, Amity felt she could deal with those objections, if only she could get Clay's attention. "I suppose I shouldn't tell you, but I don't know what to do. Everywhere I look, I see Elsa's wallpaper, Elsa's cup towels, Elsa's churn. Everything I touch belonged to Elsa. We're still eating the preserves and pickles she put up. I feel small-minded talking about it, but after a while, it wears on a person."

"I should think it would. I never thought about it in those terms before."

"I brought only my clothes into this marriage. I had quilts and linens of my own, but I thought it might be too much to bring all this way. Until now I haven't had time to sew new ones while trying to keep the house and girls clean."

"It must be a handful for someone not used to children."

Amity laughed. "At first I thought I would come apart at the seams like a rag doll. Now I can't imagine life without them. Or Clay. That's the problem. Fiona, how can I ever make him love me? How do women do that? I'm nothing like Elsa, and I've never learned to flirt." She shook her head. "It would seem ludicrous to flirt with my own husband. He would think I had lost my mind."

"What did he say when you told him you love him?"

"I've never said it. I can't."

Fiona put a clean diaper over her shoulder and discreetly unbuttoned her blouse so she could feed the baby who refused to be quieted. "Then how do you know he doesn't love you?"

"If he did, wouldn't he have asked me to move into his room? Wouldn't he act as if he cared?" She was so frustrated her voice shook. "I shouldn't be saying all this."

"Nonsense. Of course you should. You don't have family near enough to confide in. We have to stick together."

Amity reached out to touch the baby's pink feet. "I'd love to have a baby of my own," she admitted. "I love the girls, but I want to give Clay a baby. I want us to have one together."

"That's only natural. I'm surprised at Clay. I had thought he was more perceptive than that. Men can be that way, though. They mean well, but they just don't see the subtleties we women can. Sean is the same way. I have to spell everything out for him at times. I think you'll have to do that with Clay, too."

"You mean tell him I love him?"

"More than that. Move your things into his room. You'll be surprised how many barriers it brings down when you sleep in the same bed. You'll find yourself talking about things you'd never dream of mentioning in the daylight. It's harder to stay angry with each other, too."

"We rarely argue. Not really." She remembered the argument over the lace curtains. Clay had gone all the way to town, dragged two store owners back to their places of business and purchased curtains and dishes for her. Why had he gone to so much trouble if he didn't care for her? "I can't figure him out."

Fiona nodded. "You probably never will. As near as I can tell, men don't think like we do."

"Sometimes I think he cares for me. He does things that seem to indicate it, but then he pulls back, and I'm not sure."

"Take my advice. Move into his room and tell him you love him. That couldn't hurt."

Amity disagreed but she nodded. She could never have the courage to risk having him hurt her by admitting that he didn't and never would love her, that he had only made love to her that one time because he was a man and had a man's natural needs. Since that night, she had discovered needs of her own, but she was embarrassed to admit it to him. Surely no lady ever felt the urges she was feeling. Urges that didn't wait until dark but could nearly overwhelm her at the supper table, or when she saw him cross the yard or do a thousand other things.

"I should get the kittens," she said as Fiona buttoned her blouse and removed the concealing diaper from her shoulder. The baby lay dozing in her arms, perfectly contented again. "I want to have supper ready when Clay comes in."

"I'll show you where they are."

The new barn was still raw-looking, its wood not yet weathered to the silvery gray of the older outbuildings. Like the Morgan barn, it was clean and smelled of hay and feed.

Fiona held the baby with one hand and opened the door of a stall with the other. Amity could hear the mewing of kittens. They trotted a few steps toward her and watched her with open curiosity. Amity picked up the gray one. "How adorable!" The kitten tapped an exploratory paw at her finger. "I've always liked animals."

"Did you have pets when you were a girl?"

"No, I think that's one reason I'm so determined to get these for Hallie. There were a lot of times I wished I had a kitten to hug and talk to."

"All children need animals about. It teaches them how to get along with people."

"I never heard it put that way," Amity said in surprise.

"Sean says I have odd ideas at times," Fiona said with a touch of shyness in her voice as if she thought Amity might laugh at her. "He says I make too much of why people feel the way they do."

Amity picked up the yellow kitten. It had a gray spot on its side, as if part of the gray one had rubbed off on it. "They're wonderful. Hallie will be so happy."

"If they don't work out, just bring them back. We'll have room to take them in."

Amity thanked her friend and started home. The kittens curled in her arms and seemed to enjoy the journey. When she reached the house, she found Clay was already home from the field. "You're in early. I'm sorry I wasn't here."

He looked across the porch at her. "It felt odd not having you here. What's that you have?"

Amity held out a kitten. For the first time she realized she should have cleared this with him first. Elsa might not be the only Morgan to dislike cats. "I went to see Fiona. I brought these kittens for Hallie."

Clay took the yellow cat and tickled its ear. "A little girl cat. We seem to have a surplus of females in this house." The kitten purred and tried to chew his finger.

"They needn't stay in the house," Amity said quickly. "They will be quite comfortable in the barn."

His eyes met hers. "That was thoughtful of you to go all that way to get them for Hallie."

"Is she inside?"

Clay opened the door and called for Hallie. She soon came out. As usual, she ignored Amity and looked at her father. She saw the kitten right away. "A kitten!"

"Two of them," Clay corrected. "Amity got them from the O'Flannerys. They're yours."

Hallie's face lit up and she took the kittens and cuddled them to her. "Thank you, Papa!"

"Don't thank me. It was all Amity's doing."

Hallie's smile faded. She tossed Amity a doubtful look, then held the kittens at arm's length toward Amity. "No, thank you."

"Hallie!" Clay frowned at his daughter.

"I don't want them. Cats carry ringworm, and they aren't safe around babies."

"We don't have a baby here, and I don't believe they are any more likely to give you ringworm than any other animal. That's an old wives' tale," Amity said. She tried to keep her voice calm and reasonable.

Hallie glared at her. "It's no such thing. Here. I don't want these cats. Give them to Kate. She's the one who likes animals." She thrust them at Amity.

Amity took the kittens and stared at Hallie. She had been so sure this was the right thing to do.

"Hallie, apologize this minute!" Clay said sternly. "You have better manners than that."

"If she doesn't want the kittens, she doesn't have to take them," Amity said in Hallie's defense. "I should have asked her first."

"Hallie," he said warningly.

"She's just trying to look good in front of you," Hallie snapped. "She doesn't care anything about me."

"Why should she, the way you treat her?" he countered.

"I didn't mean to cause this," Amity said. "I can take the kittens back."

"No." Clay frowned at her. "We're keeping them."

"I said I don't want them!" Hallie stamped her foot as if she were Rosemary's age.

"I've had enough out of you! Apologize or I'll have to punish you!"

"Nobody loves me here anymore! I want to go live with Aunt Gretchen. I hate it here and I hate Amity!"

Clay took a step toward her, but Amity stepped in the way. "You're upset. We love you. We don't want you to live anywhere else."

"No? I wish *you* lived somewhere else. Anywhere! I don't want you here in our house!" Hallie turned on Amity, her blue eyes sparking fire. "We were just fine before you came along."

"No, we weren't," Clay corrected. "Amity has done more for us than we can begin to say."

"You always take her side." Hallie put her fists on her hips and glared at him. "You never used to be like this when Mama was alive. Then we all laughed and were happy all the time. I feel like I want to die, too. Then you'd be sorry you've treated me so badly. I don't want a stepmother, and if I did, it wouldn't be *her*. You have to choose, Papa. It's me or her!" She jerked her chin toward Amity.

"I can't choose between my daughter and my wife! You may think you're almost grown, Hallie, but you're not there yet. As long as you're a child under my roof, you'll do as I say."

"Not when it comes to her. She's mean to me when you're not around. You don't know what she's really like."

"I've never done anything mean to you." Amity gasped. "Never!"

"She's lying, Papa. She makes us work all the time, and she just acts nice when you're around. Send her away! You don't even sleep together! She's not really your wife." She glared at Amity. "Who knows what she was before she came here!"

Clay reached past Amity and slapped Hallie.

For a minute the girl stared at him, her hand pressed against her cheek. Then she turned and ran into the house.

Clay looked as if he felt terrible about what he had done. "Damn!" he muttered. "I've never hit her before in my life."

Amity looked at him miserably. "It's all my fault. I thought I was doing the right thing, and instead, I've made everything worse."

"You meant well. This isn't your fault." Clay glared at the door Hallie had slammed behind her. "She was just upset."

"I'd say she's more than upset. She hates me."

"If you ask me, Gretchen is behind most of this. I have a good mind to go and have a talk with her."

"It wouldn't solve anything. If she is causing trouble, she won't admit it, and if she's not, she will know we're having trouble with Hallie."

"I'm sure she already knows that. Hallie is over there half the time."

Amity had not realized Clay was aware of that. "Gretchen is her aunt. It's good that they can be close." She didn't believe her words, but felt she should say them. Especially since she was thinking uncharitable things about both Gretchen and Hallie at the moment. She held out the kittens. "What should I do with these?"

"We'll keep them. I've wanted a cat or two about. Elsa didn't like them, but they are better at keeping mice and rats away than dogs are." He took one and tickled it behind its ear. "I like cats, myself."

"So do I. At least I think I do. I've never had one."

"Looks like you have two now." He handed the kitten back. "Unless Kate adopts them the way she does every other animal she can get her hands on."

Amity looked at the door. "Should I go in and try to talk to her? I'm afraid it will make matters worse."

"No, let her cool down. If I know Hallie, she's not in the mood for talking."

Amity shook her head. "I don't know what to do with her," she confessed. "If I had ever said half that much to my aunts, I'd have surely been struck dead on the spot."

"Hallie's not a bad girl. Losing her mother was hard on her."

"I know. I lost mine and my father, too. But I don't think she should be allowed to hide behind that forever. Life does go on, and she has to learn to face even the unpleasant things without going to pieces."

Clay frowned at her. "You could be more understanding. Elsa hasn't been gone even a year."

Amity lifted her chin. "I would say I've been more understanding than the average woman would be. Coming here hasn't been easy on me, either."

"You're a grown woman and this is a choice you made. If I recall correctly, you had a good reason."

Amity met his eyes. She had almost forgotten she had confided in him her suspicion that she was pregnant.

"I'm sorry," he said. "I shouldn't have said that. But I can't stand to hear you talk against Hallie."

"I wasn't putting her down out of cruelty," Amity said, trying to wrap her aloofness about her like a shield. "Children must be taught how to act and how to comport themselves like adults. Especially girls who are practically grown and still shout and stamp their feet as if they were toddlers throwing a tantrum."

"I don't need your advice on how to discipline my children," he snapped at her.

"No? Then what exactly do you need me for? You could hire a housekeeper, and if you paid her enough, you could probably find one that Hallie would not drive away. You insist that I not be allowed to discipline the children and think I shouldn't even insist they do simple chores that all girls need to learn if they're ever to run houses of their own." Taking a quick, deep breath, she delivered the last blow. "You certainly don't need me as a wife."

Clay frowned at her. "Maybe if you were more like a wife and less like your spinster aunts, I would."

Amity could no longer stay and argue, because she could feel the tears building, and she refused to let him see her cry. She hurried down the steps and toward the service porch. He called after her, sounding contrite, but she could not go back, not when the tears were spilling out of her eyes and running down her cheeks.

She took the kittens to the kitchen and gave them some of the meat scraps she had set aside for the dogs. As she watched them gobble the meal up, she let herself cry.

Clay not only did not love her, but he did not even desire her as a woman. She might not know a great deal about men but she knew it could never be considered a compliment for him to tell her she reminded him of a spinster aunt. That he had never met her aunts didn't matter. She hated the idea of him thinking of her in the way she remembered Aunt Dorcus and Aunt Ophelia. He must not find her even remotely attractive.

What else had she expected? she asked herself. She was plain and had not the least idea how to make a man want her. Her hair had too much red in it, no matter what he had said that night, and her eyes were an uncompromising brown—no interesting gold or green flecks, just brown. She had no idea why the reminder of those things had the power to hurt her, since she had been told all her life that she was no beauty and never would be. Still she had hoped some man, some day, would see her and think she was beautiful.

"I should never have come," she whispered to the kittens.

She knew that was not so. If she had not come, she would never have been able to tell bedtime stories to Rosemary and Laura, never have seen Jemima blossom with her music, never have seen Kate surrounded by her animals, never have heard Clay's voice or seen his smile or have been held all night in his strong arms.

She almost groaned aloud. Now that she knew how he thought of her, it broke her heart that she had given herself to him. Before she had known what it was like for him to make love to her, she had been like a blank slate. Nothing Emmett had ever done had touched her soul as Clay had. She ached for him, even now when she was so hurt and angry at him. At least, she told herself, he need never know the anguish she felt.

"We have kittens?" Kate said behind her.

Amity hurriedly dried her tears. "Yes. They're over here."

Kate came around the table and exclaimed over the kittens as she sat on the floor to pet them. "They're so pretty! Can I name them?"

"Of course you can." Amity reached out and smoothed the girl's hair. Kate was so fond of being outside, the wind kept her hair mussed all the time. She felt her chin tremble at the rush of emotion, and she stood and pretended to be busy at the cupboard.

"I'll name the gray one Silver and the yellow Gold," Kate said. "Do those sound like good names?"

"Whatever you like. They sound fine to me." Amity was accustomed to Kate's sometimes whimsical names for pets. At least these would be easy to remember.

Kate let the kittens finish eating and took them outside to find her younger sisters to show them the newest additions to the farm. Amity quit pretending to work and sat down in the nearest chair. If only Hallie had reacted this way, she might have won the girl over, and more important, she would never have had the argument with Clay. She wished she had never learned how he saw her. How could she try to make herself attractive to him now or to be blatantly honest about her feelings toward Clay as Fiona had advised? No, that was out of the question. She was going to have to learn to accept things as they were and quit trying to change them.

Chapter Fourteen

"Amity, wake up!" Rosemary repeated as she tugged at the cover.

Amity raised her head and tried to wake up enough to focus. "What is it? Rosemary? Is that you? Are you sick?"

"No, it's Hallie."

Amity rubbed her eyes and sat up. "Hallie is sick?"

"No, no. She's gone. Hallie is gone!"

"What do you mean she's gone? What time is it?" The room was still dark, without the faintest light from the windows.

"I can't tell time yet. I had a nightmare, and I went in to sleep with Hallie, and she's gone!" The child's voice was filled with fright. "It was an awful nightmare!" she added.

"I know they can be scary but they aren't real. Maybe Hallie is in the kitchen."

"Without a lamp? I got scared coming down the stairs in the dark, and I had to run all the way across the dining room, and I hit my leg on a chair. Want to see?" She climbed into bed with Amity and pulled up her nightgown to show Amity her leg.

"It's too dark to see. Let me feel. It's not too bad, is it?" Her mind was on Hallie's whereabouts. She wouldn't have gone to the outhouse at this hour, would she? Where else could she be? "Did you wake up your papa?"

"No, his door is farther from the stairs than yours and the dining room is awful dark."

Amity scooted Rosemary to one side so she could get out of bed. "Do you want to stay in my bed while I go find Hallie?"

"Yes." Rosemary lay down and pulled up the sheet as if she was perfectly at home there. "Can I sleep here until morning so I don't have any more nightmares?"

"Of course you can." Amity placed a kiss on Rosemary's forehead. She found her wrapper and pulled it on as she slid her feet into her cloth house shoes. Maybe Rosemary had been half asleep and only thought Hallie was missing.

She stepped into the blackness of the dining room and felt around until she located the lamp she always kept on the sideboard. With one of the lucifer matches at the base, she lit it and turned down the wick until the light from the lamp was faint. She did not want to alarm the entire household until she saw for herself that Hallie was indeed missing.

Moving quickly but quietly, she went upstairs to the room Hallie shared with Kate. Opening the door silently, she held the lamp high to cast a light on the bed. Kate lay on her side, her blond braids draped across the pillow. The other side of the bed was empty.

Amity went into the room for a better look, hoping against reason that she would find that Hallie had rolled out of bed. But there was no sign of the girl on the floor or anywhere in the room. Becoming more anxious by the moment, Amity left the room and closed the door behind her.

Next she went into the room where Rosemary slept with Laura and Jemima but found no sign of Hallie. Amity was growing more alarmed. Although she knew it was most unlikely, she looked in the room that had been prepared for the baby boy. It was still and empty.

Going downstairs, Amity checked all the outside doors. The front door and parlor door were locked, just as she always left them at night. Clay had once teased her about locking up before bedtime as if she were still living in the city. Now she was glad the habit had carried over, because she knew Hallie could not have gone out either of them if the doors were locked. But when she checked the kitchen door, her heart sank. It was unlocked.

She turned up the wick and looked around outside. "Hallie?" she called softly. "Are you out there?"

There was no answer. Amity stepped inside. She would have to awaken Clay.

She went to his room and shut the door behind her so Rosemary, if she was still awake, couldn't hear their voices. "Clay? Clay, wake up."

He moaned something unintelligible and lifted his head. "Amity?" he said as his consciousness rose. Then he smiled and held out his hand to her.

She felt a stirring inside her despite her worry. "Are you awake?"

Clay nodded, his head on the pillow. He caught her hand as she reached out to shake him and pulled her down toward him.

"Hallie is missing," Amity said quickly. She thought Clay must be still sleeping, and she didn't want to hear him call her by Elsa's name. Why else would he smile and reach for her unless he had been dreaming of his dead wife?

Clay opened his eyes and became fully alert. "Hallie is missing? What do you mean?"

"I mean she's not in the house. Rosemary had a nightmare and went to get in bed with Hallie and Kate and discovered Hallie isn't there."

As he sat up, she noticed he was not wearing a nightshirt and, apparently, nothing else, either. She looked away with some difficulty. He had slept naked the night of their lovemaking, but it had never occurred to her that he always did. As he put his feet over the side of the bed, she turned her back to him to give him privacy to dress.

"I looked all over the house. The kitchen door is unlocked. I called out but she didn't answer."

"I'll check the outhouse, but I can't imagine why she would go out there before daylight." He reached past her to pick up the pocket watch he kept on his dresser. "It won't be dawn for over an hour."

After giving him ample time to dress, Amity turned to face him. He was wearing his trousers and boots but no shirt. That didn't seem to embarrass Clay. She followed him across the dining room and into the kitchen. He took the lamp and went out the door and she waited impatiently in the dark. She was glad of the darkness. The sight of his muscled torso had been more moving to her than she was willing to admit, especially at a time like this.

When he came back, she could see from his expression that he had not found her. Together, and as quietly as possible, they searched the house from top to bottom, even going into the attic. "Where the hell can she be?" he said in exasperation that barely covered his worry.

"She was so angry at both of us last night. She didn't even come down to supper. It's all my fault. I never should have brought those kittens home."

"Nonsense. This is over more than a pair of kittens." He looked at her. "It's not your fault. Hallie has been a handful lately."

"Where could she have gone? Is there some friend in town she may have run away to?"

"It's not likely she went that far." He left the kitchen and went to his bedroom, with Amity at his heels. "I suspect I'll find her at Gretchen's."

"Of course! Why didn't I think of that?"

Clay got a work shirt from his drawer and shrugged into it. Amity tried not to watch, but she couldn't help herself. As he buttoned the shirt, he said, "It's my fault, if it's anyone's. I never hit one of my children until yesterday."

"You didn't hurt her." Amity had had her share of spankings as she grew up, and she knew the girl could not have been hurt by a slap.

"I don't hit my children." His face was stiff as if he was determined to carry all the guilt. "I swore when Hallie was born that I would never lift a hand to her." He looked at Amity, his face etched with concern. "Lately I've been breaking a great number of promises I made to myself."

She didn't know what he meant and was afraid to ask. "Do you really think she's at Gretchen's house?"

"I'd bet anything you care to name." He ran a hand through his hair but didn't take time to brush it. It lay tousled and soft on his head, and Amity longed to touch it.

She carried the lamp to light his way out the kitchen door. For a long time she watched the direction he took. He might have been dreaming of Elsa, but he had reached out to her. And he had called her by name. She was afraid to hope he might have been dreaming of her instead.

Clay didn't bother saddling his horse. He could walk to Gretchen's by the time he caught the animal and saddled it. As he stormed off, he was getting angrier with Hallie by the moment. It might have been wrong for him to have slapped her, and he knew he would always regret it, but as Amity had said, it hadn't really hurt her, and Hallie had been asking for a great deal more.

He remembered his own childhood. If he had said half that much to his stepfather, the man would have beaten him severely. Why could Hallie not see that she had a good home and appreciate what she had? He wondered if Gretchen had encouraged her to run away from home. A year before he would never have dreamed any of this could have happened. A year ago Elsa was alive and expecting a baby and his future looked bright.

He thought about Amity and how glad he had been to wake up and see her standing by his bed. For a minute he had thought she had come to be with him. It bothered him a great deal that he was coming to prefer Amity's reserve that covered a passion Elsa had never felt to the memory of his wife. Elsa might have been more compliant, and she might not have had a tenth of the temper Amity had, but she also had no other passions, either. If Amity ever fell in love with him, Clay knew it would eclipse any love he had ever known. But Amity made it clear by her actions that she didn't love him and probably never would.

When Clay reached Gretchen's house, he found it dark. His heart sank. If Hallie had come here, wouldn't the lights be on? Nevertheless, he went up to the door and pounded on it. After a long time, Gretchen answered it. He had never seen her with her hair down before, and he noticed it made a much thinner braid than he had expected. "Is Hallie here?" he demanded with greeting.

"Hallie? Yes, of course she's here. What time is it?"

Relief flooded over him. "When the lights were out, I thought maybe I was wrong. I have to talk to her."

"She's asleep. She's been here since last night. Are you just now missing her?"

"She came over last night? Kate never mentioned that."

"She waited until Kate was asleep. Don't talk so loud. You'll wake her."

"I intend to do more than wake her. She can't run away like this and not tell us where she's going! We've been worried sick!"

"I'm sure," Gretchen said with no conviction. "I'm amazed you cared enough to come looking for her."

"What? How can you say such a thing?" He glared at Gretchen.

"You've changed since that woman came to Ransom. I've noticed you pay less attention to the girls than you should."

"You don't know what you're talking about. I don't treat them any different than I always have."

"That's not what Hallie says. She says you've even taken to striking her."

Clay couldn't deny it. "Go get her or I will!"

"You will not. This is my house and Hallie is my niece. As long as she seeks sanctuary here, you won't have her."

"Don't be a fool, Gretchen. I'm not going to hurt her. I just want her to come home where she belongs."

"She is at home. She moved in with me last night."

"What!" He hadn't thought to look to see if Hallie had taken any clothes with her. "What do you mean she's moved in? She can't do that!"

"She already has." Gretchen was obviously enjoying this.

Clay glared at her. "You tell her this for me. She can come home whenever she is ready, but she had better be ready to change her ways first. I don't know what is going on with her, but she deserves a spanking."

"I think she's rather too large to spank, and I'm appalled that you would even say such a thing. Hallie is a perfect angel over here, and I was under the impression she has always been your favorite."

"I don't have a favorite. I love all my children!"

"But Hallie looks the most like Elsa. I know you've noticed it. You've even commented that she is the image of her. Maybe that's why Amity is so determined to break you apart."

"That's nonsense. Amity has no idea what Elsa looked like. Even if she did, she isn't trying to tear anybody apart. She's trying to hold the family together."

"Is she? You were together quite happily before she came on the scene," Gretchen retorted. "If I were you, I'd look to her as the cause of all my troubles."

"Gretchen, I'm going to say something to you that I never thought I'd have to say. I know you wanted me to marry you after we lost Elsa, but I never cared much for you, not even as a sister-in-law. Your resemblance to Elsa only goes skin deep. Underneath you're a bitter woman. Even if I had never laid eyes on Amity I wouldn't have married you. If she leaves me today, I'll still not want to marry you. I have a feeling my troubles lie right here, not with Amity, and I'm warning *you*. Don't push me too far. Not when it comes to my children or my wife."

"Wife!" Gretchen snorted, her cheeks blazing with anger. "You don't even sleep together!"

"I don't know where you get your information, but you're wrong." He almost enjoyed the look on her face. "When Hallie gets up, tell her to come straight home." He turned on his heels and strode away.

All the way home he thought about what had just transpired. Gretchen was the divisive factor. He was sure of it now. It bothered him a bit that he had lied about Amity being in his room. It was none of Gretchen's business, but she might give up now that she knew she had no chance with him. Besides, he hoped that Amity would soon be in his bedroom to stay. He loved her, and he hoped in time she might grow to love him if they were together more often.

Now that he knew Hallie was safe, he ached for Amity. He needed her to put her arms around him and to love him. He wanted to talk to her about what to do concerning Hallie and what to do regarding Gretchen and about a dozen other things of less importance. He wanted her to truly be his wife.

By the time he reached home, the sky was paling in the east and the lamplight in the windows was welcoming. Amity met him at the door. "Didn't you find her?" Her face was drawn with worry.

"I found her. She's at Gretchen's."

"You left her there?"

"She was asleep. It seems she went there last night after we were all in bed. I told Gretchen to send her home as soon as she is up."

Amity relaxed visibly. He put his arm around her. "I was so worried," she said. "I kept thinking the most awful things. You're sure she's safe?"

"Yes. Are the others awake?"

"Yes. They're all as worried as we were. Especially Kate. She feels responsible for not hearing Hallie leave."

"I'll talk to her and the rest. Are you all right?"

When she realized she was in his arms, she pulled away. She didn't meet his eyes. "Yes. I'm quite all right."

Clay sighed. For a moment there he thought she would let him be her strength. He wasn't accustomed to a woman who could be strong by herself. He didn't know what to say to her to show her that he wanted more from her. What if he said he needed to hold her as much in order to be held himself as to embrace her? She might laugh at him or think he was weak. Clay straightened. "I'll go reassure the girls."

Amity watched him go. She had needed his arms about her, but she had been afraid he was only holding her because he thought she needed it. She didn't want him to think she was clinging to him when he had so many other worries on his mind.

Hallie didn't come home that day, and when Clay went to Gretchen's to get her, he found the doors locked. If Gretchen and Hallie were inside, they weren't answering the door. He pounded repeatedly but there was no sound from inside. In frustration, he finally gave up and went home.

Gretchen and Hallie had gone to town. Gretchen was determined to buy Hallie new clothes and the small things she would need for her new room. They selected a mirror and brush set and a lamp with a green shade to put beside the bed that now was hers.

"I want Hallie's room to be pretty," Gretchen said offhandedly to the salesclerk, a woman she had known for years.

"Her room?" Mrs. Handley asked.

"She has moved in with me." Gretchen smiled at her niece. Hallie smiled back. "It became quite intolerable at home. Her new stepmother, you know."

"I understand." Mrs. Handley gave Hallie a sympathetic look. "It's such a shame men don't think beyond themselves when they marry. I've always said they need a good mother for their children rather than a companion for themselves. But do most of them give that a second thought? No."

Hallie nodded and looked downcast as if she had been abused at Amity's hands. Gretchen nodded. "I could hardly believe he married again so quickly. It showed such disrespect for my dear sister."

"I know. We've all talked about it." Mrs. Handley remembered whom she was talking to and amended, "In the most charitable way, of course."

"Of course. It's only to be expected. If one does odd things, one has to expect to be discussed."

"We all thought he would turn to you," Mrs. Handley said.

"To me?" Gretchen feigned surprise. "Why, I'd never marry my sister's husband. That would seem peculiar, I must say." After what Clay had said about not wanting her, Gretchen wanted to be sure no one thought she was carrying a flame for him.

"Naturally. We hadn't thought."

"Anyway, Hallie has moved in with me. I'm sure we'll be just like mother and daughter in no time." Gretchen patted Hallie's shoulder. "I've always thought of her that way."

Hallie smiled again, but Gretchen saw the girl had been hurt by the references to her father. She loved Clay, and Gretchen knew it would take a while to oust him from her affection. In time, however, she was sure she would succeed. "Good day, Mrs. Handley. I'll see you in church."

"Good day, Mrs. Harris."

Gretchen and Hallie left the store and headed for the next one. Gretchen was determined that as much of Ransom as possible would know about Hallie moving into her house and away from Amity. She might no longer want Clay for herself, but she was determined that if he was to have Amity, they would be as miserable as she could make them.

Amity went into the emporium to buy bath powders for Laura. She knew her aunts would be appalled at the idea of a five-year-old wanting to smell like roses, but Laura loved to smell good, and roses were her favorite flower.

She was met at the counter by a woman she remembered vaguely from church as Mrs. Handley. Amity smiled. "Good morning. Do you have bath powder that smells of roses?"

The woman didn't so much as greet her. She turned to the shelf behind her and picked up the first box she saw and plopped it down on the counter. "That will be twenty cents." Her tone was cold.

Amity looked at her in surprise. She was accustomed to more politeness from clerks and had never noticed that the woman was unpleasant before today. "Is that a box of

Sandefur's Roses on the second shelf? I would prefer that, please."

Mrs. Handley looked as if she were pressed beyond her endurance, but she replaced the first box and got down the Sandefur's. "This one is thirty cents."

"I would also like rosewater and glycerine hand cream."

Mrs. Handley frowned at her and sighed as if this was really too much. "It's over at the other counter."

"I know that." Amity drew herself up. She was not easily intimidated. "Shall we go there together?"

The clerk stormed off, and Amity waited for her to return. She didn't know what was going on, but several other ladies had come in and were whispering among themselves and glancing in her direction. Amity touched the buttons of her dress to be sure they were all fastened, then glanced at her reflection in the mirrored surface of a soap tin. She was presentable. The women put their heads together and she heard one distinctly giggle. Color blazed in Amity's cheeks. She didn't know why they were talking about her, but she had no doubts that they were.

Mrs. Handley came back and slapped down the jar of hand cream beside the bath powder. She stared at Amity as if daring her to want anything else. Amity said coolly, "That will be all." She fished in her coin purse for the proper amount of money and held it out, forcing the other woman to hold out her hand. Then she waited as Mrs. Handley pretended not to know she was supposed to wrap the purchase. Mrs. Handley gave in and started to bundle the items in brown paper.

Amity took the package and, without a nod, left the counter. As she passed the group of women, she heard one say, "It's no wonder the girl moved out. Who could stay and be mistreated?" One of the others hushed her, and Amity gave no indication of having heard.

Clay was waiting for her in the buggy. When she climbed in and stared stonily ahead, he asked, "What's wrong?"

"Nothing. Not a thing." She didn't stop glaring ahead of her, and she clipped her words short.

"Something has happened. You were in a good mood when you went into the emporium. Did someone say something to you?"

"Mrs. Handley or whatever her name is from church was barely civil to me. There were some other women in there—" she couldn't bring herself to call them ladies "—who were actually talking about me behind my back."

"You must be mistaken."

Amity glared at him. "I'm not in the habit of making up such things. If I say it happened, it happened."

Clay frowned. "I'm going to go in there and give Mrs. Handley a piece of my mind. Her employer should know if she's being rude to customers." He wrapped the reins around the brake handle in preparation for going inside.

"No, don't. It will only make matters worse."

"What were the women saying about you?"

"I couldn't hear, but as I passed, I heard them mention Hallie having moved out. There's no telling what Gretchen has told about town."

Clay didn't deny the probability of that. His face was hard with suppressed anger. "I have one more stop to make, then we can go home."

He drove to the feed store and went in. "Hello, Charley. I need a bag of horse feed and a couple of bags of calf pellets. Also a salt block. Can you send it out? I'm in the buggy."

"Sure thing, Clay. I'll have my boy drive it out this afternoon." Charley looked across the scarred counter at him. "I was sorry to hear about Hallie having to move out."

"I beg your pardon?"

"My wife told me about it this morning. It's hard on a girl when she can't get along with her stepmother. Lucky for you Mrs. Harris is willing to take her in. Of course Hallie would be welcome in anybody's house. She's an angel, ain't she?"

"How did your wife know Hallie is visiting with Gretchen?" He emphasized the word *visiting*.

"Why, I believe Mrs. Harris told her." Charley looked as if he had assumed it was common knowledge.

"Your wife was misinformed. Hallie hasn't moved in there and she has no problem with Amity. It certainly wasn't a case of her having to move out."

"I didn't mean no harm by saying it. I had a stepmother myself. I know how hard-hearted they can be. Not that I'm saying that about Mrs. Morgan," he added hastily. "I'm just speaking in general."

"Send out the feed and put it on my bill." Clay turned and stalked out.

"What happened?" Amity asked when she saw the expression on his face.

"It seems Gretchen has been spreading lies all over town."

Amity didn't answer. He glanced at her and saw that she was struggling not to cry. Clay covered her hand with his. She looked at him pleadingly. "It will be all right," he said. It was the first time she had looked to him for comfort, and he was unable to give it. Not in the middle of the main road in town. He slapped the reins on the rump of his horse.

"If I had known Gretchen would spread it all over town, I would have made Hallie come home the morning I found her."

Amity made no comment.

"None of our friends will believe you forced Hallie to move out."

She whipped her head around. "That's what they're saying?"

"Apparently."

Amity looked forward again. "I've been nothing but trouble for you. I should never have come here."

They passed a buggy carrying a couple they knew well from church. The man nodded as if they were strangers and the woman looked away. Clay could feel Amity's distress even though only their elbows were touching.

"I'll go to everyone she is likely to have talked to and tell them the truth."

"Nothing would make us seem more guilty. No, we can't do that."

"I'll go to Gretchen and tell her to undo what she's done."

"That won't work. Do you really think she would comply? Not if her life depended on it."

"Then what can I do?" he demanded.

"We'll have to let the rumors die. As you said, our friends won't believe them."

Clay drove in silence for a while. "I suppose there are times you wish you had never seen me, the girls or Ransom."

"That's true." He felt a painful knot growing inside him until she added, "But I don't feel that way very often."

He glanced at her.

"To be more precise, there are times I wish I had never seen Ransom or Gretchen. I can't say the same for the girls and you."

He wondered what she meant exactly, but he had always been a man of few words and he wasn't sure how to ask her. Finally he said, "Amity, I want you to know that I respect you."

"You what?"

"I respect you. You're a damn fine woman."

"Thank you, Clay. I respect you, as well."

He thought he heard amusement in her voice but didn't see how that could be under the circumstances. He decided he must be mistaken. He knew Elsa had put great store in public opinion, and he didn't see how Amity could be different. If anything, he would have said she was apt to be more distressed by it.

After a while he said, "What are you thinking?"

"I was picturing Aunt Dorcus and Aunt Ophelia and what they would say if they heard I had forced my step-daughter to run away from home."

He grimaced. "What would they say?"

"They would say I'm a wanton hussy."

He looked at her. "Are you smiling?"

"Yes, I think I am. You know, if this had happened in Charlotte, I would have been mortified. I'm certainly not happy about it—don't get me wrong—but I know the truth and so does Hallie. Gretchen can go climb a tree for all I care."

"I didn't expect you to feel this way. Not at all."

"I've had time to think about it. You're right. Our friends will know better, and they won't believe it. We don't need the others. In time Gretchen will show her true colors and she will get her comeuppence. My aunts were very firm on that point. Let's hope they're right."

"I can't believe I'm hearing this. Weren't you about to cry a minute ago?"

"That was before I learned you...respect me." She turned away, but he saw her smile had broadened.

He shook his head. "I can't understand you. I don't think that I ever will."

"I believe that's probably true, Clay," she said with perfect composure.

Chapter Fifteen

Amity was determined to make a quilt for the fall fair. She had always been gifted with a needle and had no doubts that she could make a prizewinner. In Charlotte she had frequently won blue ribbons at the fairs, and she felt the competition in Ransom would be less difficult, since the population was smaller.

After the problems with Hallie over clothing in the attic, she didn't want to use any material she might find there, so she went into town to buy cloth. The crops had turned out to be promising after all, so she had no qualms about spending money on a quilt. She had a pattern in mind, the rather difficult Jacob's Ladder design, and had decided to make it in shades of pink, rose and green, and use it on Rosemary and Laura's bed. She thought of the dozens of quilt patterns she had left behind in Charlotte and wished again she had put more thought into her packing. She had confidence, however, that she could draw the pattern she would need from memory.

She stopped the buggy at the dry goods store and tied the horse to one of the iron rings set into the post. Her thoughts were so involved in the colors she wanted and how much material to buy that she didn't notice Gretchen's buggy was there, as well.

She was halfway to the fabric counters before she saw Hallie talking to a girl about her own age. Amity faltered and looked around. There was Gretchen, buying a bolt of yellow calico. Gretchen happened to look up and see her, so Amity couldn't leave. She nodded coolly, but Gretchen pretended not to see.

Amity had always detested confrontations. Her aunts and her parents before them had taught her that peace was to be preserved at all costs among civilized society and that only the lowest of women ever lost her temper in public. Thus armed, Amity felt Gretchen would be cool toward her, but that there would be no incident. She was soon proved wrong.

"I think it's a perfect scandal," Gretchen said to the clerk, a woman Amity recognized as Mrs. Pearson, "that the girls should be subjected to such treatment. Poor Elsa hasn't been gone a year and already Clay has married."

Amity stiffened but refrained from looking at the women. She couldn't, however, force herself to move away so she wouldn't be able to hear what was being said about her.

"I know," Mrs. Pearson commiserated. "Ollie Jane and I have talked about it for hours on end. I've made my husband promise that if I die he won't remarry. I think that's best for Ollie Jane."

"I quite agree. You know Hallie has already come to live with me. She couldn't take it anymore. She's the one who most resembles poor Elsa, you recall."

"How could I not? Hallie is the spitting image of Elsa at that age. This new wife must feel plain in comparison, I should think. No one could match Elsa."

Amity wondered if Mrs. Pearson had seen her and if she, like Gretchen, was being deliberately rude. Her face was blazing, and she had trouble breathing. After hearing so much, she couldn't simply walk out of the store. If she did, she would never be able to hold her head up in town again. She selected a bolt of pink, another of rose and a green one. Carrying the heavy bolts, she headed straight for the counter.

Mrs. Pearson, who was launching into the evils of stepmothers, hesitated when she recognized Amity. "May I help you?" she asked nervously.

Amity said in a carefully controlled voice, "I need four yards of the green and two each of the pink and rose." She made no effort to acknowledge Gretchen's presence.

Mrs. Pearson hurried to comply even though Gretchen was already waiting for her own cloth to be measured and cut. As she unrolled cloth from the bolt, only the thud of the bolt hitting the wooden counter was heard. The silence was stony and almost palatable.

Hallie glanced at the fabric counter, looked again and nudged the other girl. They edged closer to hear what was about to transpire. Gretchen saw her audience was growing. "I assume you will soon be leaving Ransom," she said to Amity.

Amity turned her cool gaze on the other woman. "I have no idea what you're talking about. Clay and I have no plans of leaving." She saw Gretchen's face redden.

"How much did you say of the green?" Mrs. Pearson asked.

"I said four yards." Amity was careful to keep her voice calm and controlled. The years of training with her aunts was giving her strength.

"It's not as if you two were really married," Gretchen said. "I've heard your marriage hasn't even been consummated."

Amity drew in her breath. One never spoke of such things in public. She turned to Gretchen. "Who told you that?"

Gretchen looked flustered. Apparently, she hadn't expected to be challenged. "It doesn't matter where I heard it. It's all over town."

"Then everyone is mistaken."

"You have separate bedrooms," Gretchen disputed. "I've seen that for myself."

"You've been prying into our private bedrooms? For what reason?" Amity was quaking inside, but she was determined not to show it.

Gretchen looked away first. To Mrs. Pearson she said, "When people eavesdrop on others' conversations, they can expect to hear no good of themselves."

"Mrs. Pearson, I asked for two yards of the pink. You've measured three." Amity was glad to see the saleswoman was visibly rattled. She held to her outward calm as if it were a shield.

"I see you don't even deny having separate bedrooms," Gretchen pressed. She seemed determined to put Amity to rout.

"We did at first. After all, I hardly knew Clay." This wasn't a direct lie, although it implied that they shared a room now. She knew Gretchen hadn't been inside the house lately and wouldn't know if there had been a change.

"You still sleep in the guest room," Hallie put in as she stepped to her aunt's side.

Amity gave her a level look that caused the girl to fidget. She turned away. "In the first place, I wouldn't take a girl's word for what goes on between a husband and wife. In the second, this conversation is entirely out of place. In polite society—" she let her eyes condemn both women "—such subjects are never brought up. That you chose to do so in a public place and in front of two impressionable girls is reprehensible." She looked straight at Gretchen. "I would expect no more from you, but you," she said to Mrs. Pearson, "have just lost yourself a customer. After this, I'll drive to Nacogdoches for any dry goods I may require." She picked up the two lengths of cloth that had already been cut. "Charge this to my husband's account."

As she walked out, her head held high, she could hear the whispers behind her. Tears stung her eyes now that she was leaving but she refused to let them fall. There were things a lady did in public and things a lady did not.

She laid the cloth on the buggy seat, for the first time noticing that she hadn't even had it wrapped. It didn't matter. Nothing mattered but getting away from town and the gossip that was spreading about her. She wished she had another alternative other than driving all the way to Nacogdoches to shop in the future, but she was determined to do just that. It might be three miles farther, but it was worth it not to have such a scene repeat itself.

She felt as if everyone was staring at her as she drove through town, but she was determined not to look and see. She kept her eyes straight ahead and her face stonily composed. There would be time later to let down her guard.

All the way home she thought about Gretchen and what was happening in Ransom. The woman was vicious in her gossip. That she would find Amity's weakest point and attack it was proof of that. Amity knew Hallie had told her aunt things that had happened at home, things that should never have left the house. She could imagine the two of them tearing her and her private life apart, and it made Amity ache inside. She knew Clay wouldn't miss Gretchen, but he loved Hallie, and it must be hard on him to have her feel she couldn't or wouldn't live in his house as long as Amity was there.

Since Hallie had been gone, Amity had tried not to think that thought. She had, however unwittingly it might have been, broken the family apart. Before she had come, the house might have been dirty and the children going wild, but they all had been together under one roof. Now Hallie had moved in with Gretchen, and the younger girls no longer saw their aunt at all, as far as Amity knew.

There was only one thing to do and that was for her to leave. The idea of leaving Clay hurt her more than anything Gretchen might have said about her. She couldn't bear the thought of never seeing him again. But if she stayed, he might, in time, come to blame her for Hallie's absence. Every day she loved him more. If she waited to leave, it would only be harder.

When she reached the house, she sat for a moment looking at it. She had hoped this would be her home forever. Where would she go? There was only one choice. She must return to Charlotte and to her aunts. They might not want to take her in, but she knew they would. That would give her time to think what to do with the rest of her life.

There was no reason to unharness the horse. She would pack and drive to the train station before she could change her mind—before Clay knew what she was doing. Between the two of them, she and Kate could put the trunk in the buggy, and at the station there would be a man to lift it out again.

She hurried into the house and went straight to her room. As she set the quilting material on her bed, she was reminded of how many of her plans had changed since she had left to go buy it. She would still finish it and send it to the girls, along with one for Jemima's and Kate's beds. She might be leaving, but she wouldn't forget the girls. Nor would she ever forget Clay. Through her open door she looked out and across the dining room to Clay's room. She could see the end of his bed and a rectangle of sunlight on the floor. She certainly would never forget Clay.

She opened the lid of the trunk she had brought with her and began taking out the linens she had stored there. Carefully, for her hands were trembling, she started folding her dresses and putting them in the trunk.

"What are you doing?" Kate asked from the door.

"I'm packing."

"Why are you doing that?"

Amity paused and glanced at the girl. Kate's forehead was wrinkled in a worried frown, and she was holding one of the kittens Amity had brought home. "I'm going back to Charlotte. It's best this way."

"Best for who?"

"Whom. It's best for everyone. I'll need your help in lifting the trunk when I'm done."

"Does Papa know about this?"

"You may tell him when he comes in from working." Amity looked back to add that she would miss Kate and her sisters, but the girl had gone. She heard the screen door in the kitchen bang and from the window saw Kate running across the yard. Amity sighed. She would manage to lift the trunk alone, somehow.

Packing was more difficult than she had expected. Not that she had acquired much more to take with her, but because she didn't want to go. She remembered how frightened she had felt when she had last packed this trunk and

how she had thought anything was preferable to staying in
Charlotte and being shamed by what had happened between Emmett and herself. That pain couldn't have been
more difficult to bear than the one she labored under now.
How could she never see Clay or the girls again? Somehow
she had to manage. Amity had always been able to manage.

"What's going on?" she heard Clay say from behind her.

"I thought you were in the fields." She didn't dare turn
to look at him. If she did, she might not have the strength
to leave without breaking into tears.

"Kate, go watch after your sisters," Clay said.

"But, Papa—"

"You heard me. Go on."

Amity heard Kate's reluctant footsteps as the girl left to
do as she had been told. She finally faced Clay. He looked
as upset as she felt.

"Why are you doing this?"

"I have to. If I'm gone, Hallie will come back to you. All
the talk about us in town will stop."

He saw the material on the bed. "You've been to town?"

She nodded. "I had the misfortune to run into Gretchen
in Pearson's dry goods."

He muttered a curse. "What did she say to you?"

"Not much directly. It was what I overheard her saying
to Mrs. Pearson that made me realize that I can't stay. My
being here is not fair to you and the girls, and it's certainly
not fair to Hallie. I had no intention of driving her from her
home."

"You didn't drive her away. Hallie is behaving like a
spoiled brat."

"You would never have called her that before I came."
She turned to the bed and began folding her starched
blouses.

"Damn it, Amity, stop doing that." He came to her and
took the blouse from her hands and tossed it onto the bed.
"What did Gretchen say?"

"She was telling Mrs. Pearson that we aren't really married because our marriage hasn't been consummated."

"She said that? In a store?" He stared at her. "But we have consummated it."

"That's exactly what I told her. Then I told her that it was none of her business and that she was no lady to be discussing such a thing in public."

"I can just hear you saying that. Amity, I thought you weren't going to let the talk bother you."

"I thought I could stand it, but I can't." She looked at him with tears in her eyes. "It's true that we have no real marriage. I sleep in here and you sleep in there." She gestured toward the door. "It's not what I want."

He frowned. "Neither do I."

"You don't?"

"I thought it was your idea."

"Why would you think a thing like that?"

He ran his fingers through his hair. "When you didn't move your things into my room, what else was I to think?"

"Did you believe for one minute that I would barge in without being asked?" She stared at him in disbelief.

"Why would you need to be asked after what happened that night? I thought you wanted to stay in here."

Amity didn't know what to say. She opened her mouth, but no words came out.

"I don't want you to go."

She turned away. "You miss Hallie. I know you do. This will fix everything."

"No, it won't. Yes, I miss Hallie all the time, but I would miss you, too. Hallie left to make a point. Are you doing the same?"

"No," she said after thinking a minute. "I'm leaving because I don't want you to be unhappy."

"Aren't you listening to me? I love you. If you're gone, I'll miss you even more than I miss Hallie."

She stopped and her hands remained frozen in the act of folding a blouse. "What? What did you say?"

"I said I'll miss you more than I miss Hallie."

"Before that."

He hesitated. "I said I love you."

She turned and looked at him. His face held pain and concern but also sincerity. "You love me?"

He heard a sound behind him and turned to frown at the row of girls who had crept up behind him in the dining room. "What are you all doing here?"

"Kate said Amity is leaving," Laura answered.

"We don't want her to go." Rosemary put her thumb in her mouth and her eyes were sad.

"We came to stop her," Jemima added. Kate nodded.

Clay took Rosemary's thumb out of her mouth. "You girls run along. Let me talk to Amity in private."

"You might not be able to stop her," Jemima objected.

"Go sit in the buggy," he advised. "That way you'll know she didn't leave."

The girls hurried out to do as he asked. Clay watched them with a wry smile. "It's hard to court a woman when you have so many chaperons."

"Court me?"

"Amity, I've tried for weeks to make it clear to you how I feel about you. What about the china dishes and the parlor curtains? What about all the times I've been around to carry pots of wash water for you or to drive you into town? Haven't you noticed any of these things?"

"I didn't know they weren't things you always did. How was I to know?" She added in a softer voice, "The china and curtains were a lovely gesture, but I was afraid at the time that you just did it to keep my hands off Elsa's things."

"Why didn't you ask? I would have told you that wasn't it."

"Why didn't you tell me without having to be asked?" she countered. "I didn't want to start the argument all over again."

He stepped nearer and put his hands on her arms. "I bought them for you because I wanted this to be your home. Elsa is gone. You're my wife now and I want you to be happy. I know you don't love me, but in time, if you give me a chance, you may learn to love me.''

"I do love you. That's why I'm leaving."

"Say that again? You're leaving because you love me?"

"I have to. Don't I?"

Clay picked up the trunk and carried it across the dining room. As Amity watched, he turned it upside down, dumping the contents on his bed, and went back to her room. "Put the rest of your things in it. You're moving into my room."

"What?"

"There's entirely too much distance between this room and mine. We can't talk during the day for all the little ears around here. You've made it clear you won't come to me. We're moving in together."

Amity felt a smile beginning on her lips. "That's the way you want it?"

"Yes, it is. Do you have any objections?"

"Not a one."

His eyes caressed her face as if he was memorizing it. "Do you really love me?"

She nodded. "How can you even ask?"

"Well, for one thing, you were packing to leave me."

"That was before I found out you loved me."

"You won't leave the minute I turn my back?"

"Now that I know you love me, you couldn't get rid of me if you tried."

"Good. I don't plan to try. Together we can weather all this talk. It won't last forever."

"I lied to Gretchen. I told her that we shared a room."

He smiled. "You did?"

"I sank to her level. That's been bothering me."

"It needn't. Besides, now it's true."

Amity smiled at him. "If I had known you were trying to court me, I would have been more receptive. I've never been courted by a man. I didn't recognize it."

"The men in Charlotte must be blind."

Amity blushed. She wished she could believe it. Still, it was nice to hear Clay say that he found her attractive. "I have a confession. Sometimes at night I pretend that I'm pretty and that you have chosen me from a whole room of other women. I suppose that sounds silly."

"Amity, come here." He led her to the mirror. "Look in there. What do you see?"

She gazed at her reflection. "I see a woman past the prime of her youth, red hair and eyes that are too large."

"I see a beautiful woman."

Her eyes met his in the mirror. "Don't press your luck. I'm willing to believe you care for me, but I can't believe that I'm pretty, as well."

"You seem to be deaf on top of it all. I said beautiful, not pretty, and I said I love you, not that I merely care for you."

"You were trying to make me stay."

"Amity, you could try the patience of a saint." He turned her to face him. "Why can't you believe what I say I feel?"

"Because I know how I look and that you couldn't love me. Not after what I've told you about Emmett Hamilton. I'm still surprised you didn't send me packing then. Wouldn't Gretchen have a field day if she knew about that?"

"She will never know unless you tell her. You were forced. No woman is to blame for being raped."

"You said that before. My aunts wouldn't agree with you." She looked at him doubtfully. "It must have been my fault. I led him on. I agreed to ride in the country with him."

"That's right. You agreed to go for a ride. That's not the same as leading him on. Even if you did, he had no right to force himself on you. No man has that right."

Slowly Amity felt her eyes fill with tears. She had felt so guilty for so long that she was overwhelmed by Clay's words. "You don't feel I'm tainted?"

"Don't you ever let me hear you say something like that again!" He frowned at her. "I love you. Can't you get that through that stubborn head of yours?"

"Clay," she whispered. "Will you kiss me?"

He bent his head and she stood on tiptoes to meet his lips. Her lips parted under his, and she threw her arms around him. Clay held her so close she couldn't breathe and didn't want to if it meant having to pull away from him. When he left her lips to kiss her cheek and temple and ear, she said, "I love you. I love you so much I ache all over."

"Is it the girls' bedtime yet?" he murmured as he kissed her neck.

"At three in the afternoon? Hardly."

They parted enough to smile at each other. "I think you need to go with me to the stream. There's something I want to show you."

"Now?"

"Right now."

Amity put her hand in his and they left the house. As they passed the yard he waved at his daughters, who were still sitting in the buggy. "We'll be back in a little while," Clay called out.

"Where are you going?" Rosemary asked.

"I want to show Amity the swimming hole."

Rosemary turned to Laura. "Why would he want to do that?" Laura shrugged as if she had no idea why grown-ups did half the things they did.

Amity was laughing as they crossed the feed lot and pasture and headed toward the woods. "Clay, what will they think?"

"They will be so glad to hear you're staying I doubt they will question it at all."

"Is there a swimming hole?"

"Sure there is. I found it right after I bought this place." He glanced at her. "I've never taken anybody down here. Elsa was uncomfortable in the woods and didn't know how to swim."

She knew what he meant, and her heart grew lighter. At last there was something she didn't have to share with Elsa. "I can't swim, either."

"I'll teach you, if you'd like."

"You'd do that?" She was feeling younger than she had in years. "But I'm too old and I don't have a bathing costume."

He grinned. "Neither do I."

They went into the woods, and he led her through the trees and along a cow path that eventually ended at the creek. Here the water was wider than at the crossing to Gretchen's, and it looked deep and cool. A lazy green fly buzzed past her ear, and she could see the pale outline of fish in the depths. Emerald moss studded with tiny white flowers carpeted the banks, and hairlike grass drooped over the water. "What a pretty place!" she exclaimed.

He drew her into his arms. "You don't want to learn how to swim right now, do you?"

"It can wait. Will the girls follow us?"

"No. Even if they did, we could hear them coming through the woods. See? If we are here on the moss, we are out of sight of the path."

"How long have you been planning this?"

"Ever since that night we made love. I knew we would need a place to be alone at times, and I've been on the lookout for the best spot."

"And you never brought Elsa here?" she asked.

"Not once. This is our place and no one else's. I thought that might be important to you."

"You'll never know how very important."

He began unbuttoning her blouse and Amity loosened her cuffs before starting on his shirt. "You know this is shameful," she said with a smile. "My aunts would be mortified."

"Good. Being shameful can be a lot of fun." He opened her blouse and kissed the soft flesh beside her camisole strap. He ran his tongue over her. "I love the way you taste." His voice was low and deepening with passion.

Amity experimentally ran the tip of her tongue over the hollow in his throat where his pulse beat. "You taste good, too." She caught a nip of his skin between her lips. Clay pulled her closer.

While he spread her skirt on the moss, Amity glanced around to be sure they were alone. She had never been outside wearing only her chemise and bloomers in her entire life, and it felt daring and exciting. He sat on her skirt and pulled her down beside him. The moss pillowed them from the harder ground. Above Clay's head she could see sunspangled leaves and blue sky. "I could learn to like being shameful," she said softly.

"I'm glad to hear it." He paused and said, "I was afraid that you didn't come to my room because you didn't enjoy making love with me." He waited to see what she would say.

"Not enjoy it? It was like a visit to heaven!" She looked at him. "You really worried about that? How could I not have enjoyed it?" It had never occurred to her that he might have thought that. "You're a wonderful lover. It's not just because I love you."

He grinned as if he had hoped she would say that. "Amity, girl, I do love you."

She laughed. When he looked at her in that special way, she felt like springtime. She laced her fingers in his hair and drew his mouth down to her lips.

Clay moved his hand over her breasts, teasing the nipples beneath the thin fabric. Amity murmured in delight. She had never thought it could feel so good to be touched. After he pulled the straps of her chemise from her shoulders, she untied the ribbon to let the garment fall away.

"I love to look at you," he said as he lifted his head to gaze at her pale skin. "Making love outside in the daylight may be my downfall. I may want to do this all the time instead of working in the fields."

"It could be arranged," she said. "I might start bringing your dinner out to you from time to time."

"You'd want to do that?"

She nodded. "See how decadent I may become?"

"I love it." He kissed her with all the passion in his heart. Amity responded in kind.

"Thank you, Clay," she whispered.

"For what?"

"For not letting me make the biggest mistake of my life."

He looked deep into her eyes. "Promise me you'll never leave me, Amity. Promise me that."

"I'll never leave you. I promise."

She gave herself over to his lovemaking as the dappled sunlight spangled their bodies.

Chapter Sixteen

Fiona left her horse and buggy at the fence and went up to knock on Gretchen's door. She felt out of place here and uneasy. She and Gretchen were on speaking terms but they had never been friends.

The door opened and Gretchen's face registered surprise at seeing Fiona there. "Come in," she said automatically, then looked as if she might have regretted it.

"Thank you." Fiona stepped into the parlor and removed the light blanket from her baby's face that she had used to protect her daughter's tender skin.

Gretchen glanced at the baby. "She's growing. She must be how old now?"

"Two months, almost three."

"The summer's going by so fast." Gretchen motioned at a chair.

Fiona sat and propped little Adeline in the curve of her arm. The baby looked about with solemn infant interest. "Is Hallie here?"

"No, she has gone to see Ollie Jane Pearson. I don't expect her back for several hours."

"That's just as well. It's Hallie I've come to discuss."

"Oh?" Gretchen drew herself up and wrapped coolness about her like a shield.

"Clay and Amity miss her so much," Fiona said earnestly. "Clay was over to see Sean yesterday, and Hallie was all he could talk about. Don't you think it would be in everyone's best interest if you sent her home?''

"Absolutely not! You have no idea what you're asking!''

"What do you mean? Hallie isn't your daughter. She belongs with her parents.'' Fiona had always believed that a straight line was the quickest way to get to a point.

"Hallie no longer has *parents*. Her mother, my sister, is dead. Amity is nothing to Hallie and never will be.''

"Amity has tried every way she knows to be kind to Hallie and to win her affection.''

"That's all very well and good to say, but I know differently. If you could hear the stories Hallie has told me about what happens when Clay isn't around, it would turn your hair white!''

"I don't believe it,'' Fiona stated flatly. "I know Amity quite well, and she wouldn't be unkind to anyone, let alone to a child. If Hallie told you anything else, she's stretching the truth.'' She caught herself before calling Hallie an outright liar. This was, after all, Hallie's aunt. "She may have misunderstood Amity's meaning.''

"My niece is not given to lying,'' Gretchen said frostily.

Fiona tried to soften the mood. She would do no good by alienating Gretchen further. "Sometimes a girl Hallie's age reads more into something said than is meant. My Brian has been known to do the same thing. At that age, anything at all can offend them or make them angry. At times I think Brian will explode if he didn't have his chores to help him work off the steam.''

"How you work your son is no concern of mine. Hallie, however, is of finer stock. She isn't accustomed to working like a hired girl.''

Fiona pulled back at the insult. "I think it's wrong for you to encourage Hallie to stay here. She ought to be at home where she belongs.''

"This is now her home. She came here of her own free will, and I'll not send her back to a stepmother she hates. If you'll excuse me, I have other things to do." Gretchen stood and waited for Fiona to leave.

Her cheeks blazing, Fiona went to the door. "I made a mistake in coming here. I thought I could reason with you, but now I see it's impossible."

"Good day, Mrs. O'Flannery."

As Fiona went down the porch steps, she drew the protecting blanket over Adeline's face. She had rarely been so angry. She heard the door slam behind her, but she felt Gretchen's baleful stare from the window. Fiona didn't look back.

Gretchen was still angry when Fiona's buggy drove out of sight. She was furious at the woman's gall. Imagine a woman, and one of immigrant stock, at that, having the nerve to imply *she* was doing something wrong. Gretchen was so angry she trembled. She called out to her hired girl and told her to have Jake hitch the horse to the buggy. Gretchen went to her room and prepared to go to town.

All during the drive she fumed. She could imagine Amity and Fiona with their heads together planning how next to spoil her chances of keeping Hallie. Thank goodness, she thought, the girl was gone when Fiona came over. It wouldn't do to have Hallie hear that her father missed her so much. Gretchen had convinced her that Clay was glad to be rid of her.

She drove to the parsonage and tapped imperiously on the door. It was opened by the parson himself. "Mrs. Harris, come in," he said. "To what do I owe this privilege?"

"I know I shouldn't have dropped by without warning," she said in her most charming voice, "but it's so difficult for me, living in the country as I do."

"I understand. Surely there mustn't be impediments if you're in need of my services. I assume there is a need?" he asked doubtfully.

Gretchen nodded. She had never liked Brother Crowe or his wife. They were what her mother used to refer to as country-come-to-town. "I'm here about my niece, Hallie Morgan."

"Ah, yes. Hallie. She's growing into a beautiful young woman. She's the image of her mother, isn't she?"

"Indeed she is," Gretchen said with as much pride as if she was entirely responsible for the resemblance. "She has always been my favorite niece for that very reason."

Brother Crowe smiled and nodded. When Gretchen didn't follow up, he asked, "She's well, I assume? I saw Clay only this morning, and he didn't mention her ailing."

"As if he would know." Gretchen shook her head. "It's terrible and I hesitate to mention it to a man of your profession who must necessarily think well of everyone, but all is not right in our family."

"Oh?"

"You see, Hallie has lived with me for almost a month. She is unable to live with her father because of her stepmother. I needn't tell you how things can be with stepmothers, I'm sure."

"I know Amity Morgan, and I have never seen her raise her voice to any of the children." Brother Crowe's forehead furrowed. "You say Hallie doesn't like her?"

"It's more than that. She detests Amity and will not stay under the same roof with her. Amity may put a pretty face forward at church, but we in the family know a different side of her."

"Dear me. What would you like me to do? I could drive out and have a talk with her."

"That would do no good. A talking to can't change a leopard's spots." She rather liked that simile. "No, Hallie will refuse to go home as long as Amity is there. That's why I want to adopt her."

"Adopt Hallie? She's already your niece. Why is it necessary to adopt her? That's highly unusual."

"I suppose, but as you know, Hall and I were never able to have children, and it would please me so much to have Hallie as a daughter. You have children, and you must know they are not the same as your nieces and nephews."

"True," Brother Crowe said slowly. "But what of her father? Clay never mentioned a word of this to me."

"He hasn't been approached yet. I told Hallie it would be best to keep it among ourselves for the time being. I wanted to find out how to go about the adoption proceedings before I stir up the hornet's nest, so to speak."

"He will object, then?"

"Not Clay. He knows how I love Hallie. It's Amity I was referring to. She will resist my efforts and will no doubt convince Clay to do likewise. She would do anything to keep Hallie and me unhappy."

"That doesn't sound like the Amity I know. Surely you should have discussed this with Hallie's father before coming to me. He may have strong objections of his own. I know how fond he is of all his daughters."

"That woman is turning him against his children, just as she has turned him against me. You know I've always regarded him as a dear brother. Ever since Elsa married him we've been as close as any family can be. Now he never comes to visit me, and we have long since abandoned our customary Sunday dinners together. Every Sunday for as long as I can remember, my family has gathered at that house for Sunday dinner. Thank goodness my parents didn't live to see this day." Gretchen pressed her handkerchief to the corners of her eyes as if she were crying.

"Perhaps it's not Amity who's to blame," Brother Crowe said in a placating voice. "Clay has a new wife, and therefore new interests. It's a shame that you have grown apart, but at times these things happen. I can't believe Amity would pull her family away for the purpose of being mean."

"It's not her family," Gretchen snapped. Immediately she lowered her eyes and said, "I'm sorry. I never should have spoken to you like that. You can see the state I'm in. I've worried over this for months. Ever since Amity set foot in Ransom, she has been nothing but trouble in my family."

Brother Crowe seemed to be deep in thought.

"Isn't it possible for me to adopt Hallie?" she pressed.

"Oh, yes. Yes, it's possible. The law would allow it. Assuming, of course, that her father agrees."

"How would I go about arranging it?"

"First you must discuss it with Clay. Then you both should go see a lawyer, who will in turn draw up the papers and take them to the court."

"Amity will balk at it, I know she will. Is there no way around her knowing about it?"

"None that I know of. She is, after all, Hallie's step-mother and Clay's wife."

Gretchen clenched her teeth to keep from telling Brother Crowe what she really thought of him. Surely there had to be some way of taking Hallie without Clay's permission. After a moment she said, "What if the girl's welfare is at stake? What if she would be in danger of bodily harm if she was to return there?"

"In a case such as that, I assume the court would award custody to a safe party. I'm no lawyer, Mrs. Harris. You would have to ask a lawyer that. But in this case, it doesn't apply. Even if Amity were a monster, which she is not, she and Clay would have to be informed of the proceedings. I'm quite sure you can't adopt Hallie without their knowledge. It wouldn't be right, even if it were possible. Clay loves that girl, and he wouldn't let anyone harm her. What are you implying?"

"Never mind. I've taken enough of your time." She had hoped by now to have convinced the parson that Hallie would be safe only in her own keeping and that Amity was the worst of women. She was wasting time here.

"I'll speak to Clay if you like," Brother Crowe said as he showed Gretchen to the door.

"Please. That would be of great help." She knew it wouldn't be, but at least it would let Clay know that she intended to have Hallie one way or another and that she was not to be underestimated.

Clay opened the door, surprised to find Brother Crowe on the porch. "Come in. Amity, look who's here!" he called toward the dining room.

Amity came around the corner, saw the pastor and quickly took off her apron. "Brother Crowe, how nice to see you. Come in and have a seat." She tossed the apron around the corner onto a dining room chair. She touched her hair to be sure it wasn't coming loose from the pins. "I had no idea you would be coming out. You'll stay for supper, won't you? We have a ham," she said with a smile. She knew he was partial to ham.

"No, thank you. Not tonight. My wife was making supper when I left the house. Perhaps another time."

Amity sat down so the men could be seated. Rosemary came in, smiled shyly at the preacher and climbed into Amity's lap. Amity automatically put her arms around the child. Brother Crowe was watching her closely. Amity glanced down to see if all her buttons were properly fastened. "Is someone sick out this way?" She couldn't think why he would be here unless he was stopping by on another errand.

"No, thank goodness. I know of no parishioners who are ailing. The summer is almost over now. If our luck holds, there will be no yellow jack outbreak this year." To Amity he explained, "It's our worst threat in the summer. I've seen epidemics that carry away dozens of people in a week's time."

"I've had it, I'm happy to say," Amity told him. "I was exposed to it when I was a child. At least that's what I was told, though the symptoms I remember don't seem to necessarily be the same as the ones for yellow fever."

"What does bring you out this way?" Clay asked. "Not that you aren't always welcome."

"I had a talk with Mrs. Harris this afternoon." He waited to see what would be said.

Clay and Amity exchanged a glance. Amity felt an uneasiness stirring in her. "What did Gretchen have to say that would bring you out here?"

Brother Crowe smiled as if it were nothing. "She had a rather unusual proposition in mind. She would like to adopt Hallie."

Clay's mouth dropped open. Amity tightened her grip on Rosemary. "She can't do that!"

"No. It's entirely out of the question," Clay said firmly. "She actually said that? She wants to adopt one of my children? It's one thing for Hallie to be staying there temporarily, but another entirely for her to be adopted by Gretchen."

"I thought you would see it that way," Brother Crowe said. "That's why I wanted to speak to you. Why is Hallie there in the first place?"

Amity hugged Rosemary and said, "I think you should run and play so we can talk, honey."

Rosemary frowned and snuggled closer. "I'm not making any noise."

"Rosemary, go play," Clay said firmly. The little girl reluctantly did as he said. Clay shut the parlor door behind her. "Now, what's this all about?"

"Mrs. Harris seems to think there's bad blood between Amity and Hallie, and that it's in the girl's best interest for her to be adopted."

Amity felt the blood drain from her face. It took all her strength to remain composed. "Gretchen is exaggerating. Hallie and I have our problems, but it's nothing that would necessitate her leaving us."

"Hallie has taken the loss of her mother harder than the others," Clay said as he moved to Amity's chair and rested his hand on her shoulder. "Amity has been kind to the girl. Hallie simply won't accept her."

"Mrs. Harris seems to feel otherwise. I had the impression that she was going to speak to a lawyer, then I assume she will be over to talk to you."

Amity was glad Clay's hand was there to give her courage. She covered it with her own. "I wish I could say I'm surprised, but Gretchen has done everything in her power to cause trouble since the first day she knew I was here. I just never expected anything like this." She found it difficult to believe that Gretchen would make their troubles public. That simply wasn't done in her aunts' house. "She can't take Hallie, can she?"

"No, not unless she can prove you've been mistreating her."

Clay frowned. "Hallie has never been mistreated in her life! Did she say that?"

"Hallie wasn't with Mrs. Harris. I assume she knows about the adoption, however. It would seem odd for Mrs. Harris to assume that Hallie would agree to it unless they had discussed it. At Hallie's age, the judge would most likely ask her opinion on the subject before awarding custody elsewhere."

"I'm going after her," Clay said decisively. "Hallie isn't staying with that woman another night. She's coming home where she belongs."

Amity nodded. "We've been lenient with her, but this is getting out of hand. It's time for her to come home."

Brother Crowe nodded his agreement. "I thought you'd see it that way. I might suggest, however, that you wait until tomorrow. It's already nearing dusk, and I assume that Hallie will have to pack before she can be ready to move back. It would be best done in daylight. That way it will seem less as if you're tearing her from her aunt. I've found it's best to minimize conflict whenever one can."

Clay didn't look convinced. Amity took his hand. "Brother Crowe is right. If you go over there as angry as you are, there will be a terrible scene. It's best that you wait until morning."

Reluctantly Clay nodded. "I suppose one more night won't make a difference."

"If I may ask, what exactly is the problem between the two of you?" Brother Crowe asked Amity.

"I'm not Elsa," she answered simply.

He nodded. "I thought that might be all there was to it. I remember when my daughter was that age. They can be a handful." He stood to leave.

"Thank you for telling us what is going on," Clay said as they saw the parson to the door. "I had no idea it had come to this point."

Brother Crowe smiled at Amity. "It's hard to step into another woman's shoes. Especially one like Elsa. I know it can't have been easy for you."

Amity put her hand in Clay's. "The other children are happy. It's just Hallie who won't accept me."

"Have her come to see me. We'll talk." He nodded to Clay and started down the steps.

Amity closed the door. "I can hardly believe it. Gretchen must be insane to go to such lengths. Imagine her thinking we would agree to give up Hallie!"

"Are you sure you feel that way? Hallie has been nothing but trouble to you since you came here."

"Hallie is just a child. I can't hold it against her. Of course I want her back."

Clay embraced her and Amity put her arms around him. Lately he had taken to embracing her quite often whether they were in their bedroom or not. At first it had seemed lascivious. Now it felt perfectly right. Clay was a loving man, and he had no compunction about hugging anyone he loved, wherever they might be.

"Fiona was here today. She went to speak to Gretchen," Amity said. "I was going to tell you when the girls were in bed, but I think you need to know it now. She said Gretchen was terribly upset with her."

"Fiona went to Gretchen? Did you know she was going to do that? They've never been friends."

"No, I had no idea. You know how Fiona is. She's such a good friend that she tries to take care of all of us. Gretchen apparently said some rather strong words to her."

"That could be what started this snowballing. Do you suppose Hallie is in agreement with Gretchen?"

Amity shook her head even though she wasn't at all sure. "Hallie would never want to be taken away from you."

"Wouldn't she? She left of her own will and has refused to come back."

"She won't come back as long as I'm here, you mean."

Clay drew away and looked at her. "There won't be any more talk of you leaving."

"No, there won't be," she said with a smile, deciding the time would never be better for her to reveal her great news. "There was something else I was going to tell you tonight,

but I've decided not to wait. We're going to have a baby."
She expected him to be delighted. Instead he moved away.

"A baby?" Deep concern lined his face. "We're going to
have a baby?"

"Aren't you happy?" she asked uncertainly. "I thought
you'd be glad."

He pulled her close and this time his embrace was so
strong it made breathing difficult.

"Clay?" she asked. "What is it?"

"I'm such a fool. I was so wrapped up in loving you that
I never thought about getting you pregnant."

She wasn't accustomed to a man using such a blunt word,
but she had come to expect directness from Clay. "You
don't want this baby?" she asked in a hurt voice.

He looked into her eyes. "Not want it? Not want your
baby? How can you even ask such a thing? Of course I will
love any baby of ours."

"Then what's wrong?"

"I'm afraid for you."

She saw the fright in his eyes, and she smiled. "Clay,
women have babies all the time. I'll be fine."

"You don't know that." He pulled her against him as if
his strength could protect her. "I couldn't bear it if I lost
you."

She kept her head against his chest so he could not see
that she was worried, too. She had never had a baby, and the
memory of the pain Fiona had been in when Adeline was
born was still fresh in her mind. And he had lost Elsa
through childbirth. "I'll be fine, really." She smiled at him.
"Maybe this time it will be a boy."

He couldn't be teased out of his worry. "When will it be
born? It can't be anytime soon. We've only been sleeping
together a few weeks. Maybe you're mistaken."

"I think it must have been started the first time we made
love. And yes, I'm sure. I wouldn't have told you otherwise." She hugged him. "Please, Clay. Be happy."

He cupped her chin and gazed into her eyes. "I love you,
Amity. And I'll love our baby."

She turned her head to kiss his hand, then looked at him. "I hope she looks like you."

"See? You think it will be a girl, too." He finally smiled.

"It was only habit. I can't imagine a boy in this house."

"I hope she looks like you. I've always fancied having a redheaded girl."

"My hair isn't all that red," she said with a grin. He liked to tease her about her hair now that she knew he didn't mean any of it. "But it's possible. My father had hair the same color as Fiona and her brood."

"Do you feel all right? You haven't been sick."

"Not a time. I asked Fiona today, and she said she wasn't always sick, either."

"Elsa was every time. She was sick the whole nine months with Hallie and Laura."

"Maybe its a sign that I'll have an easy time of it."

"You're not afraid?" he asked. "Tell me the truth now."

After a minute she nodded. "I'm frightened a bit. I've never had a baby, and I don't know how it will be. But I want to give you a baby. One of our own. One that's just ours together. Is that selfish?"

"No. I want that, too."

"Then I'll truly be your wife."

"You already are. You'd be my wife if we never had a child, and you know it."

She smiled. In the last few weeks she had come to accept his love and the security it brought her. "I know. But this will be even better for us, won't it?"

"We'll have to think of the perfect name. Do you want to name it after your aunts?"

"Absolutely not. Can you imagine calling a tiny baby Dorcus or Ophelia? Besides, they still haven't written me a single letter. I think I'm out of the family."

"That's fine with me. I don't think they took such good care of you anyway. You didn't seem happy to me when you first came here."

"Happy? I was scared half to death! I didn't know what I would find or what you'd be like. You and your *two* children."

"I love you, Amity. I'm glad you stayed."

"So am I." She smiled at him. "We could name the baby after your mother. Or have you done that already? I don't know what her name was. You never talk about her or your father."

"We won't name the baby after her." He drew back. "My childhood was a nightmare. My father died or left when I was too little to remember him. I'm not sure which it was. My stepfather was worse than any man you'll ever be likely to meet. I guess he's still living, but I don't know that for sure. As soon as I was old enough to make it on my own, I ran away. I've never been back since."

Amity put her hand on his arm. "They were cruel to you?"

He smiled without mirth. "Yes. It was a hard time for me. That's why I never spank my children. Maybe I was wrong in that. Maybe Hallie would be here today if I had been sterner."

"I don't think so. Hallie will come around quicker with kindness. Who wouldn't?"

He stroked her cheek and neck. "You've been so good to me and to the girls."

"I love you all. You're my family."

"You don't miss your aunts and whatever cousins you may have?"

"I don't have any close cousins. My aunts weren't loving people. I'm sure they must have been relieved to be rid of me, though they would never admit it out loud. It bothers me at times, but I've not been surprised. Not really."

"We have that in common. Neither of us has a family. At least not one we claim."

"Yes, we do. We made our own family. And now it's about to increase."

Clay counted on his fingers. "I figure she will be here in about mid to late April."

"That's my guess. Springtime will be such a lovely time to have a baby, won't it?"

"Yes, it will. You make it sound like you're planning a picnic."

"There's nothing to be gained by worrying about it."

"The girls will be excited."

"You'll tell them? I thought we were supposed to hide the fact until the baby just one day arrived."

"Kate and Jemima are old enough to know what's going on. I think we should tell them and let them get used to the idea. They may be concerned about it, too. I want them to be able to ask questions if they need to."

"I hope I have the answers." She smiled at him. "I'm glad you're the way you are."

"How is that?"

"You're so direct. You don't shilly-shally around. If there's something that should be said, you come right out with it."

"We might have had fewer arguments if I didn't," he said teasingly.

"True, but I'm getting used to it."

"When will we tell them?"

"Let's wait until after supper when we're all in the parlor. Otherwise Rosemary and Laura may not eat."

"I agree. Amity, I'm really happy we're going to have a baby. Don't think I'm not. I'm just worried about you."

"I'll be fine. I come from pioneer stock. I can have this baby and be out in the fields an hour later." She laughed until he smiled. "I really will be all right. Fiona says she doesn't think I have a thing to worry about. My hips are wide enough, according to her, and I'm in perfect health. Don't worry."

"I won't."

She knew he wasn't being entirely honest. She looped her arm about his waist and they went toward the dining room.

Chapter Seventeen

"Look out there," Clay said in disgust. "That red cow is in the hay lot again."

Amity looked past him toward the field nearest the house, where a cow with a white face was calmly grazing in high grass. "The fence must be down again."

He nodded. "I had wanted to go after Hallie early today. Now it will have to wait or we'll lose part of the hay crop."

"I could go."

"She won't come back with you. Besides, I intend to tell Gretchen some home truths about how I feel about her interfering with my family."

"My coming here has caused you a lot of trouble." Amity put her hand on his arm.

Clay covered it with his own. "You're worth it." He grinned and winked at her.

Amity blushed, but it was with pleasure. These days she was happy more than seemed possible. She remembered her aunts' dire warnings against being too happy. "My aunts used to tell me that if a person was too happy, the angels became jealous and trouble was sure to follow."

"I'm glad I never met your aunts."

"That makes two of us. You'd set them back a notch or two."

He looked at the cow. "I have to fix the fence before I go get Hallie," he repeated. "That could take most of the morning."

"I'll fix a roast the way she likes it for supper. Maybe that will put her in a better mood. And a peach pie. She always likes that."

"You're a good mother to the girls, Amity. Don't start believing what Gretchen is saying about you."

She smiled at him. "Thank you, Clay. Now you'd better get busy on that fence or it may take all day."

When she was alone in the kitchen, she looked about with pride. Under her care it was spotless, as were all the other rooms in the house. It was a far cry from the mess it had been when she had first seen it. She laughed at the way it had looked, now that it was no longer as bad. For a while she had thought she might not ever be able to scrub it hard enough and long enough to be satisfied.

She hung her apron on the peg behind the door and went to find Rosemary. The flowers would soon be gone, and the child loved picking them for the table. She tried to think of some other chore that would give the girl something to do until the spring flowers arrived.

From the parlor she could hear Jemima playing the piano. The lessons were bringing the girl's talent to life and already her voice showed promise of being unusual in its range and clarity. She glanced out the window and saw Kate following Clay from the barn and carrying some of his tools for repairing the fence. It was almost a shame Kate hadn't been a son, Amity thought. The girl loved being outdoors and was good with animals. She wondered what Kate would be like when she was a grown woman and whether she would ever be better at cooking than at riding a horse.

Amity dusted the oak sideboard in the dining room and ran her fingers along the glossy finish. She loved her home. It wasn't as expensively furnished as her aunts' house, but it was a house filled with love. With a glance at the neatly made bed in the room she shared with Clay, she smiled. It was filled with love, indeed.

When she first heard the rap on the door, she thought she must be mistaken. No one would come to the kitchen door. At the second knock she went to see who it could be.

Libby, the girl who worked for Gretchen, was backing into the yard to keep space between them.

"Libby? Is that you?" Amity opened the door to come out.

"Don't come near me, Mrs. Morgan. I'm real sick."

Cold dread began to crawl in Amity's middle. "What do you mean you're sick?"

"I was feeling real poorly yesterday and so was Pa. I didn't say nothing to Mrs. Harris about it, but today I was took real bad. Pa was too sick to come to work at all. This morning when I made breakfast, Mrs. Harris and Hallie were too sick to eat a thing."

"How are you sick? Tell me." Amity drew herself up and waited impatiently.

"It come on me quick. At first I just felt dizzy and was sore all over like I had worked too hard. Then about dinnertime I got to feeling sick to my stomach and so cold I was shivering." Libby shivered now. Amity could see her trembling all the way across the yard. "Today I feel sicker than I ever have in my life."

Amity came down the steps toward her and Libby backed away. "Stand still. Let me look at you."

Libby did as she was told. "I don't want to pass it on to your young 'uns. I've heard it can happen if a person breathes the same air as a sick person, but Pa says that's superstition."

Amity made no comment. The girl's skin was flushed and the whites of her eyes were bloodshot. She felt hot to the touch and shivered again when Amity touched her forehead. "Stick out your tongue." It was white, edged with red. Amity turned away. "Let me get my things."

"I come to see if I could borrow some cornmeal and flour. I was to go into town today, but I can't make it and we don't have nothing to cook with."

"I'll bring meal and flour with me. Go to the shed and get out the wheelbarrow. I don't want to take time to harness the horse."

She went into the bedroom and began tossing two changes of clothing into a bag she used to sort clothes. The trunk was too heavy to take. She took care not to touch anything except what she was carrying with her. When she was in the kitchen and pulling a sack of cornmeal from the shelf, Jemima came in. "Stay back," Amity said sharply.

Jemima stopped short. "What's wrong?"

"There's sickness at Gretchen's and I'm going over to tend to them. Tell your father where I've gone and that he's to stay away and keep you girls away." She paused, fearful of even saying the words. "I think it's yellow fever."

"Yellow jack?" Jemima whispered. Her eyes grew larger. "Is Hallie sick?"

"I'm going to find out as soon as I get there. If she is, I'll take care of her until she's well, then I'll be home."

"You could catch it, too!" She came a step closer.

"Stay back! I've been near Libby in the yard and I don't want you to catch it. I think I had it as a baby and it's one of those things you only have once. I think." She pulled out a bag of flour and pulled both sacks across the floor. They were too heavy to carry.

Jemima followed her to the door and stared at Libby. Amity wrestled the bags onto the wheelbarrow and put her sack of clothing on top. To Jemima she said, "Can you remember to tell your father all I said?"

"Yes, ma'am."

Amity paused to smile at her. "I love you, Jemima," she said. "Tell the others goodbye for me."

Jemima nodded. She watched until they were out of the yard, then ran to tell Clay.

Amity tried not to think what she might find at Gretchen's house. Gretchen might not even let her inside. Then what would she do? She was walking close to Libby and breathing the same air. If it was true that yellow fever spread by air, she was exposed to it and couldn't go home until she saw if she would catch it.

At the creek Amity had to wait while Libby was sick, then they went on. Amity dispelled all thoughts of sending Libby to her own house. The girl was too sick to travel that far. She glanced at her. Libby was only a year older than Hallie. "When we get there, you're to go into the guest room and go to bed."

Libby stared at her. "Me? Go to bed in Mrs. Harris's guest room? She'll half kill me!"

"No, she won't. You're too sick to go home and I can't have you passing out on me. I'll have enough to do." She saw Gretchen's house ahead. Was Hallie as sick as Amity feared she might be?

Libby took Amity to the kitchen door by habit. She was too sick now to argue about going to bed. Amity could see the girl sinking before her eyes. Yellow fever moved quickly. When they were in the kitchen, Amity said, "Where are they?"

"Upstairs. Mrs. Harris's room is the one nearest the landing and Hallie's is just past it."

Amity told her again to go to bed and gathered her skirts to start up the stairs. She could have found them by the groans. Hallie was in bed and her skin was yellowish and dull with fever. She turned her head and saw Amity but didn't seem to believe her eyes. "Amity? What are you doing here?"

Amity went to her and touched her forehead. It was burning hot. "I'm here to take care of you. How do you feel?"

"My head hurts so bad I can hardly stand it. And I feel as if there's a weight pressing on my stomach. I'm so sick I could throw up." She wet her lips and added, "I'm so thirsty."

"Wait here. I'll be right back." Amity went to the next room and looked in on Gretchen. The woman only groaned and turned her head.

Amity passed Libby in the hall, and the girl barely seemed to notice her as she went into the room across from Hallie's. Amity hurried down the stairs and into the parlor. She had seen books here and she knew there must be some sort of home companion or a medical book of some sort, however simple it might be. She pulled open the glass door of the secretary and bent to read the titles. Most were novels or poetry. She found the one she needed on the bottom shelf.

She pulled out the heavy book and thumbed through it hurriedly until she found the part on yellow fever. Quickly she read the symptoms and found her memory had been correct. The treatment called for forty grains of calomel, twenty grains gum of camphor and twenty grains cayenne pepper, to be given every hour, along with mustard plasters on the stomach and ankles. Within three hours the patient should be in a hard sweat.

Quickly, she went into the kitchen and searched until she found the cabinet where Gretchen kept all her medicines, but all she found was an empty bottle of gum of camphor. Amity took a deep breath to calm herself so she could think of what to do. If the purgatives and emetics were intended to flush the patient's system, she would not need the medicines since all three were already suffering from vomiting and diarrhea. But common sense told her they would dehydrate if they did not get fluids into their bodies. And Hallie was already complaining of being thirsty. As water was all that was available, it would have to do.

She drew a pail of water and found three glasses, then quickly headed upstairs. She started with Hallie and worked her way to her other two patients. Gretchen balked as if she wouldn't drink from the glass Amity held to her lips, but in the end she gave in and drank thirstily, then vomited it up into the pan beside the bed. Amity gave her another drink and began cleaning up the mess.

On her next round, she sponged their hot skin, working with each one until she saw some improvement, then going on to the next. Soon she was exhausted from the unaccustomed effort. As she was trying to convince Gretchen to let her sponge her face and neck to bring down the fever, she heard a loud knock on the door. Amity was sure it was Clay, and she ran down to keep him from coming inside.

"Back away so I can open the door," she called through the wood.

"Amity, are you really in there? Jemima told me where you'd gone, but I thought she must be teasing at first. What's going on?"

"Back away and I'll open the door. Do it, Clay. I don't want you to get sick."

She looked out the window to be sure he had moved into the yard, then she unlatched the door. "It's yellow fever," she said. "Hallie is too sick to move, and I can't bring her home and expose the others. Gretchen and Libby have it, as well. I'm going to stay here and doctor them."

Clay took a step forward.

"Don't come any closer! I mean it, Clay!"

He stopped. "Are you sure it's yellow fever?"

"I looked it up in Gretchen's home medicine book to be certain. They have all the symptoms." She frowned. "The treatment calls for purgatives and emetics I don't have, but I'm not sure I really need to be giving them, anyway. Do you know how to doctor yellow fever?"

"No, but I'll go to Doc Hedges and send him out. Amity, I can't leave you here."

"You have to. I've been in contact with them, and I can't go home until it's run its course. I brought the flour and meal from our kitchen. You'll need to go into town and get more to replace it. And you'd better go right away. If this turns into an epidemic, the stores may not be open."

"I don't care about meal and flour. What about you?"

"I'll be fine. I had yellow fever when I was a child." She tried to sound confident and hoped she was right. She didn't remember being as sick as they were upstairs. "It runs its course fast. Hallie and I will come home when everyone's well."

He frowned at her from across the yard. "Damn it, Amity, I can't just walk off and leave you here!"

"If you catch it, who will take care of the children?"

He glared about the yard as if he wanted to dispute her words but knew he couldn't.

"How can you be so calm? Aren't you afraid?"

"Of course I am, but there's nothing to be gained by giving in to it." She had never given in to weakness and certainly could not afford to now. "You go take care of things at home and find the doctor. I'll be back when it's safe, and I'll bring Hallie with me."

As she watched Clay leave, she wanted to run after him. She was afraid of being alone with three people as sick as the ones upstairs. What if they died? She held herself firmly erect and went back to her duties.

Two hours later she heard another knock on the door. It was Doc Hedges. "Come in," she said in relief. "They're upstairs."

"Afternoon, Mrs. Morgan," he said as he passed her. "Clay says you're determined to stay here, and I guess that's for the best. I wish I could send out a nurse to take over for you, but they're all busy."

"Then there are others sick, as well?"

"Oh, yes. It started four days ago. I had hoped it would be contained to the houses north of town, but you know how the fever can spread."

"Then it is yellow fever?" She had hoped she might be wrong.

"No question about it with the others I've seen, but let me look at our folks here to be sure. All right?" His manner was professional and businesslike, and she felt reassured at once.

When the doctor entered Gretchen's room, his expression became grave and he nodded his head. "Mrs. Morgan, have you ever had yellow fever yourself?"

"I think I have. It was so long ago. I can't remember if I had these same symptoms or not."

He was silent for a minute as he lifted Gretchen's eyelids so he could see the whites of her eyes. "You'll know soon enough. This is yellow jack, all right."

As Amity followed him into Hallie's room, she said, "I found Gretchen's home adviser. It said I should administer purgatives and emetics. Gretchen didn't have any of the medicines mentioned, but I'm not sure they need them since they are already behaving as if they had had them.''

"You're right," Doc Hedges said. "They don't need any help to purge their systems. Nature is taking care of that for us." After a moment he said, "That's how I was taught to doctor the fever years ago in medical school. But in my experience, I've had better luck just doctoring the fever—which is to say, I try to keep the patient cool and give plenty of liquids. They can't keep much down, of course, but if you keep on trying long enough, some will be absorbed." He glanced from Hallie to Amity and back again.

Amity nodded. She was relieved that she hadn't dosed them as the book had instructed.

"They are in what we refer to as the second stage. It will last for a day or two."

"Then what?" She pressed her hands together to keep them from trembling.

"Then they should feel better except for the nausea. That won't let up for another day or so. If we're lucky, they'll start to mend after that."

"And if we're not?" She wanted to know what to expect, even if it did frighten her to voice the question.

"If they start the other symptoms all over, the headaches, the pressure in the stomach, the pain in the back and limbs, this rapid breathing, you must prepare yourself for the worst. This could last a day or two longer, then the patient will start to sink."

"How will I know if that happens?"

"There will be what we refer to as black vomit. You'll notice the difference. The temperature will drop below normal, and you'll see a definite weakening in the patient."

Amity nodded. She didn't need to hear any more. "What should I do other than to give them water and sponge baths?"

"I've had good results with lemonade or cider vinegar. Sometimes it is easier for them to keep that down." He reached into his black bag and took out a bottle. "This is quinine. Give them four to six grains each hour or two."

She took the bottle. It felt alien in her hand. "How do I measure it?"

Doc Hedges showed her how to administer the medicine, then closed his bag. "I have to be on my way. I have other calls to make. If you even suspect you're getting it, get help while you can still get around. It moves awfully fast, so be careful."

Amity refused to let her fear show. "Of course."

He smiled and his eyes crinkled at the corners. "You'll do fine. Just don't give up. Remember, if you find yourself getting sick, send word somehow, and I'll find someone to come to you."

She nodded and saw him out. As she leaned against the door, she drew in a steadying breath, then dragged the sacks of meal and flour into the kitchen. She didn't think there would be much opportunity to cook nor any point in trying to get solid food down her patients, but Libby had handled the sacks, and she couldn't risk taking them back to her home. Amity wasn't so sure yellow fever traveled only by breath.

The hours crept by. After a while she lost count of how often she had made the rounds from one bed to the next. She tried to think of some way of putting them all in the same room, but there seemed to be no cots and the beds were much too heavy for her to drag. Late that night she went to the small bedroom at the end of the hall and put on her nightgown, but she was afraid to get into bed. If she put her head down she might sleep too soundly to hear them call out if they needed her.

With her body aching from exhaustion, Amity pulled the top mattress of the bed and dragged it into the hall. She positioned it within hearing distance of the sickrooms and lay down. It seemed odd in the extreme to be lying on a mattress in the hall of Gretchen's house, and she reflected on the strange twists fate could take before tiredness brought her sleep.

All night she was up, off and on, tending the sick, then dozing for as long as she dared between rounds. Gretchen continued to be a difficult patient and refused most of the lemonade and cider vinegar that Amity offered to her. When she was sensible enough to recognize Amity, she glared at her with all the hatred she could summon. It was then Amity realized that Gretchen's mind was not as sound as it might have been.

Hallie and Libby were model patients. They drank whatever Amity offered them, even the vinegar, which seemed to stay down better than anything else. Amity didn't understand it, but she kept pouring it down them between sponge baths.

On the second day, Amity thought she could see an improvement in Libby. The girl had been sick longer than the others, and Amity reasoned that she should get well sooner. The positive changes in Libby's condition gave her strength to continue her strenuous regime. By dusk Hallie was also better and could carry on a conversation. Amity began to take heart.

Gretchen, true to her obstinate nature, continued with the nausea and fever. Amity was continually fearful that she would go into the last stage the doctor had described, but the dreaded symptoms never showed. By noon the next day, Gretchen was better, and she proved it by telling Amity to get out of her house and to have a proper nurse sent in.

"No, I'm all you have," Amity said as she spooned weak gruel into Gretchen's mouth. "Swallow."

Gretchen glared at her, only her weakness forcing her to do as Amity said. Spoonful by spoonful the gruel went in, and this time it stayed down.

"Good," Amity said as she straightened. "I guess you'll live."

"Where is Dr. Hedges? I demand you send for him. Who let you in, anyway? Where is Libby? Send that shiftless girl after the doctor!"

"Libby has been as sick as you were and is still convalescing in the guest bedroom. You might ask about Hallie."

Gretchen paused as if she did not want to ask Amity for anything at all. "How is she?"

"Much better, thank you. I think she will be well enough to go home in a day or two."

"She is at home."

Amity's eyes bore down at Gretchen. "No, she isn't. She belongs with her father and sisters, not here. You know that, Gretchen."

Gretchen turned her face to the wall. "It's just like you to take advantage of me while I'm so ill."

Amity ignored Gretchen's insult and went downstairs to wash the bowls and spoons she had used to feed the others. Then she ladled herself some porridge, and as she ate it, she enjoyed the moments of rest. She had lost weight in the past few days, and this bothered her. Surely with the baby growing every day, she shouldn't be getting smaller, but her dress fit loosely now. She ran her hand over her middle. Had it hurt the baby for her to work so hard and to be so near the sickness? There was so much she didn't know about having a baby. Should she have told the doctor about the baby when he came to see them?

She rose and washed her bowl and spoon and straightened Gretchen's kitchen. What was done was done, and worrying about it would change nothing. But she worried anyway.

By the following day Libby was well enough to send home. She was still pale and weak, but Amity knew she would be able to walk that far. She knew her mother must be beside herself with worry, and they didn't know if her father had survived or not. No one was traveling the roads yet, and they were still cut off from any communication.

That afternoon Clay came over, as he had done at least once a day since she had come, and shouted for her. She opened a window in Hallie's room and waved at him. "I sent Libby home," she called down.

"How is Hallie?"

"Just a minute." Amity went to the bed and helped Hallie to her feet. Putting her arm around Hallie to steady her, Amity helped her to the window.

"Hello, Papa," Hallie called down.

Clay gazed up at her for a moment, looking as if he might be fighting back tears, before saying, "Hello, honey. How are you?"

"I'm a lot better than I was." She drew in a deep breath of fresh air. "I want to come home."

"I think we can come by tomorrow," Amity told him. "Can you find someone to take my place with Gretchen? She's mending, though slower than the others, and cannot yet take care of herself."

"I'll find someone. Hallie, you're sure you're all right?"

"I will be, Papa." She hesitated. "Do you think Kate will let me have one of those kittens Amity got at the O'Flannerys?"

"I'm sure she will."

"I like the gray one best."

Amity felt tears start in her eyes as Hallie turned to her and said, "I was awful about those kittens. I'm sorry I acted like that."

"I don't hold it against you."

"You really don't, do you?" Hallie seemed surprised. "And you've stayed to doctor us all this time."

"Why shouldn't I? You're my daughter." Amity waited for the denial she had come to expect, but this time Hallie nodded.

"I'm tired. Will you help me back into bed?"

"I'll bring the buggy over tomorrow morning to get you." Clay called. "I'll be glad to have you both home."

Amity smiled at him. "I can't tell you how glad I'll be to come back."

Knowing she would soon be in her own home helped Amity get one more night of napping in the hall within hearing distance of Gretchen's room. Hallie slept soundly and barely turned over the whole night, and Amity knew the danger was over for her.

Early the next morning, she washed Hallie's hair and helped her bathe in the copper tub, then put in fresh water and washed herself while Hallie went upstairs to dress. She imagined the tiredness and worry washing away with the soapsuds and wished she had the luxury of soaking until the water grew cold, but there was still much to do, so she got out, dressed and emptied the tub, bucket by bucket.

By the time the nurse arrived from town to take over Gretchen's care, Amity had started a stew for dinner and had all Hallie's things ready to go. The red-faced woman, who introduced herself as Mrs. Rodgers, a distant cousin to the midwife, Mrs. Willis, proved to be as efficient as Amity could have hoped for. She took over the cooking and cleaning as if she had been in the house for years. Gretchen objected to her, but Amity heard Mrs. Rodgers telling her to keep quiet or she would relapse and be sicker than ever. Her manner was rougher than Amity's, but Amity thought it might sit better with Gretchen.

When she went in to tell Gretchen goodbye, Gretchen glared at her. "I had hoped we might reach some truce." Amity admitted.

"I'm sure you did. Why else did you come to stay here?"

"I came because you and the girls needed care and would probably have died otherwise," Amity said flatly. "I had no ulterior motive."

"I don't believe you." Gretchen turned her face away and closed her eyes.

Amity hesitated for a minute, then turned and went out. There was no use trying to reason with Gretchen. The woman was filled with venomous hatred, and the words would be wasted.

Amity helped Mrs. Rodgers put the mattress on the bed in the small bedroom and felt relief at seeing the hall look as a hall should. Hallie was dressed and sitting in a chair by the window when Amity went in for her. She looked pale, but eager to go home.

"I see Papa coming up the lane," Hallie said. "He's here."

"Let's go down." She offered Hallie her arm, and as they made their way down the hall, past Gretchen's room, Hallie made no mention and showed no sign that she wanted to go in and tell her aunt goodbye. Amity suspected Hallie had spoken to Gretchen earlier that morning and that there had been harsh words between them.

By the time Clay drove up to the gate, Amity and Hallie were waiting on the porch. Amity had to restrain herself from leaving Hallie behind and running to embrace him. Instead she smiled broadly at Clay as she helped the girl down the walk and out the gate.

"Papa," Hallie said as she put her arms around him.

"Hallie, I've missed you so much. I've been worried sick about you. Are you sure you're okay?"

Hallie nodded. "I'm just tired."

Clay lifted her into the buggy, then turned to Amity. "I've missed you, too. It's been hell without you."

"There's no need for strong language," she said in mock chastisement as she smiled at him. "I've missed you, too."

She could see the admiration he had for her in his eyes, and there was no need for him to voice his thoughts. He lifted Amity into the wagon as if she were as frail as Hallie. "Let's go home."

When Amity looked back at the house, she thought she saw Gretchen's face at the bedroom window. "I'm ready, and then some."

Hallie said, "What all has happened since I was gone? Is Jemima still taking music lessons? Did you ask Kate about the kitten?"

"Yes to both." Clay looked at Amity. "Did you tell her the news?"

Amity shook her head. "I thought you might want to tell her yourself."

Clay glanced over his shoulder and grinned at Hallie. "We're going to have a baby next spring."

When Hallie got quiet, Amity's stomach knotted. Then she said, "Good! Do you have a name for her yet?"

Amity relaxed and pressed her thigh and elbow against Clay's. It felt so good to be near him again.

Chapter Eighteen

Hallie recuperated slowly but steadily from her bout with yellow fever. By the time the sweet gum leaves had turned to orange and russet, she was able to walk to the barn and back without being exhausted. And several weeks later, when the leaves lay like a spongy brown carpet on the ground, she was able to go to town and resume visiting her friends.

"I saw your stepmother the other day," Ollie Jane Pearson said with a wrinkling of her nose. "She's getting so big!"

Hallie shrugged. "She's going to have a baby." As the eldest of five children, Hallie took such changes as a matter of fact.

Ollie Jane, an only child, said, "If I were in the family way, I'd stay home where I belonged the entire time. I might not even come to town at all until the baby was old enough to walk."

"Sure, you would," Hallie said in disbelief. "You can't go three days without going to a store."

"That's different. I'm young and not that way. You'd think she would have more self-respect than to parade all over town like she does."

Hallie frowned. Since Amity had risked her life as well as that of the baby she was carrying to nurse Hallie, the girl had seen her stepmother in a different light. "I don't want to talk about this."

"Of course you don't. It must embarrass you every time you see her. Why, she and your papa must be in their thirties! That's old! Who would guess they still did—you know?"

"Papa is thirty-four and Amity won't be thirty for several years yet. They aren't that old. Thirty isn't the end of time."

"But still—for her to be having a baby!—I think it's scandalous."

"Oh, for heaven's sake, Ollie Jane! They're married! Married people have babies."

"You can't tell me you aren't upset over it. I know you too well."

"I would have felt that way once." Hallie frowned and picked absently at the ruffle on her skirt. "Ever since I was sick, things have been different. Amity came over and took care of us all. I found out later that she wasn't even positive that she had had yellow fever, though it seems she had since she didn't catch it. She risked her life for me. She even risked her life for Aunt Gretchen and Libby Larsen, and you know how Aunt Gretchen has been about her. She didn't even know Libby. Not really."

"Don't you see? That means she wasn't doing it as a special favor for you, if she did the same for them."

"It doesn't mean that, at all. If I hadn't been there, she might not have taken the chance. I didn't tell you, but she went to Brian O'Flannery's house and got me a pair of kittens just before I moved to Aunt Gretchen's house."

"What did she do that for? I don't like cats."

"I do, though, and she found out that I had always wanted a kitten so she brought me two."

Ollie Jane looked confused. "What does that prove? Anybody can bring home a cat."

"But she did it just for me. Kate ended up with one of the kittens. You know how she is about animals. The little gray one is mine. Kate had named it Silver, but I changed its name to Velvet because it's so soft. Amity even lets us have them in the house.''

''In the house?'' Ollie Jane wrinkled her nose again. ''Cats make me sneeze.''

''I think I misjudged Amity.'' It took a lot for Hallie to admit that, and she waited to see what her friend would say about it.

''How can you say that after the way she treated you? Making you work all day and not letting you have new clothes and talking ugly about your mother and tearing up the things your mother had owned!'' Ollie Jane looked outraged for Hallie's sake.

''I may have exaggerated a bit.'' Hallie could not look directly at her. ''She doesn't make me do all that much work, and that time she cut up Mama's dress, she was doing it to make a party dress for me.''

''You never told me that.''

''That's why I'm telling you now. I was wrong about her, and I think it's my duty to set matters straight. I've decided not to hate Amity anymore.''

Ollie Jane's jaw dropped as she stared at Hallie. ''That's the bravest thing I've ever heard anyone say. You're a saint, Hallie!''

''No, I'm not.'' Hallie pulled at the ruffle until she realized she was rumpling her dress, then smoothed it and looked around Ollie Jane's room. ''She even talked about putting new wallpaper in my bedroom. Kate wants green, but I think pink would be prettier.''

''Pink definitely. Kate has such ideas sometimes.''

''And she saw me talking to Brian O'Flannery yesterday and didn't make fun of me.''

''You talked to Brian? I thought you were sweet on Peter Jimmerson.''

''That was last summer. Besides, I think he's taken with Polly Fraser.''

''Mavis's sister? Mavis never told me that!''

"I think Brian is so much nicer. He came over the other day, pretending he had come to see how the kittens are doing, but I think he really wanted to see me." Hallie smiled and felt a warm glow inside. "I like him a lot. Do you think he'll start walking out with me? I'll be fourteen next month. Papa courted Mama when she wasn't much older than that."

"I don't want to grow up and settle down. I like dancing too much." Ollie Jane lay back on her bed and stared at the ceiling. "Why do you want to settle down with one boy?"

"I've been watching Papa and Amity. They really are happy."

Ollie Jane raised up on one elbow and regarded Hallie. "Are they? How can he be happy with her, if he loved your mother? Mama says it's not right to love more than one person. Not like that, you know, where you live with them."

"What if the person dies? Papa loved Mama, but she's gone. I think it's good that he's happy again."

"Do you really?" Ollie Jane considered the new thought. "That does make sense. I mean, what if you or I got married and our husband died in the first year? We would be widows most of our lives! I don't think I'd like that." She paused for a moment, apparently deep in thought. "You don't have to tell me this if you don't want to, but what do you really think about having a new baby in the house—you know, Amity's baby?"

"I'm sort of looking forward to it. Little sisters can be just awful, but Rosemary is nearly four, and I miss having a little baby around. They're so sweet and soft. I'm going to be a good mother some day. I like babies."

Ollie Jane glanced at the door. "Hush! Don't let Mama hear you say a thing like that!" In a softer voice she said, "What do you think really happens to cause a woman to have a baby?"

Hallie was thoughtful for a minute. "I suppose it must be something like what happens between dogs or cows."

Ollie Jane wrinkled her nose. "I hope not!"

"I could be wrong."

"And you really like Amity now? You're not just saying that to be noble?"

"No, I really like her. And I'm telling it to everyone I spoke badly to about her before. That's only right."

"You are so noble," Ollie Jane said in awe. "You're like a saint."

Hallie smiled but she thought she might feel more noble if she didn't have so many people to talk to in order to correct the misinformation she had given out against Amity.

Since the incident at the emporium, Amity had done most of her shopping in Nacogdoches, but with her advancing pregnancy, the longer ride was less comfortable. The next time she went into Ransom to shop, she was surprised at the number of people who spoke to her. The men lifted their hats when she passed, and the women nodded a greeting.

Her first stop was at Pearson's Dry Goods, where she hoped to buy cloth for the blankets she was making for the baby to come. The ones Elsa had used for the other children were worn from years of use and were stained from milk and juice. Besides, Amity wanted this baby to start out with new gowns and blankets. This was her first child, and she was excited about preparing for its arrival.

Frank Pearson, sporting a smile, met her halfway to the material counters. "Mrs. Morgan! How nice to see you. Is Clay well?"

"Yes," she said, trying to keep the surprise out of her voice. "He's quite well."

"And the girls? Hallie was over at our house a few days ago, and she's looking well."

"They're fine, thank you. Laura has a cough, but it's nothing serious."

"Good, good. How may I help you today?" He grinned and rubbed his hands together and looked as if he wanted nothing more than to serve her.

"I need some white outing."

"The flannels are right over here."

Amity had no idea what had come over the man. On her other visits to the store, he had more or less ignored her. Now he was acting as if she was his most treasured customer. He measured the cloth for her and even added a couple of inches for good measure, and when she selected a pale yellow ribbon to trim the blanket, he seemed overjoyed. Amity was confused but pleased that this shopping trip was proving to be more pleasant than she had expected, at least so far. But she still had to go to the emporium to finish her shopping and dreaded another unpleasant encounter there.

At the emporium's front door, she paused to square her shoulders, then went in. A saleslady met her at the first counter. The unpleasant Mrs. Handley was nowhere to be seen. "Yes, ma'am? May I help you?"

"I need some Epsom salts and iodine."

"Right this way." The lady took her to the back of the store where medical supplies were kept. "I hope no one is hurt out to your place."

"No, we're all fine. I just like to keep it on hand." She didn't recall ever having met the woman.

"My aunt is Ada Rodgers. The woman Mr. Morgan hired to look after Mrs. Harris during the epidemic."

"Oh, yes. Of course." Now that she made the connection, she could see the family resemblance.

"Aunt Ada told me what a jewel you were to look after Mrs. Harris and Hallie like that. And the hired girl, as well!"

"It was nothing anyone else would not have done. Hallie is my daughter, and I couldn't bring her home and chance infecting the younger ones."

The woman leaned closer. "Just between us, Aunt Ada also told me what a pill Mrs. Harris is. I had thought as much, but Ada confirmed it. I know there's no affection between the two of you, so I dare say it. Everybody in town knows what you did."

Amity felt her cheeks pinking. "I hope this isn't getting blown out of proportion. All I did was take care of them."

The woman winked. "The way I hear it, you probably saved their lives. Doc Hedges had his hands full with everyone so sick. He couldn't have found anyone else to stay there and do what you did—and after Mrs. Harris was talking so ugly about you, too!"

Amity was embarrassed. She had seldom heard such glowing praise, and never from a woman who was practically a stranger. "I appreciate your aunt looking after Gretchen so I could take Hallie home. She struck me as a good woman."

"Aunt Ada is that. She's a good woman, indeed. I'm the only one in the family that didn't take to some form of doctoring. You know our cousin is Mrs. Willis, the midwife."

"Yes, I know. She did a wonderful job with Fiona O'Flannery and her baby."

"She'll take good care of you, when your time comes." The woman winked again. "You'll see."

Amity blushed. She wasn't accustomed to speaking of such subjects in public, even though no one was close enough to overhear what they were saying. She paid for her purchase and left the store. Two more men tipped their hats as she was climbing into the buggy. Amity didn't know what to think. Was it possible that Gretchen had alienated the entire town against her and that her helping out during a family illness had altered public opinion this much? It seemed unlikely.

As she threaded her way through the other buggies and horses, she thought about it. Hallie and Ollie Jane Pearson were good friends. It seemed possible that the clerks at one store might be on speaking terms with the owners and clerks at another. Had Hallie been helping to remove the stigma against her? The idea warmed Amity's heart. Since her pregnancy began, she found she cried more easily than she ever had before, and she had to wipe a tear from her eye.

At Doc Hedges's office, she parked under the magnolia tree out front. There were no other horses tied there, and she hoped she might catch him when he wasn't busy.

The lady who kept his records in order smiled when she saw Amity. "Good morning, Mrs. Morgan. I hope you're not feeling poorly today."

"No, thank you. I'm here to get some cough medicine for Laura. She has a cold."

"I'll get the doctor."

Doc Hedges came to the door and motioned for Amity to come into the back office. "How are you doing today?"

"I'm fine, thank you, but Laura has a cold. Could I get some cough syrup?"

"Easiest thing in the world." He turned to a glass-fronted cabinet filled with bottles of all sizes and shapes. After a moment, he pulled one out and got a smaller, empty bottle from the adjoining cabinet. As he filled the bottle for her, he said, "What about yourself? You haven't been in to see me."

Amity pulled her shawl over her middle. "I'm quite all right. I haven't even been sick."

"Not at all?" Doc Hedges peered at her over the tops of his spectacles. "That's good. Glad to hear it. Mind if I ask when you expect the baby to be here?"

"We think it will be toward the end of April."

Doc Hedges blinked. "April?"

Amity saw the surprise in his face. "That's right. April. Or maybe even early May. I've been told the first one can be a week or so late."

He was silent for a moment and Amity was reminded of the way he had thought in silence when he was examining Hallie and Gretchen to determine if they had yellow fever.

"Is there something wrong?" she asked at last.

"Wrong? No, no, probably not. It's a delicate subject, I realize, Mrs. Morgan, but I'm concerned that you've grown this large if you aren't due until late April."

Amity looked at her rounded abdomen. "Am I too large?"

Doc Hedges observed her for a moment. "You're not putting on too much weight. Your face and hands aren't puffy. I suspect you're just farther along than you think."

Amity shook her head. "No, I'm quite sure of the date."

He smiled. "People can make mistakes. You and Clay have been married, what? About eight months now? It wouldn't surprise me if the baby comes closer to early March than late April."

"That's not possible," she said slowly.

"Why not?" His piercing eyes compelled her to tell him.

Amity lowered her eyes. Even if he was a doctor, she was uneasy talking to a man about pregnancy. "We didn't…that is, Clay and I weren't…" She drew in a deep breath. "What I'm trying to say is that Clay and I didn't have relations at first. We hardly knew each other, you see. Ours was a marriage of convenience, at first."

"I see." Doc Hedges looked as if he were thinking again. "So what you're telling me is that April is the earliest the baby could be expected?"

"That's right."

"Do you mind if I examine you? If you'll pardon my saying so, you don't look like a woman in her fourth month."

Amity's eyes widened. She had never considered that anything might be wrong with her. "But I feel fine. I get tired easily, but surely that's to be expected."

"Sit up here on the table, please." His manner was all business, but it did little to reassure her.

"Clay doesn't seem to think there's anything wrong."

"And there might not be." He helped her lie back on the table and pulled out a shelf to support her legs. Looking at the cabinet opposite, he began to feel her abdomen through her dress. "You could just be carrying well to the front," he said as if to himself.

"Or it could be a large baby."

He nodded. "That's what I'm wondering."

Amity laid her head back and stared at the ceiling. Large babies were difficult to birth. She understood now what the doctor was telling her. For the first time uncertainty crept into her. "Are you saying the baby might be too large for me to give birth to it?"

He smiled reassuringly but his eyes stayed thoughtful. "I'm not trying to scare you. I could be wrong entirely. Dresses have so many tucks and ruffles and so on. Your apparent size may be fooling me."

"This dress isn't all that gathered."

He pressed his hands against either side of her stomach. "That doesn't hurt, does it?"

"No."

"That's good." He pressed in a different spot and shook his head. "I can't feel enough of the baby to know how big it is. There's nothing we could do about it, anyway. A baby grows as big and as fast as it pleases."

"Maybe I'm eating too much. Maybe I've just gained weight."

Doc Hedges lifted her hand and pressed the skin. "No water retention." He felt her neck and jaw. "I don't think you've gained more than I would expect. At a time like this, a woman is supposed to gain some. You're eating for two, after all."

"I feel fine."

He took her hand and helped her sit up. "I'm probably just a meddlesome old man who worries too much."

"Should I come back in a few weeks and let you see how I'm doing?"

"Couldn't hurt. I'd feel better about it. Had you planned to use Mrs. Willis?"

"Yes. She's the only midwife around here, isn't she?"

"Yes, she is. And she's competent in most cases."

"Are you saying I may need more help than she is capable of giving? Be frank with me, Dr. Hedges. I want to know if I have a reason to worry."

"Well, I'll tell you. All women are different. It could be you just get larger and carry more water than most. Or it could be that you're going to have a big baby. Or there's an off chance that you counted wrong in the first place. Like I say, I can't tell. But you need to keep in mind that you may need me rather than Mrs. Willis."

Amity wet her dry lips before speaking. "I may need you?"

Doc Hedges patted her hand as if she were a child. "Let's not worry about it yet. Like I say, I could be wrong."

She nodded but she wasn't convinced. Doc Hedges had practiced medicine for nearly half a century. It wasn't likely he was wrong, and she knew the man was not an alarmist. "I don't want Clay to know."

He raised his eyebrows.

"He's already worried. He lost Elsa through childbirth. If he knew there might be cause for concern this time, he would spend the next five months worrying."

"You'd be the best judge of what to tell him. I just wanted you to know and to be prepared for the eventuality that a midwife might not be enough."

She nodded. "I'll tell Clay that I'm nervous about having it and that I want you to be sent for instead. He will agree to that." She frowned and clasped her hands together. "If you're right and this is a big baby, what can be done about it? I mean, if you see it's going to be too big to be born?"

Doc Hedges avoided her eyes. "There's not anything to be done that I know about. I've heard of some doctors in cities back East trying to bring babies early, but I don't think they've had much success. Not without endangering the mother or the baby."

"I don't want to chance hurting my baby." Amity pressed her hand against her middle protectively.

"I know and I understand. For now, just take care of yourself and keep your feet up as much as you can. Let the older girls do more around the house. It won't hurt them. Whenever you can, sit down and rest. Don't overdo."

Amity nodded.

"And don't worry. I may be fretting over nothing. Let's just wait and see. Can you come back in about a month?"

"Yes. Yes, I can come back."

"Good." He helped her off the table and handed her the bottle of cough syrup for Laura. "If this doesn't help your little girl, let me know and I'll come take a look at her."

"Thank you," she said, keeping her voice calm and her face unruffled, but inside she was in a turmoil. For some reason she had never thought she would be in any danger from having this baby. She didn't feel any different than she had for a month or so. Every woman, according to Fiona, got tired as the baby grew inside her. Doc Hedges was just blowing it out of proportion. That had to be it.

As she paid the lady for the medicine and told her she would be back in a month, it was as if she were standing apart from herself and watching a stranger perform the actions. Babies who were too big to be born seldom survived, and neither did their mothers. There was only one way to have a baby, and sometimes nature did not cooperate. For a minute she wondered how the doctors in the East—the ones Doc Hedges had mentioned—managed to bring a baby early. At once she rejected the idea. Babies born too early also had a low chance of survival. She would do nothing to endanger her baby.

She went to the buggy and drove toward home without giving a thought to what direction she was taking. Fortunately, the horse knew the way and was eager to get home. Her thoughts were in a jumble. On one hand she wanted to tell Clay what the doctor had said, and on the other she wanted to shield him from more worry. He was already treating her as if she were made of spun glass. No, she couldn't tell him. She would have to keep this to herself, at least until she saw the doctor again and had him confirm that there was reason to worry.

In the meantime, she would work on the baby blanket and think of names and try to imagine what it would be like to hold the baby in her lap and how Clay would love it. She felt more tears welling in her eyes, but this time she let them fall. There was no one on the road to see her cry, and she had to shed them all before she reached the house and had to put on an unconcerned face.

Chapter Nineteen

"I want to be a veterinarian when I grow up," Kate announced one night after supper.

"Do you now?" Clay said with a smile.

"Yes, I do, so don't smile at me like that." Kate put aside the nightcap she was embroidering and frowned at her father. "I've given it some thought, and that's what I want to do."

"Honey, you might not have noticed, but you're a girl."

"I think she would be a good veterinarian," Amity said calmly. She pulled the green silk through the cloth and started another stitch. "She's good with animals and makes good grades."

"She's a *girl*," Clay repeated.

"This is almost 1888, not the Dark Ages. I think it's time women were free to do whatever they want to do."

"Amity, you surprise me. If Kate can't vote or testify in court, why would she be able to attend veterinarian school? I don't even know where one is."

"Neither do I, but I suspect I can find one." She smiled at Kate. "I'll start looking and asking around."

Kate grinned and picked up the embroidery, which she detested and only did to please Amity.

"You shouldn't get her hopes up," Clay said. "I never heard of a woman vet."

"Neither did I, but I can't see any reason there shouldn't be women doctors. I should think they would be particularly good at attending childbirth." She lowered her eyes. She wasn't comfortable discussing such things with children in the room.

Clay gazed into the fire as he thought. "A woman doctor instead of a midwife?"

"I've thought I might like to have Dr. Hedges here when the time comes." She held her breath. She had been unable to think of a way of telling Clay that the doctor had stressed the importance of his being there.

For a long minute Clay didn't answer. Then he said, "When the time comes and you think it's necessary, I'll ride for Doc Hedges."

"And I can be a veterinarian?" Kate asked.

"I'll find out. But don't get your hopes up. I don't know if such schools take women."

"I should think there ought to be a beginning for everything," Amity said with composure. She lifted her eyes and winked at Kate, who grinned.

"I'll see." Clay went back to staring at the fire.

Christmas came and went. Gretchen had been inactive during most of the fall and winter, sending Libby or Jake to town for most of her needs. She had been determined to play the role of invalid for as long as possible, but few of the women she considered to be her friends came out to see her. Then bad weather set in, and the chill in the air, which had made her bones ache in recent years, kept her inside.

On the first day that promised to be neither frosty nor rainy, Gretchen had Jake harness her horse and she drove into town. It was a Thursday, and she knew her women friends would be sewing at Lola May Grizzard's house.

When she was shown into the parlor, two of the women exchanged looks of surprise, and Lola May said, "Why Gretchen, we didn't expect to see you today. You're looking well."

"As well as might be expected. The cold bothers me so much these days. I've not even been able to attend church."

"We've missed you," Esther Crowe said automatically, but with a marked lack of sincerity. "My husband was out to look in on you, but he said you weren't at home."

"I didn't say I was bedridden," Gretchen said more sharply than she had intended, then realized she had better soften her tone, because something odd was happening. "I may have been gone to tend poor Elsa's grave and, of course, Hall's. We should have brought them into town to the city cemetery where the graves would have been properly cared for, but at the time it seemed the thing to do, to keep them close." She waited for the customary murmurs of consolation, but there were few.

"How is Hallie?" Clematis Osgood asked, and immediately Lola May shot the woman a silencing look.

Gretchen put on a long face. "I have no idea, Clematis. Since that Amity woman took her away from me, the child has only come to see me a handful of times. She looks thin and tired."

"Young women do like to starve themselves to keep their waists small," Lola May observed. "My Fern does the same."

"There's a difference between being starved and choosing to slim down," Gretchen snapped. She mentally warned herself to be careful. It would not do to turn these women against her, no matter what her personal thoughts of them were. "Hallie is being mistreated, of course. There's nothing I can do about it. It breaks my heart."

Myrtle Smith spoke up. "I saw Amity the other day. She looks ready to have the baby and it's only February."

"She's going about in her condition? Shameless trash!" Gretchen waited for agreement. There was none. She looked around sharply.

"I've gotten to know her," Myrtle continued, her cheeks blazing with restrained emotion, though she kept her voice steady, "and I like her. So does Hallie. She told me so herself."

"That's what she told Fern, too," Lola May said with a firm nod. "Hallie comes here often, you know."

Esther added, "Amity has asked if she may join the church choir once the baby is here and she's out and about again. I told her she'd be welcome."

"Amity? In the church choir?" Gretchen looked as if she would like to choke the woman. "I'll bet she can't even sing!"

"I imagine she can," Esther said calmly. "She seemed to be quite talented."

"Have you seen the quilt she's entering in the fair?" Myrtle asked, her eyes fixed on her sewing. "It's a beauty. We'll have to do some work to even compete. The stitches are so tiny and all the corners meet perfectly."

"When did you see it? Is she dragging it all over town to show off what she's done?"

"No, of course not. Will and I have started visiting them, and she took me in the back room and showed it to me. It seems she frequently won prizes in Charlotte."

"I'm entering a Tumbling Block myself," Lola May said. "It's almost finished."

"Do you have the pattern for Log Cabin?" Esther asked.

"Would a crazy quilt have a chance in the competition?" Myrtle asked. "I'm better at embroidery stitches, and I've done one with each block surrounded with feather stitches and with wildflowers embroidered in each solid color piece."

Gretchen didn't want to talk about quilts. She looked around the room. The women were ignoring her, and she had a feeling it was intentional. "So Amity has turned you all against me," she said slowly. "I would never have thought it."

Lola May sighed and shook her head. "It's not that she's turned us against you. It's just that we've gotten to know her, and we like her. We don't want to hear bad about her.

If you want to get out your sewing, you're welcome to stay and visit with us. What are you working on?"

Gretchen stood and surveyed the group. "I had thought better of my friends than for them to side with my enemies."

"We don't want to have to choose," Clematis said. "We would prefer to be friends with you both. Ransom isn't that large. It would be so much easier if you made up with Amity and buried this animosity. She never speaks ill of you."

Gretchen tried to wither her with a glare. "So after all these years, this is how I'm to be treated? You should be ashamed, all of you."

"We mean you no ill will," Esther said. "Please, get out your handwork and show us what you're working on. Is it in your bag there?"

Gretchen clutched her sewing bag as if she thought the woman might try to pry it from her hands. "I'll be on my way," she said stiffly. "I can see there is no room for me here." She jerked her head up and left.

"I can't help but feel sorry for her," Esther said when they heard the door slam.

"She brought it all on herself," Myrtle replied. "We tried to be friendly. But I can't sit here and listen to my friend being attacked and not speak up in her defense."

"I know," Clematis said. "Gretchen does love to ride a horse into the ground. I can't believe that, at first, we all took her at her word about Amity and never bothered to get to know her for ourselves. I blame us as much as her."

"Well, it's set right now," Lola May put in. "If Gretchen wants to stop running Amity down, she knows we will accept her." She looked out the window at Gretchen climbing into her buggy. "I had hoped she would give in." She sighed. "We have been friends since we learned to walk."

"Maybe she'll mellow as the weather warms," Esther said.

"Will you show me how you did this stitch?" Myrtle said as she leaned forward to look more closely at the cloth in Esther's lap. "I've never been able to do that one."

As the conversation turned back to sewing, Gretchen drove away.

The February rains gave way to tentative blue skies and the earliest flowers raised their faces to the sun as March blew in like a lion. Already, the days were somewhat warmer.

"Are the Texas winters always as cold as this one was?" Amity asked Fiona as they sat quilting by the fire. "I thought Texas would be warm year around."

Fiona laughed. "This was a particularly hard winter, but it's always cold here. Sean says it's warmer closer to the Gulf of Mexico, but I think it's probably cold everywhere. I'm looking forward to springtime."

"So am I." Amity pressed her hand against her middle where the baby was kicking particularly hard. She had been aching all day, off and on.

"You don't have much longer to go," Fiona said, divining Amity's thoughts.

"I'm glad of that. I don't have energy to do half of what I should be doing these days." She could hear girlish giggles upstairs and hoped she wouldn't have to go up and see what was going on.

"It's always like that toward the end." Fiona bit off a length of thread and knotted it. Adeline played on a pallet on the floor beside her. Fiona smiled at her. "Adeline will be talking soon. She babbles all the time. Sean says he doesn't know how he will get a word in edgewise."

Amity laughed. "You should hear our brood at mealtime. I don't see how we hear half the conversations. I had to get used to that—my aunts never talked at the table."

"In my family we chatted constantly. That was one thing we could afford to do, Ma always said," Fiona laughed. "I wonder what my little sister looks like now. She's all grown up now, maybe even married.''

"Have you heard from your brothers lately?"

Fiona nodded. "I was saving that good news for last. You'll never guess! Two of them are thinking of coming here. To Ransom!"

"To live? Why, Fiona, that's wonderful!"

"If they come, my parents may come, as well. The ones I'm talking about are the older boys, and they're the ones who usually take care of Ma and Pa. Wouldn't it be something if my ma was here?"

Amity was smiling when the first real pain hit her. She frowned slightly and ran her hand over her middle, which felt hard and and rigid.

"What's wrong?"

"I'm not sure. I guess the baby has kicked me until I'm black and blue inside." She laughed. "It's stopped now."

Fiona went back to sewing. "Brian tells me he's taking Hallie to the dance next week."

"I know. That's all Hallie has talked about for days. You'd think she had invented love."

Fiona laughed. "If they don't change their minds, our families may become connected through more than friendship."

"Fiona, how you talk. Hallie is only fourteen and Brian's not much older. It will be years before they think about marriage."

"Maybe, maybe not. One of my sisters married at fifteen."

Amity drew in her breath sharply as the pain hit again. She poked her needle in the fabric so she wouldn't lose it and met Fiona's eyes.

"You're having pains, aren't you," Fiona said rather than asked. "How long have they been going on?"

"I'm not sure. Up until now, I thought they were just the usual twinges. It's only the first of March. I can't be having pains yet." Her body made a liar of her with her next breath.

"You're going to bed. I'll send Kate to find Clay." Fiona put her needle in the quilt and stood.

"No, this is silly. The pains don't hurt much, and it's too early for the baby to be coming."

Fiona shook her head. "Babies arrive in their own time. Kate?" she called over her shoulder. She unknotted the rope that held the quilting frame and started to raise the frame to the ceiling so it would be out of the way.

Kate came into the room. "Did you call me?"

"Yes, go get your father."

Kate put her head to one side. "Get Papa?" Then she looked at Amity's pale face and her eyes widened. She rushed from the room.

"She'll run all the way," Amity said as the door slammed. "Kate never walks when she can run." She stood and went to the dining room door. "I feel foolish."

"You won't for long."

As they went across the dining room, Amity had to pause again to let a pain subside. Her eyes searched Fiona's face but neither said a word. Both knew it was too early for the baby to come.

"You could have counted wrong," Fiona said as she shut the bedroom door and helped Amity pull off her dress. "I've done that before. You lose track of time with children in the house."

"It couldn't be earlier than I figured. I'm sure of it."

She slipped a cotton gown over her head and went to the bed. Fiona was taking the birthing sheet and clean linens from the closet. "Dr. Hedges asked me the same thing the first time I went to see him. He thought I was growing large too fast."

Fiona glanced at her. "I didn't know you were seeing Doc Hedges. He thought that, too?"

"I didn't want to alarm anyone. Yes, I've seen him a time or two." She paused to let a contraction pass before climbing into the bed. She heard someone running through the house. "I hear Kate found Clay."

He burst into the room and stared at Amity. "Kate said I should come." His eyes, filled with concern, searched her face.

"It's probably nothing," Amity said.

"Go get Doc Hedges," Fiona told him. "It's time."

For a minute Clay hesitated as if he couldn't bear to leave Amity, then his eyes grew wide and fearful as it dawned on him that Fiona had told him to get Doc Hedges. "You don't think Mrs. Willis will do?"

Amity knew she had to tell him the truth. "I'm sure it's nothing to worry about," she said to calm him, "but several months ago, I went to see the doctor, and he suggested we have him attend the birthing."

"For what reason?" Clay demanded.

"I don't know. Doctors rarely tell their patients anything. I'm sure it's nothing to be alarmed about."

Looking more worried than ever, he kissed her forehead, then he went out. They heard him tell Kate to go tell Sean what was happening, then the doors slammed as he went out one way and Kate the other.

"My family isn't overly quiet," Amity said with a smile. "Fiona, this doesn't feel the way I expected it to. I'm not in all that much pain."

"They start slow and build. You're just getting started good."

Two hours later Clay returned. His face was white. "I can't find the doctor anywhere, and Mrs. Willis is visiting her sister over in Louisiana."

"Sean is in the kitchen," Fiona said. "Go talk to him."

"How is she?" He came closer to the bed. "How are you, Amity?"

"I'm fine. It's uncomfortable, but that's about it."

"Her water broke a few minutes ago," Fiona said with her customary bluntness. "She's in labor, all right."

Clay took off his jacket and began rolling up his sleeves. "I'm staying."

"You'll do no such thing. Go help Sean boil water."

"No. I have to be here." He went to Amity and took her hand.

"What good will you be once you pass out?" Fiona countered.

"I won't do any such thing. Have you ever delivered a baby? Other than your own, I mean?"

Fiona shook her head. "But neither have you."

"No, but I've pulled enough calves and foals to make me something of an expert in comparison." His eyes met Amity's. "I'm staying."

Amity didn't want to say so, but she was glad. It might be completely improper, but she felt safe when Clay was in the room.

"In that case, I'll go tell Sean to ride back to town and keep looking for the doctor. He doesn't have anything else to do. Hallie and Kate have Adeline upstairs."

Amity gripped Clay's hand as a stronger pain hit her. She made no sound, but she saw his face grow pasty. "I'm all right," she reassured him. "If you faint, Fiona will have to pile you in a corner until we have time to deal with you."

"Don't you worry about me. I'll be fine."

In the next hour Clay grew accustomed to watching Amity in labor. She became silent when a pain began and she held tightly to his hand, but other than that, she gave no indication of what was happening.

Clay tried not to look worried. All he could think of was Elsa and how she had died, here, in this very bed. Amity was calmer than Elsa had ever been, even though she was farther along with her labor than any he had ever seen. With Elsa, by the time the pains had become constant, she had always been closeted with the midwife, and screaming. Amity was so quiet he had seen no reason to send the girls to the O'Flannerys' house.

Amity's face was damp with sweat and her auburn hair curled at her temples. Clay thought she was even more beautiful now than when every hair was in place. Her cheeks were flushed from her efforts and her eyes bright, but she smiled at him between contractions and talked of everyday matters. Clay's admiration for her soared.

"Is Sean still gone?" Fiona asked after raising the sheet to see what progress was being made.

"Yes. He would tell us if he were back."

"I told him to keep looking until he locates the doctor." She smiled at Amity. "We may have a surprise to show him when he comes in."

"Is it that close?" she asked.

"Maybe." Fiona's eyes met Clay's. "I don't think it will be much longer, but I could be mistaken. I've never seen a labor from this angle. I'm always where Amity is."

Clay lifted the sheet. "I think we'll have to assume the doctor won't make it in time." With a degree of nervousness in his voice, he said, "Go get Amity's sewing scissors, the ones she uses to cut cloth. And a needle and thread." He gave Amity a reassuring smile. "You're doing fine."

She nodded, unable to speak until the pain subsided. He reached for her hand. "You can cry out," he said. "I can send the girls away."

Amity shook her head. "I'm not one to carry on. I'll be fine." Her voice was firm, but her eyes were worried.

Clay held her hand in both his and said softly, "I love you, Amity. I'm not going to let anything happen to you. This is no different than any other birth, as far as your body goes."

"It's too early," she said. She had been reluctant to have such a personal conversation in front of Fiona. "It's too soon."

"I know, but this way the baby will be smaller and easier to birth. It may not be as bad as Doc Hedges thought. Not with it coming so soon."

"We may lose her," Amity whispered.

"Not if I have anything to say about it. I want a pretty little girl just like you." A pain gripped her and he said, "Breathe shallow so you can push better. That's the way."

"How do you know I should do that?" she asked when she could.

"It's the way the animals do it."

She laughed even though another contraction was starting. "You say the sweetest things!"

He helped her through it and glanced over his shoulder as Fiona came back with the scissors, needle and thread. "Good. Now go to the kitchen and put them into the boiling water Sean has started."

"Boil my scissors?" Amity asked. "They'll rust."

"No, they won't. I've found that my animals have fewer infections if I have clean hands when I doctor their cuts. I can't see how this is any different."

Fiona looked doubtful, but she went to do as he had said.

"You're going to ruin a perfectly good pair of scissors," Amity told him.

"If I do, I'll buy you another. Push."

For the next hour Clay held her hands and talked soothingly to her, just as he would to a frightened mare. He didn't know what he was saying, nor did Amity care. His tone was all that was important. Fiona lifted the sheet and nodded to him. He went to stand at the foot of the bed.

Amity raised her head. She was tired and she hurt worse than any pain she could recall ever having had, but she could sense the end. Her eyes met Clay's and she managed to smile. He tried to smile back, but she could tell he was terribly frightened.

Within minutes the contractions changed, becoming stronger and almost constant. Amity groaned and clenched her teeth to keep from crying out. Clay bent and said, "The head is out!" His voice was as excited as if he had never seen a baby before. He guided out a tiny shoulder and suddenly the baby was in his hands. He stared at it.

"What's wrong?" Amity demanded. "Why are you looking like that? Clay, what's wrong?"

He laughed. "Nothing! Nothing is wrong. We have a baby boy! It's a boy!"

For a minute Amity was stunned. Then she laughed. "We have a boy?" She looked over at Fiona, who was grinning and nodding.

Clay began tying the cord off as another contraction hit her. She looked frantically at Fiona, who stepped closer at once. "Clay? What's happening?"

He looked up in surprise. After glancing at her, he said in amazement, "I think it's twins!"

Although Amity thought she was too exhausted to push again, she managed to do so, praying it would not be much longer. She didn't know anything about twins. If it was going to take as long to have the second one as it was for the first, she was afraid she would not hold out.

Fiona took the baby and placed it on the sheet she had folded on top of the dresser. As she wiped the infant clean, she glanced over her shoulder at Clay and what was happening on the bed. "It's coming, Amity," she said. "I can see its head!"

Fortunately, this one came much faster, and Clay let out a whoop that would have startled her if she had not been so exhausted. "Another boy! Damn, Amity! *Two* sons!"

Amity listened to the cries of her babies and smiled. There were a few more contractions, but she knew it was over. Fiona had her hands full cleaning the second baby. "They're as alike as two peas!" she said to Amity. "Wait till you see them!"

"Hurry," Amity said in a tired but happy voice.

Clay was finishing up the birthing. As soon as all was taken care of, he went to the washbasin and washed his hands as he stared at the babies. Then he took the first one and carried it, naked and qualling, to Amity. "Look," he said in wonder. "Look at him!"

Amity held the baby in the crook of her arm and felt absurdly like crying. "He's the most beautiful thing I've ever seen." She tentatively touched the downy dark hair that was plastered close to the baby's head.

"Do you think he's an odd color?" Clay asked.

Fiona laughed. "They all look like that at first. He'll be pink in a few minutes."

Clay relaxed. "Listen to those lungs!" He went to Fiona and took the second baby. "This one, too!"

"He's so little," Amity said. "They're so little."

Fiona nodded. "They're early. They'll grow." She was smiling as she patted Amity's foot and said, "I'll go into the kitchen and give you two some time alone."

Amity barely heard her. She was looking from Clay to their sons. "They look like you."

"I was thinking that they look more like you." He grinned. "I'll bet you their hair is red once it's dry."

She laughed and reached past the babies to touch his cheek. "I love you."

His eyes grew moist. "You still do? Even now?" He was remembering how Elsa had never wanted him near her after a birth and how she had looked accusingly at him as if he were entirely to blame for her travail.

"Of course I do." Amity looked deep into his eyes. He could see the love and knew his own must look the same.

"You're beautiful," he said. "You really are."

She laughed. "I'm sure I must be." She reached up to smooth her hair, which had long since come loose from its pins.

He lifted a strand and touched it. "I hope the babies have your hair. I've always been partial to this color."

Tears of happiness welled in Amity's eyes and ran down her cheeks. "I love you," she whispered again.

"I love you more than I can ever say." He heard the sound of footsteps outside the door. "I think news has spread to the girls."

"Let them in. They should see their new baby brothers."

With one baby still in his arms, Clay went to the door and opened it. All the girls were there, Adeline having been delivered to Fiona already. Their eyes fastened on the baby.

"It's a boy," he said proudly. "And so is the other one."

Hallie's eyes widened. "Two of them?"

Clay stepped aside and let them come into the room. "We have twin boys." The word sounded odd in his mouth. He had been so sure this would be another girl that the idea of not only one son, but two, dumbfounded him.

"What will we name them?" Kate asked.

"They're so little! Was I that little?" Rosemary asked as she tiptoed to see the baby Amity held.

"Not quite this little," Clay told her. He knelt so she and Laura could see the baby better. "We don't have a name picked out."

Amity laughed. "I don't think Rebecca will fit either of them."

Clay grinned at her and said to Rosemary, "Touch him easy, honey. He's still new."

Rosemary gently put one finger on the baby's hand. He reflexively grabbed it and held on. "He likes me!" she exclaimed. "He's holding my hand. See?"

Clay thought he'd never been happier. "Of course he likes you," he said. "You're his big sister."

Rosemary looked proudly at the baby. "I'm your big sister," she informed him.

When the girls had examined each baby and left the room, Clay went to Amity. Both babies lay beside her, their crying hushed for the time being. Clay tucked the blanket more snugly around them. "They're beautiful."

"We have to think of two names," she said, her voice filled with wonder. "I want one to be named after you."

"Won't that be confusing?"

"Not to me."

"Amity, I'm going to make you a promise. I'm never going to put you through this again. No, I mean it. I've seen what you went through, and I don't ever want you to be in such pain again."

"You may not have a choice." She smiled at him. "I'm not going to move back into the guest room. I'm in here to stay."

"You know what will happen. I can't keep away from you."

"I know. That's why I'm staying in here." She put her hand over his. "I want more babies. The pain wasn't more than I'm willing to go through again."

"How can you say that? I was here. I saw what went on."

"And you saw that I did just fine. You're experienced as a midwife now. We can't waste that talent."

He knew she was laughing at him, but he was firm. "I want to take care of you."

"Clay, just love me. That's all the care I need."

"I couldn't stop doing that. Not ever." He reached out and smoothed her hair from her face. "I've never loved anybody as much as I love you."

"Not anybody?" she asked hesitantly.

He smiled and shook his head. "Not anybody at all."

"I have my work cut out for me, you know. I have three more boys to deliver before the family is balanced. We're still girl-heavy."

He gazed down at the sleeping faces of his sons. "I never thought it would be twins, and certainly not that it would be boys. It's like a miracle, isn't it?"

"Yes." She touched one tiny face much as Rosemary had touched the baby earlier. "Our miracle." She darted her eyes at him teasingly. "Maybe they'll become veterinarians like their big sister."

"Maybe so. If we can have twin boys and if I can deliver them, there must be some way for Kate to be a veterinarian."

"My thoughts exactly."

He looked at the babies. He still couldn't believe his eyes. "Two boys," he repeated in wonder. "Wait until Sean comes back!"

"Won't Dr. Hedges be surprised? He never thought it might be twins, either."

"What will we name them? It's all right if one has Clay for a middle name, but he needs his own name, as well."

"We'll think of something. What about Matthew and Mark?" She tried it out. "Matthew Clay and Mark...?"

"How about Mark Becker? If we use my name on one, the other should have your maiden name."

"Perhaps. Luke and John can come next time." She smiled at him and he had to smile back.

"And you still really love me?" He could hardly believe his good fortune.

"Of course. I love you with all my heart. Especially now."

Clay felt his eyes watering and tried to blink back the tears. She covered his hand with her own and squeezed it, and he responded by reaching across the sleeping babies and hugging her gently.

Amity was tired and ached all over, but she had never felt so happy and alive. It was almost overwhelming to have Clay and her babies, as well as the girls. She felt ridiculously like crying. "No one has ever loved me this much," she whispered in his ear. "Not anyone."

"I'll always love you." He touched her cheek tenderly.

"That's all I ask." She smiled from him to their sons and back again. "That's all any woman could ask."

* * * * *

HISTORY IN THE MAKING!

Join Harlequin Historicals as we celebrate our 5th anniversary of exciting historical romance stories! Watch for our 5th anniversary promotion in July. And in addition, to mark this special occasion, we have another year full of great reading.

- A 1993 March Madness promotion with titles by promising newcomers Laurel Ames, Mary McBride, Susan Amarillas and Claire Delacroix.

- The July release of UNTAMED!—a Western Historical short story collection by award-winning authors Heather Graham Pozzessere, Joan Johnston and Patricia Potter.

- In-book series by Maura Seger, Julie Tetel, Margaret Moore and Suzanne Barclay.

- And in November, keep an eye out for next year's *Harlequin Historical Christmas Stories* collection, featuring Marianne Willman, Curtiss Ann Matlock and Victoria Pade.

Watch for details on our Anniversary events wherever Harlequin Historicals are sold.

HARLEQUIN HISTORICALS . . .
A touch of magic!

HARLEQUIN®

THE TAGGARTS OF TEXAS!

Harlequin's Ruth Jean Dale brings you
THE TAGGARTS OF TEXAS!

Those Taggart men—strong, sexy and hard to resist...

You've met Jesse James Taggart in FIREWORKS!
Harlequin Romance #3205 (July 1992)

And Trey Smith—he's THE RED-BLOODED YANKEE!
Harlequin Temptation #413 (October 1992)

Now meet Daniel Boone Taggart in SHOWDOWN!
Harlequin Romance #3242 (January 1993)

And finally the Taggarts who started it all—in LEGEND!
Harlequin Historical #168 (April 1993)

Read all the Taggart romances!
Meet all the Taggart men!

Available wherever Harlequin Books are sold.

ROMANCE IS A YEARLONG EVENT!

Celebrate the most romantic day of the year with MY VALENTINE! (February)

CRYSTAL CREEK
When you come for a visit Texas-style, you won't want to leave! (March)

Celebrate the joy, excitement and adjustment that comes with being JUST MARRIED! (April)

Go back in time and discover the West as it was meant to be . . . UNTAMED—Maverick Hearts! (July)

LINGERING SHADOWS
New York Times bestselling author Penny Jordan brings you her latest blockbuster. Don't miss it! (August)

BACK BY POPULAR DEMAND!!!
Calloway Corners, involving stories of four sisters coping with family, business and romance! (September)

FRIENDS, FAMILIES, LOVERS
Join us for these heartwarming love stories that evoke memories of family and friends. (October)

Capture the magic and romance of Christmas past with HARLEQUIN HISTORICAL CHRISTMAS STORIES! (November)

WATCH FOR FURTHER DETAILS IN ALL HARLEQUIN BOOKS!

HARLEQUIN®

my Valentine
1993

The most romantic day of the year is here! Escape into the exquisite world of love with MY VALENTINE 1993. What better way to celebrate Valentine's Day than with this very romantic, sensuous collection of four original short stories, written by some of Harlequin's most popular authors.

**ANNE STUART
JUDITH ARNOLD
ANNE McALLISTER
LINDA RANDALL WISDOM**

**THIS VALENTINE'S DAY, DISCOVER ROMANCE
WITH MY VALENTINE 1993**

Available in February wherever Harlequin Books are sold.   VAL93

HARLEQUIN ROMANCE®

Norah Bloomfield's father is recovering from his heart attack, and her sisters are getting married. So Norah's feeling a bit unneeded these days, a bit left out....

Orchard Valley

And then a cantankerous "cowboy" called Rowdy Cassidy crashes into her life!

"The Orchard Valley trilogy features three delightful, spirited sisters and a trio of equally fascinating men. The stories are rich with the romance, warmth of heart and humor readers expect, and invariably receive, from Debbie Macomber."

—Linda Lael Miller

Don't miss the Orchard Valley trilogy by Debbie Macomber:

VALERIE   Harlequin Romance #3232 (November 1992)
STEPHANIE   Harlequin Romance #3239 (December 1992)
NORAH   Harlequin Romance #3244 (January 1993)

Look for the special cover flash on each book!

Available wherever Harlequin books are sold.   ORC-3